ITALY
in the 16th Century

miles
0   20   40

RAVENNA

PESARO
URBINO • SENIGALLIA
• CAMERINO
PERUGIA
• ASSISI
PAPAL
STATES
Spoleto
NEPI
PESCARA

ADRIATIC
SEA

ROME
• MARINO
CAMPAGNA

BISCEGLIE
GAETA CAPUA • BENEVENTO   BARI
NAPLES
ISCHIA   TARANTO

THE
SCARLET
CITY

A Novel of
16th-Century
Italy

THE SCARLET CITY

A Novel of 16th-Century Italy

HELLA S. HAASSE

Translated by Anita Miller

ACADEMY CHICAGO PUBLISHERS
1990
OUR 15TH YEAR

Academy Chicago Publishers
213 West Institute Place
Chicago, Illinois 60610

De Scharlaken Stad
Copyright 1952 by Hella S. Haasse

English Translation: Copyright © 1990 by Anita Miller

The publisher thanks Mary Dennis for her helpful research.

Printed and bound in the U.S.A.
Printed on acid-free paper

First Edition

Library of Congress Cataloging-in-Publication Data

Haasse, Hella S., 1918–
  [Scharlaken stad.   English]
  The scarlet city / by Hella S. Haasse : translation by Anita
Miller. — 1st ed.
     p.   cm.
  Translation of: De scharlaken stad.
  ISBN 0-89733-349-7 (acid-free) : $22.95
  1. Italy—History—1492–1559—Fiction.   I. Title.
PT5838.H45S3613   1990
839.3'1364—dc20   90-39547
                                                          CIP

THE
SCARLET
CITY

A Novel of
16th-Century
Italy

CONTENTS

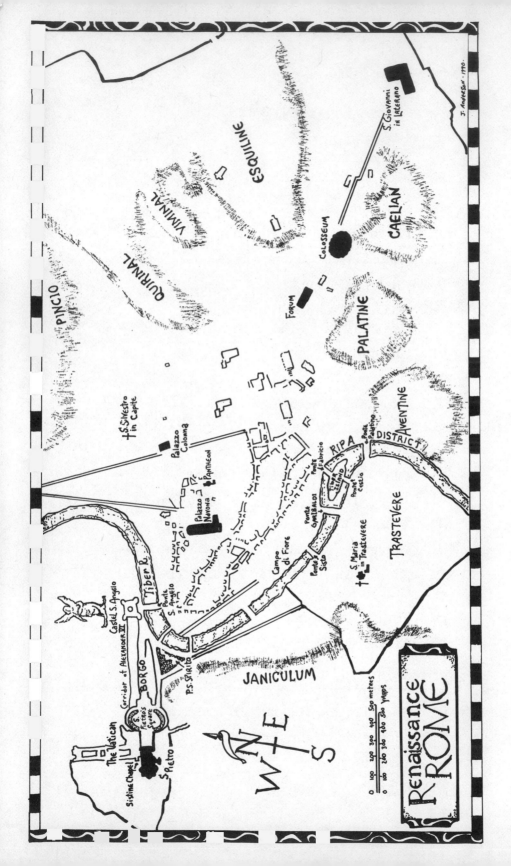

Renaissance ROME

INTRODUCTION

This book is set against the background of the protracted and somewhat complex conflict known as the Italian Wars, which began roughly in 1495 and ended, more or less, after the Sack of Rome in 1527. The antagonists were chiefly Francis I of France, who inherited the war to establish France in Italy from his two predecessors, Charles VIII and Louis XII, and, on the other side, the Emperor Charles V of Spain and the Holy Roman Empire, who wished to establish his own power base in Italy. Swiss and German mercenaries fought under the Emperor's banner along with Spanish soldiers. Between these two were the Italians themselves; the popes attempted to palliate both the French and the Emperor, an impossible task. Powerful Italian families threw their lot in with one or the other: Cesare Borgia was a partisan of the French and was made a duke by ~~Francis I~~ *Louis XII*; the Colonna family fought for the Emperor. Italian city-states like Florence, Venice, Genoa, Milan, were at the mercy sometimes of the French, sometimes of the Imperial forces. Intrigue abounded, in which the popes took a hand.

The protagonist of this labyrinthine story, Giovanni Borgia, a mysterious figure known in history as the *infans Romanus*, or child of Rome, was born in 1497. We meet him first in Rome in 1525: he had been fighting for the French and was captured by the Imperial forces at the Battle of Pavia; he was rescued from the Imperials by a friendly prelate who remembered Cesare Borgia and taken to Rome, where he has been awarded the office of speechwriter in the Vatican: he is not sure who pulled the strings for him.

But as he stands at his writing desk in the Chancellery of Pope Clement VII, Giovanni confides his past only to paper: he cannot talk to anyone in Rome because he trusts no one. His only release is to write down everything that has happened to him. And he does not do this chronologically: his mind travels over his past in a sort of circular movement: he is searching for his identity. He does not know who he is. As a child he believed he was the son of Cesare Borgia by an unknown woman, but over the years he has come to doubt this. He is in a kind of maze, and he recalls his life as a maze. Before he joined the French army, he had been living in the court of the French King Francis I where he had met Luisa, Cesare's daughter by his marriage to the French noblewoman Charlotte d'Albret: when he first came to France, Giovanni took Luisa to be his half-sister. Cesare, who had died in 1507, had then been dead for ten years.

From recent experiences, his mind moves to his earliest memories: his visits to Pope Alexander VI whom he took for his grandfather; the fearful time after Alexander's death in 1503 when Cesare was fighting for his life against a legion of enemies. . . .

So the drama of Giovanni's search for his identity is played out against the violent background of the Italian Wars: Italy and indeed Western Europe are in the throes of the birth of national consciousness and religious upheaval as they emerge from the feudal Catholic stasis of the Middle Ages. We meet not only Giovanni but other memorable characters: Vittoria Colonna and her husband, the Emperor's brilliant general, the Marquis of Pescara; the tormented artist Michelangelo; the Italian patriot Machiavelli who is involved in desperate intrigue to free the country of the Emperor; Lucrezia Borgia and her unpredictable husband, the Duke of Ferrara. And the scurrilous writer Pietro Aretino and the courtesan Tullia d'Aragona. Each of these characters has his/her own story, each struggles with a private quest for fulfilment.

The book can be read as a puzzle, dominated by the mystery of the *infans Romanus*. Hella Haasse has broken chronological time into time as it is called up by memory: the narrative circles and circles in a sort of widening pool, until the story is revealed.

—Anita Miller
Chicago, Illinois
June, 1990

CHRONOLOGY: THE ITALIAN WARS

[Events occurring in *The Scarlet City* are bracketed.]

1492: Election of Alexander VI, Borgia Pope. His daughter Lucrezia marries first husband, Giovanni Sforza.

1494: Charles VIII of France invades Italy.

1495: Charles VIII seizes Naples, but is forced to retreat by a coalition consisting of Spain, the Holy Roman Emperor Maximilian, Pope Alexander VI and the city-states of Venice and Milan.

[1497: Birth of Giovanni Borgia. Lucrezia's marriage is annulled. Her second husband is Alfonso of Aragon, illegitimate son of Alfonso II of Naples.]

[1498: Cesare Borgia, made a cardinal at age 17, resigns after the death of his brother the Duke of Gandia. Becomes papal legate to the court of Louis XII with whom he makes an alliance.]

1499: Louis XII of France invades Milan, after first working out agreements with Ferdinand V of Spain and Pope Alexander VI whose son Cesare is made Duke of Valentinois by Louis. [Cesare marries Charlotte d'Albret of the French court. Begins to attack and conquer cities of the Romagna (territory northeast of Rome).]

[1500: Cesare Borgia conquers cities of the Romagna, one by one in the name of his father the Pope. Arranges murder of Lucrezia's second husband Alfonso.]

1501: The French successfully occupy Naples, but disagreements flare between French and Spaniards. [Cesare Borgia is made Duke of the Romagna by his father Alexander VI. Lucrezia marries for the third time to Alfonso d'Este.]

1502:   Spain and France are in open warfare. [Cesare lures chief enemies to castle of Senigallia where he has them strangled.]

[1503:   Death of Pope Alexander VI. Succeeded by Pius III who also dies in this year and is succeeded by Julius II, a Della Rovere pope and enemy of the Borgias. Cesare is arrested but escapes and flees. Louis XII too has turned against him.]

1504–1505:   Temporary peace ensues when Louis XII signs the Treaty of Blois, pledging Naples to Spain and keeping Milan and Genoa for France. [Lucrezia's third husband Alfonso becomes Duke of Ferrara.]

[1506:   Cesare Borgia finds refuge at the court of the King of Navarre. Meets Niccolò Machiavelli, who uses him as the model for the ideal ruler in *The Prince*.]

[1507:   Cesare dies in battle fighting for the King of Navarre.]

1508:   War begins again in Italy when Pope Julius II makes an alliance with France, Spain and the Holy Roman Emperor Maximilian I against Venice.

1509:   The French conquer Venice.

1510:   Pope Julius II makes peace with Venice and begins martial action to expel the French from Italy.

1512:   The Swiss enter the conflict on the side of Spain and the Emperor. They storm Milan, defeat the French and return Sforza to the throne.

1513:   The Swiss rout the French at Novara and take over Lombardy. Death of Pope Julius II; his successor is Leo X, a Medici pope.

1515:   Francis I of France, successor to Louis XII, defeats the Swiss at Marignano.

[1517: Giovanni Borgia goes to the court of Francis I in France.]

1519: Death of Emperor Maximilian I. His grandson Charles V, King of Spain, is elected Emperor, defeating Francis I of France and Henry VIII of England for this throne. Strong enmity exists between Charles and Francis. [Death of Lucrezia Borgia.]

1521: Hostilities between Francis I and Charles V break out afresh in Italy. Death of Pope Leo X; he is succeeded by Adrian VI.

1522: Francis I is defeated by Imperial forces at La Biococca.

1523: Death of Adrian VI, succeeded by Clement VII, Medici pope.

[1524: Francesco Guicciardini is made President of the Romagna.]

1525: Francis I is defeated, this time disastrously, by the Imperial forces under the Marquis of Pescara, at Pavia. The French King is taken prisoner there and sent to Madrid. [Giovanni Borgia, who has been fighting for the French there, is also captured by the Imperials, but is rescued by Cardinal Aleandro who takes him to Rome where he becomes a speechwriter in the Vatican.] Death of the Marquis of Pescara.

1526: Francis I's mother, Louise of Savoy, becomes Regent of France during her son's imprisonment in Spain. To win his freedom, Francis signs the Treaty of Madrid, ceding victory to Charles V. But immediately upon his release, Francis repudiates the Treaty and signs the League of Cognac against the Emperor with Pope Clement VII, Henry VIII of England and the city-states of Venice and Florence.

1527:   The Emperor punishes the Pope for the League of Cognac by sending an army of mutinous German mercenaries and Spaniards under Charles de Bourbon, an enemy of Francis I, against him. In May of 1527 Rome is sacked for a full week by this army, and the Pope is trapped in the Castel Sant'Angelo. Francis captures Genoa and is advancing to Rome to release the Pope when Clement submits to Charles V to win his freedom. Charles had disavowed the sacking but he takes advantage of the Pope's plight to extort money and concessions from him. [Guicciardini loses office and retires to write history. Death of Niccolò Machiavelli.]

1529:   The Treaty of Cambrai is signed with France. Francis gives up all claims to Italian territory. The Peace of Barcelona is signed, between the Emperor and Pope Clement: this confirms Charles's position in Italy.

1530:   Charles V is crowned Emperor by the Pope at Bologna.

[1534:   Death of Clement VII. He is succeeded by Paul III, a Farnese pope.]

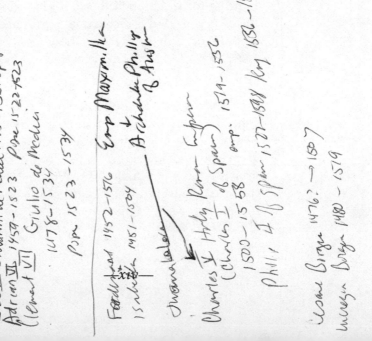

THE FAMILY OF THE BORGIA POPE, ALEXANDER VI

Rodrigo Borgia
(1431-1503)
POPE ALEXANDER VI
1492

Vannozza dei Catanei
(1425-1518)

unknown women

?

Pedro Luis
(1462?-88)
First Duke of Gandia,
1485
(betrothed to
Maria Enriquez)

Isabella
(1467?-1541)
m.
Pietro Matuzzi

Girolama
(1469?-83)
m.
Gianandrea Cesarini

Giovanni
(1497-1548?)
INFANS ROMANUS
Duke of Camerino
and Nepi

(possible offspring
of Lucrezia
or Cesare?)

Rodrigo
(born 1503)

Cesare
(1475-1507)
Bishop of Pamplona
Cardinal,
1493
Duke of Valentinois,
1498
Duke of Romagna,
1501
m.
Charlotte d'Albret

Louise

Juan
(1477?-97)
Second Duke
of Gandia,
1488
Captain-General
of the Papal Army,
1496
m.
Maria Enriquez
(died 1520)

Lucrezia
(1480-1519)
m.
1. Giovanni Sforza
of Pesaro
2. Alfonso of
Bisceglie
(died 1500)
(brother of Sancia)
3 Alfonso d'Este

Gioffredo
(1481?-1518?)
Prince of Squillace
m.
1. Sancia of Aragon
2. Maria de Mila

second wife

4 children

second
husband

third
husband

Rodrigo of
Bisceglie
(1499-1512)

Ercole
(1508-59)

6 children
(3 died
in infancy)

Isabella
(1498-1557)
Abbess of Convent
of Poor Clares,
Gandia

Juan
(1494-1543)
Third Duke
of Gandia

Giovanni Borgia

1 5 2 5

Borgia am I; two, perhaps three times a Borgia. To others, my lineage is a riddle; to me, it's a secret—no, more than a secret—a source of torment. In Italy, for a quarter of a century, no name has had a more evil sound than Borgia; if I didn't already know this, I would discover it anew every day. Anyone who wants to curse wholeheartedly says Borgia! Anyone who wants to sum up the wretchedness of these times, the corruption in Rome, the decline of Italy, spits out his bitterness: Borgia! Deceit, decadence, fornication, black arts, murder and manslaughter, incest: Borgia! Quarrels and dissension, endless discord among towns and principalities, invasions by rapacious foreigners in North and South, hatred, avarice, failure, hunger, disaster, pestilence and approaching doom: Borgia! To grasp fully all the connotations of the word Borgia, I had to come back to Italy.

God knows that in France—at least during the last years of my stay there—I was proud of my name. If the court secretly slandered me and my lineage behind my back, I wasn't aware of it. The King was well-disposed toward me: after all, I was considered to be a protege of the House of Este of Ferrara, and in those days France had no better friend and ally in Italy than Alfonso d'Este, Lucrezia's husband.

Equally important to me was the good will of another blood relative: Luisa—or Louise as she was called there—Cesare's daughter by his French marriage. Since I still believed then that

Cesare was *my* father too, I set great value on the influence of this woman whom I thought was my half-sister.

Luisa was four or five years younger than I; we shared the same mixed feelings toward our lineage. On the one hand, pride, inborn Spanish pride in the fact that we both belonged to a race that had dared to challenge kings and emperors; but on the other hand, a secret gnawing doubt, a sense of shame which neither she nor I could put into words and which we both tried to hide behind a great show of arrogant self-confidence. This was easier for me than for Luisa, because she was cursed outwardly as well: sickly, thin, her face disfigured by scars . . . living proof of the truth of the rumors circulating about Cesare before his marriage to Charlotte d'Albret. By now everyone knows that he suffered from the illness that the Italians call the French disease—a high price to pay, in my opinion, for the pleasures of love. He poisoned Luisa's blood with it—and, they say, the blood of most of his bastards. I suppose I should consider myself fortunate that I've been spared physical infirmities. *My* suffering is invisible: my soul has been poisoned.

So in France I could—in spite of certain earlier events—still maintain my self-respect. When I came to the court of Francis I, Cesare had been dead for more than ten years. People seldom talked about the last period of his life in Navarre, and never—in my presence—his inglorious end. If his name came up, it was usually in connection with current Italian politics: compared to my other countrymen who supported the French cause, Cesare appeared in a favorable light: he, at least, had shown himself to be *hardi homme*—a man of courage.

At those times I was always struck at how strongly his name, his personality, still held the imagination. Even then Cesare was more than a memory; he was a legend. In him good and evil had assumed dimensions that went beyond the powers of human judgment. In speech and in writing he was always referred to by his French titles; it was not forgotten either that his escutcheon bore the lilies of Valois and that his daughter Luisa was married to one of the greatest lords of the kingdom.

All this tempered any possible negative connotations of the Borgia name. In addition, I had been presented at the French court by Alfonso d'Este himself, and further, I wasn't officially called Borgia, but Duke of Nepi and Camerino. An imposing title, but a hollow one, nothing more than a string of names, because the possessions and the rights that went with them had been taken from me when Julius the Borgia-hater became pope; he returned the territories to the former owners—the Varano and the Colonna. For my fine titles, worthy of a prince of the blood, I have Pope Alexander to thank, the father of Cesare and Lucrezia. As the bastard of the illegitimate son of a former vicar of Christ on earth, I could in a certain sense consider myself to be a member of a dynasty.

In my first years at the French court, I lived in the customary style. I had a permanent place among other young nobles in the King's retinue. I held an honorary post and received an annuity. But the office and the salary were purely symbolic. Most of my companions served the King for the honor of it; they had solid backgrounds: money, castles, lands—and they bore ancient il-lustrious French names—their escutcheons were unblemished. I was poor, a foreigner. I had no fortune, no income beyond the handful of ducats doled out to me each year in the King's name, and gifts sent by Lucrezia. After her death in 1519, I received nothing more from Ferrara.

I kept a horse, a valet and a groom; beyond that all I possessed was a trunk with clothes, books and a few valuables. I rode in the royal hunt, sat at the banquet tables, indulged in my share of diplomatic intrigue and amorous adventure, like everybody else. In the halls and parks of Chaumont, Poissy, Chambord and Fontainebleau, life whirled past in a kind of happy intoxication. It was all a game—we knew that. We played against each other with courtly flourishes: move, countermove, attack and retreat . . . as much in love affairs as in the unending struggle for rank and precedence in the King's good graces. But all this was carried on with ceremonious restraint; the intrigues and maneuvers were like the movements in a ballet, executed with compliments and bows and well-chosen words. To be deeply serious or openly pas-sionate was considered tasteless. At first my mixed Spanish and Italian blood played me false; eventually I managed to adapt.

I never forgot that the world extended beyond palace walls and the borders of a royal park. How could I? I carried the memory of my youth, of the early years with Cesare in the Romagna and at the Castel Sant'Angelo, of isolation in the Castle of Bari and the long period of wandering after that. I remembered events and faces—at night, especially. My childhood passed before me—a furious cavalcade lit by torches; most of it was lost in blood-red smoke, but sometimes a glaring light played upon an image that I recognized: the angel Michael on the Citadel of Rome silhouetted against an angry sunset . . . a series of flags hanging from the ledge outside the great hall of the Castle of Camerino . . . a landscape filled with heaps of rubble, scorched black and still smoking, seen from the window of a palanquin . . . hollow-eyed heads on pikes, grinning above a city gate . . . .

Faces of the men and women of Cesare's retinue: his mother, Madonna Vannozza, stout, faded, with a shadowed upper lip, but regal in bearing and gesture; the shy, quick-tempered Gioffredo, his youngest brother, who was comfortable only with children and animals; his fortress-builder and engineer Messer Leonardo da Vinci, that man with the penetrating eyes, who could use a lead marker to create landscapes and figures from mildewed blotches on a damp wall; Micheletto, Cesare's advisor and right hand; Agapito, his secretary—and finally, the children, my playmates: Camilla, Carlotta and of course Rodrigo, the confidant and bosom friend of my youth.

I was five or six years old then. I knew that we were in danger, but the how and the why were beyond me. Much later it all became clear to me. In the silence of the night, in antechambers and alcoves of French royal palaces, lying sleepless next to tossing, snoring French nobles with whom I had to share a bed, I had plenty of time to connect the facts I had learned over the years with my memories—the shreds and fragments of what I had heard and seen as a child.

There are reasons why I want to write all this down here: the adventures of my youth, my life in the French court and the experiences which I've had since then and still have every day. A man who feels himself threatened and spied upon from all sides, who knows that he can't confide in anyone and that there's no security anywhere, has to keep his own counsel. To speak one's thoughts, even to whisper them, is out of the question. The Vatican galleries are as crowded as the streets on market day; the walls have eyes and ears here and anyway, only fools, prisoners or madmen talk to themselves out loud. My writing doesn't attract any attention; it looks to be part of my work. Nearly every day I stand at a desk in the papal library, covering sheet after sheet with words: drafting letters and speeches to oblige the lesser diplomats of His Holiness Clement VII. Papal scribe: a curious occupation for one who was brought up as a nobleman, who has fought for France in Navarre and before Pavia.

They probably think here that I aspire to the purple—or at least to a red hat. Considering my lineage, anything is possible, I suppose. Of course there's nobody in the court of Rome who would dream of asking me openly what my intentions are. No one dares—at this stage—to show himself either for or against me. My name creates space, a no-man's-land between me and the others. *Borgia*—it's like the warning sign on the door of a plague-stricken house. They keep their distance, I still can't quite tell why. All I have are my suspicions, because whatever might be planned against me remains cloaked in darkness for the moment. I'm left in peace because they think I'm in the good graces of His Holiness's favorites. But I know perfectly well that I have to make good use of this quiet time, this respite. Uncertainty makes one vulnerable . . . Now, first of all, I have to find out why people are avoiding me. The poison is hidden in the name: Borgia. They don't know who I am, what I want, what connections I have, what friends and relatives I protect, what enemies I can hurt. They know less than I do, and what do I know myself?

I'm not certain of the exact day and year of my birth, any more than I know who my father and mother were. There must be records of my birth in Ferrara, but I haven't seen them. I'm roughly twenty-eight years old, my name is Giovanni Borgia, or—to employ the Spanish title which is mine by right—Don Juan de Borja y Llançol. When I was still a child, I thought Cesare was my father, probably because no one said he wasn't, and because I lived in his immediate entourage with two of his other bastard children, Camilla and Carlotta. Later, Lucrezia's son Rodrigo joined us; we knew that Cesare had taken pity on him because Alfonso d'Este refused to have the boy at his court in Ferrara; he didn't want to be reminded of his wife's previous marriage.

Cesare took the four of us everywhere with him; we had a secure place in his retinue with the women appointed to look after us. I spent the first years of my life in palanquins and coaches, in tents, in halls of newly captured or hastily abandoned castles in the Romagna. I no longer remember names. Later I heard about Imola and Forli, Cesena, Senigallia—I've probably been there, too.

I remember Camerino only because when Cesare took possession of it, I played a role in the solemn ceremony that was performed there. The previous owners of the castle and estates, the Lords Varano, had been murdered or driven away by Cesare; Pope Alexander issued a bull that made me, the male heir of the Borgia family, Duke of Camerino. At the same time, I received also the castle and lands of neighboring Nepi, which had belonged to the Colonna family—almost half of the Romagna. At that time I was scarcely—if at all—aware of the great honor which had befallen me.

I sat in front of Cesare on his horse; surrounded by soldiers, we rode through the steep and narrow streets of the town. Cesare's standard was flying from the damaged tower of the castle. *Duca! Duca!* the people cried, packed together in the alleyways and on the roofs of the houses. Cesare's armored hand lay on my knee.

In a gloomy hall filled with armed men he held me under the armpits and lifted me up high.

"Behold the new Lord of Camerino, the first Duke, by the grace of Pope Alexander!"

He pushed a heavy ring, too wide for it, onto my finger, and told me to make a fist. So for the first—and up to now the last—time in my life, with Cesare's seal which was also mine, I sealed official documents as Duke of Camerino. Coins were struck with my head on them. When I was in France I still had one of those coins, a silver carline with the legend: *Joannes Bor. Dux Camerini.* But I seem to have lost it somewhere.

In the following year, Pope Alexander—whom I took to be my grandfather—died. With him went Cesare's power in the Romagna and also my dukedom, forever.

When I came back to Rome two months ago, I didn't recognize the Vatican. The rooms where Pope Clement usually lived were unfamiliar to me. When I went looking for the Borgia apartments, I found only closed doors. The section of the palace where Alexander had lived and where Cesare had spent time now and then, is no longer used. I've heard that no one has entered there since the days of Pope Julius. I haven't requested admittance yet—if only to avoid giving away a long-cherished, secret desire.

Sometimes, standing in the Belvedere court, I look up at the open galleries which circle the outsides of the apartments. The ground floor rooms belonged to Alexander; the floor above was fitted out for Cesare. Whenever he put up at the Vatican for a while, Rodrigo and I lived in a house in the Ponte quarter where two Spanish cardinals looked after us as our guardians.

Of our many visits to the Vatican—Alexander couldn't seem to see enough of us when we were in his neighborhood—all I remember are the papal apartments.

In a room with brightly painted walls which sparkled with gilt and sky-blue enamel, was a fat old man leaning comfortably back against the cushions of a state chair. He permitted us to kiss the ring on his forefinger, and his hand, which was broad, soft and always very warm. Then he bent forward and squeezed us against him, breathing heavily with emotion; his velvet cape smelled of stale incense and musk.

"Are you here again, my boys, my fine, handsome boys, my falcons, my cubs You, Rodrigo, from my beautiful Lucrezia, and you, Giovanni, Giannino *mio*, my little dukes; I'll make you rich and powerful, you'll rule Italy like kings, Borgia kings!"

He kissed us and petted us, put his hand in blessing on our heads, groped in a dish of preserved fruit next to him and scattered sweets over us. Sometimes he threw a ducat, a jewel or something similar between us and watched us romp and scuffle for it. With applause and shouts he urged us on until Rodrigo and I, excited, overheated, paying no attention to our surroundings, rolled through the chamber, dragging carpets with us, knocking over candlesticks. Those present—shadows in the background, prelates, nobles, a handful of servants—smiled and clapped, echoing Alexander's childlike pleasure in our roughhousing. But Cesare, who usually came with us on our visits to his father, didn't look at us or give any sign of enjoyment.

Now, after all these years, I know that his unwavering dark look was not for us, but for Alexander. Whenever I think of Cesare, I see him with that expression on his face—a look at once mocking, contemptuous and wryly amused: the sourly indulgent smile of one whose patience has been tested for all too long a time.

These visits to the Vatican must have taken place in the last months before Alexander's death—that would have been in the summer of 1503. I was about six years old then. The summonses calling us to the papal palace which usually came every day from Alexander or Cesare, suddenly stopped. After that our guardians the cardinals barely showed themselves in the house in the Ponte, cool and dark as a tomb, where Rodrigo and I were believed safe from the fevers which rose from the marshes in August.

Finally our nurses came, crying, wailing, repeating rumors about poison: Pope Alexander dying, Cesare seriously ill, the Vatican in an uproar, Rome a place where those who support Borgia will go down to perdition . . . The servants' agitation spread to us too. While the doors were being bolted, shutters nailed over the ground floor windows, Rodrigo and I crept away to crouch in deadly terror inside the darkness of the bedcurtains, listening to sounds inside and outside the house: muffled voices close by or resounding in the distant galleries; quick footsteps beneath us, above us; chests and pieces of furniture being dragged over the floor; horses snorting in the courtyard.

When the curtains were suddenly thrust roughly apart, we expected to see the dreaded assassin. But by the light of the candles which the women hurried to hold high, we saw Don Michelle Corolla, called Micheletto, Cesare's captain, friend and confidant, the head of his bodyguard, his constant companion and frequent deputy: a Venetian with such dark skin and eyes that he was always taken for a Spaniard. We had learned to respect him; he seemed to us to be a part of Cesare himself, as inseparable from him as his shadow, but a shadow of flesh and blood, a replica, a creature emanating from Cesare, obeying his unspoken will.

The chamber was full of people, servingmen and women taking down tapestries from the walls, throwing linen and silver into chests; from the open door came the tumult of armed men striding through corridors and across landings.

Surrounded by Micheletto's men, we hurried on horseback through an unfamiliar nocturnal Rome. The newly risen moon shone yellow and swollen through the shimmering haze of heat which, day and night, hangs over the town in August. With a clatter of hooves, creaking and bumping of wagons, with cries, curses and a great hubbub, the procession squeezed through a labyrinth of narrow streets. Black clouds of dust swirled high behind us between houses and churches and the steep, window-less walls of palaces.

Later, I woke in a strange bed. Rows of Borgia bulls in parallel lines, climbed the stiff shiny cloth of the bedcurtains. Next to me, as usual, Rodrigo slept peacefully. I turned my head toward the light. By an open window, in the cool dawn breeze, stood Cesare's mother, Madonna Vannozza. I called her by the name which we sometimes heard Cesare use: *matrema*, little mother. She came to me, her black garments rustling, so quickly and angrily that it seemed as though she had been waiting for me to wake.

"Be still, you'll wake Rodrigo. Lie down."

She pushed me ungently back onto the pillows. I could never understand why she loved Rodrigo and not me.

"Is there danger, *matrema?*"

"Yes, danger to *Borgias*," she said, stressing the last word.

She stood half-turned away, looking at me over her shoulder while she tucked stray wisps of hair under her kerchief. Her eye-lids were swollen, there were deep lines at the corners of her mouth. What I remember most clearly about Vannozza are her eyes and mouth: the sparks in her black pupils, alternately glow-ing and dying, the shadows on either side of her broad fleshy upper lip with its faint moustache, which gave her face a look of bitter pride. Her harsh, probing stare frightened me.

She always treated me roughly, resentfully. She spoke to me only if it were unavoidable, and then with perceptible antipathy. This attitude of hers, for which I can now easily find an expla-nation, filled me then with anxiety and insecurity. Of all the time which I spent in Vannozza's company, that early morning hour of the day after Alexander's death remains the most vivid in my memory. Silent and unmoving, she stood with her back to me at the open window, while the sun rose in the hazy sky and the bells of Rome pealed, alternately and together. The daylight brought the heat; a faint swampy smell rose from the town. From a distance came a sound that I could not identify. It must have been going on since I woke, but I had not been conscious of it earlier. Not the sound of the sea or the wind, which rises and falls; this was a continuous rustling murmur like falling rain or the splashing of a brook.

"What is that outside, *matrema?*"

Even before Vannozza replied, I sensed that there was a connection between the distant noise and her air of motionless, tense listening.

"Shouting and screaming in San Pietro's square. They must have come from Rome by the thousands last night when they heard the news."

"Why are they shouting, *matrema?*"

"You don't remember much of what you're told. What did Fra Baccio say in the story when the stranger asked him when Rome was at its most cheerful? —When a pope dies."

"Where are we now?"

"In my house in the Borgo. Be quiet now, lie down. Don't let me hear from you again."

The harshness of her voice frightened me more than her severity. I broke into a sweat. I did not dare to stir, or to push aside the covers. Rodrigo was sleeping and I felt that the woman at the window was aware of my every movement, although she did not look at me.

The bed in which I lay was her bed; I was suddenly certain of this. I recognized the scent which rose from the pillows as Vannozza's, but mixed with another, stale smell, fleeting but still persistent: an odor from the past, an odor of musk and incense, a strange faint animal smell, both exciting and repulsive. The linen was clean, aired in the sunlight and stored with perfume, but neither fresh air nor all the oils of Araby could dispel from its folds that scent of dead lust. Without knowing why, I felt oppressed to the point of suffocation in that bed. I sank slowly into mattress and bolster as into treacherous quicksand; under the brocade coverlet, I lay bewitched, condemned to immobility.

Wherever I looked, above me, before me and on both sides of me, I saw, in an endless procession on the bedcurtains, gleaming gold on a scarlet background, the Borgia bulls climbing toward a hidden goal.

❧

I am describing these events as they arise in my memory and as I experienced them as a child, when I could not understand the reasons behind them—although much that was important must have been discussed by the adults around me. When, as a young man, I wandered about Naples, and later before I left for France, when I stayed for a short while with Lucrezia in Ferrara, I heard things. I know now why Micheletto rushed us headlong to the Borgo. The chests carried by packhorses and mules on that nocturnal procession contained, apart from our possessions, gold, silver and valuables from the pontifical treasury, taken from the Vatican at Cesare's command by Micheletto with a dagger in his fist, as soon as it was known that Alexander was dead.

Cesare himself, weakened by poison or an intestinal illness— no one knew the truth—took action from his bed to forestall popular uprisings and attacks by the Colonna, the Orsini and other lords whom he had driven out of the Romagna. His soldiers took over the Borgo, which was fortified. I remember that Gioffredo, Cesare's youngest brother, and his wife Sancia of Aragon, that man-crazed, unpredictable shrew, had fled from their palace on the other side of the Tiber to Vannozza's house, in deadly terror of the vengeful crowds which raged and threatened before their door day and night.

We didn't see sun, moon or stars in those days. Behind closed window shutters and bolted doors, we awaited the outcome of Cesare's negotiations with the Spanish and French envoys, and with the College of Cardinals. Vannozza, her vigilant eyes upon us, told her rosary quickly and loudly; Sancia started quarrels or sat yawning. Gioffredo bit his nails in silence. Rodrigo, Camilla, Carlotta and I amused ourselves as well as we could, throwing a ball or playing with Sancia's lapdog in the stifling, darkened chambers. Visitors were incessantly announced and admitted: messengers from Cesare in the Vatican, Micheletto, the Spanish cardinals. Over our heads disputes raged, accusations, arguments, bursts of fury. We heard it as we played, without listening to it. All that I remember is the account of Alexander's deathbed and burial, probably because particular details made an impression on me: the blue-black swollen body, already decaying, which no one wanted to touch and which had been dragged by the feet to San Pietro's where it was forced into the coffin with blows of the fist; the black dog—Alexander's soul or the Devil in disguise?—which roamed restlessly through the basilica as long as the corpse remained above ground.

At the beginning of September, we left Rome in an endless procession: armed men—on foot, on horseback—protected the column of wagons and the sedan chair carried by halberdiers, in which Cesare, too weak to ride, lay hidden behind black curtains. We were on our way to the Castle of Nepi, which was still my property and thus a haven for Cesare.

We didn't stay at Nepi long. Before the chests were unpacked, they were tied once again on the backs of the pack animals. That return to Rome was sheer flight; even at the time I realized that. The vindictive barons followed us to Rome. For safety's sake, Cesare put up at the palaces of friendly cardinals, sometimes here, sometimes there. We children scarcely had time to get used to the strange beds, had hardly learned to find our way through the series of unfamiliar rooms, before the signal was given once more for departure. To our questions, Vannozza gave the surly, off-hand response that our lives would be in danger from the Colonna, the Orsini, Varano and other Borgia-haters if we stayed in that particular place an instant longer.

I remember this time of confusion and uncertainty as being endless, but in reality it lasted only a few weeks. One morning we were awakened before sunrise, wrapped in cloaks and brought outside. This time no sedan chair was waiting. Horsemen carried us before them on their saddles. In the glimmer of torchlight I saw Cesare mounting; he had to be supported by grooms. We went through Rome at a quick trot. The rider who held me shouted something at a comrade over my head. I heard, "Ostia . . . ships . . . sea. . ." But before I could grasp the significance of these words, an uproar broke out in the troop. The battle cry of the Orsini reverberated between the houses; fighting was already at fever pitch in the vanguard.

It didn't last long. Our column dashed back at full speed by another route, this time over the Tiber Bridge into the Borgo, where the Vatican buildings and the basilica rose darkly against the sky tinted yellow by the dawn. There were threatening shouts behind us—life or death!—and the pounding of horses' hooves, while we pushed our way into a forecourt of the papal palace. I was pulled from the horse, half-carried, half-dragged between armed men rushing forward shoulder to shoulder through galleries and halls where the frightened screams of Carlotta and Camilla raised infinite echoes.

Suddenly we found ourselves under an open sky. I almost cried out when, accidentally, I was held away over a parapet; I looked down on the roofs of Rome. But after I had been swung around on the shoulder of the man who was carrying me, I saw, at the end of a narrow uncovered passage, the outlines of the Castel Sant'Angelo and the angel on its highest battlement glittering in the sunlight. I realized that we were fleeing through the corridor which connects the Vatican with the Castel.

I know now that Cesare thought he would be safe there, inaccessible to his enemies, under the protection of Pope Pius, Alexander's successor, a timid sick old man who—out of self-interest, incidentally—spread his mantle over us Borgia. In actuality, Cesare sat in the Angel Castle like a mouse in a trap. We hadn't been there five days when Pius died . . . following an operation, it was said. With his going, Cesare lost his last base of support; now all he had to depend on were his own cunning and sagacity. Of what followed, Cesare's bitter struggle for self-preservation, I was—then, at any rate—unaware.

The apartments in the Castel Sant'Angelo where we lived with Vannozza were low-ceilinged, dark and chilly, situated around a semicircular garden. On roof cornices and doors, and on the walls of the well in the garden, Alexander Borgia's arms were painted: crossed keys crowned with the papal tiara and the Borgia bull. We played there every day amid the symbols of Borgia power. It scarcely occurred to us that this power had been destroyed. We seldom saw Cesare. He remained secluded in the section of the fortress where he had taken up residence, writing letters, receiving trusted friends, negotiating with messengers sent from the Vatican and foreign countries.

Vannozza sat sullenly for hours, not speaking, at a window overlooking the garden. Now she would pray, now she would rub the beads of her rosary between thumb and forefinger. She was often overcome by fits of rage and despair; she called us to her and punished even the most minor infraction with blows and kicks, or she cried, lamenting, for help to a long series of saints, ordering us to pray too. Sometimes she burst into complaints; then she chose to heap pity on Rodrigo, her pet: my boy, my child, *duchetto mio*, what will become of you? Your father is murdered, your relatives are our enemies, your mother can't take you in, our family is going down in ruins, our power is broken, we're lost.

At other times she allowed herself to be carried away by less comprehensible feelings. Her eyes closed, her head thrown back, rocking back and forth as though she were in pain, she whispered accusations, entreaties, curses . . . these toneless whispers had nothing to do with us. When she behaved like that, she was truly alarming. We didn't understand the sense of what she was muttering; her words were as enigmatic as the words of a sybil. Later, much later, I remembered this oracular talk and realized that it wasn't gibberish. I could have been spared much uncertainty and doubt if I had been able to forget Vannozza's dark mumbling. When we lived in Bari, in the formal elegant court of our foster mother Isabella, my youth was disturbed by the suspicions roused by the courtiers' behavior: odd glances, stray words picked up by chance, conversations quickly broken off when I approached . . . I asked Rodrigo then what he thought Vannozza had been saying. But Rodrigo couldn't remember anything about our stay in the Castel Sant'Angelo. That's understandable: he was two years younger than I.

Our sojourn in the Castle of Rome was suddenly interrupted. That didn't upset us; we had become quite accustomed to unannounced journeys and house-movings. We were brought to take leave of Cesare. He was lying on a couch, his legs crossed. I looked at him with curiosity. I hadn't seen him since we had come to the Castel Sant'Angelo. In his eyes, his face, his behavior, I sought an explanation of Vannozza's mysterious complaints. Peeling, raw patches—the result of his recent illness—stood out sharply against his sallow skin, already disfigured by old scars. He had grown thin; at intervals a restless light flickered in his eyes. I found this odd: an unwavering, lackluster dark stare had always been characteristic of Cesare. I believe that others had noticed this too.

It didn't surprise me to hear it said later that Cesare had the evil eye. Many—and especially those who had reason to fear him—must have believed that with that stare he could read their most secret thoughts and feelings.

When I saw Cesare for the last time in his murky apartment in the Angel Castle, that magic power seemed to have left his eyes. As always, he had perfect control over his body and the expression on his face. He lay on his side, propped up on his left elbow, letting a perfumed ball roll back and forth—an habitual gesture—on the palm of his hand. Behind him two prelates from his retinue sat at a table playing cards. We stayed only a short while; I no longer remember what was said. Vannozza wailed softly and whispered into his ear; but when she tried to embrace him, he thrust her away. He raised his hand in farewell, his eyes resting for a moment, absent, indifferent, filled with secret disquiet, first on Rodrigo, then on me. "Take them away now," he said finally, with a shrug.

That night we left the Castel Sant'Angelo by a secret door; our departure had to remain hidden from Cesare's enemies in the Vatican. The two little girls remained behind in Rome under Vannozza's care, but Rodrigo and I travelled quickly, with our guardians the cardinals, southward to Naples.

❦

I ask myself who is that man with the insolent face who roams about the Chancellery for a while every day and then chooses apparently to dawdle near my reading desk? He's there now too, extravagantly decked out, like an actor, and literally drenched in musk. He might superficially be taken for a nobleman, but his face, posture and manner give him away. A newly rich flunky, an artist, a favorite, or even Ganymede to a powerful man here at the court? It's obvious that he considers himself a man of great consequence. He walks back and forth like a strutting peacock, poisoning the air with his perfume. He knows everyone, greeting people left and right; he has a really adroit and rather amusing way of indicating, with a nod, a gesture, a bow, how high—or low—a value he sets on the person in question. A conceited co-median and undoubtedly an adventurer. He betrays himself by the way in which, obsequious, humble, with a thousand and one bows, he approaches the dignitaries who pass through here on the way to the audience chamber of His Holiness.

Yesterday the most powerful man in the court, Monsignore Schomberg, the Archbishop of Capua, visited the Chancellery with his retinue. On these occasions anyone who has the oppor-tunity comes forward and salutes. My friend in the peacock blue literally flung himself at Monsignore's feet, pouring forth a be-wilderingly eloquent stream of flattery and praise; after that he proceeded to act as though he belonged to the august company.

Whatever he might be—parasite, buffoon, adventurer—it's ob-vious that some people find it in their interest to cultivate him as a friend. Glances and comments are exchanged as soon as he turns his back, but if I'm not mistaken, everyone is actually afraid of him. I'd like to know who he is. He's different from the others. In that respect we're alike, he and I. With this difference: that *he*'s a familiar figure at court. No one can allow himself the luxury of snubbing him. What concerns *me* is that in the two months of my stay here I haven't held a conversation with anyone beyond strictly necessary exchanges. I must admit that I've consciously kept my distance. It's not in my nature to rush into intimacies. I feel that my comings and goings are being closely watched—but again, I don't know by whom and why, although I have my sus-picions.

Before I came to Rome I tried of course to get a feeling for the current situation and relationships at court and to find out the names of the most influential people. I thought that that kind of knowledge would be useful to me. But as it happened the opposite was true. The French court is structured on unvarying principles: everyone has a fixed place there and belongs to a clearly defined circle. The rules of the game are complicated, but they're always strictly maintained, under all circumstances. Here, I feel as though I were living inside a chameleon. Things are continually changing: titles, benefices, appointments, new parties, come and go with mysterious rapidity. One must adjust constantly: he who was powerful yesterday appears today to be out of favor, and vice versa. And there's no way of predicting which way the wind will blow.

The papal household is a tangled mass of functionaries, spiritual and secular, all with their own retinues, relatives, friends, favorites, servants and hangers-on. I have gradually learned to recognize the most important cardinals, the Monsignori, numerous as they are, at least distinguish themselves from the multitude. But the rest: prelates, lords-in-waiting, secretaries, masters of ceremony, valets, officers of the watch and other people with more or less clearly defined duties . . . From sunup to sunset they all swarm through the Vatican's series of rooms. Half of Rome seems to have free access here.

They say it's busier here than ever, not so much because of the Holy Year—one consequence of the Battle of Pavia is that far fewer pilgrims have been coming to Rome from the provinces—but because of the continual arrival of legations. A day doesn't pass without meetings with ambassadors from Venice, Milan, Florence, Ferrara. Official and unofficial representatives of France and Spain are trusted guests. The events at Pavia have caused great confusion, because nobody knows where they stand now. The defeat of the French was completely unexpected here. It seems that Pope Clement was half-dead from fear. No wonder, if the truth is that this time he had counted upon a victory for King Francis without leaving himself a loophole.

It's beginning to be realized in Rome that the Emperor holds Italy in his power. The defenses of cities and principalities are in a sad state, according to reports from the ambassadors who are continually arriving and departing. The Imperial troops have suffered few losses and have not yet been disbanded. Who would dare to deny that this is an extremely dangerous situation? The Emperor has given repeated assurances that he has only the best intentions, that he wants peace and nothing but peace. As far as I can judge, there's no one in Rome naïve enough to believe these pronouncements. It's being said openly that the Emperor plans to come to Italy to teach His Holiness a lesson. It may be true that the Emperor received the news of the victory at Pavia with humility and prayers of thanksgiving. But his thoughts, his deepest desires, are known to no living soul. All princes are ambitious and as a general rule a prince doesn't become more self-effacing after a victory. Anyway, one thing is certain: his advisors and more especially his agents here in Rome are trying to spur him to further action. At the moment a joke is circulating about the Pope: His Holiness, they say, must now rely for the first time upon the authority conferred through papal dignity.

On the subject of the spiritual prestige which His Holiness should possess as God's representative, I prefer to be silent. I'm not qualified to judge matters of faith. Every day wiser men than I take it upon themselves to speak and write about these things. Apparently the Pope wishes to be considered a temporal authority—only as such, then, should he be judged. Clement has neither troops nor money; no one supports him with enthusiasm. It's difficult to believe that only three years ago the selection of this Pope was greeted with shouts of joy. The Ecclesiastic State is lacerated by party strife: Rome, more than any other city, is polluted with the evil of political dissension.

At the court, two conflicting points of view are embodied in His Holiness's two most influential advisors—the real rulers here: on the one hand, the Datary Giberti, a childhood friend and favorite of the Pope, an avowed partisan of France, and on the other, the Archbishop of Capua—a Fleming or German named Schomberg—who exerts his influence on the side of the Emperor. The Pope stands between them: he turns first to one, then to the other. This waffling and wavering seems to have infected His Holiness's entire entourage. Add to this, mutual distrust, fear of treachery, general insecurity. The situation is discussed incessantly: meetings, conferences and audiences follow one after another, but it all comes to nothing.

Still, there must be capable and sharp-witted men enough in Rome. Left and right I hear gloomy predictions from insiders, or from those who pretend to be insiders. In this court I have yet to find one man whom I would wish to follow, one group which I would be willing to join. I'm following a wait-and-see policy. On this turbulent sea, fraught with currents and cross-currents, I'm an inexperienced helmsman. I must know more, see more and hear more, before I risk deciding on a course. Anyone like me, without money and without protection, who has to rely on his own resources, can't be too careful.

It was by a stroke of luck that I came to Rome. Most of my comrades, friends from France, were killed, wounded or taken prisoner at Pavia. Now I don't know what direction to take. When I was in France, I had a clearly defined goal: I wanted to make a career for myself in the King's army. I believe that I have all the necessary qualifications for military service: courage, skill, adaptability. My men respected me and I knew how to obey my superiors. After the disturbance in Navarre, I was given a permanent appointment in the Bayard cavalry as a reward for my services. I want to continue on this path. I don't have friends or relatives, I'm free of obligations—that can surely only help me in the military profession.

As I stand behind my reading desk in the Chancellery, it looks as though I must forget these plans for the time being. Strange as it seems to me even now, I'm a speechwriter; I perform a function which is usually reserved only for scholars or aspiring scholars. I gained this post through the influence of Bishop Aleandro, who was papal nuncio at the French court for a considerable time. He knew that I speak French and Spanish, have some Latin and a passable handwriting. Presumably the pious man wasn't able to think quickly of a more suitable occupation for me.

However it happened, here I am then, commissioned by one of the secretaries of His Holiness's secretary to frame a speech which will be read by the *podesta* in the square of some hamlet or other: "Good people, the taxes have been raised again, the cost of bread has gone up once more . . ." Because of these and similar regulations here and there, the starving, plague-ridden populace seems to have arrived at the conclusion that His Holiness is the Devil incarnate. This puts my work in a peculiar light. What am I doing here among these clerks? Few laymen practice this profession; those who do, consider it an honorary post: they scoop up the annuity and take a monk into service to do the work. If I saw a chance to spend my time in a better way, I would follow their example.

Does the man in peacock blue, that walking scent-bottle, belong in that category? I don't know. On further reflection, I have decided that he is less of a shallow braggart than I thought he was at first. He's not stupid. That boisterous affability, that overbearing geniality, is a show, a display, designed to mask the fact that he's constantly watching and listening. He has an obsessive desire for information. He considers me, too, his prey. I've noticed that. Whenever I look up, I see his eyes fastened on me: a flashing, arrogant stare which troubles me. An honorable man doesn't stare at someone like that. I have to know who he is and what he's up to.

❦

Borgia, Borgia. Under the vaulted ceilings of the Vatican, my name has taken on another sound for me. Never have I felt such an incessant, overwhelming need to call back memories of my youth. What possesses me, to return again and again to a past that holds nothing for me but confusion and upheaval?

In France I was able to get rid of my constant secret uncertainty for the first time. Once I entered King Francis's household, I felt freed from ghosts and shadows. The men accepted me because I was a good rider, hunter and fighter; the women were amused by my Southern gallantry. Why did I need to be anyone but myself? I shook off my uneasiness the way a snake slips out of its withered old skin. Perhaps Luisa helped to bring back my childhood belief that Cesare was my father. Occasionally after a dream-filled night the old doubt stirred; but I knew how to fight it off. I was no longer oppressed by thoughts of my lineage. I believed that once and for all I had lost the feeling that I had to drag the Borgia name with me always, as a galley slave drags his chain. I was used to living with the dregs of uneasiness buried deep within me.

Knowing it was there—and probably for good reason—made me dress and behave more formally. I noticed the same tendency in Luisa: she led an exemplary life at the frivolous court; proud reserve was her armor. We were both trying to emulate the stiff dignity of the Spaniards, a style which suited us better than French elegance or the Italian grand manner. Speaking of this, I remember something that happened when I was fighting in the Pyrenees for King Francis. That was in '21. The Spaniards were occupying Navarre. We were marching to win back the territory under the command of the Duke of Navarre. In the main the army was made up of Gascons, Basques and Navarese; I belonged to the King's men-at-arms. After some skirmishes near the city of Pamplona, my men found a wounded Spaniard among the bushes by the side of the road.

I spoke to him in his own tongue—asked him his name, where he came from. He listened attentively, measured me from head to toe with a sharp look.

"You're a Spanish nobleman, as I am," he said finally. "Why are you fighting on the wrong side?"

I took this remark as a compliment. At that time, under the influence of Alfonso d'Este and my friends in France, I was opposed to Spanish policy. In addition, I knew even then that the Borgia family was permanently out of favor in Spain. In spite of all that, I decided after that encounter to model myself on the example of the hidalgo: the best part of the Borgia heritage which had—I found—fallen to me. The Spaniard was later ransomed. I remember his name: he was called Ignacio de Loyola.

A constant interaction existed between my new-found self-respect and the soldier's life I was leading. The journeys and marches, filled with hardship, over the southern and southeastern borders of France, the sieges and battles, the companionship of experienced soldiers, steeled my body against discomfort of every kind, my mind against feelings that I thought I had banished to its most profound depths. I couldn't guess that they had flourished there. Now that I'm breathing the air of Rome, they're sprouting up, a poisonous growth. The man I was during that life of action under the open sky—riding, fighting, free, unfettered—no longer exists. When I put aside my cuirass and coat of mail, I gave up my identity as a knight. The speechwriter in court dress, who sees only the rooms and galleries and adjacent symmetrical inner gardens of the papal palace, is a stranger whom I don't like to identify with. Who and what am I here? I shall know that when I find out how others see me.

I haven't been able to present myself at court as Duke of Camerino. Aleandro told me tactfully that doing that would get me into considerable trouble. Apparently the present holder of the title, Giovanni Maria Varano, is in Rome now. But even if he weren't, there isn't a living soul here who would acknowledge my claim. To tell the truth, even *I* don't believe that I can assert a claim to the dukedom. Varano is the legitimate heir of a family that has been settled in Camerino since before living memory—naturally he's the legal owner of the lands and the title. What have I ever been, but a usurper? If I were to mention the gratuitous role which I had unwittingly filled as a little child, I'd only make myself ridiculous.

In this environment the name of Borgia has more significance than I can quite grasp just now. People don't see *me* as a man in myself; all they see is—a Borgia. If I knew what facts, rumors, myths and invented or half-forgotten mischief I'm identified with, I could at least take a stand, defend myself. But there is silence all around me. There's plenty of courteous bowing, gracious saluting, a readiness to let me share in superficial conversations, but no one takes me into his confidence, there aren't any efforts to draw me into the intrigues of any cliques. Of course, on the other hand, I've also been spared the feeble jokes which newcomers here are sometimes subjected to. Every day in the Belvedere garden, a new courtier tumbles into a branch-covered pit, dug and filled with muck for that purpose. Up to now, no one has dared invite me to take a stroll like that, with a surprise at the end.

II.

Pietro Aretino and
Giovanni Borgia

Ah, Messer, my apologies! A man can't see where he's stepping in this crowd. It would be worth the expense to widen these galleries a little—what do you think, Messer? At least the gentlemen who are received in audience by His Holiness can wait in the antechambers. But people from their retinues are forever blocking these loggias. Crowded and noisy as a fishmarket! Listen, you can hear every Italian dialect here. And arguing and bragging and telling jokes ... Those cardplayers and dicethrowers there have found a more amusing way to spend their time ... That's right, go on, gentlemen, let the money roll! ... Pretty soon they'll start drawing their knives again ... Just yesterday the guards had to step in, there were some flunkies from the Venetian and Sienese legations threatening to cut each other's throats. Later on they had it out in San Pietro's square. I don't know how it turned out ... Where are you going, Messer? You don't still resent my treading on your toes?"

"I'm in a hurry, Messer."

"Surely not in as much of a hurry as those two Monsignori there ... Look at that, the guards give lots of room to red gowns. Lesser gods like you and me have to give ground, don't we? ... Listen, Messer, I advise you to wait a minute. Unless you want a punch in the chest from the blunt side of a halberd. Those Swiss mean business."

"Messer, I must ask you not to delay me. I have been instructed to go immediately to the Datary's secretary."

"Oh, really, to Berni? Watch out, Messer! Keep on your feet—
you almost tripped over the purple! The richest whores in Venice
and Rome don't wear such long trains as the cardinals nowa-
days."

"Thanks for your help. Now do let me go on."

"With pleasure. But it's too late; another company is coming
out of the audience chamber. You must be patient until the gentlemen have gone past. What am I saying, there are ladies with them
this time! I see it is the Marchioness of Pescara. There goes the
only chaste woman in Rome, Messer. She doesn't often show
herself in public when His Excellency her husband is away with
the Emperor's army. 'I'll be with you as often as Pescara is with
his Vittoria.' That's a sarcastic refrain from a street song about
a man who wants to get rid of his sweetheart. I must say, Her
Excellency bears her lot with admirable patience. A beautiful
woman, don't you think so? Too cool maybe for my taste, too
serious, but what bearing, what eyes, Messer! A woman like an
ancient statue; no Aphrodite—an Artemis rather, or a Nike. . . .
One of the Colonna family, noble blood, proud race!—Your servants, my lady!—Look, Varano condescends to notice me this
time!"

"Varano?"

"He there, walking one step behind Her Excellency. The big
woman with the horse face next to him is his wife, Caterina Cibo,
a niece of the Pope."

"Varano, Duke of Camerino?"

"Precisely, Messer . . . Both close friends of Her Excellency.
They've taken up residence with her in Ascanio Colonna's palace.
I hear that the high-toned company amuse themselves by reading
the Epistles of the Apostle Paul together and attending meetings
of the Brotherhood of Divine Love. Could there be a more edifying
pastime? You're going out the wrong side, Messer, you're following the retinue. If you have to go to Berni, shouldn't you go
through the fresco gallery? What a rush . . . I can't keep up with
you . . ."

"I haven't asked you to walk with me, Messer."

"I'm not the slightest bit surprised that Varano and his wife
have been with His Holiness. The Medici and Cibo families are
hand in glove, as they say. But what's the significance of the

Marchioness being here too? Pescara is more sympathetic to Spain than the Spanish themselves and for years the Colonna have been openly at odds with all the popes—they're Ghibellines of the first water. And Her Excellency has been out of favor for a year."

"Does the Duke of Camerino have duties at court?"

"Oddly enough, he does not. Through his connection with His Holiness, he should in a manner of speaking be able to have whatever he wants. Apparently he's not ambitious. He and his wife are more interested in spiritual than in worldly affairs. The rumor is that they're the patrons of a new mendicant order. They're here often, asking favors for their protégés . . . But Her Excellency? If she's trying to get closer to the Pope again, then it makes sense that the Varanos would act as intermediaries . . . Ah, now I see—you want to cut through the procession . . . This way then, between these pillars; from here you can still see the company passing by . . ."

"That place is already taken, Messer. Will you kindly leave that man in peace. I'm not in the habit of pushing myself forward like that."

"If it involved anyone else, I would say, Don't give it a thought; pushing oneself forward is a question of skill. But in this case I think it's better for us to give way. Do you know who that is standing there, Messer? Shabby, dusty, unkempt as usual, always eccentric, always inaccessible, our Michelangelo Buonarroti! But a great man. One must be somewhat understanding. But not everyone is as broad-minded as I am . . . He has many enemies in Rome. No manners—rude, really—goes for days on end without saying a word, moody, unsociable. Things are said about him . . . collects advance payment but doesn't deliver the work on time, or doesn't deliver it at all; runs after handsome boys, and not only to immortalize them in stone or paint . . . But a great artist, Messer, a giant among giants. I know what I'm talking about . . . I understand art."

"And who and what are you yourself, Messer? A guide who explains everything that's to be seen here, without being asked?"

"Ah, you consider me an intruder; you find me annoying. But don't try to deny that you were eager to hear about the Duke of Camerino. What a stroke of luck that I was on hand to satisfy

your curiosity. Without exaggeration I can say that I know everything about everybody at court. I'm at your service."

"Your name, Messer?"

"Are you claiming that you don't know who I am? You must
certainly have heard people talking about me. I am Pietro Aretino,
recently made a Knight of Rhodes, poet, orator, pamphleteer,
eulogist, critic, satirist, biographer of saints, mediator in the ac-
quisition of works of art, antique and modern, confidential agent
and correspondent of important personages both in and outside
Rome . . . at your service. My name rhymes with Pasquino . . .
does that tell you anything? Also with *divino* . . . a small but
significant detail."

"And one in which, in my opinion, half of all Italians can take
pride. You're certainly extraordinarily sure of your own accomplishments."

"As sure as two and two make four, as sure as I want to smash
that hypocritical stone face there to pieces—who is it, San Ono-
frio, San Pasquale . . . some obscure martyr or other—"

"Let's move on before you do anything outrageous. I'm in a
hurry."

"But seriously, Messer, do you find the faces here in this gallery
artistically successful? No expression, no life in them, flat, hack
work from a time when sculptors didn't know how to render
warm, breathing flesh. Now the work of Messer Michelangelo
Buonarroti, whom we so recently met: it creates life, it's eloquent . . ."

"I can imagine that you have a penchant for eloquent art."

"Ah, ah! You're trying to make fun of me, Messer. Figuratively
speaking, you can't trip me up . . . This way out, to the right—
don't trip—there are a couple of treacherous steps around the
corner. I notice that you're still not completely at home in this
pontifical labyrinth, Messer Giovanni Borgia."

"You apparently know me too?"

"I know everything about you that's worth knowing. You come
from the French court, you fought in King Francis's army at Pavia,
you were taken prisoner by the Emperor's forces, but you were
released inside twenty-four hours because you were sensible
enough to join the retinue of His Eminence Geronimo Aleandro,

also taken prisoner, but naturally, out of consideration for the Pope, sent on to Rome with the requisite compliments."

"You really are amazingly well-informed."

"My specialty, Messer. I have a keen nose. You came to Rome with Aleandro and, upon my word, the days of that journey weren't wasted if it's true that you have His Eminence to thank for your post here. In Pope Leo's time it was easy enough to get a position: anyone who could hold a pen and had brains enough not to look at a book upside down was in; there were swarms of fellows here who dared to call themselves scholars or men of letters. Now things aren't so simple . . . You can't do anything without substantial backing. Pope Clement is frugal and he has no taste, but he takes good advice before he spends money on art and scholarship. You're not a poet by profession, so it's a testimony to your skill and perseverance that you've managed to become a papal speechwriter . . . Or to the special favor of influential people . . ."

"Why not a testimony to my personal ability?"

"I've taken the liberty of getting hold of a couple of your speech drafts to have a look at them. The style is completely correct, all the instructions are followed, but it's colorless, it has no fire, no spirit. No dash, no cleverness at the outset, in style, metaphor, closing phrases. It doesn't show a particle of insight into people; you don't know how to play on the feelings of readers or listeners. You have to flatter them, entice them, excite them, rouse their curiosity, lead them along the path you have chosen for them; you must offend them, taunt them, challenge them, if that's called for. You don't know the secrets of true rhetoric; you don't have a passion for words. In short, Messer, you don't have a speck of talent. You've been named speechwriter for some other reason."

"And consequently you're positive you know what that reason is. I don't underestimate your flair for ferreting out information."

"Ah, this promises to become an interesting conversation . . ."

"Not today, Messer. I'm already late for my appointment."

"You're right. Above all, don't keep Berni waiting needlessly. It's not a good thing to have him for an enemy, I could tell you a little about that . . . It's an honor to be summoned by him, Messer. Perhaps it's a commission for you from the Datary?"

"I don't know anything about it."

"We must get together again soon. You're a stranger here, I don't doubt that you want to be informed about all sorts of things. I'm at your disposal. I know all about everything, I have the best contacts. I can show you the ropes in the Vatican and in Rome. Naturally, you want to see the city. I advise you not to go alone, particularly to Trastevere, Ripa and Sant'Angelo which are infected with riffraff. What you need is a trustworthy guide, a friend, a man of the world, who knows the right addresses, who can provide introductions. Pantasilea, Antea, Tullia, our great courtesans, I know them personally. All you need to do is give me a wink and Rome lies open to you."

"Thanks for the offer; I'll bear it in mind. I bid you goodbye, Messer . . ."

"Aretino, Pietro! Don't forget it. Aretino Pasquino, an epigram in two words, if you follow me. Is it possible that there's a man knocking about Rome who doesn't know me? Hey, hold on, Messer—or are you just playacting? We'll have a talk again soon."

III.

Michelangelo Buonarroti

He walked swiftly, his hands behind his back, through the deserted side galleries. A far distance behind him, voices and footsteps echoed among the colonnades of the great vestibule; a never-ending stream of sound reverberated everywhere around him. To his left: a long row of closed doors studded with gilt and bronze ornaments; on his right, glimpsed through the tall arcades, an inner garden. On the pavement, pots of flowering plants stood in the sunshine. A group of workmen were repairing a wall under the supervision of a builder. Fallen hunks of lime, old stones, flakes of colored plaster, lay scattered about. It was quiet here compared to the noisy bustle in the loggias outside the papal reception halls. In the air hung an odor of incense and decaying wood, mixed with the smells of spiced food, long-unaired apartments, musty carpets, Tiber mud, blooming oleander, overripe fruit and horse dung.

He had come to Rome against his will. Pestilence had broken out in the city, his enemy Bandinelli predominated among the artists at the court, and on top of that, he had had to leave his work in Florence—work which he found fulfilling and which, indeed, obsessed him. He was embittered at the loss of valuable time. The affair for which he had been summoned was too complicated to be resolved in a few days. He had sent letters and messages repeatedly stating his point of view, and he considered it a personal insult that despite this, the Pope was forcing him to be present for the prolonged investigation into charges and defenses.

The facts were well-known, after all; the pertinent papers were in the Chancellery. In the contract which he had signed with the heirs of Pope Julius in 1513 or '14, all that was mentioned was continuation of the work on the tomb which had been ordered by the deceased. No date had ever been set for its completion. He had not violated the agreement when he had temporarily given precedence to other work. Besides, he could prove that he had done this on Pope Leo's instructions. True, he had received a large part of the seventeen thousand ducats which were to be paid for the purchase of materials and for wages, but substantially less than the Lords della Rovere contended. Anyone who took the trouble to look at the figure of Moses, at the blocks of marble and supply of bronze intended for the tomb could surely understand what this amount had been spent on. Pope Clement could easily have settled the matter to everybody's satisfaction: that he preferred endless discussions, putting on a grotesque show of listening to both sides, provided more evidence that His Holiness was totally incapable of coming to any kind of final decision.

Honesty compelled him to amend these irascible thoughts. He knew that he was largely to blame for the misunderstanding between himself and the heirs of Pope Julius. Once he had begun the work, he had not bothered about fulfilling the commission in a businesslike way. He could never remember precisely how it had happened. In impatience and haste, he made promises without realizing the extent of their impact. A portion of the advance payment he had sent to his father and brother: what was wrong with that? Everyone knew he had to support his relatives. Had he actually received more than the amount which he thought they had given him? He cursed his carelessness, the confusion in his business records.

All he knew was that he had worked for ten, twelve years, day in, day out and most nights too, on that monument and on the new commission in Florence—a torment because he could no longer force himself to keep at the one nor let go of the other for a moment, so that he had not allowed himself a single hour of freedom. It was only right and reasonable that he had now been called to account. But what could he argue in his own defense?

He was prepared to accept the blame, to promise to repay the money, to complete the tomb on short notice, if they would only leave him in peace for the rest of the commissioned time. He did not dare to hope for the fulfilment of his most secret wish: that he would be released from a task which no longer inspired him, which had become a torment for him, a yoke chained to him, a millstone dragging him down to the depths of despair.

The days in Rome were a long drawn-out agony. He had nothing to do, he had to be constantly available to obey a possible summons. He visited the workrooms of painters and sculptors of marble and metal, who were in the papal service; there he found much facile skill, much smooth perfection in form and color, but no trace of the inspiration which had consecrated these rooms earlier, in the days of Raphael and Perugino, Francia, Bramante and Signorelli.

Everywhere he went, he encountered the enmity of Bandinelli, that plagiarist and seeker after cheap success who dominated the herd of third-rate luminaries. Because he considered Bandinelli's work inferior, he refused to allow himself to be disturbed by certain persistent rumors. He could not, even in fits of the deepest despondency, imagine that the Pope would take an important commission away from him and give it to Bandinelli. As soon as he had arrived in Rome, he had felt the movement, the unrest that betrays the undercurrents of rumor. He closed his ears to the echo of this intrigue, but it remained audible around him during his stay at the court—an attendant whisper, like the troublesome buzzing of flies.

He knew who was responsible for the lion's share of the criticism, slander and opposition which he had had to endure for the last few years. Just now, between the pillars near the bronze gate: that bloodsucker Pietro Aretino, a rat who rummages in filth, a maggot who can thrive only on stench and corruption. As soon as he had seen that look, heard that voice, loathing and rage rose up in him. Venal and rotten, a fellow who sells his pen to the highest bidder, who feeds on the secrets of bedchambers and confessionals, who mints coin from the passion and despair of others less hypocritical than he. He himself lies with the lowest form of catamite, so naturally he thinks great admiration of a beautiful face or body can be prompted only by physical lust.

Again he had a friend with him, this Aretino, a young man whom he was holding familiarly by the arm, pulling him through the crowd. Slanderer, making a display of his own shamelessness! What does he think, *quod licit Jovi* . . . He's arrogant and cocky enough. Although at one time Messer's preference had been for youths with painted faces . . . This companion didn't seem noticeably effeminate. . . .

He spat angrily on the ground. He felt polluted, forced away from his concentration on the work left behind in Florence. Enforced idleness, the worst torture. Keep moving physically and think, think . . . without that counterbalance, he would go mad.

That part of his mind which relentlessly examined his thoughts and feelings for purity raised an objection: no physical lust? . . . no trace of it? Never—while contemplating a well-proportioned body—the hot mist clouding thought and vision, never the desire to touch for the sake of touching? Why deceive himself by denying it? His soul bore—didn't it?—the scars of his struggle to overcome this urge through sculpting. Whenever he transmitted to clay or marble or paper those bodies which his principles forbade him to possess, he experienced an emotional climax that was more of a deliverance than any ecstasy of physical love could have given. Still, a sense of guilt and shame tormented him. It was useless to claim that he had subdued lust, that he had not become enslaved by desire. This lust could not be thought away; it affected every accomplishment. He knew that for that reason, he was not invulnerable to the rumors spread by Aretino: it was as if the slander were vermin, endlessly multiplying.

In that man, that adventurer in words, he saw his own feelings grotesquely deformed, as though they were reflected in a distorting mirror. What was the use of defending himself? He could say truthfully that he had never practiced sodomy, in the usual sense, with any friend or model. That the lines of a body, male as well as female, could take him out of himself, fill him to bursting with a rapture that could not be due only to the creative impulse—how could he explain that? He was dominated by Eros, but it was Eros the divine, the winged, the Phoenix-Eros rising from the ashes of blind lust.

That nagging inner voice, which would not leave him in peace, forced him to descend to the depths. Not the friends whom he respected, not the young men who served as models—their beauty, which he considered godlike, made them seem unattainable—but the stonecutters, the painters' companions, who shared his sleeping quarters ... Fellows accustomed to the coarsest pleasures, the filthiest jokes. The provocation and satisfaction of lust, with or without women, acts performed without thought, in dull heat, like beasts. . . .

This pollution accompanies me wherever I go. Would I have had this sense of inferiority if I had dared to approach women? I have gone grey without knowing that love. But a whore is an affront to nature, an abomination without equal. The others—the virginal daughters and sisters, the virtuous mothers and wives—are strange to me, beings from an unknown world, beings whom I can observe, recreate, but whom I cannot comprehend to the depths of their flesh as I can comprehend myself and others like me ... That shyness, a curse.
Speaking of this, it's symbolic that it was Messer Aretino who thrust himself between me and that magnificent, impressive woman there in the gallery. With one hand she held the folds of a veil against her breast. A jewel fastened to her hair above her forehead sparkled with the rhythm of her movements. Flawless, lustrous, the skin on the curve of cheekbone, temple and chin. Full lips, sternly compressed. A slender, supple body under that load of velvet and silk skirts. Long limbs, well-proportioned, she walks proudly, with perfect bearing, her head up, her shoulders straight. This is a beautiful, healthy being—the dawn, Demeter, a Winged Victory. Outwardly, at least. The soul in that superb form remains a mystery. A body that is striking, stunning, in its beauty all too often harbors an inconceivably cowardly, petty, twisted soul.

He stood still, staring vacantly at the white patches of light behind the pillars. Humble servant of the divinity that he saw in youth and revealed beauty. The human body, miraculously animated flesh, each movement, each pose so deeply, harmoniously sensual that it brought tears to his eyes, made his heart pound. Those who gave him this experience, he loved, he honored, he cherished. He was ready to humble himself, to do violence to his shy, surly nature. Surprised by the realization that the adored one had misunderstood him and was trading on feelings that he had permanently conquered, he thrust that person from him. The deeper the disappointment, the more intense the aversion. And with it came the torments of uncertainty about his own honesty. That voice told him that he had obligations to each of those whom he could no longer bear to have near him—was it their fault that they had misunderstood him? Although he felt abused, deceived, he gave the money and gifts that were asked of him, begged forgiveness for his violence and crude words and withdrew with his bitterness where no one could follow him—into his workroom or the marble quarry.

He had a clear memory of one of these episodes. The humiliation and pain of that last abortive friendship awaited him in Rome in the form of epigrams with double meanings which flowed from Messer Aretino's pen, with no other purpose than to embitter his stay in the Vatican. On every gust of wind, from every nook and cranny of the papal palace, the dirty mocking words blew at him. He kept silent, acting as if the halls and galleries were peopled with ghosts. He had become a stranger in Rome. The city seemed an empty shell, a glittering form without substance. This new Rome looked as it had ten years before when he had watched it being built, but over the palaces, basilicas and bridges hung a cold empty light. The life had been blown out of it.

He chose to spend his time in that part of the Vatican that bordered on the Sistine Chapel. Amid the scaffoldings of the builders and painters who were there every day demolishing walls, breaking out new doorways, restoring frescoes, he was able to think. Slowly he made his way around broken or collapsed pavement, piles of wood and stones in the deserted galleries. Sometimes he stopped and sketched quickly with his thumb in a layer of dust on a balustrade. He stared at the lines he had made, rubbed them out with his sleeve and walked on.

A little further on, he stopped and began to scribble again—crosses, triangles, gallows, plans for lathe constructions which he would need for his clay models. From time to time he swore, his face distorted by a sort of spasm. The thought of the work he had left behind and all the uncompleted work awaiting him, of his inability to finish what he had contracted to do, was like being touched on a raw wound. Not a single commission completed in ten long years. The time had slipped past him, had left him nothing, no tangible result of his drudgery, no gratification, no peace of mind. . . .

The Borgia courtyard and the Cortile della Sentinella: diamond-shaped patches of dazzling white. A fresh wind was blowing from the hills; it was cool in the shadows of corridors and porches. In the midsummer months, it would be impossible to escape the heat even in the most shadowy vault of the old part of the palace.

He greeted the sentry posted at the side door of the chapel. As usual in this place he felt uneasy, like a swimmer about to dive into unsounded waters. He stood irresolute. He felt he should turn back, but desire, vexation and pleasure, warring in him, pushed him on. He opened the leather-covered doors and went inside. There, leaning against the wall, he crossed his arms on his chest and looked up.

From the vaulted ceiling and the arches above the windows, they stared down at him: prophets and sybils, titans, angel children on supporting columns—his creatures, born out of the inner chaos which he himself did not dare to probe. He saw in them the embodiment of his own doubt, despair, bitterness and fear. From this distance, he could hardly see the expressions on their faces, the subtleties of their gestures. He had to shut his eyes to lose himself in details: glance and bearing, the curve of muscle under the flesh, the luster of eye and hair, the arrangement of folds in the garments.

During the years that he had lain, day in and day out, like a martyr on the high scaffolding, groaning from the almost unbearable cramp in his outstretched arm and in the fingers which clutched the brush, every part of his creation had engraved itself forever on his memory. Coming from him, returning to him, his creatures had a two-fold existence: high up on the vaulted ceiling, visible, spirit become form; and within him, not perceptible to the senses, approachable only in the most profound concentration, closely akin to the magic darkness from which it had sprung. The pictures above his head, inviolable as the starry heavens, were estranged from him. Only their reflection, which he carried about with him, seemed to him still full of warmth and life, still animated by the power of his passion.

His face had been wet with sweat and tears and fallen drops of paint, his throat and nostrils prickled with the dust and fine grit which always hung in clouds about the scaffolding; muttering, swearing, praying, whispering adjurations to the still unborn as he had suffered in labor. From sunrise to sunset, as long as the light was good, the isolation of the high scaffolding, and, at night, the torture of sleeplessness. His body had ached with exhaustion, his mind with doubt. Mornings, sickened by his own impotence, he had climbed the scaffolding, obsessed by the desire to destroy the failed work, wipe it out irrevocably.

Squatting under the ceiling, he had mixed lime, water and sand for a new background. Then he had lain on his back and fumbled for his brushes.

God the Father had swept toward him out of highest Heaven like the very whirlwind; from the folds of the violet mantle which billowed rustling about him, curious angels peered. Sun, moon and stars receded into the firmament. Adam slept, part of the earth, a body kneaded out of clay and dust, perfectly formed but without consciousness, sunk defenseless in the dream state which precedes life, and which seems as deep and imperturbable as death. The Almighty pointed to him: rise! But Adam could not arise; he slept, with his cheek pressed against the earth, a fully developed unborn child not yet able to separate from its mother's womb.

When one morning, after days of desperate toil, nights filled with inward struggle, he had surveyed the fresco, suddenly he knew where he had failed: the creation of man—the body had been created, the soul had not yet been revealed. The only significant thing is that crucial moment when the new creature, perceiving for the first time that it has become distinct from inanimate matter and animals, turns to God, raises itself from its sleep.

He had brushed out the sketch of the sleeping Adam with lime and sand until nothing remained except a shapeless, colorless blot. Now, leaning against the wall, he looked up at the work which, sixteen years before, he had painted on the ceiling from a new design. He was completely alone in the chapel, an insignificant insect at the bottom of a treasure chest. With every breath, he drew in the sharp, sweet smell of incense. Now that the doors to the hall were closed, no sound from outside penetrated the sacred premises.

The relationship between God and man, between man and the world which was created before him. On the last day of the Creation, a desire awoke in the Almighty to bring forth a being who would be able to comprehend the meaning of His work. But the universe was perfect in all spheres; in the archetypes of things, God found none on which to model a new creature. He made man after His own image and blew life into him.

"Rise, Adam! No fixed sphere, no immutable shape, no defined task, do I give you. All other beings on earth have been given their own nature, must obey the laws of their species. For you, Adam, no ties, no boundaries, no restraint except the will which I breathe into you. Neither of Heaven nor earth, neither mortal nor immortal, have I created you. In you sleeps the seed of all forms of life. You can decline into bestiality or be regenerated into divinity. Yours is the choice. Adam, rise!"

Adam, reaching out to God, his knee bent, his eyes open, was aware for the first time of his will. He wanted to rise.

The silence under the painted, vaulted roof seemed disturbed suddenly by a rustling, as if an immense multitude were approaching in mortal terror, an apprehensive, lamenting horde, a swelling tidal wave of fear.

The man below, cringing at the door, pressed himself against the wall, his hands raised in the defensive gesture of one caught by surprise, although he knew that this sea of sound existed only in his own mind. It was not the first time that they had called to him, the still unborn creatures of his imagination, beings without form, faceless, whose fate he did not know. He heard only their voices, that chorus of the doomed, which woke an echo in the deepest fibers of his heart. The seers and seeresses up there with angry faces, warning gestures, kept watch—sometimes startled, sometimes desperate or often sunk in gloomy silence—over the destruction of Adam and his race; they seemed to want to force him to answer a question to which he did not know the answer:

"Explain this inner pain, this longing which torments us. What is the mainspring of our thought, the hidden tone which our ears strain to hear, the thing unseen for which we hungrily seek? Explain this anxiety which weighs upon us like a curse. How much longer? And why, why?"

Why? He took his hands from his eyes. The disquiet of those above filled him, as it had innumerable times before, with helpless horror. The prophets and sybils, solitary in their niches, challenged him to account to them for the tragedy which he had dared to create.

Who am I ... how can I know myself? Your cry—Rise!—rings in my ears; day and night I hold the echo of Your voice. But I cannot rise. I lie chained by my lust, my pride, my lack of wisdom. Acting in free will—Your gift to him at birth—man has chosen evil. The urge is in us to be tempted and damned, an urge which You cannot have inculcated in us but which undeniably exists, poisoning life on earth. Was the clay polluted on the day of creation?

Up there, the reflection of the fear of doom which had never left him in peace since, as a young man in Florence, he had heard Fra Girolamo Savonarola preach with superhuman passion about approaching damnation. Naked, without possessions in their flight from the flood, driven together like a herd of animals, Noah's fellowmen see the sea rising toward their last refuge. The cold wind piercing to the marrow of their bones, the odor of death from the boundless sea ... God, God, must there always be a deluge to cleanse the earth of us?

He could not bear the tension which confrontation with this work evoked in him. He cursed himself: he should have known it. It always ended this way. Above him hovered the projection of his own fear and guilt like clouds in a stormy sky, swirling here like a whirlwind, there massed together, heavy with lightning and rain. The storm was going to explode, when, when?

He turned and fled blindly, stumbling over his own feet, out of the chapel.

IV.

Vittoria Colonna

The procession split at the Tiber Bridge. Giovanni Maria Varano and his wife went toward Trastevere—they wanted to visit the basilica of Santa Maria—but the Marchioness of Pescara turned back with her retinue to the Palazzo Colonna, where she spent the rest of the day in her apartments.

I shouldn't have gone to visit the Pope. His friendliness is a mask. There's too much distrust between us; Pavia can't be erased. He blames *me* because the peace plans failed, as preposterous as that is. I threw myself into it completely at the time—Giberti knows that. I didn't do it from ambition or love of intrigue; I was convinced that this suffering must end. I deeply wanted mediation, I wanted to help create a pleasant climate so the adversaries could reach common ground. I didn't do it from self-interest . . . actually it was against my interests to do it because Ferrante wouldn't accept my suggestions, some plan that the enemies could come to agreement on . . . that was my goal. Harmony, for the sake of Christ.

I didn't suspect that His Holiness and Giberti were only promoting their own interests. They thought they could use me to win Ferrante over. That's the most bitter disappointment—in retrospect I have to admit that their suspicions were justified. But I certainly wasn't even thinking of playing diplomatic games. I was willing to let myself be used as a link between the Pope and Spanish sympathizers so that I could help bring about a peace.

Was I working only for peace? I pray God to help me to be honest with myself ... Why do I doubt myself again? Of course I was trying to pave the way for harmony, for mutual understanding ... If I were really doing it only on account of Ferrante, to bring him closer to me—wouldn't I have known it? I've always hated self-deception; I've known for a long time that I can never conquer Ferrante. True, there was a time when I would have given everything I had to possess him. But that's over now, that's over ...

Why did His Holiness ask me to come to the audience? He spoke almost the whole time only to my friends from Camerino. He was polite to me, but his voice was cold, he gave me sharp looks—when do I expect my husband home from Novara, how long does he plan to stay in Rome? Have his wounds healed which he received at Pavia? A formal question-and-answer game, chilly and conventional after the friendly letter he sent me last year. And just before the end of the interview he lashed out—

"Your Excellency must now desire peace more passionately than ever ... if only to be able to enjoy wedded bliss at long last without interruption. His Imperial Majesty makes too many demands on your husband ... Let's hope that he'll know how to value and reward the merits of the Marquis of Pescara."

A world of meaning in a few words. The Pope, Giberti, everyone who was there knew her circumstances too well to be misled by a self-possessed smile. The blood left her heart, her lips felt cold and stiff. She didn't answer. Wedded bliss. A pretty, melodious phrase, a phrase for poets. Did it really exist outside the sphere of testimonial speeches, panegyrics, pastoral idylls?

She had been seventeen years old when she was married to Ferrante Francesco d'Avalos, Marquis of Pescara. That was an alliance with favorable terms for both parties. She spent the years between the betrothal and the actual marriage at the castle of Ferrante's relatives in Ischia; that was a breathing-space for her after an early youth full of disturbance and danger. The Colonna had been driven from their lands by the Borgia Pope Alexander, who had taken Nepi from them, their estate in the Romagna. They had fled to Naples where Vittoria's father Fabrizio became general to the Viceroy. He arranged Vittoria's marriage because he knew that he could become influential in the pro-Spanish South only if he were connected to a leading family of Castilian blood; the D'Avalos family were seduced by the Colonna's ancient name and military reputation. Ferrante and Vittoria were the same age—healthy, attractive young people, carefully brought up The negotiations for the wedding went forward smoothly.

From time to time over the years between the betrothal and the marriage Ferrante came to visit Vittoria at Ischia. They spoke little on these occasions; Ferrante's aunt, who acted as duenna, took note of Ferrante's covert glances, Vittoria's blushes. It was the aunt who saw to it that the nuptials were not delayed any longer.

Amid the blooming lemon trees in the park of the Casa d'Avalos stood a statue of an ancient god. Fishermen had hauled it up out of the Bay of Naples. It was made of smooth yellow marble: a winged figure of a youth with closed eyes, who held a warning finger to his lips. When he was brought in, algae and seaweed hung on his body like dark green slime; shellfish were clinging to him. Young Vittoria often stood motionless before this god. She saw him as Eros, but Ferrante was convinced that the statue represented Mors, the personification of death. Later that double identity seemed significant to her. When had love become synonymous with death?

She realized one day, still early in her marriage, that she was not satisfied by Ferrante's embraces. In her arms he remained a stranger, closed-off, inaccessible. It was a brief pleasure that they shared; a tempestuous sensual appetite which flared up and vanished without a trace. Vittoria knew that she really had nothing to complain about: her husband respected her, behaved in a friendly way, came to her bed every night. What royal bride could expect more?

She didn't understand the longing which tormented her. Why did she feel lonely? Glances, smiles, gestures, the private language of lovers . . . she looked beyond these to find the secret ardor of the soul. She found Ferrante difficult to understand; she was fascinated by the depths that she suspected lurked behind his Castilian reserve. She brooded constantly about the qualities which must be hidden in him; these only were what she desired to find. She never talked about this; she couldn't put it into words.

She didn't enjoy the banquets, hunting parties and tournaments which she had to attend during those first years in Naples. Her pleasures lay in serious conversations, quiet gatherings; raucous noise she found paralyzing. As time passed she detected growing hostility in the exciting sexual currents and countercurrents flowing between her and Ferrante—currents which swept her off-balance and left her exhausted and embittered. She did not trust this intoxicating ecstasy; she was afraid it would sully the purity of the ideal love, the heroic feeling between two kindred spirits which was her model of perfection. She held back out of fear of spoiling that ideal love.

Gradually her stiff behavior destroyed Pescara's desire: when he saw his wife becoming cold, withdrawn, unresponsive, he drew away from her. He began an affair with the Vicereine of Naples who captivated him so that he forgot his resentment against his wife. Vittoria was crushed by his unfaithfulness; he didn't realize that her emotion stemmed from suppressed passion. He seemed to respect Vittoria; he appeared reconciled to the fact that she was barren. He appreciated her beauty, her intelligence, her dignity. Her piety, her interest in poetry and philosophy, her preference for seclusion over attendance at banquets and fêtes—he accepted all this as part of her nature; her austere chastity he saw also as an integral part of her. She had his respect, but he was no longer attracted to her.

She had the statue of the blind winged god placed in a chamber where, she said, she intended henceforth to sleep alone. He accepted this too, with a smile; her seriousness and religious devotion, he thought, were beginning to border dangerously on religious mania. There was a touch of mockery in his attitude.

In the autumn of 1511, Pescara rode, under the banner of Pope Julius, against the French who were occupying Lombardy. He was gone for more than four years.

❧❧

Wedded bliss. His Holiness certainly knows how to choose his words. For years Ferrante has avoided living under the same roof with me and God knows I feel closest to him when we're apart. His letters don't destroy that illusion of affection: "Your Excellency, my dear wife, to learn that Your Excellency enjoys good health is my most heartfelt wish . . ."

We have many things in common: the estates in Ischia, Marino, Benevento . . . Money matters, family affairs . . . And everything that concerns our stepson Alfonso, Ferrante's heir and successor. When I write to Ferrante, when I read his replies, I have the feeling that we're united. But to see him again, to speak with him, to touch his hands—I don't dare to think about what that means to me. I don't want to repeat the homecoming he had in '15—never, never! I'd rather escape to the farthest, most remote corner of the world!

❧❧

Pescara was taken captive by the French at the Battle of Ravenna. But after his release, years passed before his return to Naples. He spent the greater part of the time in Mantua, at the friendly court of the Gonzaga. It wasn't a secret that he stretched his visit to the very limits of hospitality because of Delia Equicola, a beautiful woman in the retinue of the Marchioness. He decided to travel to the South only because of the death of the Spanish King and the subsequent questions of succession. Vittoria received him with deceptive calm; she was determined not to betray her deep bitterness by word or manner. Pescara saw her coolness, her self-possession; it was from courtesy, not desire, that on those first nights he visited her bed.

At the foot of that bed the winged god exhorted her to be silent, and close her eyes.

> He doesn't know anything, he doesn't suspect anything. After he left me, I couldn't sleep. I prayed, I begged to be delivered from that inner conflict. My body demanded the pleasure I had denied myself for so long. Never before had I grasped the full meaning of desire. Night after night, I betrayed myself, I betrayed my deepest convictions. Then, after that brief oblivion, boundless emptiness . . .

Pescara was more surprised by her passion than he had been by her coldness in the past. He tried to think of an explanation for it: was she hoping to become pregnant, did she begrudge the succession to his young nephew Alfonso del Vasto, who had grown up in their house? He was slightly repelled by her physical appetite: tears, sighs, those fits of silence seemed unnatural to him. With a feeling of relief he accepted the commission to go to Brussels to swear vassalage to the Emperor in the name of the pro-Spanish nobility. A year passed before he saw his wife again. It was a short, formal meeting with no opportunity for private conversation.

> We were guests at Bona Sforza's wedding, honored guests. We couldn't avoid even one of the countless cer-

emonies. Day after day and part of every night we sat next to each other, like strangers. Smiling masks, lifeless, stuffed robes of state: the Marquis and Marchioness of Pescara! The apartments they gave Ferrante and me were far away from each other—and there was so little space that we had to share our bedrooms with the members of our retinues. We were never alone together for an instant. And we didn't want to be alone together.

Despite all his courtesy to me, I could *feel* Ferrante's aversion toward me. Those feasts were a hell. And yet I didn't really want it to end. It was out of the question now that we could live together again in the quiet of the Casa d'Avalos or in the castle in Ischia . . . Ferrante had no place in my life, and I didn't fit into his. He was close to me only in the letters he wrote me, in the conversations I had about him with Alfonso.

Ferrante is a shadow, but he's part of me. His actual physical presence was—and still is—an intrusion into my peace of mind. He himself can't exist along with the image I form of him when I'm alone. I can't be deprived of that image; it's the only consolation which I have created for myself. Physical desire can be overcome . . .

❦

The couple seldom met after the year 1517. Pescara was rising rapidly in the Emperor's esteem. In the struggle against the French in Lombardy, he was distinguished by his courage, his energy, his ability to organize. Vittoria heard him praised as the most capable general of his time. She couldn't think clearly when Ferrante was always with her; she could deal more easily with the man who turned up for a few days' visit once or twice a year. She wasn't blinded by praise or flattery. She knew what qualities made up his character under his formal Spanish courtliness: ambition, an extremely vulnerable sense of his own importance, cold calculation. . . .

Silently, secretly, her eyes were on him always. She knew every line of that face, that body: the thin, proud lips, the scars on his cheeks and forehead, the way he moved his shoulders when he spoke, his habit of emphasizing points in an argument by patting chair or tabletop lightly with the palm of his hand, his firm, disciplined step, the way his hand rested on the hilt of his sword. . . .

During the business discussions they had whenever they met, Vittoria began to object to his harsh judgments, his tendency to cruelty. But when in the heat of argument she met his eyes—smoldering under frowning brows, dark, annoyed at her opposition, derisive—then in her confusion she forgot all her objections. She knew that feeling: it was a prelude to the passion which had driven her into his arms in the past. Now the only affection shown between them were formal kisses of greeting and farewell. She tried to distract herself from the restlessness she felt when he was near her, by engaging in all sorts of busy work. Whenever she knew he was coming to visit, she upset the peaceful routine of her household by inviting guests, preparing elaborate fêtes and hunting parties.

Pescara found his wife's moods incomprehensible: she alternated between periods of nervous vivacity and tense silence. He couldn't force himself to pretend desire for her any more. He was completely preoccupied with Delia Equicola, the young woman at the court in Mantua. She usually stayed with him in the army camps or fortresses which he commanded. She was uncomplicated: warm, responsive, blindly devoted to him, and she gave him children. Vittoria knew about her, but neither she nor Pescara ever mentioned her. Delia was, however, the unnamed, unseen third person who was always between them. Ferrante did not call her up with words but his look when he was lost in thought, the language of his body, called her up—the other, the desired, fertile one—out of nothingness.

He treats me with formality, pretense, irony. When his eyes cloud over while he is taking wine, listening to music, when we dance or when he returns from a strenuous hunt, then I know he's thinking about *her*. It's *she* who makes him restless when his visit with me lasts too long. I know he respects me: he leaves everything to me, lets me handle things as I think best. Not long after Pavia, he sent me that flattering letter:

". . . that our nephew Del Vasto bore himself with notable courage and dignity is thanks primarily to the way in which Your Excellency has formed and guided him over the years. I have been away a great deal and have been able to contribute less to his upbringing than I would have wished. I shall always remain deeply grateful to Your Excellency, because in Alfonso del Vasto she has presented me with a worthy successor. . . ."

Those words are explicit, they're sincerely respectful. He was in the fortress of Novara when he wrote that. Was *she* standing behind him, next to him? And I'll never be able to meet Alfonso again without remembering that he has seen Ferrante with that Other. . . . Alfonso. My ward, for years the center of my life. The only real peace I've ever known came from him. All the time I was raising him, I kept thinking of Ferrante: the stronger the tie between Alfonso and me, the closer I felt to Ferrante. My body is barren, but I can call Del Vasto my own son; he couldn't be more a part of me if I had borne him myself. Ferrante thinks so too. Now Alfonso is grown up, he's detached from me, circumstances have pushed him to Ferrante. As successor and heir he'll have more control over the administration of money and estates than I will. I accept that completely. But how can I bear the thought that I'm not needed any more?

When young Alfonso left her in '21 to join the Emperor's troops in Lombardy, Vittoria began again the laborious task of filling the empty space in her life. She stayed for a while in Naples, visited for a while with her only brother Ascanio in Rome. But it was Ischia that she loved, the castle where she had spent the first years of her marriage. She returned there, gathered a circle of poets and scholars around her, gave commissions, bought their works for her library, invited them to meet under the cypresses and laurels of her park. She forced herself to take her patronage seriously; what had once been no more than a pastime for her, a conventional game, had now become a necessity.

Later she looked back on this period as a time of sterile repose, of artificially cultivated peace. The poetical works dedicated to her, the eloquence of the debates—these were technically perfect but they were as pale and lifeless as the statues among the foliage lining the avenues. With secret annoyance she thought about the sonnets and canzoni celebrating her in courtly fashion and about how, with the echoes of that fervent praise and elegant admiration in her ears, she tossed sleepless during the long nights in her lonely bed. The amorous literary declarations of Sannazaro, Britonio, Gravina and a half-dozen other court poets left a bitter aftertaste. The gap between pretense and reality was too wide. She was the Muse of professional flatterers—Pallas Athena, Aphrodite and Artemis rolled into one, rival of the sun and the moon, mistress of Parnassus . . .

But far more difficult to forget than these lyrics were the taunting words of a street song she had heard once while she was riding through Naples next to Ferrante:

> Sweetheart of mine,
> I'll be with you as often
> As Pescara with his Vittoria.

❦

I played their game; I became tainted in order to survive with the evil I've always hated: self-deception. I became intoxicated with words. I wrote verses glorifying wedded bliss, faithfulness in marriage—it was a strange satisfaction after that to hear Ferrante and me praised publicly as the ideal couple. I produced insincere, stilted strophes about the love between the hero away at war and his patient, waiting wife. I sent them to Ferrante who always reported punctiliously that he had received the pages in good condition. No more than that—and that taciturnity brought me to my senses. I was surfeited with flattery, and sick with loneliness.

I visited my brother Ascanio in Rome. But although I had a change of scene, I still suffered from the same affliction. I went to churches, convents, chapels . . . a futile pilgrimage. My prayers rose no higher than the ornate altars, there was only emptiness beyond the candlesticks and images. Confession didn't relieve me, the mass seemed a meaningless jangle. God had become unreachable. Fasting, mortification of the flesh, self-chastisement . . . I tried everything, but it wasn't any use. I was struggling for grace; I went through the same suffering I had endured over Ferrante. I thought that God's peace would fulfill that need that had driven me to Ferrante in the past. In surrender to God, I thought, the desires of the body, the turbulence of the blood, would fade painlessly away. I couldn't understand why that comfort was denied me.

It was at her brother Ascanio's court that she first met the ducal couple from Camerino—Giovanni Maria Varano and his wife Caterina Cibo. The Varano and Colonna families had fought together in the past against the power of the Borgia; their alliance remained even when their enemy's name was only a memory. The Duke and Duchess of Camerino came to Rome regularly: two serious people noted for their somber dress and habits. They never attended a single fête; in fact, they were seldom seen in public. When they were not visiting friends, they went with a small retinue to certain private gatherings, which were the real purpose of their visit.

Vittoria had heard good things about the Company of Divine Love, but she didn't know who went there or what they did there. Caterina Cibo was still young, a woman with a long, thin face and deep-set narrow eyes: ordinarily she faded into the background, but she came to life vividly when she began to talk about the beliefs which obsessed her. Varano was more open-minded than she, more inclined to choose the middle way. He had been badly wounded in his youth when he was fleeing from the assassins serving Cesare Borgia; since then his delicate health had forced him to use diplomacy, compromise, patience—the weapons of the uncontentious.

When he finally came back to his estate of Camerino after years of exile, he found fortresses and villages in partial ruins, the fields neglected, the people apathetic from fear and poverty. He summoned the hill farmers to bring their complaints and petitions to him. But fewer came than he had expected: he had become a stranger; he was distrusted.

It was a Franciscan monk from the monastery of Montefalcone who had supplanted him as the people's authority: Fra Matteo da Bascio had endangered his own life to help the people of Camerino survive plague and famine. They looked upon him as a benefactor who stood in the odor of sanctity: his word was law, the people would follow his judgment of the ducal pair. Varano invited the monk to come and see him; he thanked him for everything he had done, promised to support his good works, and kept his word.

Thus without threats or a show of force Varano made sure of the people's loyalty; they identified Fra Matteo's patrons with Fra Matteo himself—an inviolable trinity. Varano was pleased with his accomplishment. And a deep friendship developed between Caterina and the monk. They were kindred spirits: both passionate, militant, willing to make any sacrifice for their beliefs. Varano contributed money and other help to the monk's causes, but Caterina did what Fra Matteo did: cared for the sick, fed and clothed the poor, comforted the afflicted.

Vittoria took the couple into her confidence; they shared their views with her. They propounded Fra Matteo's doctrine to her: the necessity for simplicity, self-discipline, repentance. Every time they visited Rome they became stronger in their belief that peace of mind can be achieved only through a mercilessly honest recognition of one's faults. The halls and galleries of Ascanio Colonna's palace rang with Caterina's loud, somewhat harsh voice raised in a rhetorical catechism:

"Where does the catharsis begin? In our minds. Who has the right to form and direct that mind? The Church, which calls itself holy. To be called that, it must be as pure as spring water, as spotless as snow, as cleansing as fire. But the Church is a breeding ground for pollution. The ritual is only a surface thing. The cardinals and bishops, all the prelates high and low, give themselves over to worldly lust and ambition. In the monasteries idleness and immorality run riot—monks steal, they beg and whore! The sacraments are bartered, the Ten Commandments are rolled into one command: give us money! Rome stinks of corruption, all of it . . .

"Listen to what Fra Matteo says: even the elect have become unfaithful; the world is the Lord's vineyard and He is waiting for righteousness but there is no righteousness, there is no justice, there's only rot and cacophony. The Church can't show us the way. Faith doesn't mean anything to most of us, don't tell me it permeates our lives—that's a lie! Everything is superficial—the talk about the will of God, Jesus, Maria and all the saints . . . just words and gestures, superficial, like bows and compliments at court. Faith is just a formal game to us . . . The stupid mob is superstitious, the educated show off their paganism, they should set an example but they're unbelievers, they're rotten to the core. The Church gives us stones when we ask for bread. So she's become a joke, a curse. So therefore let us begin at the beginning. A broom to sweep through the Curia, the Orders, the monasteries . . .

"That's what Fra Matteo says, and he's right . . ."

Caterina leaned forward, fixing Vittoria with a forceful stare. Her face, leathery and yellow-brown from wind and weather, was glowing with emotion.

Varano had kept nodding as his wife spoke. Now he broke in with a palliative smile. "You're defensive, but you forget that no one is attacking you," he said to her mildly. He turned to Vittoria. "After all, Fra Matteo is fighting against abuses which all right-thinking people hate, our friends in the Company are working for the same goal. There's nothing new under the sun; as long as I can remember people have been demanding reform. But now the time's ripe for action. Now don't think for a moment that we're like those German hotheads who actually repudiate the authority and the tenets of the Church; please understand me: the leaders of the Company don't think like that at all—not Fra Matteo, not Caterina or I. We want to support the foundations of the Church, we don't want to undermine them. We want to go back to the pure source, the Word of Christ and His disciples, we want to use that fountainhead to reanimate the laws and practices of the Church, do you see? Many people close to the Pope feel the same way, they see that it's necessary. The Datary Giberti himself is the driving force at meetings of the Company. We're trying to set an example, to influence public opinion—"

"Be quiet now!" Caterina cried. "Let *me* tell her what Fra Matteo says. *I* think like him, *you* want to tread the middle way! Now is the time to choose a position, to define our attitude. Everything that separates us from God must be cast out, banished, annihilated! Love of God can never be great enough, He must be loved eternally, cherished above everything else, never forsaken! I would make any sacrifice, bear any pain if I had to, all privation for His sake . . ."

Vittoria tried haltingly to put her thoughts into words. "I feel that it must be possible to give oneself up to the service of God, but how can I reach that love? No one can serve two masters— those who want to give God their love must renounce everything. If you're chained by earthly possessions, you can't ascend to Him. Tell me how it can be done."

Caterina rushed up to her and threw her arms about her. Vittoria let herself relax into that vigorous protective embrace. She felt Caterina's thin strong shoulder against her cheek and, palpable through flesh and clothing, the slow, regular, restful throbbing of Caterina's heart.

"I can't go on," Vittoria whispered. "Show me the way, tell me what I must do to find peace. . . ."

"Peace is where God is, in ourselves. He will still all desires, seeking satisfaction elsewhere is like trying to slake your thirst with salt."

"Is the only way then to forsake the world, to live in a prayer cell, to wear a habit and cowl?"

"No, no, that's all superficial too. What does it matter where you live and what you wear if you've dared to change your whole life? If you've put a stop to desires and evil thoughts, you don't need to shave your head. If you're filled with thoughts of God, you don't need to pray night and day. The *will* is what matters. Why else have we been given a will if not for the sake of God?"

"But I'm afraid of the power of nature—it works within us, it undermines our will, it poisons our blood—"

"But that's precisely our task! To subdue nature and make it serve God!"

"Oh, teach me," Vittoria said, "teach me how to do that! I will certainly do it if I can . . ."

"Don't lead her astray," Varano said to his wife. "All we can do is stimulate the will, each must find his own way alone. What do I know about your pilgrimage—what do you know about mine? Isn't that precisely the crux of our teaching—that everyone must learn to know God in his own way?" He looked at Vittoria. "Invite Madonna to attend a meeting of the Company with us—to be our guest in Camerino—maybe what she hears and sees there will strike a chord in her heart."

The figures of the ducal couple moved into the foreground of Vittoria's field of vision: everything sank into oblivion beside them. She drew strength from their confidence, even though she didn't fully understand them. But they gave her the impression that it was possible to cross the boundaries at which she stood frozen in hopeless despair, that it was possible, without losing one's faith, to recognize that the Church did not offer sufficient means of consolation. One could condemn, even reject, things about the Church, in the growing consciousness of God's grace. So perhaps after all her doubts did not mean an ending; they might mean a beginning.

Has my life really changed since I began attending the meetings in San Silvestro and Santa Dorotea? At first I really believed that it had. After all that clever, pointless chit-chat in Ischia, the empty hours alone in Rome, I was comforted by the straightforward seriousness of the Brotherhood. Giberti, Sadoleto, Contarini—I knew their names, but there in Trastevere I enjoyed the privilege of associating with them as if we were old friends. I was impressed by their learning, their firmness of character, their piety. Their aims became mine too. Every week, the meetings in the little church on the slope of Monte Janiculo near the spot where Peter died a martyr's death. Every week the renewal of the promise to dedicate ourselves to meditation and the practice of charity, to follow Christ's teaching in word and deed . . .

Have I kept my promises? I give alms to the poor, I help the hospitals, I visit the cloisters. I live simply. I lose myself in the writings of Paul and Augustine. But I don't have Varano's peace of mind, Catarina's inspiration. The form of my life is altered, but not the content. Under the surface, the constant passion lies in wait, ready to burst out at the first sign and catch me off-balance.

What do I really care for the notions of that far-away Fra Matteo or the Company, for the books on my prayer stool, now that I know Ferrante could be here at any moment? This is a betrayal and a defeat at the same time. I try to recapture the thoughts that had comforted me over the last few years, but they're pale, unreal, next to the certainty that Ferrante is coming.

I haven't seen him since '21. Three, four years have passed . . . an eternity. He writes me that the wounds are healed which he received at Pavia. But I hear other rumors. The messenger who brought me his letters let something slip toward the end: "The Marquis is in pain, it's hard for him to walk, he's not the man he was." God grant that I can persuade him to stay with me for a while. Not in Rome . . . they say that the district along the Tiber is infected with pestilence. I want to go with Ferrante to Marino, to Ischia. I would even put up with his summoning that Other if he longs for her. . . .

It's not peace I have to thank for his presence, but

war. An insult of fate, a mockery of my struggle to bring about a reconciliation between the parties. Would I have thought of doing that without Giberti's influence? In retrospect I'm inclined to think he had a hand in this matter. We became friends in the Company; he had my confidence. In the first year we often had long talks about the disasters in Italy, about the bitter necessity for peace.

When he was the papal ambassador in France and Spain, I wrote to him regularly. And it was he who brought me into direct contact with His Holiness. In one letter I implored the Pope to work for a reconciliation of the hostile powers for the sake of Italy and the Faith. At Easter His Holiness sent me a palm branch which he had blessed himself—I saw that as a symbol, a promise. I wrote to Ferrante about that—I asked him if he would plead for peace with the Emperor. He answered me by courier from his army camp in Lombardy: I mustn't make any attempt to lure him or my Colonna relatives into a political trap . . . I was really hurt and offended by his distrust. Of course I had never consciously been a tool in the hands of the French sympathizers. And I didn't doubt Giberti's good faith until recently. Really, I should have realized even then that you can't rely on the Pope's word. I was misled by his apparent sympathy. . . .

The news caught Vittoria by surprise that Pescara and her nephew Prospero Colonna had led the Emperor's troops across the French border. Giberti behaved in as friendly a manner as ever, but she felt that he was on his guard, that he didn't really believe that she was upset about this latest move. Pope Clement lost control of himself and openly accused her of violating his trust. Vittoria thought that his words smacked of hypocrisy. She began to suspect for the first time that it was not peace he had been working for since the beginning, but the French cause.

Ferrante informed her that as the Emperor's Commander, his

business at this stage was to wage war and not to make peace. His strategy had the desired effect: it lured the French armies into the field. Skirmishes, sieges, brief confrontations here and there in Lombardy culminated finally in the Battle of Pavia. From the day that the news of the Emperor's victory reached Rome, Giberti avoided Vittoria. She was told that she was in disgrace with the Pope. She immersed herself in good works and meditation, but she could not forget the bitterness of that experience.

In Rome the mood was divided between dismay and high excitement. Ascanio Colonna hung out the Emperor's colors and received the Spanish sympathizers at extravagant fêtes. But Vittoria never left her apartments. In her letters to Pescara she dwelt more on his wounds than on his victory. It seemed to her that his replies didn't reflect a mood of triumph. She read discontent between the lines, self-pity. He told her that he would arrive in Rome ". . . as soon as these cursed injuries have healed."

On the hills, the almond and lemon trees were in blossom: the air was filled with the perfume of oleander and honeysuckle. The fields were rose-red and white with anemone. Outside the city, amid some ancient ruins, the Colonna owned a country house in a setting of vineyards and olive groves. Vittoria often spent a few days and nights there. The silence, the pure air, were refreshing after a long stay in Rome. She walked alone in the carefully laid-out gardens, along the narrow straight spaces between the vines; she sat alone for hours in the shade of a trellised arbor. Sometimes she followed an overgrown path that led through woods and undergrowth to the remains of a temple.

A single fluted column still stood erect among broken fragments and heaps of stone. There was a faint rustling under weeds and trailing vines: a stone fell, leaves flickered—a glossy green snake glided away into the shadows. Cicadas sang in the grass . . . no sound beyond that except for the flapping of a wood pigeon's wings and the bleating of goats higher up on the slopes.

Rome lay at the foot of the hills: domes, towers, a sea of irregular, slightly sloping roofs. Seen from this height, the city appeared to be a confusion of colored chips thrown higgledy-piggledy into a basket: brick-red and yellow ochre, grey, cream, white. In the bright April light, all the colors looked fresh and bright, as if they were shining with dew. Outside the city walls a branch of the Tiber wandering through the open fields gave off a dazzling glitter. Stinking rubbish heaps, collapsed buildings, filthy narrow alleys, patches of waste . . . none of these were visible. No signs of life except wisps of smoke which rose here and there above the housetops. The statue on the Angel fortress sparkled like a star.

Pavia, worry about Pescara, fear of the future, her own doubts and inner struggle . . . these sank back into the depths of her mind. They were always there, like memories and bad dreams, but less real, less painful than in Rome. She might have stayed on at the country house until Pescara's return, if she hadn't heard that Giovanni Maria Varano and his wife had come once again from Camerino to pay a short visit to Rome.

For the first time since I met them, I had the feeling that their zeal is excessive. Possibly because of my disquiet over Ferrante's homecoming and my stay in the country, I feel somewhat removed from the work that occupies them. They're fulfilling Fra Matteo's vision: Saint Francis appeared to him in a dream, calling: "I insist that the Order keep my rules to the letter, to the letter, to the letter!" The brothers of Montefalcone were evidently not ready for reform, because Fra Matteo and a half-dozen followers have separated themselves from them. Now they live as hermits in the forests of Camerino, under the protection of Varano and Madonna Caterina.

The Franciscans here in Rome have demanded their excommunication and execution. Of course my friends came to plead with the Pope for Fra Matteo. His Holiness granted their request—how could it be otherwise? Madonna Caterina is his blood relative.

But it was completely unexpected, frankly astounding, that *I* was invited to be present at that audience. For the first time since Ferrante invaded France, I have been to the Vatican again. Without enthusiasm. I still don't understand His Holiness's purpose. A show of forgiveness? I don't believe it. I have a trained ear: his voice was affable but there was a note of irony in it; his eyes remained cold. He must have known that his words would hurt me. "Wedded bliss"! The Emperor's "appreciation" of Ferrante's service! Sore spots which no one should touch. Is it still a secret from anyone that Ferrante and I seldom meet, that we're heavily in debt because the Emperor doesn't keep his promises?

Giberti stood next to the Pope's chair and watched me. All the while my friends were speaking with the Pope, I could feel his eyes on me. This seemed strange, because we have had no contact for a long time. The audience was brief: a legation had apparently arrived from Milan; the Chancellor Girolamo Morone and his retinue.

I've never seen the Vatican galleries so crowded. The guards had to clear the way for us. I thought I saw Messer Michelangelo Buonarroti in the crowd—it's not a face you forget easily. What can he be doing here? I thought he had moved to Florence for good. The encounter had a violent effect on me, I don't know why. He's suffering, he's exhausted, embittered—that's obvious, even to a stranger like me. I'd like to hold that head in my arms and comfort him like a child . . . But you couldn't approach him with pity . . . pity is for the helpless. I don't understand my own thoughts, much less the feeling that made me forget time and place for a moment.

I don't know the man; I've never exchanged a word with him. Without so much as a nod, he gave me a sad, surly look. But it almost seemed as thought I were walking past a part of myself. I felt a shock of surprise: I recognized something I can't identify.

Varano and Madonna Caterina are pleased with their visit with the Pope. I'm not going with them to Holy

Year ceremonies in the basilica of Santa Maria in Trastevere. I don't feel capable of listening to any more talk
about Fra Matteo and his heavenly visions.

She sat in her bedchamber and watched the bands of sunlight
creep back across the floor, to vanish finally through the window
niche. A book lay open on her reading desk; she did not look at
it.

Toward evening, the courtyard echoed with the sound of horses'
hooves. A servant announced the early arrival of the Marquis of
Pescara. At the head of the grand staircase, Vittoria waited to
greet him. He had not yet appeared, but she could hear, in the
vaulted passage which led from the courtyard, an unfamiliar shuf-
fling step, the steady tapping of a stick. She pressed her nails into
her palm in a vain attempt to control the trembling that overcame
her.

V.

Niccolò Machiavelli to Francesco Guicciardini

L ord President of the Romagna, dear friend:

I'm writing this letter to you from Rome. I came here three days ago to pay my respects to His Holiness. The audience was a disappointment. I had fixed my last hopes on the Pope, to get me a position better suited to my talents than the job of postman which they think is good enough for me in Florence now. His Holiness knows me. He's spoken sympathetically about me more than once, even if he were a hundred times a Medici. I took that into account when I dedicated the eighth book of my *Florentine History* to him.

At the beginning of this year, I sounded out Vettori about whether I should come here. He's never very encouraging: when he replied that the Pope had read a part of the *History* and thought it was good, I made up my mind to take a chance. I was properly received: Strozzi and Salviati immediately promised to use their influence on my behalf. I must admit that I was counting on a great improvement in my circumstances. This time I didn't go out of my way to be modest. My petition is crystal clear; it leaves nothing out. The water is climbing to my lips; day and night I look desperately for a way to serve this unhappy, afflicted country.

What is there for a man like me in that farmhouse at San Casciano, surrounded by chickens, geese and yokels? I've told you often enough how I spend my days: strolling back and forth between my orchard and the inn, drinking wine and playing little games of backgammon and reading, reading, reading the works of my Greek and Roman friends, whose only shortcoming is that they've been dead for fifteen hundred years.

Francesco, you know what I'm worth. When I'm forced to be idle, I become as musty and bitter as forgotten fruit in the drying loft. I ask you: what kind of existence is that? I never have any peace: I see Italy going to rack and ruin helped along by the stupidity and corruption of our high lords—which shrieks to heaven. I could advise them. I'm the apothecary with the bitter medicine, the last resort. I don't guarantee recovery, but in a time of emergency, surely any suggestions should be welcome. If only I had the necessary authority. Do you know what's going on? They want to sip the medicine at their pleasure, and without paying attention to the prescription. I see every fool in the Vatican making a mess of the remedies which turn to poison in their hands. All I can do is look on the whole tragedy as a farce—as incredibly true to life, as heart-rendingly comic as my *Mandragola*—which, by the way, I gathered to my pleasure from your last letter, reduced you and your closest entourage to tears of laughter.

Really, it doesn't happen every day that an ex-envoy of Florence, ex-confidant of princes and prelates, still makes a career as a writer of farces. Even His Holiness was good enough to direct a few flattering remarks to me: the comedy had amused him particularly; he was thinking of having it performed for the court, surely to add some luster to this unsuccessful Jubilee at the eleventh hour. But about a suitable post, a proper salary for the author—who, by God, has surely earned his spurs as a politician and diplomat—not one word.

So I offered the *History* to His Holiness with death in my heart, because at that moment the formal presentation seemed like an empty gesture. Other than the vague promise of an allowance— When? How much? No one said a word about that—I received nothing. I was amazed to hear His Holiness announce that he was thinking of allowing the papal press to print *The Prince*. It remains to be seen whether he means it. But if that should happen, it would be the fulfilment of one of my most fervent wishes. Let them only seek in black and white what power means, possessing authority, ruling, keeping order, bearing arms and being vigilant—in short, what it means to be a prince. Let them take heed from that example, those lords who don't know what they want and if they did know, wouldn't be able to translate their wishes into action. God grant that this situation doesn't go on for too long. It doesn't seem that we have much time left to act in some way. If something isn't done soon, we're lost.

I take it that you—probably better than anyone else—know about the preparations that the Datary Giberti and Messer Alberto Pio, the French ambassador, are making to develop a new strong League against the Emperor. But what can come of it? An indissoluble alliance to fight against His Majesty's dangerous power? How many indissoluble treaties have we all seen forged over the last twenty-five years? Both for and against the Empire? I've lost count, my worthy friend. I don't give a fig for this plan either. The essence of a League is that the results are noticeable only in the long run—certainly if everything is handled in the usual way, with endless scribbling and gabbling on both sides, not to mention all the mutual internal intrigue.

The way things are now, we need immediate action. His Holiness's attitude—that eternal spinning in all directions—would make sense if its purpose was to gain time for effective measures . . . but it is frankly irresponsible now because there's no fixed policy behind it. His decisions—taken too early or too late, or not taken at all or completely wrong anyway—spoil whatever little chance we still have.

The German and Spanish mercenaries are not being paid, they're restless, capable of anything. Who's going to defend France, Venice—the Ecclesiastical State when it comes to that? A spark in the powderhouse and then? *Actum erit de libertate Italiae.*

I know you think the way I do. Giberti and Alberto Pio are pushing the Pope toward a League, but you're making a contribution there too. Giberti is very capable—a noble man—but not progressive enough; Pio is a diplomatic weathercock. The ingenious moves must come from you, Francesco. You're not blind; a man with your experience and background can't be. We mustn't be dependent upon foreigners. French support doesn't mean a thing: as long as they're negotiating with Madrid over the release of their own King, they won't steer a single horseman or foot soldier or ducat in our direction. And if they did, what then? I know a little about mercenaries. You never know if they're coming, and if they are, when; they're more of a hindrance than a help. Nothing binds them except pay and if they don't think it's enough, they won't fight, or they'll go over to the enemy. What do the self-styled allies say when it comes to the point? What did the English spokesman say the other day? *Quid ad nos Italia!* What's Italy to us . . . They're fighting for themselves, not for our freedom. And as far as Italy itself is concerned, how many fraternal quarrels and border disputes must we settle first before Venetians and Florentines and Milanese and Neapolitans trust one another?

If our struggle for independence has any chance to succeed, the whole thing has to be approached in a different way. Do you remember my idea about a national militia? That would be our salvation, that or something like it. We must defend ourselves. Of course it's inconceivable that on short notice a hundred towns and states would move together in unanimous agreement. But we have to make a beginning—a seed. When that exists, and people see that it's possible, then we'll all join together. What once happened in Florence is possible in the Romagna under your leadership. After all, you're the great man there: civil and military governor, pro-consul—we may safely say absolute ruler. Does the Pope ever dare to object to anything you decree?

Arm and train the populace. That's one point. Then comes a second one at least as important: what we need most urgently is a leader. Not just anyone, but a man who inspires us with confidence and who is respected even by the Emperor's followers. In short, an illustrious man, courageous, subtle, able to make decisions with far-reaching consequences. An ingenious commander. After Pavia, is there any necessity for me to name names? At the moment born leaders are a rare breed among us. What I'm going to say will probably strike you as reckless or even ridiculous, because you know that the man I'm singling out is fighting on the wrong side. But times like these demand bold measures.

Politics has private expedients and goes its own way, which has nothing to do with what you and I in our private life call good or evil. There's only one criterion that counts: efficiency. Not wavering, not hesitating, but choosing with determination the precise course that circumstances dictate. Who's going to squabble over the means once the end is attained! The goal: Italy's salvation. Now or never, Francesco. We must take our fate into our own hands. You, republican in heart and soul, have served the Medici all your life, you're an enemy of the worldly power of priests who has to do your duty as a papal official; now you have to realize the stake in this game: a new conception of the State.

The Sforza's Chancellor, Messer Girolamo Morone, has come to Rome from Milan. He had a long conversation with Giberti and later with the Pope too. I've heard one or two things about this visit from Giberti's secretary, Berni. Since then I haven't been able to think about anything else. Francesco, I can't emphasize this enough: this concerns an extremely important matter which is closely connected with everything I've been touching on here. Apparently the ideas I've had for years are shared by others. A daring plan: to grasp freedom! According to what I've heard, the man I would choose if I could select a leader, is perceived also in influential circles as the obvious person to take command in our struggle for independence. You'll understand that I can't go into these things in detail just now. See if you can arrange to have me appointed to the post of envoy between you and the court at Rome. I've made attempts in that direction myself, but who am *I*? *I* don't pull the strings of the papal puppet show. Only your influence might make such an arrangement possible. It's urgent that we speak privately with each other before too long.

Nothing has changed in Rome since I was last here, except that the court is not as brilliant as it was in the time of Pope Leo. I've spoken with many old acquaintances, called up many memories. I had a remarkable encounter in Giberti's offices. While I was chatting with Berni, a young man was announced: Messer Giovanni Borgia. That name is not often dropped so casually. A name associated with many memories, a piece of the past, a decisive period in my life. This Giovanni was one of the children in Cesare Borgia's retinue. The little Duke of Nepi and Camerino. Unless I'm mistaken, there was something wrong about him: there were too many conflicting explanations for the boy's presence there. I don't want to rake up old rumors—let them be dead and buried with the Borgia.

In any case, since that meeting in Berni's office, I've been thinking continually about the time I spent as envoy with Cesare in the Romagna. Those were the days when I still had hope because I believed he was the leader Italy needed. Francesco, you know better than anyone else that I was convinced that the dawn of our unity and independence lay in Cesare's actions against tyrants great and small in the Romagna. If he had been able to complete what he began with such cunning deliberation and careful calculation, France and the Emperor would never have been able to make us their slaves. He's been called base and treacherous, they've called his conquests in the Romagna a barbarous bloodbath. I've thought about it a great deal, and I don't see what else he could have done. It seems that evil will bow only to evil. Bitter necessity may force someone to take actions that can't bear the light of reason. Ends justify means. . . .

I've never tried to pretend that Cesare Borgia wasn't, from first to last, thinking of his own interests. But what I admired in him: his coldbloodedness, his ability to keep his plans secret, his tactic of sudden strikes, catching the enemy off-balance . . . Compared with him, the other princes and their *condottieri* were a troupe of amateurs. It's a question of size. He was the great snake who swallowed the little ones. If it should have become necessary to render the great snake harmless, then all the reptiles would have been destroyed at one blow. I remain convinced that similar measures are needed to form a whole from the patchwork quilt which Italy is at the present time. It's the senseless mutual hostility of the Colonna, Orsini, Montefeltre, Baglioni and so on that has weakened this country and that weakness will lead to our destruction.

You know that I've had to acknowledge that Cesare Borgia wasn't the man I had taken him to be at first. After his father's death he wasn't able to manage, and that speaks against him. He should have considered all eventualities, including the possibility that when Pope Alexander died, he himself might be too ill to act. Reverses made him uncertain, and that was the beginning of the end.

I visited him once more—it was the last time I saw him—in 1503 in the Castel Sant'Angelo where he was awaiting the Cardinals' conclave. I was in Rome constantly then as an envoy of the Signoria. Cesare knew that his enemy Della Rovere was going to be elected pope—he had even supported that choice himself for diplomatic reasons—in my eyes an incredible mistake. How could *he*—who used to break his promises arbitrarily—trust the word of an adversary? He always played the role of the superior, self-assured man. Perhaps he could deceive those around him, but *I* saw the uneasiness in his eyes. For the first time, I felt resentment, contempt . . . as well as pity. For me, the man was finished. I realized that he was not the personification of the Prince who could create *la Patria* out of a muddle of states great and small.

I had to make a great effort to cope with this disappointment. Later I learned to look at the thing in a different light. What did he mean to me, this man Cesare Borgia, who had failed? In spite of everything, his actions in the Romagna are still the practical application of those ideas I spelled out in that work of mine that you know so well.

See what thoughts can come out of a chance encounter! I haven't thought of Cesare Borgia for years. Incidentally, the young man at the Chancellery doesn't look like him, although he has dark eyes and skin like Pope Alexander. Anyone who didn't know his name wouldn't think of the relationship immediately. He's living proof of the speed with which the wheel of Fortune spins. His family were the powerful of the earth; he's an unassuming clerk at the papal court. The ducal crowns and the princedoms . . . some of them fell to him in his youth . . . now all gone up in smoke. If he's ambitious, he'll have a hard road to travel. But what do you and I care about this man—he can't alter the destiny of Italy by a hair!

I want to talk to you face to face about Messer Girolamo Morone and the matter which brought him here. This is in all our interests. God grant that I'll be able to talk to you about it myself very soon. I've fastened all my hopes on your intercession in this affair. Your voice can be decisive. *That* is a comfort in my bitterness . . . that at any rate fate has granted you in abundance what it withheld from me: influence upon those who set out policies.

A long letter this time. Reply quickly; I'm longing for favorable news from your end. I salute you.

Your Excellency's servant,
Niccolò Machiavelli
in Rome

VI.

Giovanni Borgia

Since the interview with Berni, I seem to have been appointed to a post. Without, by the way, knowing why, I have suddenly been added to the retinue of no lesser personage than Messer Girolamo Morone, Chancellor of Milan, who has come here for discussions. I still don't understand what service is expected of me—is there a point to this new job or is it purely decorative? Berni spoke in vague terms about a few things. But he promised me a large salary. He gave me at the most five minutes of his time. Berni's anteroom was filled with people waiting; there was, in fact, someone with Berni when I was announced. The visitor showed some surprise at hearing my name—Why?— and stared fixedly at me from a corner of the apartment while I was speaking with Berni

Later I found out who he was from one of my colleagues at the Chancellery. A certain Messer Machiavelli from Florence—envoy, poet, philosopher, apparently an excitable eccentric who wants to change the world. I believe I may well have heard that name before, but I don't know where or when. I can surely find out all about him if I ask for information from my remarkable friend in the peacock blue, Messer Pietro Aretino. Of course it was not by accident that I came upon him in the loggia. He was lying in wait for me or he had followed me. From the first word that he spoke, his intention was obvious: he wanted to strike up an acquaintance with me. He was as difficult to shake off as a leech. The meeting, incidentally, was useful. Without Messer Aretino's eloquence, I wouldn't have known that the Duke of Camerino was passing by. A strange sensation to hear someone else called by that name which I myself, rightly or wrongly, bore for a time. This Giovanni Maria Varano must be the one, the only member of his family who escaped Cesare's ambush. A slender fellow with a soft, dreamy face, grey-haired . . . I'd guess about fifty years old. He's a patron of mendicant friars, he goes every day to the Company of Divine Love.

But Camerino is a fortress in steep mountain country—it's an inheritance for a soldier, not for someone who spends his time studying the Letters of the Apostles with a bunch of women and scholars, and dabbles in Church reform. Apparently he is friendly with the wife of the Emperor's field commander. He'd be better off offering his support to Pescara himself or—depending on his convictions—to the French. When the fighting is prolonged and moves to the south, as it probably will, Camerino will be strategically important. If I were Varano, I wouldn't waste my time with theology; I'd prepare myself for what's going to happen in the near future.

I followed the procession to get another look at Varano so that I'd be sure to recognize him the next time. But actually I had eyes only for the woman Vittoria Colonna, Pescara's lady. This is the second time I've come across her by accident. The first time was in '17 in Naples—she passed me, riding next to Pescara in a royal procession. That was more than three years after I had left Bari and I was no longer on an equal footing with the high lords of Naples and its environs. I stood among the crowd in the street, a nameless spectator. The Marquis and Marchioness were greeted with cheers and applause: he was looked on as the hero of the battles in Lombardy, and as for her—the people wanted to honor her father, Fabrizio Colonna, the General of Naples.

I cried *"Viva!"* along with the multitude. I had just completed a period of service with the mercenaries drilled by Fabrizio Colonna for the Emperor's army; my admiration for the capable warrior, the great commander, was unbounded. *His* star guided me in my time of wandering. It was his example which led me, in those crucial years, to choose military service as a profession. So for his sake I too cheered the woman. Otherwise I was not interested in this beautiful, stiff, bejeweled doll.

The other day, in the colonnade of the Vatican, she made more of an impression upon me. A stern mouth, eyes full of shadows. But what caught my attention above all else: her striking resemblance to the woman at whose court I was brought up—my stepmother, Isabella of Aragon. The resemblance lay in her bearing and her expression. When I saw her approaching slowly, with downcast eyes and, around her mouth, the trace of what for lack of a better word I must call a smile, it seemed as though time had stood still.

They say that one's outward appearance bespeaks the soul within. A queerly exciting thought—that the chaste and yet ripe beauty of women like Isabella and this Vittoria should be the fruit of a secret grief, of privation endured with dignity. Messer Aretino hummed a ditty for me:

> Sweetheart of mine,
> I shall be with you as often
> As Pescara with his Vittoria.

Derisive promise of a lover who plans to desert his sweetheart! Street songs, in spite of their exaggerations, generally hit the mark. In Naples, when the Marquis and his wife rode past in the bridal procession of Bona Sforza, I heard joking remarks among the spectators: it had taken a lavish feast to lure Pescara home. What's the reaction of a beautiful woman scorned?

I bowed deeply when she went past me in the portico of the papal palace. I thought for a moment that she was looking at me. But she probably didn't even notice me. She was looking back over her shoulder at the man standing in front of me in the crowd; he—as Messer Aretino did not neglect to inform me—is apparently the painter and sculptor Michelangelo Buonarroti. I don't know much about arts or artists. When I saw the paintings on the arched ceiling of the Sistine Chapel, I had the notion that a man who could portray the human body that way must be especially well-favored himself. But the opposite is true: he's stooped over, has coarse wide, gnarled hands, and his hair and beard are tangled. His nose is broken—his whole face looks askew. When Messer Aretino spoke to him—"Evidently Her Excellency wishes to honor you with a greeting"—he didn't answer. He brushed his fingers quickly over his mouth and chin a few times as if he were wiping something away, and gave us an oblique look filled with nervous suspicion. Then with a sudden awkward movement he pushed his way into the crowd. Later, when I was back on my way to Giberti's office, I saw him walking in the distance. He hastened his step. Obviously he wasn't eager to be overtaken and addressed by Messer Aretino.

By that time the Marchioness's procession had reached the steps outside the bronze doors. Her husband Pescara is a great man: without him the Emperor's forces would never have won at Pavia. His energy and resourcefulness are inexhaustible; his attacks and skirmishes forced us to be constantly on our guard. His soldiers threw up ramparts all around our camp; that ring of fortifications tightened around us every day. Three days before the battle he stormed our bastions with a few thousand Spanish foot soldiers, pushed his way into our camp, seized our big guns as booty, inflicted heavy losses on us. Finally, on the twenty-fourth of February, the infamous day of Pavia, his musketeers slaughtered our horsemen and carried the day.

I'd like to fight under this man. It wouldn't pay badly to serve in a victorious army, and anyway I wanted to follow Pescara's banners long before I went to France. And if I hadn't gone to Ferrara, I'd surely have a worthwhile post now with the Emperor's troops. I felt so flattered that Alfonso d'Este wanted to help me that I followed his advice. And for a long time I really hoped that I'd make my fortune in France. I know better now. Of course they treated me courteously, but they considered me an adventurer; they'd never have given me a high rank in the army or a responsible post at the court. No man with an illustrious name would ever have given me his daughter. Now that I look back on it, I realize that visitors who aren't French are received with patient courtliness but they're never fully accepted.

Although it's true that I spent years serving the French cause, I wouldn't be a turncoat if I tried my luck on the Emperor's side—after all, I was born and brought up in Italy. My compatriots are free to choose whatever side offers the greatest advantage. I have no obligations to King Francis's army or his country. But I can't begin anything without the advice and help of influential people here at the court in Rome. So I have to wait and see. Maybe Messer Aretino can shed some light on my problem; he's an unreliable sort of fellow, but he's interesting and amusing and anyway he seems to be a useful connection.

I've tried to find out about him. No one at the Chancellery would answer my questions; they seem frightened to death of my friend in the peacock blue. He's the favorite of Paolo Giovio, the head of the papal library; if you make an enemy of him, it means dismissal. A clerk hinted that I could ask whatever I wanted to know at the Datary's office, and I gathered from Aretino himself the other day that he's not on good terms with Berni. So presumably people will be more communicative there. My years of experience in the ways of the world tell me that in everything associated with that inquisitive and eloquent gentleman, caution is the watchword. First problem: to discover why he seeks my company. He wouldn't be so obliging without a reason. He wants to be my guide in that labyrinth of Rome. To take me to Bramante's new palaces—which, incidentally, I saw when I was here in '18—or to antique ruins and displays of newly unearthed statues and vases? No, probably to show me around taverns and bordellos. He says he knows the great courtesans of Rome. Women who charge a fortune for a few nights. So far as I know, all those kisses and embraces leave only one tangible keepsake: the French disease.

I haven't touched a woman since I came here. Rome is infested with prostitutes at all prices: in the strada del Popolo and near the Ponte Sisto, they hang out the windows of house after house, calling out their fees to the passersby. Pimps are doing business in all the galleries of the Vatican. But I've known experienced ladies of the French court and half-savage suntanned country girls who want to amuse a lonely rider . . . these whores who can be bought for a handful of *scudi* have no appeal for me. The others, the beautiful seductive ones who live in palaces like royalty— invisible to everyone but invited guests—are still beyond my reach. Even an introduction from Messer Aretino would probably not bring me much further than the anteroom.

Today I met him again. He greeted me smartly with a bow and a wave of the arm—eloquent mimicry. In passing, he wished me luck with my appointment to Morone's retinue. Apparently he never needs to be told anything.

⚜

Seeing the Marchioness of Pescara has reawakened memories of my foster mother. In my childhood, Isabella of Aragon was the symbol for me of injured defenseless majesty, of dignified resignation to adversity. Beneath her signature on her letters, she used to write: *unica in disgrazia*—no one knows misfortune as I do. Anyone whose eyes met hers believed that too. I was in France when I received the news of her death. Never have I surrendered myself like that to prayers that the soul of the dead might rest in peace. All that Rodrigo and I knew about mother love we learned from the affectionate way in which she looked after us.

The lonely castle of Bari became our home, set on the Adriatic Sea. Weren't we exiles, like Isabella and her two daughters? After a short stay in Naples—under the supervision of our guardians the cardinals and then with our kinsman Gioffredo and his lascivious Sancia—we were taken to Bari. We knew nothing about Isabella of Aragon except that she was a sister to Sancia and Rodrigo's father and that she had at one time been Gian Galeazzo Sforza's wife, and Duchess of Milan. When we rode through the castle gates, I thought we were going to be imprisoned there for life. Cesare was locked up like that far away in Spain, guarded by implacable enemies.

We were led through a series of small empty rooms, dark as mole-holes. Rodrigo and I held hands; I felt him trembling with fear. A door was opened; daylight streamed out, dazzling us. We came to a gallery bordered on three sides by a row of narrow pillars. Outside this arcade stretched the cloudless sky, the sea gleaming in the sunlight. Among pots of small blossoming trees sat a woman, solemnly looking at us. She did not move; not a fold of her clothing, no lock of the long hair that hung over her shoulders, stirred in the warm still air. Her eyes drew us to her. When we were standing close to her, she smiled, a slight flicker at the corners of her mouth. She turned her palms up and took our hands in a firm cool grasp.

Our life with Isabella: a peaceful routine. We were not accustomed to living in the same place for more than two or three weeks. We had never had any lessons; the only games we knew were leapfrog, tag, wrestling and various kinds of mischief to which children resort out of boredom. Now, in the company of Isabella's daughters Bona and Ippolita, we were introduced to more courtly accomplishments and pastimes: singing, dancing, playing the lute, reading and writing. Rodrigo and I each had his own tutor; mine was named Baldassare Bonfiglio—he was also Isabella's librarian. Spanish as well as Italian was spoken at the court of Bari—we were already familiar with that custom.

Isabella never forgot that she was from Aragon. She had a regal manner, the austere distinctive grace and restrained passion of the great women of the romances—Dōna Ximena, Dōna Inès. Fate had given her the opportunity to demonstrate how deeply rooted these qualities were in her nature. I never heard her utter a complaint, an accusation, a reproach. No woman could keep a secret better than she.

Once in my presence, an envoy from Milan praised her resignation in adversity.

She answered with a smile, "My horizon has shrunk to a single point. My eyes, my thoughts, are fixed upon that. Faith moves mountains, Messer, and my will is as strong as faith. But what is will without patience?"

He asked her what satisfaction she found in waiting that must surely seem hopeless.

"Form, style . . . Who dares to say hopeless? I don't waste my patience, Messer. You may go."

Looking back on all this, I know now that the belated realization that her waiting had actually been hopeless must have been the most bitter experience of her life, more difficult to accept than humiliation, banishment, the death of her children, the loneliness of her last years.

When Rodrigo and I came to Bari, Bona was fifteen years old, a marriageable age: a tall, thin girl with the arched nose and pale complexion which are said to be characteristic of the Sforza family. She dominated us, led us in games and lessons and in other things as well. Her decisive manner and sharp tongue gave her the authority of a grownup.

Isabella's thoughtfulness toward us was reflected in the books and music chosen for us, the dishes set before us, the clothes given us to wear, in the words and attitudes of the tutors, the fencing master, the marshal and other members of the household whom we saw every day. Isabella listened, observed and then quietly considered what course of action to follow. She rarely acted on impulse.

Bona, on the other hand, scolded, punished or rewarded us on the spot, acted as arbiter in all our quarrels and as comforter in our sorrows and misfortunes. She knew everything—or behaved as if she did—and that more than anything made a deep impression upon us. Sometimes, seized by a desire to unburden herself, she called us to her in some deserted chamber or in one of the roof gardens and gave passionate details of the past in Milan: how her father, the lawful duke, was deposed and finally poisoned by his blood kinsman Ludovico il Moro; how her mother was insulted and humiliated, and her brother, still a child, was taken away and rendered harmless.

"Il Moro, that brigand, that murderer, he brought the French to Lombardy so that together they could enslave the rest of Italy and then share the spoils. He thought he could deceive and betray the King of France just as he had deceived and betrayed my father, but he walked into a trap and now he sits in France behind locks and bolts, chained like a common thief, and the French control Milan, where my brother should be lord and master. He can never claim his inheritance because they forced him to become a priest when he didn't even know what that meant.

"The only successor to Sforza is abbot of a French monastery, and we here, my mother, Ippolita and I, are helpless exiles. And in all Italy and outside it, there is not a living soul who will help us to stand up for our rights. I am the eldest of my father's children; I should have been a man. I will go mad thinking that I must bear witness all my life long to our defeat, without ever being able to lift a finger to relieve this disaster."

What Bona said did not fall on deaf ears. I had a wish: to grow up quickly so that I could drive the French usurpers out of Milan and restore the Sforza's honor. I wanted to serve them; if necessary to give my life for that restitution. Bona's narrative merged in my mind with Spanish heroic romance which I was learning to read with Messer Bonfiglio's help. The ducal castle of Milan, which Bona said was a series of palaces surrounded by a gigantic fortress, dominated my dreams. I saw myself adopted into the Sforza family. I forgot that I was a Borgia. All connections between Rodrigo and me and our past seemed to be broken, although we knew quite well that every year, from Ferrara, Lucrezia sent gifts and money for our support. I saw myself as Isabella's champion; I could foresee no other future but a life consecrated to knightly protection for her and her daughters. Rodrigo talked as I did, but for him it was all mostly a game.

Gradually I became aware of the tension existing under the apparently calm surface of Isabella's court. The peace was deceptive. In the castle an exemplary quiet and order reigned: every member of the retinue had his own daily task, which was carried out with dedication. The air was filled with the fragrance of the flowers in the roof garden and the sound of singing to the lute. Isabella moved about quietly with a faint smile on her lips and her eyes cast down in thought.

Over the years I learned to understand why she so seldom looked directly at anyone. Her eyes gave her away; behind a thin veil of melancholy, they were sharp and tense, searching and at the same time clear and hard. All of life at Bari was permeated with an air of expectation. Isabella and everyone who shared her exile considered Bari to be merely a way-station. Our hearts, our thoughts, were in Milan. Messengers came and went, reporting events in Lombardy, bringing letters from Isabella to trusted friends from earlier days.

Isabella rarely mentioned these things in front of us. But Bona knew, and told us that her mother was in communication with Milanese citizens who wanted to rid the city of the French yoke. Her most important correspondent was Girolamo Morone who had been secretary to Il Moro, but had later deserted to his enemies—a betrayal that did not really matter to us because in our eyes Il Moro, the usurper, was a criminal who deserved every punishment.

"But what's the use, what's the use?" said Bona; angry and angular, she paced back and forth before us. "What will we gain from my mother's persistence and Messer Morone's intrigues? We are too far away from Milan—we have no friends, no money, no troops, nothing—and even if one day all the French were to be driven away, my brother could never be the duke. Why does she go on hoping? It's senseless.''

But that hope dominated Isabella's life. The sounds of the wind and the sea, the unalterable prospect of the city of Bari and the blue mountain range in the distance, the quiet of the castle, the monotony of the daily routine, did not distract her attention from the goal which she had set for herself.

In 1506 Ippolita died of a throat infection. Sorrow made Isabella easier to approach. She had, now that Bona was grown up, no other children except Rodrigo and me. We filled the place for her of her absent son, of the dead Ippolita. Alone with us, she would sometimes lay aside the mask which she wore for the outside world. She spoke little and seldom laughed. But the woman who received us in the intimacy of her own apartments was quite different from what she appeared to be when she was surrounded in public by courtiers and servants.

Those who knew her only slightly saw her silence and self-possession as mere coldness. At the French court I encountered several people who remembered Isabella from the time of King Charles's first campaign in Lombardy. They spoke of her as brave and clever, but had words of greater praise for the charms of Beatrice d'Este, Il Moro's young wife. It doesn't surprise me that next to the proverbial splendor of the usurper and his duchess, Isabella's qualities were not noticed. She permitted few people to guess that under the ashes, the fire still smouldered. One would have had to be as close to her as I was, to realize that. Even now I am haunted by the memory of her faint inscrutable smile, her eyes filled with bitterness, melancholy and determination.

I saw something similar in the face of the Marchioness of Pescara. And there is another similarity between them. In France there was a rumor that Sforza fulfilled his marital duties only under pressure from his kinsmen and his advisors. Isabella had the body of a woman who had been a mother but had not known love: despite her age, a maiden still in movement and bearing. Even if Messer Aretino had not praised the chastity of the Marchioness of Pescara, I would have known perfectly well that she lives like a nun. What does that stranger mean to me, why do I keep thinking about her? Women have aroused my desire, but have never occupied my thoughts, never touched my heart. Does she fascinate me because she reminds me of Isabella? My shock at seeing her made me realize what a strong influence my foster mother had upon me.

I wanted to win her approval, to model myself on her standard. I was still a child; I had no opinions of my own, I knew nothing about myself. Chivalry, proud self-esteem, dignified self possession . . . I adopted all these like attractive but borrowed garments: you strut about in them without realizing that these clothes don't fit because they have been tailored for someone else. Probably I was identifying with Rodrigo, who looked and behaved more like a little prince in Bari than he had in Vannozza's hothouse atmosphere. I forgot that Rodrigo was Isabella's own cousin, the son of an Aragon—and I was not.

Two events changed my life again: an unexpected journey I made with my tutor Bonfiglio and a visit to Bari by Alfonso d'Este, Lucrezia's husband. It wasn't until later that I began to suspect a definite connection between those two events. They brought me into a situation I didn't understand, based on facts I didn't know. Precisely because of these mysterious circumstances, the journey was an adventure, but I sensed from the beginning that there was something ominous about the visit of Alfonso d'Este, Duke of Ferrara.

One day—I was nine or ten years old then—Isabella summoned me to her *studiolo*, a room where she kept books, paintings and pieces of antique sculpture. When I came in, I saw her handing a letter to Messer Bonfiglio.

"Here comes Don Giovanni," said my foster mother. "Follow my instructions, Messer, unless something else is decided in Carpi."

I knew that these words marked the end of a long conversation which I wasn't told about. Messer Bonfiglio went out of the room with the letter. Isabella sat looking at me for a while in silence. Finally she told me that I was going to take a long journey to Carpi, a territory ruled by Alberto Pio near Ferrara. I must not ask her any questions; she couldn't explain the why and how to me.

"If one thing or another is not made clear to you there, don't act surprised. We'll see each other again shortly. Trust to Messer Bonfiglio in everything."

I asked her whether Rodrigo was going with me. She shook her head.

"Come here. Look at me. What do you remember about the time before you came to Bari?"

I can repeat this conversation word for word primarily because I have never forgotten what a violent response these words evoked in me. Before I came to Bari my life was bound up with Cesare. My first thought was of him.

"Is he free? Have they let him go? Has he escaped?"

"There are people who are never released once they are taken. You will probably never see him again. You're shaking with excitement. Are you so attached to him?"

"He's my father."

Isabella knit her brows and looked at the floor. Her silence confused me. My words echoed in the silence. It was the first time that I had openly called Cesare my father.

I was excited at the prospect of traveling in a ship at sea; I couldn't think about anything else. I forgot that I didn't know why I was going to Carpi, or even what I was going to do there.

The voyage passed quickly with bright weather, a calm sea. A tent was set up in the forecastle for Messer Bonfiglio and me; we sat in its shade all day, and at night the carpets protected us from the wind. It was August: the sun filled the sky with fire. The coast was always in sight. By day, Messer Bonfiglio read or slept in the tent; I shaded my eyes with my hand to look out over the sea at villages and castles, while the sailors worked on the 'tweendeck, the rows of oars regularly rose and fell alongside us and the dolphins leaped playfully out of the foam. Finally, well before sunrise, the galley dropped anchor at Tolle near the mouth of the Po.

On the shore Alberto Pio's armed servants were waiting with horses. There followed a long, exacting ride through a landscape that seemed as strange to me as if I were at the other end of the world: flat, green and watery. Toward evening we came to a great stretch of marshland where the air was filled with the monotonous croaking of frogs; I dozed off, leaning forward against my horse's neck; I was still asleep when we reached our destination.

I remember only certain events about our stay at the Castle of Carpi. I didn't see Alberto Pio more than once or twice during those weeks. He was as important in the Spanish party then as he is among the allies of France today. I saw him go by the other day on his way to the audience chamber. He's French envoy in Rome now. He has lost Carpi, which is occupied by the Emperor's troops. But by all accounts he has a reasonable hope of getting his property back again. This doesn't seem to be the first time that he has changed his allegiance and lost castle and land because of it.

He probably doesn't remember my visit or he doesn't want to remember it. Apart from that, there's the question of whether he can give me any help at the moment, even if I remind him of our earlier meeting. That was seventeen years ago. I spent almost all my time with Pio's young sons. We hunted birds in the marshes, played catch in the castle or sat listening to music with the women and girls of the household in a gallery overlooking the gardens. Pio's friends and relatives frequently arrived as guests, with great retinues, horses and dogs. The only topics of conversation were the Pope's military actions—that was Julius then, who was busy extending the Ecclesiastical State at the expense of the small princedoms. While I was at Carpi, Perugia fell. I felt that I had come of age because I was allowed to be present at these discussions. So I listened attentively, aping the grownups, although I didn't understand half of what they said.

One day at noon Baldassare Bonfiglio came to fetch me from the stables where Pio's sons and I were watching the shoeing of a horse. I had to put on my best clothes, was sprinkled with perfume and taken to the apartments of the lady of the house. Madonna Emilia herself opened the door.

"Here he is, Your Ladyship," she said. She half-turned toward someone who was sitting on a bed of state in the gloomy chamber. I was pushed forward so that I stumbled and fell to my knees.

The stranger leaned forward to help me get up. Her gloves smelled of jasmine. She held my wrists in a caressing grip and laughed softly. A veil covered her face to the chin. I could see her eyes glistening faintly through the thin material, but I couldn't make out anything more. She pulled me toward her with a sudden, violent gesture. Her fragrance intoxicated me; I felt her lips moving, pressed under my ear.

"Juan de Borja? Giovanni, Gianni, Giannino?"

Caressing names that sounded like a question. I didn't understand what she meant, so I stood before her in silent confusion. A green stone in the shape of a dolphin hung between her breasts from a chain around her neck. She began to ask me questions in Spanish: was I happy, did I like Bari, was there anything I would like to have? Was I fond of Rodrigo, was he smaller than I, was he like me, what did he like best? I gave the expected answers; Messer Bonfiglio filled in with what I had forgotten or suppressed out of an inexplicable feeling of shame.

Later in the evening the unknown woman came into the chamber that I shared with Messer Bonfiglio. I lay in bed, hovering between sleep and waking. I heard her voice and my tutor's, but I did not understand what they were saying. Finally I half-opened my eyes. They were standing near the table. I saw Bonfiglio give her Isabella's letter; she in turn shook gold out of a purse. After that when she came up to the bed, I pretended to be asleep.

Bonfiglio drew open the curtains and held up the candle. "Don't wake him," the woman whispered. She touched my face, my hair and then carefully pulled the sheet away. The awareness that I lay naked and was being looked at like that by a stranger made me sweat with embarrassment and annoyance. I was physically well-developed for my age; with Rodrigo and other playmates in the bath or at games I usually exhibited myself with a certain pride. But this was different. I felt myself helpless, at her mercy, pulled into a hot, irritating stream. Finally the woman covered me up, slowly, caressingly, but without a semblance of maternal feeling; that above all was a new, confusing experience. The dolphin brushed my cheek.

Long after she was gone, her jasmine perfume lingered under the bed canopy. I asked myself why she found it necessary to hide her face behind a veil, why she had spoken Spanish. For the first time since I had left Bari, I faced the fact that I did not know the purpose of my journey. I identified that purpose with the mysterious female figure. Later, during my years of wandering in Naples, when I was violently tormented by doubt about my origins, I reproached myself for that childish, unquestioning acceptance of these riddles. Before that time I had never seriously believed that the visitor to Carpi could have been Lucrezia, even though that thought sometimes crossed my mind. Why shouldn't Rodrigo's mother, our blood relative and guardian, make herself known to me?

At Carpi I had the feeling that I, together with Messer Bonfiglio, the Pio family and, in the background, my foster mother, were playing a game; one of those apparently senseless, mysterious and complicated games that one reads about in chivalric romances, in which the hero of the tale is put to the test in one way or another. What lay behind it was of minor importance. To me the main thing in this case was the promise I had made to Isabella: to show no surprise no matter what happened. Therefore, I asked no questions when I noticed that the woman with the dolphin had vanished again. No one mentioned her; it was as though she had never existed. I understood that keeping silent was an indispensable element in this game.

Later I spent a lot of time thinking about the experience I had had at Carpi. That journey was my initiation into the world of thought which comes after the barely conscious reactions of childhood. I had heard Pope Julius abused in a way that hinted of complicity in a conspiracy; with Pio's sons I had secretly laid snares in the marshes and later wrung the necks of the birds we caught. I could never forget the scent, the body warmth and the caressing touch of the strange woman.

Messer Bonfiglio and I returned to Bari. During the trip I kept watching the dolphins. Messer Bonfiglio told me that they always play in the waves in pairs. If a dolphin loses his mate, he dies of grief. They are playful, loyal companions of Venus Anadyomene.

When I came back to Bari I looked upon Rodrigo as a small boy. And I viewed Isabella differently too. Her face was not hidden behind a veil, no scent of jasmine hung about her, she did not have caressing hands, her voice did not coax or flatter. Now that I am more experienced in that sort of thing, I know and can quickly recognize the peculiar physical attraction that emanates from a woman who has been much loved and desired. Isabella did not possess this power of attraction, no more than the Marchioness of Pescara.

My foster mother never asked me about my experiences in Carpi. When she first greeted me after my return, she looked curiously at me, but she gave me no opportunity to ask questions or to talk about what had happened to me out there. What I took to be the authoritative behavior of a wise woman was really a reflection of impotence and feelings of discomfort. But I did not realize that at the time. Rodrigo bombarded me with questions, but I did not want to tell him anything. For the first time, I became sharply aware of the difference in age between us.

❦

With the visit to Bari of Alfonso d'Este, Lucrezia's husband, my childhood ended for good. His coming had a two-fold purpose: to announce that Cesare had died in Spain, and to take Rodrigo back to the court in Ferrara. But Rodrigo did not want to go. He couldn't remember his mother, and he didn't trust Alfonso, who had so emphatically rejected him while he himself did not yet have a legitimate heir. Rodrigo's resistance caused his removal to Ferrara to be postponed indefinitely. *I* wasn't mentioned. Until then Rodrigo and I had been equals. We had considered ourselves to be closer than cousins—more like brothers with the same parents. We had been treated alike, with the same deference. We both bore ducal titles of territories in the Romagna that had been conquered by Cesare: Rodrigo of Sermoneta, I of Nepi and Camerino. Although we knew perfectly well that we couldn't assert our claims, we never doubted that we both had the right to a royal upbringing, to royal marks of homage. In the world which we knew, the world of Isabella—who was the deposed ruler, the exiled daughter of a king—no one lost his prestige if fate turned against him.

I noticed that Rodrigo was given precedence in everything by Alfonso d'Este and his retinue and, after a short time, by Isabella's retinue too. This attitude wasn't just the result of courtesy to the son of Ferrara's duchess. There were glances at me, insinuations about me, which I didn't understand. There was whispering among the courtiers which was hushed abruptly when I came near, but which began again as soon as I walked away. Alfonso's treatment of me was even more hurtful to me. He inspected me at our first meeting as if he were selecting a horse or a hunting dog. He stood in the middle of the room with his legs apart and his thumbs thrust into his girdle. A jacket with puffed sleeves accentuated the width of his torso, the strength of his arms and shoulders. His beard had a ruddy glow.

I approached him with awe. Even then he was a famous man; it was said that he cast his cannon and shot singlehanded, that he could lift his horse and himself on a crossbeam. For a long time, without saying a word, he examined me attentively from head to foot. There was not a trace of sympathy in his look. I waited for a gesture, a greeting such as he had given Rodrigo. But he turned away abruptly, leaving me standing there, and walked over to Isabella, who had been a silent witness of this inspection which inexplicably reminded me of how at Carpi I had lain naked under the eyes of the nocturnal visitor.

During the following days, the Duke of Ferrara took no more notice of me, although I was always part of his company. But far more incomprehensible to me was the fact that my foster mother and Bona treated me with perceptible reserve. I was unprepared to be thrust into the darkness and left all alone. As soon as I had gotten over the first feelings of terror and confusion, I set out to discover whom I had to thank for this treatment. After Alfonso d'Este's visit, I began to consider myself, my own fate, the cause of my exceptional position infinitely more important than the weal and woe of Isabella and her family. I realized that my foremost duty was to serve myself. I consider myself fortunate to have achieved that insight so early.

Words which I had picked up by accident put me on the scent: in my birth, my descent, lay the key to the mysterious behavior of the people around me. For the first time, I took into account the difference in birth between Rodrigo and me. He was the legitimate son of Lucrezia, and a prince of the House of Aragon. And I? Cesare Borgia must, I believed, be my father. I had never even given a thought to the existence of a mother. When I was still a child, I had heard talk about Cesare's wife, Charlotte d'Albret whom he had left behind in France after the honeymoon. It was clear that she could not be my mother: my birth occurred in the period when Cesare still wore the purple. I was the bastard of a cardinal. And what of it? Pope Alexander had considered me worthy of a dukedom. Why should I be less than Rodrigo?

Every time I came to this point, Vannozza's words and behavior would flash into my mind. She had disliked me, she always treated me with secret contempt. She never allowed me to want for anything, but despite the care she gave me, her antipathy was palpable. Once in a while she fondled even Camilla and Carlotta, Cesare's other illegitimate children, with as much warmth as with Rodrigo, the apple of her eye. Me alone she never took into her arms. Then finally there were her strange outbursts during our stay at the Castel Sant'Angelo. I racked my brain in fruitless attempts to find connections between these half-forgotten puzzling words of an old woman.

Rodrigo looked at me in amazement when I talked to him about these things. He didn't understand what I meant: his memory went no further back than our arrival in Bari. He did not notice the chill in Isabella's and Bona's behavior toward me. He and I played together as always, took lessons and practiced with weapons together. Nothing had changed for him; for me everything had changed. Rodrigo was a carefree child, fascinated by trifles: a ride on a horse, fools' capers, the pretty flight of a falcon, a new cap or sash, a galley sailing by far away at sea. The only thing that bothered him was the fear that he would be sent to Ferrara.

Even then I was uncommunicative, inclined to self-examination. I refused to shed a tear over Isabella's coldness, but day and night I brooded over the possible reason for it. Outwardly she seemed as pleasant and composed as before. I might not even have noticed the change in her if I hadn't set so much value on her opinion of me.

Once some farmers brought her a young eagle that had fallen from its nest before it learned to fly: a misshapen animal, naked and blind, its beak wide open, wild with hunger. The household amused itself with this squeaking, floundering bird. Isabella looked on silently, her face reflecting both aversion and pity. Whenever I saw her eyes fixed on me in the days after Alfonso d'Este's visit, I remembered that look. Day by day my insecurity grew greater. In addition, I felt my body changing. I knew that I was growing up; new urges, new sensations overcame me; I looked at the people around me with different eyes. I was curious and restless, sauntering from room to room without knowing what I was looking for or exerting myself excessively in fighting- and riding-lessons. I was, as is usual at that time to life, more interested in the visible and concealed charms of the damsels who served Isabella than in Messer Bonfiglio's book learning. I could not talk to Rodrigo about this either; he was a child and I was a man.

In the year 1510 Isabella's son broke his neck at a hunting party at the French court. It is dangerous for anyone in whom the hunting instinct is inborn to go out riding in a soutane.

When Isabella received the news of this disaster she seemed unmoved. It was now ten years since he had been taken away from her; she had never seen him again, never received a letter or a message from him. She knew that he had forgotten her, that he felt content in his role of worldly abbot of Noirmoutiers. She had hoped herself that this might happen so that he would be spared regret and useless longing. When he was torn from her arms, she had mourned for him as though he were dead. Since then for her he was no longer primarily her child, a part of herself painfully missing, flesh of her flesh, blood of her blood, but the personification of the dream which dominated her life: to return to Milan, to restore Sforza and Aragon. According to Bona, she had never given up the hope that her son would one day attain the dukedom. She was ready to plead with the Pope on her knees for a dispensation. The fatal news from France destroyed that hope. Isabella, a model of stoical self-control, donned mourning.

Although I no longer felt the unity with Isabella, Bona and Rodrigo that I had felt earlier, I was still hit hard by the discovery that Rodrigo was gradually beginning to play the role of heir and successor in Bari. In itself that was a natural enough development. Rodrigo was the son of Isabella's brother. She could, as far as birth was concerned, lay almost as much claim to him as his own mother, Lucrezia—and as far as devotion was concerned, she had a stronger claim. He himself viewed it as a given that he belonged with his father's relatives. He was an Aragon, of royal stock. He sat and walked at Isabella's right hand. It was murmured at court that now nothing was impossible any longer: son, heir, successor, one idea flowed easily from the other.

During that period a decisive change took place in my rank. I passed from the circle of blood relatives to the *famiglia*, the household. The process was executed so gradually that I could not complain about any definite humiliating treatment. I felt the difference without being able to say exactly how it had happened. From being a member of Rodrigo's family and his equal in rank, I became a sort of foster brother, a playmate of lower birth. I still went in and out of the royal apartments, kept my place at the head of the table, at the front of the procession to the hunt or on the way to church, but it seemed to me that this honor no longer came to me as my self-evident right. It had become a favor which I shared with Isabella's fools and lute-players, the physician and the court philosopher.

At the outset Rodrigo was certainly not aware of this change. For him I remained the elder, the trusted friend to whom he turned without prejudice. He really knew nothing about the conspiracy against me, which I felt involved all of Bari. Nevertheless, I felt unsure of him. I looked at him with suspicion, snapped at him, or preserved a wounded silence when he began a conversation. Later I felt ashamed of my obviously groundless suspicion.

This rapid change of mood demonstrated how estranged I felt from Rodrigo. I preferred to go my own way. His presence annoyed me, provoked me to continual carping and sharp words. I was driven to torment him, almost against my will. I used all my strength against him in wrestling and fencing. He hid his pain and swallowed his tears—but that precise chivalry irritated me. Sometimes he became really angry: what began as an exercise deteriorated into a bitter scuffle. At these moments we hated each other. When I struck out at him, pinned him down with my knee, I told myself I was triumphing over Alfonso d'Este, over Isabella's haughty Neapolitan and Lombardian courtiers, over the mystery which tormented me, over my own feelings of inferiority. I couldn't forgive Rodrigo for being sure of himself; I couldn't forgive him for his past, and for his future.

I enjoyed knowing that he secretly feared me. He never complained—not to Isabella, not to anyone. I knew I was doing him an injustice but I was too proud to admit shame or regret. Whenever I had the chance, I assaulted him with jeers or blows. In the beginning, these clashes bore the guise of playfulness, but gradually that changed for good. We never discussed these things. But Rodrigo knew—I didn't doubt that—quite as well as I that our relationship had been damaged at the core.

From the corner of my eye I saw him staring at me often with dark suspicion. He let himself be bested less frequently; he was on his guard. He began to avoid me, as I avoided him. We drifted apart, like swimmers separated by a dangerous current. Sometimes I was overcome by a feeling that bordered on despair, when he passed a few steps away from me without a greeting, his lips pursed nonchalantly in a soundless whistle. Our order of rank had now reached a point where I always walked behind him in Isabella's retinue. Rodrigo was small and slender for his age; in spite of his dignified demeanor he gave the impression that he could not really meet any definite challenge. There were moments when I was sorry I could not put my arm protectively around his thin shoulders as I used to do. That regret vanished whenever I realized that of the two of us, *I* was the one who was lonely and threatened. I could not forgive him for that. Why must I feel sullied, rejected; why was my life so miserable compared with his?

I had gradually come to see that the Borgia family had an evil name. Cesare and Pope Alexander seemed to have systematically made enemies of all the great lords of Italy. Again and again during my years with Isabella I was reminded of that whenever politics were discussed. Apart from the well-known offenses—the accusations of usurpation, murder, treachery—there was more that was not openly mentioned. As I grew older I learned to recognize the insinuating tone, the significant look, which accompanied every reference to Borgias' words and deeds. I was on the watch for these signals which I did not know how to interpret. Even then, one thing was clear to me: whatever it might be that the Borgias were suspected of perpetrating, it was not held against Rodrigo but against me.

He was privileged in other respects. It appeared that as a member of the House of Aragon, he stood under the protection of the Spanish Crown and that he received a large annual income from his father's estate. No such provision had been made for me. I possessed nothing but a couple of gold pieces which Lucrezia sent me from time to time. I believed then that Cesare's enemies had prevented him from taking definite measures on my behalf.

When Rodrigo was twelve years old he took his father's title: Duke of Bisceglie. From that time he was always present when messengers and agents from his properties appeared at Bari with the annual accounts. This new evidence of his worth made him noticeably more self-assured, more independent. Now whenever the tension between us was released in insults and fights, I was no longer the undisputed champion. Fear had given way in him to contempt. Although he always got the worst of it, I read in his eyes his opinion of my undisciplined assaults and that was as bad as a defeat.

The Castle Bari is built on the sea. A path, originally intended as a means of escape but long neglected, led from the castle to an inlet. This path was reached by going through an opening in one of the outside castle walls, and down a flight of narrow steep stone steps. We were strictly forbidden to go near that opening in the wall. Probably for that very reason, we played at that spot inside the opening in the wall whenever we had the chance to do it unobserved. We pretended that we were sitting in the cave of the winds. Cold air was sucked through the opening, it was murky inside there, and beyond a panel, which was easily moved, yawned the abyss, echoing with the sounds of the sea. From the first, I was irresistibly attracted by the idea of scrambling down there.

When I put this desire into action for the first time, Rodrigo squatted silent, motionless, behind me while I thrust my head out to estimate the distance and fastened a rope I had found to a ring in the wall. That was in the time before Alfonso d'Este's visit; no shadow lay over our friendship then. But I was annoyed at Rodrigo's lack of zest for this adventure. I looked over at him and talked to him but he didn't hear what I was saying. He was white, there were beads of perspiration on his forehead, his nostrils quivered. Over my shoulder he stared tensely at the white line of the breakers far below us. Hanging on the rope, I let myself fall through the opening and dropped onto the narrow flight of steps. The bright daylight and the glittering sea dazzled me; dizzy, I clung to the stones in that empty space. When I had climbed up again, I found Rodrigo lying unconscious in his own vomit.

As time went on, I ventured further, down to the place where the gulls' nests, like grey scales, covered the face of the rocks. While I was busy emptying nests, I heard Rodrigo's voice above me, shrill with fear: "Be careful, Giovanni, come back! Come back!" But I always stayed away as long as I could, because I wanted to impress him with my bravery and also to make him realize that his fears were unfounded. If I happened accidentally to look down—I knew I must avoid that—I was warned by a sick tingling sensation in the soles of my feet that it was time to go back. Sweating, out of breath, I would haul myself up and crawl back inside the hole in the wall. Rodrigo was usually sick afterward. Even in his dreams, the fear of being dashed to pieces, or seeing me go crashing down, pursued him.

He never dared to do what I did, and Isabella's older pages did: to sit recklessly astride the battlements or the railings of the roof gardens. He would stand, white as a sheet, his lips compressed, watching us from a distance. We laughed at him, but his fear was stronger than his shame. Even then I knew perfectly well how much he suffered from it. Eventually I began maliciously to use his weakness as a target for my shafts of mockery: when we quarreled, I never neglected to ridicule him for his fear of heights, which I considered childish.

"Look out, Rodrigo, there's a mouse hole behind you! . . . The footrest is too high for Your Highness—you might lose your balance!"

I enjoyed embarking on dangerous climbs when he was nearby: on a wall, a rock, a scaffolding. Once I was aloft, I dared him to come after me. Sometimes when he was frustrated to the point of madness, he did dare to make some attempts, but he always had to give up when he was halfway there. Those were cheap victories for me. I celebrated them more boisterously as I began to lose my grip on Rodrigo in various ways.

I suppose I'm going on about these memories at such length because for a long time I felt so guilty about his death. I didn't want him to die, I had no part, no share in that unfortunate accident . . . or did I? Men are skilful at turning their most secret wishes into their opposites. When I saw Rodrigo's shattered body lying exposed in the great hall at Bari, for a moment I was blinded by an insight into myself that made me shudder. It would mean a great deal to me if I could remember what it was.

One morning in September, 1512, shortly after dawn, I was walking to the armory through the open gallery above the inner court. I looked below and saw Rodrigo's groom waiting before the opening which led to the flight path. I called to him and asked what he was doing there, but he shook his head and waved his hand in warning back and forth before his mouth. I climbed into the old catwalk that faced the sea and hoisted myself between two battlements so that I could look out over the rocks.

Rodrigo had already passed the spot with the gulls' nests; I had never ventured that far. A landslide had left the step there dangerously narrow, the slippery rock offered no purchase. Rodrigo lurched wavering forward step by step, hunched over, groping about him for some support. Finally, he stopped for a rest, on hands and knees. In that ludicrous position he looked like a frightened, helpless calf that had wandered away from the cow and did not dare to go forward or back. I had to laugh. Rodrigo looked up. His shirt was torn, his hair clung dark with sweat to his forehead and cheeks. He seemed to scan the walls of Bari. Then he saw me. I did not move, I made no sound. Leaning against the battlements, I looked down at him. He opened his mouth and cried out. Fear, triumph? I will never know. He threw his arms up in a violent, uncontrolled gesture and fell backward.

✿

Over the course of the last few days I have received no instructions, except the order to remain in the Vatican. It seems that Messer Morone can have me summoned at any moment. Thus once again the Chancellor of Milan is playing a role in my life. Looking back on what I have heard and seen of him, I have the impression that the approaching meeting between us is preordained; a continuation and at the same time an extension, a rounding off of a series of contacts begun earlier. I once saw a painting by a Flemish master of the last century. It portrayed the visit of the Queen of Sheba to King Solomon. Out of naïveté or thrift, the painter had depicted on the same canvas, in a single landscape, all stages of the journey. Far away on the mountains in the background, smaller than a little finger, was the figure of the queen setting out; more clearly, nearer by, she was speaking to envoys halfway to her destination; but in the foreground, painted as large as life, the first meeting between her and Solomon was in full swing.

In much the same way the image of Messer Morone comes to me out of the past, growing larger, more sharply defined, at every turn. What does he want of me or is he perhaps not responsible for this approach to me?

There is not a single reason why he should remember me. I saw him a few times at Bari surrounded by his retinue and Isabella's courtiers; I was never introduced to him nor did he ever speak a word to me. He could not know that twice his presence and news of his activities have had a decisive influence on my life. It was on *his* advice that Isabella made peace with the son of her enemy Il Moro and that reconciliation led to my departure from Bari, later it was his betrayal of Sforza which caused me to take service under the commander of Naples, Fabrizio Colonna.

After Rodrigo's death, I began to think of leaving Bari. I was fifteen years old, old enough to stand on my own feet. There was nothing for me at Isabella's court. I should never again hold a place with my equals in rank and I did not belong among the serving folk. Bari lay in an out-of-the-way place, far from everything that attracted me. I wanted fame, and to win honor, chiefly to silence my doubts about myself, and to escape from Rodrigo's death. Somewhere, I thought, it must be possible to find men who were still loyal to the name of Borgia, who would be ready to give their support to me, the offspring of a once powerful family. Where were Cesare's army captains, the cardinals who were showered with gifts and favors by Pope Alexander?

I sought an opportunity to tell my foster mother about my intentions. With Rodrigo the last semblance of friendship between her and me had faded away. She lived secluded in her own chambers with Bona and a few confidants. I saw her seldom and then mostly at a distance.

Clothes and money came for me regularly from Ferrara; the

letters enclosed with them were intended for Isabella—I never saw them. Messer Bonfiglio had resumed his work in the library; the lessons had run out. I went hunting with the gentlemen of Isabella's retinue and practiced with weapons. They tolerated me without paying much attention to me. I listened to their political discussions, their mutual boasting and arguing. I learned to swear fluently and talk smut and, like them, had a series of brief adventures with damsels of the court and local girls—these flings weren't worth much; after a few jocular words and some pawing, they simply surrendered. What followed then gave me little satisfaction in the long run.

There was really nothing else to do in Bari. But worse than the tedium was the uneasiness which plagued me by day, the fear which tormented me at night. I thought I kept seeing Rodrigo in the shadows and in the dark; I kept hearing his voice in the rustling of the wind and the sea. *I* had not thrown him off the rocks—but I felt inexplicably guilty. I have carried that feeling with me everywhere ever since then. I've come to believe that my sense of guilt goes beyond what happened to Rodrigo—that it's an old feeling, hereditary, like a physical resemblance. This disquiet is my atonement . . . for what thoughts and actions of my dead family, God alone knows.

In the spring of 1513, a messenger from Lombardy reported that under the Emperor's protection, Maximilian Sforza, Il Moro's eldest son, had accepted the lordship of Milan, now at long last freed from the French. To my annoyance, Isabella immediately sent her congratulations to the heir of the man who had been her most bitter enemy. Not long afterward, the new Duke's envoys appeared in Bari. The leader of the deputation was pointed out to me: an ugly man in a black judicial robe—Messer Morone, former secretary to Il Moro, now appointed Ducal Chancellor.

Initially the purpose of the visit was kept secret, and no wonder. Unquestionably Isabella had to overcome great internal resistance before she could come to her decision. Before the envoys departed, she gave a banquet and announced in the hall, to the household and the invited guests, that she had promised to her worthy kinsman Maximilian Sforza, the Duke of Milan, the hand in marriage of her only remaining child, Madonna Bona Sforza. As the bridegroom's representative, Morone shoved a ring onto Bona's finger. He did it quickly and silently, making an apologetic gesture before touching Bona's hand. The marriage contract, signed by both parties, was shown to the gathering.

Afterward Isabella held the rolled-up, sealed parchment in her hand as one holds a scepter. When I saw the two women standing next to each other—Bona tightly controlled, Isabella trembling with emotion that could no longer be concealed—I realized that for me the moment had arrived. They had reached their goal— on Morone's advice the only possible route to follow: Milan, no longer a mirage, but the promised land, attainable on the horizon. In Bona and her future offspring the legitimate branch of the Sforza family would be restored to honor. There remained only the trip to Lombardy, the solemnization of the marriage in the ancestral Castello. Although I had to admit that Isabella could behave in no other way, in my eyes she had lost her invulnerability.

I waited until the guests and the envoys had departed before I asked to speak with my foster mother. While I spoke she sat motionless, with downcast eyes, a faint smile on her lips, in the attitude which I remembered so well. I looked down at her. For the first time I saw grey streaks in her hair, deep grooves running from her nostrils to the corners of her mouth. Finally she raised her head.

"So you want to leave? That's all right, I can understand that. We will write to the Duchess of Ferrara."

"I'm not going there."

"She's your guardian, your blood relative. She can support you."

"I decline the help of people who consider me an unwanted bastard."

Mother and daughter exchanged glances. I went on the attack, trembling with emotion because I could finally say what I wanted to say.

"I have eaten the bread of charity long enough. More than a servant, but less than a gentleman. Always in Rodrigo's shadow. I'm not a whit worse than anyone else. Bastards have become rulers, army captains, bankers, cardinals. I come from a powerful family. I am more of a Borgia than Rodrigo was."

Isabella raised her brows and Bona, who was standing behind her chair, made an abrupt gesture.

"What have you heard?" asked my foster mother.

"I've heard that we are a family of traitors and murderers. But aren't they all? Este, Montefeltre, Baglioni, Gonzaga, Medici? I keep my ears open. Why is it worse to be a Borgia?"

Bona moved a step toward me.

"Cesare had Rodrigo's father stabbed to death on the Vatican steps, because he—"

"Hush, Bona," Isabella said in a clear, hard voice. "Those are assumptions. We can't be positive of anything. I don't want certain charges repeated under my roof. I have never based my opinion on rumors. It's bad enough that doubt has poisoned our thoughts, blurred our vision . . . Giovanni, I shall write to Ferrara that I support your decision to leave. A man is what he *wants* to be. I think that you must be given the opportunity to show what your inclinations are.

"I've watched you grow up. I had reason to pay very close attention to your actions. Rodrigo never presented me with riddles. I will tell you frankly that I do not like the look in your eyes, the set of your mouth. I think that you have to strive against a deep darkness in yourself. Don't ask me why. How can I express something that I don't understand myself? I wish this for you— that you learn to know your own nature and force it to nobility."

She turned toward the wall—we were in the *studiolo*—and beckoned to me to come closer. Over her head I looked at the canvas she was pointing to. I knew it well. It had been there as long as I could remember. Always, whenever I entered Isabella's *studiolo*, my eyes were drawn to that painting.

Against the background of a dusky landscape, rocks, cypresses and a distant blue lake: a figure, half-turned away from the viewer, kneeling among ferns and low brushwood. The face was alive, moving in some inexplicable way. No bright, clearly defined colors, but gradations of light and shadow, degrees of depth in the ingeniously rendered perspective. It was as though one were looking through a window. I did not know if the figure in the foreground was a woman or a man, a child or an adult, a human, an angel or a demon. The expression on that face seemed to change as one looked at it. During that brief moment, with Isabella and Bona there, I saw at first cruelty and malicious mockery, then sorrow and compassion and finally it seemed to me that the mouth and eyes smiled, mysteriously, sweetly and playfully. I turned around and met Isabella's searching look.

"Messer Leonardo da Vinci painted that for me when I came to Milan as a bride. He gave me an explanation of it: that is the face that nature turns toward us; it shows our most secret passions, hidden away and unknown even to ourselves, part of our blood. A puzzle, but Messer Leonardo was fond of making puzzles. Sometimes I shudder at that look. Sometimes I think: if there are angels, they look like this. Often I stand before the painting as I stand before my own mirror. Look at it, Giovanni, and tell me what you are."

Later in France when I saw a similar painting by Messer Leonardo, I knew what Isabella meant. He had worked there for King Francis. The canvas hung in the Castle of Amboise. It was enigmatic and disturbing; indeed, as strange and at the same time familiar as our own reflection in a mirror can be. The man who knows how to reproduce human likeness from spots of mildew, wreckage and excrement showed, in the faces and forms of his people, their affinity with the inanimate that surrounds us. I remember the magician from the time when he was an engineer with Cesare's retinue.

What had Isabella intended when she confronted me with that painting in her *studiolo?* That I, in describing what I thought I saw, would betray my innermost self?

My days at Bari were numbered. I had asked Isabella to send me to Milan. I wanted to serve Sforza. With the intercession of the former and the future duchesses I must always get on well there. Everyone said it would not be long before the war in Lombardy broke out again; France was preparing to reconquer Milan. The threat of war was the reason for the postponement of Bona's wedding. Presumably Lucrezia feared that I was going to meet a sure death as I rode northward. I did not see her answer to my foster mother's letter. From Ferrara she sent me money and clothes and a good horse. Isabella wrote letters of recommendation to friends and relatives in Naples. She did for me what she could. Yet I was aware of the relief beneath her sympathy. She was absent-minded, restless. Bona's wedding, the journey back to Milan, the end of a long exile—these things preoccupied her.

When we took leave of each other she gave me a dagger that had belonged to Rodrigo. I had always been jealous of his having it. He had received it from Pope Alexander when he was a little child. Since then I have carried that weapon continuously; it is a stiletto from Toledo, beautifully chased. On the hilt are the heraldic signs of the De Borja and Llancol families. I still remember vividly that Cesare went into a fit of laughter when Pope Alexander handed the gift to Rodrigo. Alexander became angry; they had a heated argument about it. Later Cesare helped fasten the dagger to Rodrigo's girdle; he said that he had used the weapon himself for a long time. He kept bursting into laughter. I believed then that this was because Rodrigo looked ridiculous with the huge dagger at his side. Later on, I began to suspect that Cesare's merriment was caused by something else.

The last person I took leave of at Bari was Bona. When I wished her happiness, she frowned impatiently.

"Happiness, happiness! Are you being malicious? Maximilian Sforza is a drunken brute, a womanizer, lazy and stupid. If I were a man, I would kick him out of Milan. But I'm a woman and the only way I can reach my goal is to creep into his bed. I'll recognize my son as a true Sforza because he'll have my father's blood in his veins. Of course no one should feel sorry for me; that's what I'm here for. Only wish with me that the war will be decided in our favor quickly so that I can travel to Milan. And you must admire my mother: it's her work, you know, that they've chosen me over there. I only wish for you that you'll be able to play the trump card of your life like that. You hold a strange hand, Giovanni . . . . Do you remember how we used to sit down to cards with Ippolita and Rodrigo? I have to say this to your credit, at least: I've never seen you cheat."

She patted me lightly on the shoulder and turned away. I looked after her. An angular, unbending figure, the head set proudly on the long, delicate neck . . . Her gown was decorated with the colors of Milan.

Not long after that, I left Bari forever.

The only way I can look back on my first wandering in Naples is with self-ridicule. Although I had a groom, a horse and a well-lined purse, I was a beggar. I rode about presenting Isabella's letters of recommendation to the high lords in the hope of being taken up at one court or another: to the Viceroy, to the Marquis

of Pescara, to Prospero and Fabrizio Colonna. I was received courteously through the mouths of majordomos or secretaries; I was
considered a guest like others who came and went every day. The
Viceroy received me personally, was most affable but promised
nothing; Pescara, the two Colonnas, were not in Naples—they
were defending Milan with the Imperial troops in Lombardy. I
was burning with the desire to go there too. If I had support from
some influential man, I would certainly have achieved that goal.

I was disappointed because Isabella's letters had not been more
of a help and I was annoyed at my own inexperience. When I had
left Bari on my new spirited horse with my groom behind me
and the mules piled with my baggage, I had considered myself a
man of the world, free, grownup.

Very little of that haughty attitude survived in Naples. I spent
my days waiting endlessly in unfamiliar palaces. I didn't know
what I should say or do, to whom I should direct my request, to
whom I should not direct it. Nobody bothered about me. As I
rode through the streets of the city, I was so impressed by what
I saw and heard that I forgot to assume the careless bearing that
characterized the nobleman. It was curiosity and clumsiness that
destroyed me.

I was flattered when, in front of an inn, two well-dressed young
fellows spoke to me in Spanish, respectfully but with a touch of
familiarity. I took them for courtiers of the Viceroy's. Over a glass
of wine I told them about the place I had come from, what I
wanted. They promised to recommend me to a powerful man in
the court. But first they wanted to let me see the attractions that
Naples offered. In the following days: a frenzy of wine, purchased
love, heated brawls with other celebrants.

When I came to myself, I was lying half-naked on a table in a
public house somewhere in the brothel district. I had lost my
horse, my purse, my cloak and my boots. The clothes which I was
still wearing were soiled and torn. In addition, in the course of
everything I had lost my groom. I have never seen him again and
don't know what became of him. Unsteadily, I tried to find my
way back to the familiar part of town. The sun burned on the
narrow steep streets, I stumbled over heaps of rubbish; shrieking
with laughter, women wrung out their washing over my head.

I had to turn the contents of my traveling chests into money. I
would not go back to Bari at any price or ask my guardian Lu-

crezia for help. I bought another horse; he was no longer young, but could walk tolerably well. For a while I roamed around the neighborhood of Naples, accidentally got into a robbers' den, was pursued by them as a traitor when I decided to get out of it.

After that I served for a few months in the retinue of a nobleman at an estate not far from Benevento. There I heard—that was in September, 1515—that the French under the command of King Francis had defeated the Imperial armies at Marignano and that the city of Milan had fallen into their hands once more, although Sforza was still entrenched in the Castello, waiting for reinforcements. In the South it was expected that he would persist. The Castle of Milan was considered to be impregnable.

But before winter, the news came that the Chancellor Morone had betrayed his master and sold him to the French just as he had betrayed and sold Il Moro fifteen years earlier. Later on in France I heard another version of that rumor. It would seem that Maximilian Sforza who had little interest in ruling Milan or in his marriage to Bona, was taken—not unwillingly—as a sort of prisoner to France where he had been promised an honorary post and a comfortable life. Whatever happened, it is undoubtedly a fact that Morone had a hand in it. Perhaps for the good of Milan, but decidedly to the detriment of Bona and Isabella. For these two women, it seemed, the opportunity of returning to Milan was gone forever. Pope Leo left the Emperor's supporters in the lurch and concluded a peace with King Francis.

Not long after that, the Lords Pescara and Colonna returned to Naples from Lombardy. They were—Pescara still is—the leaders of the Spanish party. It was generally thought that they would not accept the Pope's politics but would continue to fight against French influence with everything in their power. It was announced in Benevento that Fabrizio Colonna was recruiting men for training. That was my chance. I wanted to go to Lombardy, to fight against France, to free Milan, if possible to punish Morone single-handedly for his treachery, eventually to bring Isabella and Bona back to the Sforza throne and, finally, reap, along with their gratitude, recognition of my complete equality with them. A childish dream. I didn't hesitate: packed my possessions into a bag, saddled my horse and rode to Naples.

VII.

Vittoria Colonna

S he knew what disease her husband had contracted at Pavia. She knew also that she must not mention her discovery, not to Pescara himself, not to others. His attitude made that clear to her from the beginning. After every attack of dry, tortured coughing when she was with him—how could the spots of blood on the handkerchief be hidden from her?—he looked at her with suspicion and defiance: don't dare to pity me. Her proposal that they take a trip to their estates in the South, he dismissed out of hand; he had not come to Rome for a rest, he said; he hadn't needed to leave the fortress in Novara in order to recover his health. He had been well cared for there.

Vittoria kept silent and bowed her head so that he could not see that this remark wounded her. She knew him too well not to be aware that he would not stand for the slightest encroachment upon his habits, his decisions. He rose early every day and rode his horse out of the city, although the scars on his thighs made riding very painful. Later in the day he received relatives, friends, members of the Spanish party. Since Vittoria had last seen him, he had grown a beard in the Spanish fashion. He went about clad in black. His posture was stiffer, his gestures more measured, his whole being petrified with Spanish formality. He used up his strength attempting to deal stoically with pain, to hide attacks of weakness. He appeared perfectly in control of himself. Only his choice of words betrayed his irascibility and anger.

All conversations revolved around politics. Pescara did not

spare sarcasm and ridicule when he talked about the combat tactics of the French, the Pope's diplomatic policy and the wait-and-see attitude of the Italian states. He declared scornfully that France deserved defeat and Italy had earned destruction ten times over. The Emperor's best chance lay in the incompetence of his enemies. The most important event that spring was Pescara's arrival in the city: friend and foe alike wanted to know his opinion of the current situation. Every day he granted audiences like a prince.

Because I'm next to him, I share the honor and the interest. I see what the visitors, even the members of our retinue, our relatives, don't see: the deep shadows at his temples and nostrils, the way he sometimes runs his tongue over his dry lips, how in the middle of a conversation his smile suddenly tightens into a grimace of pain. Only I hear him sigh, swear under his breath, stifle a moan. Thanks to his relentless self-discipline, he can convince strangers that he's still the man he was. The cut of jacket and mantle hides the fact that he's grown thin, that he limps. When he plays the courtly game of question-and-answer at table, he displays his old wit and dash so well that he sometimes makes me think that I'm silly to be frightened. I want to believe then that I've only been dreaming, that this is one of those bad dreams which I've had for years—phantoms of sickness and death, of sudden frightful news . . .

But I'm awake, it's not a dream: Ferrante is sitting beside me, leaning carelessly back in his chair, his teeth gleaming in that familiar ironic smile . . . Torchlight, the disorder of wine glasses and fruit on the table; in the distance the sound of singing to the lute, and outside the arched windows, the blue night sky . . . it's a time-less scene, it's the scene of other evenings ten, twelve years ago, in Ischia, in Naples. When I think about those other evenings, an old feeling wells up in me, a shadow of the passion I felt when I was a bride . . . We're young again, there's no distance between us, no bitterness. . . .

I want to lose myself in that pretense; I want to forget that time can't stand still, that I'm in Rome sitting at the table next to a sick man with a deceptive glow on his grey, thin face. The melody of a madrigal breaks down my resistance and tempts me to a world of senseless dreams. But when the guests have departed, the torches in the hall put out, then the mask drops away. Hollow-faced, leaning on a servant's shoulder, Ferrante seeks his bedchamber. I don't know anything about his nights.

To avoid friction, they both acted as though his suffering was a secret from her. She waited for him to tell her what was troubling him, what reason lay behind this show of authority, this feverish activity. Despite every appearance to the contrary, she had no doubt that he was restless, uncertain, bitter.

It was a long time before he took her into his confidence. Her involuntary gesture of horror, the look of alarmed comprehension on her face when he came home, caused him to feel a greater hostility toward his wife than he had ever felt when he had seen her again after a long absence. When he was away from her, he was usually well-disposed toward her; he could respect and appreciate her; he even felt compassion for her loneliness. He was sometimes overcome, as he lay in his Delia's arms, by a certain guilt. He would make up his mind, then, to be more affectionate to her when they met again.

But when Vittoria came forward to greet him, antipathy welled up in him. She was not behaving naturally. He could see that she was making every effort to hide her real thoughts and feelings. He knew that she constantly made sure that he had care and attention, that she never stopped thinking about him, that she was always watching, always listening. This secret concentration bothered him immensely at all times, but especially now when he was feeling ill. There were moments when he hated that woman with her false serenity; her suppressed feelings disturbed the silences between them.

He tried to escape from her by holding conversations with friends, although these left him dissatisfied because they weren't serious, because they didn't alleviate his irritation and uncertainty. It was Vittoria alone who was completely trustworthy: she had shown that she could keep a secret, that her advice was valuable—a fact that increased his resentment over her association with people he considered silly idealists, like the Datary Giberti. Peace, freedom ... sweet enticements to trap women. Anyone who understood the situation as he did, knew that peace was out of the question at this stage; Italy was fated to be dominated by the Emperor. How could people who sat in their palaces playing at politics know anything about what was involved in this war?

Only those who had stood on the field amidst the smoke and roar of battle could know the importance of the ability to handle the demands of a horde of mercenaries—that ability was more important than all the promises written on paper by all the diplomats. Vittoria's attempts at a peaceful settlement appeared to stem from stupidity and not from a conscious intention to thwart him. It was only when she assured him that she had no more contact with Giberti, that after Pavia she was distrustful herself of her old friend, that he decided to tell her what was bothering him. He sought her out in that part of the Palazzo Colonna where she liked to spend her mornings: in an open gallery which overlooked a courtyard but which was screened from view by rows of potted blossoming orange trees; it was ornamented with fragments of antique statuary which had been unearthed during a recent rebuilding: tombstones, fountain basins, truncated pillars.

Slowly the couple strolled up and down between the blooming trees and the broken marble.

"Do you really have a reason to be so annoyed? I know from your letters that you feel wronged . . ."

"Not a single one of my requests will be granted! It's always the same: gracious letters from Madrid overflowing with praise and promises. And then nothing further. De Leyva and Lannoy don't have to wait for tangible proof of favor, because they enjoy the privilege of being fullblooded Spaniards . . ."

"But you've made it clear to the Emperor what you want, he's aware of it . . ."

"Oh, naturally he's aware of it. I've been letting him know what I want directly now for three or four years. I certainly think I have the right to make demands. But he ignores me. God knows he's made good use of my services; he thinks I'll never forsake him. I'm his vassal, after all—my father and grandfather before me supported the Spanish cause; all my actions prove I'm following their example. But the Emperor is damned suspicious: he won't take me at face value because I was born in Italy, he distrusts me. He hates Italians. It's true, they're a cowardly, treacherous people—"

"Ah, now you're going too far!"

"All right, to spare your feelings, I'll except the Colonna. But seriously you know my position. I won't go into it, but you know as well as I do what the average Italian is—I don't care whether he comes from Milan or Florence or Venice or God knows where—He has no principles, he brags, he has more cunning than intelligence, he puts on a great show of heroics but he has no real courage . . . I've seen plenty of proof of that under all sorts of circumstances, believe me."

"Well, but isn't it possible that you have met a certain kind of Italian in the Emperor's service? Maybe they're not the best—you really haven't come into contact much with other Italians."

"You mean those dreamers and talkers—Heaven protect me from them! I certainly have no desire to have anything to do with them. Listen, I've dedicated my life to the glory of the Emperor, to help consolidate his power in Italy; he has a lot to thank me for. I think I can say without exaggeration that I'm the one who has kept the Spanish party together here over the last ten years. I've paid the troops out of my own pocket, I've provided their weapons . . . But I don't have to tell you how much we've had to sacrifice—you know how deeply in debt we are. Soon the mortgages on our estates will elapse and then we'll have lost them forever. By any standard of justice, I have the right to ask to be paid back now. There couldn't have been a victory at Pavia without me, and I'm the one who took the French King prisoner. So I certainly believe I'm entitled to repeat the request I made two years ago: I want to be named supreme commander of the Imperial army. Who else would qualify for that appointment?

"But here again I haven't received any definite answer and I sit biting my nails, waiting, always waiting. My money has run out. Neither you nor I have anything left to sell or pawn. I can't pay my men, so I have to let them plunder the territory around them—that certainly hurts the Emperor's name and it hurts the Spanish cause, and I'm going to be held responsible for all the damage they've done. My enemies think I'm the cruelest scoundrel who ever walked God's earth . . . I have to put up with this insubordinate behavior, this disorder and confusion—it drives me mad!"

"Does everybody know about this situation? Is it public knowledge?"

"No doubt about it! There aren't any secrets in this country. Everybody knows that the Emperor has no money. The French have good reason to laugh—they're counting on that lack of money to finish him off. And what's more, the dukedom of Carpi has been vacant ever since Alberto Pio went over to the French. My troops control that castle and the estates. I've asked the Emperor to award me Carpi—and there hasn't been any response to that request either! Now what do you think about that?"

"Well, I think the Emperor might just be extremely cautious . . . He gives things a lot of thought . . . Or maybe—isn't it possible?—he's planning other things for you, better things . . ."

"Oh, you're very trusting! He soothes me with promises to keep me in his service, but he doesn't plan to follow through on a single one of them."

"A little while after the victory was announced, I got a letter from Madrid. It was congratulations from the Emperor on your military performance. I wrote back that it was an honor to receive praise for *proven* service from a mighty sovereign, but it's a still greater honor to hear from his own lips that he's in our debt."

"That's very good, my compliments! If he's going to answer, he'd better hurry before I'm forced to an expedient that he won't like. The French King is *my* prisoner—why shouldn't I be the one who collects his ransom? With a little planning, I can get the French to pay for the Spanish troops and recoup my losses at the same time."

"Oh, but you'd never stoop to doing a thing like that! It's beneath your dignity."

"Oh, is it? Why? I repeat: the French King is *my* prisoner. Lannoy shoved his way forward at the surrender and took the King's sword, but that doesn't mean a thing. He goes around saying that he won the victory, but everyone who fought at Pavia knows he's lying. In fact he went crazy with fear in the heat of battle and started screaming 'We are lost!' like a maniac. The Spanish soldiers can bear witness to that. If I hadn't intervened, there would have been irreparable chaos, and now the man wants to scoop up all the honor for himself. God only knows what his relatives in Madrid are saying to the Emperor."

"Well, I can understand your frustration. But please don't do anything hasty until you get an answer from Madrid."

"I have no time to go on waiting. Help that's delayed will come too late for me. Don't say anything—I hope you understand what I mean. That's enough."

His look silenced me, as usual. Why does he refuse to spare himself? Is he really afraid that he'll be shoved aside as soon as the Emperor and his advisors learn that he's ill? But a man like Ferrante surely can't be just ruled out, and I'll never believe that the Emperor is keeping him waiting deliberately before he grants his requests. Maybe De Leyva and Lannoy are trying to create that impression because they're jealous. But still. . .

How can the Emperor treat his best general like that, how can he put Ferrante's patience to the test like that, how can he be so careless with him? Doesn't he realize that there are people who could take advantage of this situation? Ferrante says that everybody knows about it. I remember that remark of the Pope's when I was in the Vatican with Varano of Camerino: "Let us hope that His Imperial Majesty will know how to reward the worth of the Marquis of Pescara. . . ."

I suspected at the time that there was something behind those words. And there was a short significant silence after he said them. Varano and Madonna Caterina seemed to slip into the background while Giberti, the Pope and I were the actors in the foreground in a play in which everyone but me knew the plot and the dialogue. The two men looked at me—they seemed tense, expectant: Pope Clement was leaning forward, he had his palms flat on the arms of his chair as if he was about to get up after I answered him . . . there was an expression of undisguised curiosity on his face, and a condescending smile . . . The light was falling from tall windows above, the folds of his shoulder cape were glowing in nuances of color from silver white to blood red. Giberti was standing behind the Pope's chair; he was stiff and silent—he seemed to be waiting with the same tension to see what I was going to say. I noticed that he kept running his fingers slowly down the row of buttons on his gown.

At first I thought they were making fun of me. Why else would they make those insinuations about my marriage, about the miserable state of our finances, about the Emperor's indifference? I didn't answer; the Pope ended the audience with a few brief words.

But now that I think about the things that Ferrante has just told me, I see that moment in the reception room of the Vatican in a different light. The Pope wasn't trying to insult me when he mentioned Ferrante's homecoming and his dissatisfaction with the Emperor . . . There was some other purpose behind that.

But she discovered that Ferrante had not told her the whole truth in that conversation in the gallery. He had planned from the beginning to ransom the King of France for an amount that would pay for the maintenance of the Emperor's troops. He and Lannoy had had violent arguments about it—Lannoy thought the royal prisoner should be taken to Madrid and all action after that should be left to the Emperor. There were personal resentments behind this difference of opinion: Lannoy wanted to prevent Pescara from taking advantage of the circumstances; Pescara knew that Lannoy wanted to scoop up the honor for himself in Spain. Finally, each decided that he would checkmate the other through a compromise: until further orders, the King would be kept in fitting style in the Castle of Naples. When Pescara left for Rome, Lannoy was at the point of setting off for Naples with his prisoner.

Vittoria knew that her husband was waiting with growing impatience for reports of the King's arrival in Naples. Finally he sent out a courier for information. The man returned at full speed with unsettling news: the fleet had gone to sea, headed for Spain.

Pescara shut himself up in his apartments; he refused food and drink. Vittoria, listening outside his door, heard the muffled sounds of a fit of mad rage, which ended in a vomiting of blood. When at last she was admitted to him, she found him lying on his bed. He seemed to have become quite calm, but his dull dark stare alarmed her more than his fury had. She brought him a letter: Messer Girolamo Morone, the Chancellor of Milan, was requesting an audience. She suggested that this should be put off until a more convenient date, but he dismissed that with a curt wave of the hand. He got up and dressed carefully in Spanish black. A messenger was dispatched to Morone to announce that the Marquis of Pescara was ready to receive him.

VIII.

Francesco Guicciardini to Niccolò Machiavelli

M y dear Machiavelli,

It wasn't possible for me to answer you by return post. I have my hands full these days. Besides, I really wanted to let the contents of your letter sink in first. Whenever you put forward certain possibilities, one is apt to catch fire oneself from that flame. You're an idealist, my friend. You build a dazzling castle in the air, but you lost sight of reality. "Drive foreigners from Italian soil, unite cities and states into *la Patria*, curtail the secular power of the priests!" That's my life's goal too, dear friend. We've often discussed these things together: you know how I feel about the disunity of Italy, how I've cursed it. I share completely your opinion that we'll be ruined by the discord, the corruption, the licentiousness and open greed of princes and prelates. In all my years as governor of the papal territories, I've tried to think of some way to prevent this calamity. And if there were one, I'd be the first to implement it, I'd use every effort to fight for it. But I've come to the conclusion that there's no way to do it. The present situation has been formed so rigidly by the behavior of previous generations that there's little chance for change or improvement.

In this sea of disasters which is our life on earth, I recognize only one goal: man doesn't have the power to change the course of events, but he can study the phenomena and learn from them. To keep a sharp eye and a cool head—that seems the most important thing to me. To allow nothing to blind you, not to let yourself be carried away by anything—to resign yourself to conditions—that's the way it is now. As I said, there's no remedy for the evils of the world. Heroism leads to nothing. A sensible person can do only one thing, my dear friend: he can try to avoid the blows of fate as far as possible, and if he's hit anyway, he must bear his suffering with composure. Our only consolation comes from absolute honesty, which gives a realistic insight into events. I wish you such an insight.

The war which France and Spain have been waging on our territory for a quarter of a century must be fought out now to the bitter end. The victor there will determine Italy's destiny. It's not possible to check an avalanche once it's begun. All we can hope for is that the Pope will begin to realize the effect that his choice of allies is having on Italy. Without a League, we will surely be trodden underfoot.

I don't see salvation in the organization of a popular militia in the Romagna. The populace here isn't fit for anything like that. The Romagna is a breeding ground for feuds; it swarms with bandits, preachers of sedition who have escaped from other places, roving bands of deserting or discharged mercenaries . . . to say nothing of the Spanish and German soldiers whom we've had to feed and pay ever since Pavia, in accordance with the new agreement between the Pope and the Emperor. On top of that, the people are split between support of the French and support of the Emperor . . . few support the Church; they still remember the destructive acts of earlier popes. You're suggesting the formation of an army made up of men who don't belong to any party. There are no men like that. If only out of self-preservation, everyone has had to make a choice. Not a living soul here is sure of his life or his property—small wonder, after half a century of robbery, murder, plunder! Think about how dangerous it would be to arm these fellows if there were a war. It would take a great deal to rouse their enthusiasm for notions like unity and independence.

Now about the question of a leader—if we suppose that the selection of a leader really matters, and you can see from what I said above that I don't think it will make any difference—then I would be strongly opposed to the candidate whom you mentioned. I know all about Messer Girolamo Morone's plans. By the

way, he didn't originate them—they were hatched in the immediate neighborhood of His Holiness, although I don't know exactly
who first came up with this idea that we're talking about. I don't
believe that the Pope and Gilberti understand that they're treading on dangerous ground. I've been told about it in confidence,
although I don't want to get involved in this affair. It speaks
volumes that Morone was instantly in favor of it. You know him:
he's sharp-witted, a skilful lawyer. But he's served too many
masters for my taste, he's too good an actor. I've always been
suspicious of the smooth way he justifies his diplomatic moves
after he's made them.

Morone can be trusted only when he's sure of great profit for
himself in the near future. And can he be sure of that in this case?
Take a sober look at the facts, my dear Machiavelli. We don't need
to be mysterious about it—I'll bet that more people know about
this conspiracy than the Pope and Giberti realize. So Morone is
going to talk with Pescara. And then? He can receive yes or he
can receive no for an answer. But it's not that simple. Who really
knows Pescara? He was born in Italy, yes, but he feels and thinks
like a Spaniard. Even if he hates the Emperor with a deadly
hatred, there's still the question of whether he can reconcile
treachery with his sense of honor. I simply refuse to believe that
he's for sale. Morone is playing with fire—he must know that
himself.

I remember four or five years ago I once had a conversation
with him. He said then that he thought there wasn't a more malicious or unreliable man in all Italy than Pescara. And now does
he want to trust Italy's destiny to this man?

Call me a pessimist, accuse me of excessive caution. I'm a practical man, I know people. You're assuming that Morone loves *la
Patria*. He doesn't love it in the least and neither do the other
lords who are involved in this affair. Each serves his own interests.
That quality is the only thing we Italians have in common. We
don't even understand the concept of a unified endeavor—how
can we work together then? And that's our ruination.

That is the secret of His Majesty's victories and his growing
power—that his servants are capable, at least, of placing the glory
of Emperor and Realm above their own immediate interests. I
speak from experience. You know that I spent a long time in Spain

as envoy to the court of King Ferdinand. Fanatical devotion to an idea that transcends personal interests—that's a Spanish characteristic. True, it often degenerates into an obsession with grotesque fantasies, but it also manifests itself in proud chivalry and loyalty to the monarch. And you can't criticize that. I believe, Niccolò, that nothing can be accomplished without honor, without trust, without loyalty. God forbid that the Spanish should gain still more influence here than they have had since they invaded us in the wake of the Borgia.

You mention Cesare Borgia in your letter. He accomplished more in the Romagna at that time than I can do now: order, peace, immediate adjudication of rebellion and crime. But I'm not an unscrupulous adventurer like him, and I don't have an indulgent pope behind me with money and authority. That's the reason, my dear Niccolò, that I can't do as I would like in the Romagna, as you seem to think I can.

I'm having a very difficult time keeping the savage people here in check. When I was appointed in '24—I was supposed to purge the region and restore peace—I acted at once to eliminate the most unruly elements. I had scarcely pronounced the first death sentence in Forlì (on a fellow who had murdered his father and had eighteen cases of manslaughter and numerous robberies on his conscience) when the trouble started. The criminal and his relatives had powerful connections in Rome, who put in a good word for him with the Pope. I was forced to revoke my death sentence and to grant safe-conduct to the murderer and all his followers. I was made to look ridiculous in the eyes of the populace, and that certainly damaged my authority.

After that they had no compunction about robbing and killing one another under my very windows, so to speak. You're envious of my power and you're bitter about your enforced idleness—but if you were in my shoes, you'd know how hard it is to hold your ground in high office, how much humiliation and disappointment even the governor has to swallow when at the same time he's held responsible and hobbled by those who appointed him. I know you—you have a violent nature. You'd scream with indignation and run away even before they took your post away. This demonstrates the value of those precepts I mentioned earlier: be silent, take things as they come, wait patiently, and in the meantime study the situation calmly. I had every reason to rage against the Pope. But I tried to take his character and position into account. As soon as he was distracted by more serious worries than the disturbances in the Romagna, I went my own way. Now I can safely say that I have the situation more or less under control.

You've often reproached me for having made a career of serving the Medici popes even while I was a staunch champion of the Republic of Florence and an enemy of the rule of priests. Dear friend, without the Medici, without the papacy, I could never have gotten where I am today. It's only in the office which I hold now that I can achieve, in the long run, something perhaps of what I set out to do when I was younger and more hopeful.

Forget about conspiracies against the Emperor, forget about political tinkering, Niccolò. There's only one thing that might still save Italy from catastrophe: a League, provided that the agreement is cleverly drafted, quickly concluded and maintained to the letter. If I give my support to anything, devote myself to anything, it will be that goal: a League.

Don't talk to me any more about Morone or people's armies. That's romantic, my dear friend Niccolò, and I'm interested only in sober reality. I'll recommend you with pleasure to Rome or Florence as envoy in the Romagna. But if I were you, I'd prefer to read Cicero or Livy in the shade of the olive trees and thank all the gods for the peace and quiet to put my thoughts down on paper. Write more of your *History*, give us a second *Mandragola*. Few possess your gift of words. Paint the State for us, the Prince the citizens, as they should be if this were a better world Leave to sober men like me the reality, which is compromise.

In friendship,
Guicciardini

IX.

Giovanni Borgia

M uch ado about nothing. I had expected at the very least to travel outside Rome, to be part of an embassy to Venice or Florence. It's not clear to me why Messer Morone needed an escort of a hundred riders—along with his own retinue and the gentlemen added to it here in Rome—just to pay a visit to the Marquis of Pescara here in the city. Did he expect an attack, a hostile reception? No one in the company knew what was going on. Before we left the Vatican, we were told that we must remain vigilant and follow Messer Morone's instructions under all circumstances.

Our procession attracted a good deal of attention. There's very little going on in Rome: compared to '18 when I was here with Alfonso d'Este, the city looks dirty and decayed. At that time new palaces had just been built in the piazza Navona; their facades were painted in various colors. I had trouble recognizing the piazza when I rode past it in Morone's retinue. The pavement has fallen in, the paint's flaking off. The roads are quagmires or refuse dumps, the squares have become real wildernesses—you can hardly tell them from other vacant overgrown land. Because of the unsettled situation and the unsafe roads, no pilgrims hurry to Rome. It seems that a number of ceremonies which are normally observed during Holy Year are being dropped this time. The pestilence is spreading. The Ripa district along the banks of the Tiber is all closed off to try and contain the sickness. That won't help much. It's growing warmer every day; they predict an unusually hot and dry season.

We were welcomed suitably at Ascanio Colonna's palace. The men of the horse guards waited in the courtyard while Morone went inside with his confidants from Milan and the two or three papal functionaries—of whom I was one. But we members of the retinue were allowed to come no farther than an anteroom. Morone saw the Marquis alone. It's said that Pescara is ill.

The interview lasted a long time. The gentlemen from Milan thought they knew what was being discussed. They said that Morone is contacting influential men in the Emperor's party, one after the other, to make sure that Francesco Sforza has the proper support to win the dukedom of Milan. Francesco is yet another Sforza, the younger brother of Bona's ex-bridegroom. There's nothing new under the sun: Francesco seems to be incompetent too, a puppet in Messer Morone's hands.

Waiting in the anteroom that day, I learned about the other side of things that happened long ago. The men from Milan see the Chancellor as the defender of their interests, the captain who has to maneuver the dukedom between Scylla and Charybdis. No one dreams of accusing him of treachery although he was responsible for the downfall of Il Moro as well as of Maximilian Sforza, when he turned against them. Milan is fighting for her independence, and she's well aware of her importance: she's the key to Lombardy, to all Italy. It seems that Morone has full power to put this key into the hands of anyone who promises not to violate the city's rights.

Listening to these and similar observations, killing flies and looking out the window, I passed the time until Messer Morone reappeared. He sat down for a moment and wiped his brow. It was a hot day and Morone is no longer young. But I had the impression that there was another reason for his exhaustion. However, he seemed satisfied. He gave us a jocular apology for having kept us waiting such a long time. When we were walking back through the gallery, I saw him bite his lips repeatedly to hide a smile.

The Marchioness was waiting in the portico, presumably to see us off in Pescara's stead. This time I got a good look at her. The woman rouses an odd feeling in me. I would like to bury my face in the folds of her garment, as I used to do with Isabella of Aragon when I was a child, to draw tranquillity from her cool pure composure.

When I saw her a while ago in the Vatican she had looked older to me, more austere, clad in steely self-control. Inside the walls of the Palazzo Colonna, she seemed to have shed a part of her inaccessibility along with her cloak and veil. She showed her neck and shoulders down to the swelling of her breasts: lustrous ivory-white flesh. There was no trace of coquetry in her attitude or her glance; her eyes were serious and alert, her lips severely compressed. The contrast is exciting: it rouses an urge for conquest which is deeper than physical desire. Perhaps Pescara prefers women who are more easily overcome than his opponents on the battlefield. He must want love that's relaxing, not intellectually demanding. Reducing a woman like this Vittoria to submission must give him the kind of satisfaction he can get only from victory over a powerful enemy or taking a supposedly invincible fortress.

I stared at her, but she didn't notice me, or pretended not to because she found my look too bold. Behind her, through an open door I could see a hall; in front of a high fireplace stood two people whom I recognize: Giovanni Maria Varano and his wife.

My thoughts always follow the same circular course; I always return to the same point: Borgia. Both my desire for power and my sense of inferiority can be reduced to one idea: Borgia. My ambition smashes up against the secret of my birth which I know about but which I cannot solve; I am made uncertain by the realization that I am inwardly unformed, a prey to influences which have pushed their way into my blood, God only knows how. I believed that I could resign myself to the fact that I cannot make any reasonable claim to the dukedom of Camerino. But that was asking too much. I despise Varano, who has emasculated his fortress by turning it into a monastery, a hospital, an almshouse. A man who jumps about like that with his inheritance deserves to lose it. He supports renegade monks with advice and money and is zealous in the cause of church reform. Renegade monks are men enough to defend themselves and to attack the power of the Curia on their own—witness the case of the German Brother Martin who threw the Diet at Worms into confusion in '21. I happen to have heard a great deal about that from a reliable source. Bishop Aleandro, my patron, was present at the Diet at the time as a representative of the Pope and he personally pronounced the excommunication. During our long journey from the battlefield at Pavia, he talked again and again at length about the words and actions of the German.

Aleandro is a man of the old stamp: rigid, of unimpeachable integrity, ascetic—and at the same time distrustful and naïve, he is an example of a kind of prelate who, so far as I can judge, has died out in Rome. Because it was in my interest to keep the old man as a friend, I said yes and amen to everything even when he, in his zeal to defend the actions of the Church, advanced arguments which seemed to me ludicrous in their refined subtlety. Well, but all that is beside the point. Church reform is, as the word implies, a matter for the Church. Presently everyone thinks that he has a role to play in matters that aren't his concern. Priests act as war commanders, statesmen want to be philosophers, princes call themselves poets and scholars. All that is wanting is for highly-placed gentlemen whose first duty is to bear arms, to withdraw into the forests to brood over the lapses of the Church.

I should be the last to deny that the lordly prelates serve their own ambition and avarice before anything else; the higher their rank the more striking the contrast between the dignity of their office and their behavior. But isn't that the case everywhere? The world has respect only for power.

Pope Adrian, Clement's predecessor, was apparently a devout and righteous man. Aleandro could not find words enough to praise his simplicity, self-discipline and incorruptibility. In France at the court the Pope was spoken of only with mockery and contempt because he did not know how to make a stand and was too simple-minded to be a good diplomat. Homely virtues are not expected of a pope any more than of a king. Apparently Varano takes these and similar things much to heart. Why don't he and his wife take monastic vows? A red hat would suit him better than a ducal crown. Who knows how wholesome his influence on the Curia would be!

He has no male heir—only a daughter, still a small child. If he does not beget a son, Camerino will pass into other hands. With money and the support of influential men behind me, I should perhaps have a fair chance. That makes the thought all the more unbearable that I have absolutely no means, I have no foothold. What I am I have created for myself.

When I was roaming around Naples at the age of seventeen, I could have developed into anything—a bandit, a hanger-on in the *famiglia* of a country nobleman, a beggar, God knows what. I chose military service because I wanted to fight for Milan and Sforza. I offered myself as a mercenary to Fabrizio Colonna. There could not have been a better school for a soldier. What I know of combat tactics I learned when I served as one of his men. And not only riding, handling weapons . . . Fabrizio Colonna had the men lined up every day. First he rode his horse slowly past the rows. With his staff lifted, he looked down on us. Under his raised visor his eye was sharp and stern; his long grey beard stirred in the wind. Finally, standing in the stirrups, he addressed us. His voice carried a long way. I remember some of the things he said.

"Everyone these days does his best to imitate the ancients in externals. Let us rather take our example from their spiritual and moral strength. Simplicity, order, discipline are usually hard to find among fellows who make their living through war the way you mercenaries do. You can only steal, murder, commit violence. Your kind must have long wars. In peacetime you become criminals. A soldier without a feeling for honor, without a feeling of shame, is a tool of the devil, he causes incalculable misery . . . .

"It's not enough for me simply to be the commander of an army. I intend to educate you to be what I call soldiers. I won't tolerate undisciplined rabble among my troops. I'm teaching you to fight, the art of taking up a position, attack, encirclement, withdrawal—but that's not enough. I will show no mercy for malice, greed and treachery. . . ."

Probably he was casting pearls before swine but in any case his sincerity and animation ensured him our affection.

There was talk now and then of our embarking for Lombardy. But the battles there never seemed to last long. Before all the preparations for our departure were completed, news usually came that the hostilities were suspended indefinitely. Fabrizio Colonna wanted to keep us under arms, but lack of money forced him to disband the carefully trained troops. A good many of the men made their way on their own toward the north to join the armies which were roaming about there. I would certainly have followed their example if my life hadn't taken a different turn.

At that time I always called myself Don Juan de Borja y Llancol. In Naples there's a special advantage in belonging to the Spanish aristocracy. Only the oldest men serving with me in Fabrizio Colonna's mercenary troop connected the name of Borja with Borgia. Whenever I was asked if I belonged to that disreputable family, I said yes, but I didn't tell them *how* I was related. Twice this sort of conversation ended in a dagger fight between me and an impudent scoffer. My prestige rose because I was obviously prepared to defend the honor of my family instantly with a dagger in my fist. It wasn't only out of injured pride that I reacted like that. The remark which caused me to draw my dagger—Rodrigo's dagger, Cesare's dagger—made me realize how much I *didn't* know.

The first time it was a question which led to a duel: did I know the secret of the *cantarella,* the poison which had repeatedly served Pope Alexander and Cesare so well?

"Look, we're friends—just between us—come on, out with it, refusing makes you look guilty, man! Copper filings and urine, we all know that, but what else? It's a perfect remedy that doesn't leave a trace behind. Didn't your blood relatives, the murderers, leave you the formula?"

And another time, after I had mentioned that Gioffredo and Lucrezia had both married members of the House of Aragon: "Have they swallowed that kind of bragging in Rome? Here in Naples, everybody knows that the old King Alfonso considered his lawful children too good for a priest's bastards, pope or no pope! So he gave them his own bastards instead. Birds of a feather . . ."

What? The conceited Sancia, and Rodrigo's proud father—were they both bastards? I won the fights, but inwardly I was completely confused.

One day I encountered a procession on its way to the gallows field. Bailiffs were dragging a man and a woman along; a shouting mob was following them. The condemned couple were already half-dead; they had been tortured since dawn at another spot in the town. The people were hurling dirt and stones at the two of them, yelling abuse and raving with striking violence. The man, grey and fat, bleeding from many wounds, let himself be dragged along like a sack. The woman was still young, naked to the waist, her head shorn. The nature of their crime was shrieked at me from ten directions at once without my asking. One man who stood next to me was shaking both fists above his head and ranting:

"Those swine must hang, they must hang! Father and daughter, there's no filthier sin!" He turned to me. "Where I come from, in Foligno, last year two people were hanged for incest. There was a child too. Tied it in a sack and drowned it, that's what we did. An abomination against nature. No Christian people can stand for that!"

Someone else bobbed up in the crowd to respond to him. It might have been a piece on the stage where speeches had been worked out to the last detail: "There was a time when we had to put up with it whether we wanted to or not. Speaking of Christians—what Christian people would be the first to throw muck and filth at a tiara?"

"That's twenty years ago, we've never seen anything like that since. The Borgia are dead, they're burning in hell, and *e basta!*"

"But that bitch is still living in honor and virtue in Ferrara! Where's her kid? That's what I want to know!"

I didn't go after the man, I didn't seize him, I didn't force him to explain himself. Deep inside myself, I was not surprised. What had remained incomprehensible in the insinuations of Isabella and her courtiers in Bari seemed to me now glaringly illuminated, sharply defined. So during a nocturnal thunderstorm one sees trees and houses standing out in a single instant white against the darkness, motionless in the lightning flash. At long last words and gestures which I hadn't understood but had also not forgotten became clear to me. An abomination against nature. That wretched creature from Foligno had been tied in a sack and drowned. I remembered Alfonso d'Este's contemptuous expression, Isabella's eyes filled with aversion and pity, the woman in Carpi who came secretly to look at me and handle me, and—

deeper still in the past—Vannozza's distaste for me, her soliloquies . . .

To be the bastard of a bastard, without possessions, friends or patrons—that's a drawback, but it's not a disgrace. Actually, it's more like a spur to be self-assertive, to force Fortune to smile on you. But self-loathing, looking on yourself as an incurable disease, always tortured by guilt for something you had nothing to do with—worse still, to be in constant doubt about whether your suspicions are true—that's a curse.

I made up my mind to go back to Bari, to demand an explanation from my foster mother. But I was spared the journey. With trumpet flourishes and proclamations in the squares and at the street corners, the Viceroy's heralds confirmed the vague rumor that had been circulating around the city: before the end of the year a royal wedding feast was to be held in Naples. Bona Sforza was betrothed to the King of Poland. I had to believe this news although I thought then—and later, even after the nuptials—that it was absurd that Bona should rule over a distant barbarous country and not over Milan.

I waited until Bona and Isabella came to Naples. On a day in autumn they rode into the city—a long procession in the pouring rain. The curtains of the palanquins, the caparisons of the horses and mules, were dripping and faded, riders and mounts and the attending foot soldiers were spattered with mud from head to toe. They put up at the palace of the Viceroy, De Lannoy.

The beginning of winter was wetter than usual in Naples that year. A salt vapor hung over the coast. Under grey skies, in muddy streets, triumphal arches were erected and festooned with garlands. I stood among the people along the road and watched the cavalcade of distinguished guests go by in a rain of mud clods. The spectators expressed only derision for the bridal couple: Bona was certainly ten years too old to be a blooming bride and the Polish King was wearing a ridiculous tall, hairy bonnet. But Pescara and his wife were greeted with applause and cries of *"Imperio! Spagna!"*

I was more interested in the Commander of the Imperial troops than in his spouse. Pescara's bearing on horseback was especially impressive—erect, unmoving, one hand at his hip. To me he was the model of everything I wanted to be: the Spanish aristocrat, proud, brave, obviously always self-disciplined. By contrast I was in a frenzy of impotence at that moment; I felt farther from that goal than ever.

When the festivities were over—I had seen Bona, pale and tense at her husband's side, leaving the city forever—I went to the Viceroy's palace. I had to bribe various members of the household before I managed to get my request for an interview conveyed to Isabella.

She had scarcely changed, although her hair was white. I could understand less than ever what caused that secret smile of proud satisfaction to appear on her lips and in her eyes. She had after all nothing more to hope for in her life but a peaceful ending to it. She showed no surprise when I suddenly appeared before her. I had the impression that she knew why I had come, that she had expected this final encounter for a long time. She sent away the women who sat near her.

"I don't know the answer to your questions," she said, when I had spoken. "But I want you to understand how it happens that the question can be asked."

She was silent for a while. I remained standing motionless before her.

"The lives of people like us are determined by the destinies of our families. Without his name, power, possessions, a man doesn't count. The pawns in this game don't think or feel. Few rebel, few realize that it's ignominious to allow yourself to be shoved about like a piece on a chessboard. The first marriage of your kinswoman Lucrezia Borgia with a Sforza was dissolved on the grounds of impotence. Even before the divorce was pronounced, Pope Alexander was negotiating with my father about an alliance between Borgia and Aragon. It was an open secret that Sforza had to disappear because he didn't fit into the Borgia policy any longer, he was standing in the way of new arrangements. I knew that man Sforza quite well, he was my husband's cousin. I believe it's possible that he really did suffer from impotence. All the Sforza have weak constitutions; my own marriage was not consummated for three years. And even then . . .

"But anyway the Borgia made the error of publicly opposing Sforza. That was unforgiveable, and more unforgiveable precisely because the accusation was probably true. So Sforza of course responded to the slur with an accusation of incest. And the Borgia's enemies—too many to count, even then—made good use of that accusation."

"So it's a lie?"

"I can't prove anything. All I'm telling you is what I know. Don't be in a hurry to judge; after all, truth has many facets, you know. At about that same time there was a rumor that Madonna Lucrezia had had a child. Whether that was slander or not, the echo of that rumor has reverberated for a long time. My father demanded an official denial from Rome before he would allow my brother to travel to Rome as Madonna Lucrezia's second bridegroom. I can certainly assure you that if my father had had any reason to doubt the denial, that marriage would have come to nothing."

At this point I came out with what I had heard in Naples. I asked Isabella if perhaps a blind eye had been turned to one thing or another because the young Bisceglie was also a bastard.

"Legitimate or illegitimate, that makes no difference to us where education and marks of honor are concerned," Isabella said haughtily. "Those are the facts. I can't give you any assurance."

"You despise me too. You have an aversion to me."

"When I took you in years ago, I wanted to protect a lonely child—not a Borgia. After the cowardly murder of my brother, I had little reason to feel well-disposed toward the Borgia. They drained the power of Aragon and finally destroyed it. I regret that through circumstances beyond my control I was forced to take notice of the Borgia in you. Since then we have become estranged from each other, Giovanni."

"Why was he murdered? Did Cesare do it?"

Isabella shrugged. I saw the corners of her mouth turn up in a bitter smile. "Do you really expect me to know the answer to that? The House of Aragon, as I have just told you, lost a good deal of influence and power at the time. Pope Alexander chose to support France because Cesare, the apple of his eye, had interests there. Alfonso of Ferrara was even then an ally of France and, moreover, a widower. No one could accuse my brother of impotence—Rodrigo had just been born—so he had to disappear in some other way. Draw your own conclusions."

"So it's true that all Borgia are traitors and murderers . . ."

"They know how to reach their goals. Their opponents will never forgive and forget that. I say to you once more: I can't judge. There's no sense in raking up old rumors. That won't help you. You're grown up. You want to know yourself. You belong to a new generation that won't rest until it understands everything under the sun."

She said what I myself thought.

"That's how it is, I want to know who I am."

"What do you *want* to be, Giovanni? A man *is*, through a belief, a conviction, a concentration of his whole being on a consciously chosen goal. Everything that's worth having and dying for exists by the grace of our human will."

I commented that despite belief, conviction and concentration, her will had never led to the desired goal.

She looked down. "I've learned to desire my destiny. Whatever happens to me doesn't hurt me any more because I devote all of my being to will myself to resignation."

Again I thought she was showing signs of cowardice. "But that resignation is a lie to cover defeat."

She shook her head. "The will to a noble life can never be a lie. To surrender to hatred, bitterness, rage—*that* is suffering a defeat, in my eyes. To desire control, the preservation of ceremony, form, just when it looks as though everything is giving way—that's acting consciously. If you act, you can never be a puppet, a victim. Because of my will to preserve formality for myself under all circumstances, I'm free. I don't collapse under disappointment, under grief."

"Yet you call yourself *unica in disgrazia* . . ."

"I have earned the right to call myself that. I see that you don't understand me . . . You must live before you can grant that I'm right, Giovanni."

The only thing I could or would understand then was that royal pride prevented her from admitting that her world had collapsed like a house of cards. I respected her elevated sentiments, which undoubtedly reflected the only attitude she could possibly take, but I didn't believe her. It was difficult for me to conceal my impatience and resentment. From her lips I would never hear what I wanted to learn: she was indulging in philosophizing which left me cold. I did feel sorry for her: Milan lost, Bona gone forever to the other end of the earth. She was a lonely woman on the brink of old age. That she wanted to be generous, to avoid judging harshly, to draw a veil across rotten patches of the past— how could I blame her for that?

Her calm words soothed my doubts for a time, but didn't expel them. She hadn't answered the questions which tormented me the most. She had evaded those questions just as, in the old days, her eyes had evaded mine.

So to Ferrara . . . a voyage which I wouldn't forget in a hurry. The sea was turbulent, the wind unpredictable; near the middle of the Romagna, within sight of the coast, the merchant ship foundered. I swam to shore, my baggage was lost. In the town of Pesaro I joined a group of travelers. On a borrowed horse, in a borrowed cloak, with a borrowed bonnet on my head, I rode to Ferrara. Again that flat, colorless country, filled with swamps. The continual croaking of frogs reminded me of my trip to Carpi— I think I've already mentioned that Carpi is not far from Ferrara. Fresh nourishment for the misgivings that would not leave me in peace.

As I stood before the Castel Ducale, I was overcome by an unusual feeling of oppression. Between me and the high, red-brown walls of Lucrezia's dwelling—fortified, crowned with battlements, reinforced with towers—was only the mirror of the moat. Rows of dark window openings stared at me from the fortress. I walked my horse slowly across the bridge. Every hoofbeat seemed to remove me irrevocably from the freedom which I had enjoyed in Naples. But I no longer had any choice: I could not turn back, I had been observed. From the way I was received in the gloomy courtyard, it was apparent that my arrival had been reported.

Isabella had apparently sent a messenger to say that I was coming. An apartment had been prepared for me. Along with the water for washing, a servant brought new clothing that fit me. I watched the people whom I encountered in my first hours there, to see if I could read from the looks on their faces and their general attitude what the feeling toward me was in the ducal palace. But I found only a welcome servility; I hadn't been treated that way for a long time. Later I was greeted by Lucrezia's secretary and a couple of gentlemen of the household. They addressed me as *Vostra Signoria*, a title reserved for distinguished visitors. Through long, badly lighted passages, I was led to the apartments of the Duchess.

I hadn't been able to imagine what the woman looked like whose name called up not only the picture of the stranger in Carpi but also the woman condemned for incest whom I had seen dragged through the streets of Naples. Not a day of my youth had passed without reports and rumors about Lucrezia; consciously or unconsciously I had taken it all in: praise, blame, mockery and double entendre. I had heard descriptions of her elegant appearance and manners, heard her letters read aloud, heard her conduct both praised and criticized. Vannozza had spoken of her with awed respect, Cesare with indulgent irony, Sancia with envy, Rodrigo with indifference, Isabella with formality and Bona chose never to speak of her at all.

I always knew that more was held back than was said about her. A haze of mystery hung between me and the woman whom the whole world was talking about. In my thoughts she kept appearing in different shapes. Later—after the whispers, the glances, the insinuations—my image of her became still cloudier. As I was traveling from Naples to Ferrara, my heart was filled with aversion and secret fear.

Rodrigo and I used to look for snakes on the rocks around Bari. An old woman in Isabella's retinue had told us that if you knew how to surprise a reptile in its hole, you would become proof against snakebite for the rest of your life. Cautiously, armed with stick and knife, we stole through the low shrubbery. The thing to do was to find a snake which lay coiled asleep in the sun and follow it as it glided back into its hole. But the snakes were always quicker than we were. Then once I ventured into a narrow deep crevice in the rocks. In the darkness before me I saw two points of green fire glowing, the eyes of a startled animal—a wildcat perhaps, or a ferret. I crouched down, my heart pounding. Even with my knife, my sharp pointed stick, I had the feeling that I was helpless in this darkness. The beast could see *me;* I was blind. My limbs, my powers to think, were paralyzed by fear. I wanted to run away, but I couldn't do it. The sound of Rodrigo calling me outside put an end to that cramped tension. Wildly I scurried back among the loose stones. Much later I realized that that animal in the darkness must have felt fear as great or greater than mine.

On the bridge before the Castel Ducale in Ferrara, I was seized for a moment by a similar paralysis. That sensation of terror returned when I was being conducted through murky vaulted landings and gloomy anterooms to see Lucrezia. I told myself that I had better appear to be haughty and in command of myself, prepared for any revelation which Lucrezia might make, for any fate that Alfonso d'Este might have in store for me. After all, I had gone to Ferrara of my own accord, driven by the desire to learn the truth about my birth. Now that I had taken this step, I preferred to accept whatever followed rather than to go on living in uncertainty. With my hand on the pommel of Rodrigo's dagger, I stepped across the last threshold.

The chamber was full of people. The entire household seemed to have gathered in that confined space. When I entered—no sound, no movement. Apparently everyone had been waiting in silence, with their eyes on the door, for me to appear. There was an oppressive smell of strong perfume and the exhalations from many bodies. I didn't see Alfonso d'Este.

A woman rose with difficulty from her chair and came toward me slowly with the rolling walk of advanced pregnancy. Small, plump, beringed hands held the folds of a loose gown against her breast. Under a ridiculous melon-shaped headdress: a faded child's face, light-blue eyes. When she stood close to me I saw that the curves of her chin and cheeks were spongy, obviously the result of dropsy; her pouting mouth, charming at a distance, was really soft and weak, her eyes were bright with fear and repressed tears. She looked at me and put out both hands toward me. Her welcome sounded shrill and loud; with a gesture of her head she included all those present in the greeting.

"Welcome to Ferrara. This is Don Juan de Borja, my brother."

The hands I took in mine were clammy. A polite murmur traveled through the rows of courtiers; the women sank with a rustling of skirts onto the benches along the wall. I led Lucrezia to her chair.

"Stay next to me. Tell me about the voyage. How is our kinswoman, Doña Isabella? They say that her daughter's wedding was *the* event of the year in Naples. To our regret, we couldn't attend."

Her voice was melodious and light, but her eyes avoided mine. Her fingers, crumpling up a handkerchief, were trembling.

"I suffered a shipwreck."

"We had heard that. We will compensate you for the damage you sustained."

"What I owned wasn't worth much . . . a burden which I carried with me against my will. I can think of no better destination for it than the bottom of the sea."

"At flood-tide perhaps it will be washed ashore."

"I'm not obliged to acknowledge ownership of it."

"To lose everything sometimes means the beginning of a new life."

"I have lost my baggage, Serene Highness, but not my memory."

"Time is greedy; it swallows everything. Today we live through what will be a memory tomorrow. So make good use of the time here in Ferrara. There are many amusements here in the winter months: the hunt, horse races, shortly the Carnival. Our ballets and stage performances are famous; I have the best fools and dwarves in Italy. Where are they, let them come in. My dwarf Anna la loca can dance a moresca. Ask her to do her 'wading across the river'. She lifts up her skirts as if she were stepping into the water. It gives you the feeling that your own feet are wet."

She shivered and brushed the handkerchief over her lips. From an adjoining apartment the monsters came in, singing and leaping. A fat, gaudily dressed little female flung her legs so high in the air that her thighs were visible. This was Lucrezia's favorite, Anna la loca, an impudent half-idiotic creature. The jingling of the tambourines and the harsh singing drowned out our conversation.

"I don't need any dwarves to keep me busy," said I. "Your Excellency has posed me a fascinating riddle by calling me 'brother'."

"Don't show any surprise," she answered in Spanish, without taking her eyes from the dancing dwarves. "We shall have plenty of time to speak in private. For God's sake, behave naturally. Everyone is watching us."

She laughed and clapped her hands. La loca came rolling toward us like a ball to kiss the hem of Lucrezia's gown. As she did it she threw me a jealous and malicious look.

"Cross the river, sweetheart," said Lucrezia. She laid her white, plump hand on my sleeve. "Watch this, it's a pretty sight."

The dwarf growled uneasily, like an animal who will tolerate no stranger near its mistress. I have never liked to bother with these misshapen little people. It's a mystery to me how people can find amusement in seeing themselves and others aped by deformed creatures with enlarged heads and crooked legs. So most dwarves dislike me. Anna la loca hated me from the first moment she set eyes on me. Neither slaps nor caresses from Lucrezia could induce her to show off her tricks for me. She was finally dragged away, kicking and screaming, by her comrades.

The failure of this diversion made Lucrezia even more nervous than she was already. Her lips quivered, beads of sweat stood on her forehead below the border of the brocade turban. It was obvious that it required an effort for her to continue to sit there and smile. Her eyes shone opaque as enamel; the life seemed to have gone out of them; they betrayed nothing. I looked down at her, resentful and disappointed. In that faded face, that body deformed by pregnancy, I could find no trace of the beauty which I had heard so often praised, nothing that reminded me of the woman at Carpi. Beyond a certain grace in the curves of arms and shoulders, the light porcelain-blue eyes and the melodious voice, I could discover no trace of that charm which would justify her reputation. Through a thin layer of powder the unhealthy yellowish color of her skin was visible. The nose and chin were rather coarse and fleshy. She didn't resemble Cesare in any way. I had expected to find something in her that would bring back Cesare's character-istic dark, feline suppleness. Lucrezia gave the impression chiefly of indolence, limpness, weak features, a malleable character.

She seemed helpless, a prey to every outside influence, easily frightened yet just as easily reassured, childishly delighted or grieved over unimportant things. I had the feeling that it was my duty to protect her, but often at the same time I felt an uncon-trollable urge to torment the naïve, oversensitive creature to the point of tears. Her dignity, restraint, formal conversation were just appearance, pretense for the sake of the retinue.

Later in the day as soon as we were left alone, she dropped the role she had been playing. She burst into tears, overloaded me with kisses and caresses. In a torrent of Spanish endearments she called me her Juanito, her little brother, her one remaining be-loved blood relative. She begged me to forgive her, to have pa-tience with her, swore that all mysteries would be cleared up, that she would fulfill all my wishes, pave my road with gold. I asked her what Alfonso d'Este thought of my coming to Ferrara.

"He's away now on a journey. But he's your best friend; he will do everything in his power for you," said Lucrezia. From her agitated manner I gathered that she herself was really not so sure of that. She had me tell her about my stay in Naples, surely to prevent me from asking questions myself. While I talked she walked with difficulty, restlessly, massaging the hollow of her back with her two hands, back and forth in the dusky chamber. After a while I noticed that she was not listening to me, so I stopped. She stood still and over her shoulder threw me a be-seeching, guilt ridden look, like a child caught playing a forbidden game. Because she was afraid of irritating me, she resorted to a pouting coquetry that would have been attractive in a young woman but which no longer suited her. She sensed my distaste and tried another tack.

"Oh God, my head, my poor head hurts so much that I can't think any more."

She sat down and jerked the buckles and pins out of her turban with trembling fingers.

"I have never been able to wear heavy finery. The weight of my hair alone makes me ill. I put this on to please my husband. His sister, the Marchioness of Mantua, introduced this headdress. Her ideas are law here. I take my cue from her insofar as I possibly can. Excuse me for a moment."

While her coiffure was being put in order in an adjoining room, I stood looking out the window. The inner courtyard lay below, dark and deep as a well. Chilly air rose from the paving stones. Under the arcade, the faint glimmer of torches and lanterns could be seen moving from time to time. The overhanging galleries deadened all sound. I took a step back and saw Lucrezia standing behind me, her face a white spot against the darkness.

"They were beheaded there in the courtyard, Duchess Parisina and her stepson Ugo. That was long ago, a hundred years now. Those D'Este are inexorable in their passion. My husband too would show no mercy if he caught me being unfaithful. A lot has happened inside these walls. I could tell you things . . . Imprudence, frivolity are severely punished here. Only those without principles or without sin can breathe freely in the Castello. Come along now; it's warmer and lighter next door."

In candlelight she looked less faded. Her eyes sparkled, she talked continuously. She had her children brought in, a row of heirs to the House of Este. Later a meal was served. While I ate and drank, she talked with downcast eyes about Rodrigo. I assured her that he had not been unhappy when he was far away from her.

"Please try to understand—my husband's suspicions prevent me from doing what I want to do. Even toward you, my little brother, I have fallen short."

"No one has ever told me before that I was Pope Alexander's son."

"I didn't know it myself. You were so young when my dear papa entrusted you to Cesare. Recently papers have been brought from Rome. They are here now in our chancellery . . . A bull, a long piece entirely in Latin signed by my dear papa the Pope. In there it states clearly that you are his son."

I asked whether the name of my mother was known. Lucrezia shrugged.

"What difference does it make? You enjoy all privileges."

"In writing, perhaps. In reality I am a wanderer without a *soldo* to my name."

"That will change now. I shall help you. I shall do for you what my dear papa would have done for you. That is my duty."

"Why?"

"Why, why?"

My look upset her. She cut a piece of meat into strips and fed her two little greyhounds.

I did not believe her. The longer I spoke with her, the more convinced I was that she was hiding something. She was uncertain, nervous.

Servants and women took the remains of the meal away; we were alone again.

"We Borgia must stand by one another. We belong together like grapes in a cluster. My dear papa said that. He was good, whatever was said against him. No one ever loved his children more than he. He never cared about anything except my happiness. Yes, yes, that's true!" said she vehemently, although I had not uttered any objection. "All that he did, he did for us, our fame, our power, our wealth. Love for us—nothing else made him weak. After the death of my brother Gandia, he wouldn't eat, wouldn't drink. Only for my sake, because he couldn't stand to hear me crying, he got up from the floor.

"'What happens to my children, I feel as pleasure or pain in my own body'—those were his words. He was always pointing out to us that blood relationship is a holy bond, worth all sacrifice, demanding all our service. We were brought up to believe that. I obeyed my dear papa. Whatever he asked of me, I always did. Perhaps that wasn't good, perhaps I should have acted differently. I've heard and seen so much since then. Oh God, who knows what's true and what isn't? You couldn't understand that. To serve my relatives, that has become second nature to me, to do whatever my dear papa willed, my brothers willed, my husband wills. How then should I not help you?"

She spoke excitedly, breathing fast, her hands continually in motion, plucking at the folds of her garments, the trimmings on her sleeves and bodice. The rings glittered on her restless fingers. While I listened to her, I let my dagger, which I had unhooked from my girdle, roll effortlessly back and forth on my knee. Everyone has his own habits or gestures like that, while his thoughts are elsewhere: an ornament, a coin, a pair of gloves, a tassel or cord are always at hand to toy with. I take my dagger, let it turn on the blade's point, test the shape of the shaft with my fingertips. I used to do this without giving it a thought. Since that conversation with Lucrezia, I am not so careless about it. But for most people whom I meet my dagger is a weapon like any other.

"How then should I not help you?"

With these words Lucrezia leaned forward and lightly touched my knee. At that instant, her whole body began to tremble. I heard her teeth chattering. She covered her face with her hands and turned away. With difficulty I made out her whispers.

"Take it away, take it away! Who gave you that dagger? Take it away, hide that thing. I don't want to see it, ever again!"

I asked her if she had forgotten that the stiletto had belonged to Cesare. When she, still with her hands over her eyes, nodded speechlessly, I told her how Pope Alexander had given it to Rodrigo and how later, in Bari, it had become mine.

She let herself fall backward in her chair, her body jerking convulsively. When I lifted her up, I saw to my amazement that she was not weeping but laughing, a convulsive soundless laughter, more pitiful than tears.

"Ferrara is renowned for its maskmakers. All of Italy orders masks here for the Carnival. Those artists are rubbish compared to me. Little Lucrezia, beloved daughter, beloved sister, Lucrezia, laugh and dance, make yourself beautiful, there are always festivals, always Carnivals, always weddings . . . One, two, three times a wedding . . . Why not? Bridegrooms are puppets to make and break at will . . ."

This unnatural laughter ended as abruptly as it had begun. She lay quiet in her chair, her attention fixed on something that I couldn't see or hear. Groping, she brushed her spread fingers over her belly. She sighed a few times and asked in a whisper if I would call her women and then go away myself.

Weeks passed before I saw Lucrezia again. On the day after our first conversation, she gave birth to a child that did not live. As soon as she was able to stand up, she arranged to be taken quietly to San Bernardino, a convent in Ferrara where, I was told, she often stayed for a while to regain her health. While she was gone, Alfonso d'Este returned from his journey. More than half of the ducal suite returned with him. I understood why it had been so quiet in the Castello. Alfonso brought life and activity with him. Lucrezia's absence was scarcely noticeable.

I didn't have to wait long for a sign of interest. Alfonso greeted me with careless joviality as though he were welcoming a distant relative of lower rank. He didn't allude in any way to our first meeting at Bari. For that matter, I had little desire to remind him of it. He hadn't changed at all despite ten years of involvement in government affairs and in warfare against aggressive popes. His thundering step, his loud voice, filled the Castello. Everywhere he went, he was surrounded by the atmosphere of the hunting party or the army camp. Bulldogs and greyhounds followed him or lay around his chair. Lute players and fools were banished to the servants' quarters.

"Frippery and finery—women's business! Keep all that stuff out of my way until the Duchess comes back. Give me decent food—no gilded nightingales' tongues or perfume pies—all those fine things which cost me a fortune! It's a more expensive hobby to hold court than to make war. All that nonsense that's part of a court—good. I won't object to it when the Duchess comes back; she can arrange all that, she has the time for it. So long as I'm alone, we'll leave it."

To guests and retinue he offered masculine diversion: heavy meals, long horseback rides over the marshy fields outside Ferrara and—a still more exhausting occupation—nocturnal visits to his mistresses and women friends. Alfonso had a penchant for fat, dark women, pleasure-seeking and sensual, but at the same time taciturn, placid, with indolent movements—the opposite in all respects from Lucrezia.

He led me himself around the galleries behind the battlements to show me cannon from his own foundry which were mounted there. Everyone assured me that this was an exceptional mark of favor. Bareheaded, without a cloak, he walked out before me over the platforms of the watch towers, pointing to important parts with the handle of his whip.

The winter sky hung low and heavy with rain over the land. On three sides of the Castello, as far as the eye could see, grey-green, flat country, broken up with marshes, tributaries of the Po and the thickets of the ducal deer park. At the side of the draw-bridge: the town of Ferrara, an irregular jumble of low dark houses encircled by a wall. The wind blew a fine wet mist into our faces.

"The weapon of the future!" Alfonso caressed the smooth bronze of his cannon. "Experience proves it. Yet I'm the only one in Italy who realizes that. You don't agree with me? You come from the school of Fabrizio Colonna. A vigilant man, a good strategist, yes, but he still lives in a time that's gone forever! The Spanish troops trust too much in foot soldiers and archers. The Swiss think that lance technique constitutes the ABC of the art of war. The French used to swear by the cavalry. They have cannon too, but that was good for nothing. At Ravenna I showed them what cannon are worth. They see the error of their ways, they listen to me. The French King sends his cannoneers to Ferrara to learn the art from me."

He called the cannoneers, had them show me all the details. His legs wide apart, his hands thrust into his girdle, he stood under the roofing over the gallery. He took an obvious delight in my astonishment. Later we went down to the foundry in the vaults of the Castello. I thought of the harangues of old Fabrizio Colonna, his fiery demand for discipline and a sense of responsibility without which he considered the waging of war to be a repulsive business. Alfonso's passion for guns was one of a different order. The perfection of firelock, fuse and powder chamber was a goal in itself for him. Calmly, in a loud cool voice he went into the fine details of all the advantages of design and material, computed for me the range of various sorts of balls, described the effect of the shot. For him, war presented the opportunity to test the efficiency of cannon. Fellow fighters and adversaries were important only as users or victims of artillery fire. The main thing: the duel between the muzzles, the suitability of the entrenchments, the efficient organization of ammunition supply.

Until that moment I had considered war a necessary evil, an unavoidable phase in every disagreement between groups of people with conflicting interests. The belief in one's own right or the other man's wrong, ambition, revenge, rapacity: a hundred, a thousand times personified in the armed men in the field. And, moreover, every man prompted by his own motives—fear, the instinct for self-preservation, the hope of booty, whatever it might be. Listening to Alfonso d'Este's technical exposition, I saw all combat as destruction for the sake of destruction. The cause and purpose of the conflict no longer mattered, the men were mere supernumeraries, slaves of bronze and iron monsters belching fire; the towns and villages only targets, defenseless ant hills. An oppressive vision.

For a long time after my stay in Ferrara, I believed—not surprisingly—that an army couldn't be invincible unless it had enough proper cannon. But I found out at Pavia that that wasn't true. King Francis prided himself on his guns, great heavy pieces which can be aimed by means of a team of horses—that latter was a novelty suggested by Alfonso d'Este. And at first on the morning of the battle the Imperial forces were certainly thrown off by the French fire; they had to run head over heels for cover. The result was general confusion. But then King Francis made a technical error which wiped out his advantage, and Pescara deftly exploited that error. He forced a melee; artillery was useless when that was going on; it would have hurt the French more than it helped them. So at the Battle of Pavia it was proven that the art of the warrior and especially the decisions of a commander are more valuable than cannon, no matter how tricked out with the latest innovations.

But I didn't know that yet when I was in Ferrara: at that time I was deeply impressed with Alfonso d'Este's knowledge and authoritative manner. Cesare was dead, Fabrizio Colonna was an old man, Pescara was too far above me. So Alfonso seemed to me to be the personification of masculine authority, the model of a perfect ruler. I saw him against the backdrop of the greatness of the House of Este: a giant, a hero.

Once he pointed out to me the tower where he was keeping his two half-brothers—caught in a conspiracy to murder him—prisoners for life.

"There's no sense in trying to enforce strict laws in Ferrara if

I close my eyes to the crimes of my own relatives. That's a tradition with us—we are relentless toward the weaknesses of family members . . . we maintain our authority because of this policy."

I admired his attitude then. Later on I had plenty of opportunity to learn about his cold, small-minded, suspicious nature.

He treated me with affable indifference, inviting me occasionally to take meals with him and his eldest son Ercole, a youth of fourteen, and allowing me to ride directly behind him at the hunt and in processions. He also showed me his workshop where he liked to paint crockery and potter about with iron locks. He seldom mentioned the absent Lucrezia and never said a word about me and my past.

Finally he summoned me to his bedchamber one morning. When I entered, he was standing in the middle of the room in his shirt; servants were handing him pieces of clothing, helping him to tie his shoulder knots and lace his cords. His two mastiffs were lying on the bed. Outside the window was the misty dark of an early winter day. The reflection of the hearthfire flickered on the walls which were painted with a fresco portraying, larger than life size, Alfonso's illustrious ancestors in the time of Duke Borso.

"I've sent orders to my wife to come home tomorrow; she's stayed with the nuns long enough this time. In the past she didn't suffer from the need to go and shut herself up in a convent—on the contrary, Madonna used to prefer less pious occupations. Dances and feasts every day of the week, long private conversations, pleasure trips to a country seat with the admirer of the moment . . . and if by chance there was no enamored idiot in the neighborhood, she'd take a bath with one of her damsels, those creatures are sly, they know all sorts of Moorish love tricks. There wasn't any talk then about prayers or fasting. That's the way women are—changeable, they go from one extreme to the other. Of course one thing has stayed the same: my wife is just as ridiculously clannish as the rest of her family. And then she certainly knows how to get her own way—she sulks, she pretends to be ill or she runs away . . . Apparently she learned as a child that that was the only way to get anything done among the Borgia trash. I see right through that behavior, but if it doesn't hurt me in any way, I give in—otherwise, I don't. She wants to help you along in the world. Only time will tell whether you deserve help. You never met Madonna until you came here?"

The question was put off-handedly. But something in his look and the tone of his voice told me that much depended on my answer and the manner in which I gave it. "Never," said I. "No more did I know that I was the brother of Her Excellency."

Alfonso sat down before the fire and allowed them to put his boots on. After that he sent his servants and retinue out of the chamber. I remained standing before him while he polished off his morning meal: meat, wine and fruit.

"At her request, an inquiry concerning your birth has been instituted in Rome. There are two bulls which have come to light in the papal Chancellery."

"Her Serene Highness spoke of one."

"Did she? Remarkable. Why should she mention one, when she knew that there were *two*? You must be mistaken, my friend."

I ignored the question in his cold, dark eyes, showed no surprise, and kept silent.

"So there are two bulls! In the one you are recorded as the son of Cesare Borgia; in the second Pope Alexander declares the contents of the first null and void, calls you his own child, his most beloved Giovanni, Duke of Nepi and Camerino, Infante of Rome. That sounds like crown prince of the Ecclesiastical State or something similar anyway. That makes you sit up, doesn't it? No wonder. I don't understand what's behind these two contradictory declarations which seem to have been drawn up with a great deal of legal frippery on one and the same day. Personally it leaves me cold whether you stem from the father or the son. The one seems as likely a possibility as the other. What interests me more is the attitude of my wife in this affair. Your surprise is sincere. So I will accept that she really did mention only one bull, the last one. Can you guess, Messer, why she didn't tell you the full truth? The Duchess is a creature full of surprises—for a long time mild as a dove, agreeable, meek; then suddenly without any apparent reason, obstinate and uncommunicative, or praying and weeping like a penitent sinner."

He stood up; his shadow climbed the wall across the painted procession of nobles.

"I thought I was getting a Magdelene when I married her. There were good reasons for that assumption. But at the time Madonna was apparently not plagued by her conscience. My father didn't care much for this marriage—nor did I, nor our relatives. But we needed money. When Pope Alexander seemed to be prepared to pay well for Madonna's acceptance into the House of Este, we turned a blind eye to one thing and another. And, incidentally, we knew how to tame her. To her credit I must say that she does what is expected of her, relapses aside. But I don't care much for her whims. Understand me, here in Ferrara we have never let ourselves be dazzled by Borgia arts. I'm a hard-headed man, I keep my eyes and ears open. Madonna's tender-heartedness and melancholy are all on the surface. Underneath, she's just like Cesare, with his mysterious intrigues and Pope Alexander, with his lust. All Spaniards are sensual and secretive and fickle; anyone who closes his eyes to natural traits like these is a fool. They knew damned well what they wanted, those Borgia—clever, sly, inflexible characters all of them, Madonna Lucrezia not excepted. . . . And you, Messer Giovanni, what do you want?"

He turned toward me and stood flatly in front of me. I answered that it was impossible for me to know my own will until I knew who I really was. Alfonso made an impatient gesture.

"Don't represent yourself to be a blank page. You're not. You have all the characteristics of a Borgia. You are able to conform like a courtier, obey like a soldier, you have the bearing of a nobleman, the effrontery of a Spanish Marrano, the low self-esteem of a bastard. Teach me to know men! You're ambitious, and discontented with your lot. You have brains, you can wait. There is undoubtedly more in your arsenal. When will you reveal duplicity, cunning, treachery and ingratitude to your benefactors, Messer? Will these characteristics suddenly pop up as they do with my lady the Duchess who's always lying to me and deceiving me while she pretends to be submissive? She sentimentalizes over a father and a brother whom she was actually deathly afraid of— no, stronger than that—whom she hated . . . Yes, certainly, that's right, but it's a question whether she knows it herself. My lady the Duchess, who looks up with great innocent eyes and claims that all insinuations about her are slander, but then has fits of fasting and praying like a penitent . . . I will not put up with that secrecy, that unpredictability. As soon as other people's whims bother me or threaten to become dangerous, I know no mercy. I'm always on my guard, even if it doesn't seem that way. I hope you'll bear that in mind, Messer?"

"I'll leave today if my presence here doesn't please you. I had a feeling that I might not be welcome. I remember that in the past at Bari, Your Serene Highness didn't wish to speak to me."

"Ah, so you remember that?" Slowly, carefully, Alfonso chose a piece of game from a dish; he looked at it and sniffed it before he set his teeth in it. "I knew that Don Rodrigo existed. Madonna was sensible enough to know that she couldn't have the boy here with her while he was still a child. It was handsome enough of me to be ready to accept her two previous marriages in the bargain. And to accept the rest too: the gossip, the insinuations not very pretty, I can tell you that. There was supposed to be a bastard of my wife's running around somewhere, father unknown. I believed for a long time that *you* were that child, Messer."

He chewed the meat without taking his eyes from me. I thought about it and in that instant I understood him perfectly. My own safety in Ferrara, Lucrezia's peace of mind, Alfonso's willingness to support me—all that depended on the way I behaved now.

I said I had always considered myself to be Cesare Borgia's son and I was sure that everyone else considered me his son too.

"He had an extremely bad name here in Ferrara. And the memory of him and of what he did still hasn't faded. So therefore I advise you in your own interests to make use of the possibilities offered by that second papal bull. As half-brother to the Duchess, you have a claim upon us."

This whole conversation with Alfonso d'Este was—I knew it even then—playacting. Our real concerns weren't put into words. What was tormenting *me* was the question of whether I was a product of incest; the two bulls with the contradictory contents gave no decisive answer on that point—on the contrary, they presented me with new riddles. In fact the documents weren't shown to me, then or later. Alfonso d'Este's motives were different from mine. Later on, the situation became clearer to me: Alfonso was obsessed day and night by the desire for proof of Lucrezia's guilt. He wasn't thinking of one definite transgression; it wasn't her guilty thoughts and actions which interested him primarily, but the satisfaction he would apparently get from being able to catch her committing an outrage against him and the House of Este. Alfonso was one of those men who are incapable of admitting that they have made a mistake.

Neither of us got the answers we wanted during that conversation. We both knew that.

Lucrezia's return coincided with the beginning of Carnival. As if by magic, the city and castle of Ferrara showed a new face. They were no longer dead and grey as they had been in the first days of my sojourn, no longer filled with grim military activity— but a place now swarming with fools and lovers, obsessed with wine and dance.

Through the streets of the town and the passages of the Castello, which had been opened to everyone, the celebrants paraded, shouting, singing, wearing masks: cocks' heads, false pointed noses, devils' faces, monsters of forest and sea . . . a swirling tornado of motley cloth, plumes, tinsel and confetti. There were processions everywhere, competitions, feasts, and—on the meadow along the Po—horse and donkey races. Day and night torches burned in the castle, the tables were never cleared away, ballet and comedy shows alternated continually on the platforms; all sense of time was lost.

In one room an endurance contest was going on between the musicians and the dancers—*piva, saltarello, mezzacrocca*, all going on without a pause. And further, through a doorway, there were groups of exhausted, drunken merrymakers sleeping soundly wherever they had happened to drop. Daylight came and went unnoticed in the cloudy sky. There was no reality—only a craving for pleasure that bordered on madness. I realized during this time that I lack the ability to give myself up to any delirious ecstasy. Despite masks and fancy dress I couldn't lose myself for one instant in all this exuberance. You have to be an Italian, lighthearted and easily enflamed, to be absorbed into the frenzy of Carnival.

The close tepid air in the festive rooms, the glow of torches, the uncontrolled laughter and shrieking, the ambiguous effect of animal masks on human bodies, the studiedly shameless costumes—

all this roused conflicting emotions in me: contempt and boredom, but also—I was aware of the danger—the urge to make
something serious out of everything that was being done in jest—
to pitch into the harlequins and clowns who were rolling drunk-
enly over the floor wrestling, or pelting one another in groups
with sweets and pastries; to throw a torch among the ribbons
and trumpery—to hear the foolish laughter change to screams of
fear, to outrage the women—they imagined that because they
were in disguise, they could permit themselves any word and
gesture—until they stopped their lascivious, reckless behavior.

While the couples dancing the *balla della catena* twisted and
turned for hours in an endless chain through the series of rooms,

> *il ballo s'intreccia*
> *braccia con braccia*
> *mentr'un s'allacia*
> *l'altro si streccia,*

I stood in a corner, masked, hung like the others with frills and
bells, attacked by misgivings. I remembered the stifling feeling
that had seized me when I teased Rodrigo about his childish fears.
I stood again on the point of stepping across a border: why? To
where?

Through anterooms, down some stairs where I tripped over
sleepers and couples making love, I looked for a way out. I pushed
open a window and saw that it was snowing. After that, in France,
I became fed up with white winters. But then in Ferrara, snowfall
still had the charm of unfamiliarity for me. I remember thinking
of Bona Sforza out there in Poland, who must look at frost and
ice for six months of every year. The thought of Bona, the drifting
light flakes, tempered my anger and brought me to my senses.

I took a cloak and was about to ask for my horse when a troop
of masked figures stormed over the bridge into the courtyard,
daring the court to a snowball fight. *"A fare alla neve!"* Those who
were not too drunk to stand came down from the festive halls.
No one took more pleasure in this foolish game than Alfonso
d'Este.

Women thronged the galleries above the courtyard. Among the
excited, screaming damsels of the court, Lucrezia stood, unmoving and silent, recognizable by her gilded mask. For the first time

I felt akin to her. Behind the gold leaf of the bacchantic face, I sense the same feeling of pride and disapproval which tightened my own lips.

The court of Ferrara had a reputation to keep up, of offering the most elaborate, costly ballets and comedies. Carnival time in the Castello was a series of divertissements. I won't deny that they were grandly designed and had obviously cost a great deal of money. Fireworks, waterworks, machinery which could lower nymphs and angels invisibly through the air, luxurious costumes and decorations, a mass of dancers and singers and what-not. But the scripts without exception seemed long-winded to me, the action was unintelligible, the jokes and buffoonery as old as the road to Rome. And over all this was what I considered a cheap varnish of classical culture. They used all the gods of Olympus. Every play, each allegory, was a sort of puzzle that could be solved only by those who were steeped in mythology. No wonder the guests and the household sat around yawning.

I thought it was really amazing that Alfonso d'Este would put up with performances like these, that he would remain to watch them, one and all, to the end, and that he would even throw displeased glances at those who made no attempt to hide their boredom. I enjoyed the privilege of being allowed to sit next to the ducal couple and their children under the baldachin. But I was forced to witness not only what was going on on the platform, but also the conversation between Alfonso and Lucrezia.

A gigantic silver dolphin was brought out which spouted first colored water and then fire, after which the sea gods who were sitting on its back, sang an endless series of verses celebrating the recent alliance between Ferrara and Venice.

"Ha! Very handsome! But what did it cost?" said Alfonso. "Couldn't it have been done for less, my lady? I certainly know who taught you to throw money around like this. I can't understand why you don't seem to realize that in the past few years Ferrara has spent a fortune on defenses."

Lucrezia didn't move. "*My* fortune, *my* dowry," she whispered. "I didn't start these Carnival celebrations. I'm carrying on a tradition. You're so strong on tradition here. That allegory there was suggested by the Marchioness of Mantua."

"Oh, don't put the blame on my sister! You ought to be grateful to her because year after year she did her utmost to bring credit to our traditions while you were so busy looking as if you were ill or meditating, you couldn't think of anything yourself. My sister is a princess through and through, she's the first woman in Italy! *She* knows how to run a court. But of course those who haven't inherited the distinction of being part of a noble house can't understand that."

Lucrezia coughed and raised her fan before her face. "It isn't out of friendship that she meddles with arrangements for the celebration. But I don't protest any more; I grant her that pleasure."

"Oh, but you don't grant it so meekly, Madonna. You correspond so diligently with my worthy brother-in-law, the Marquis. Have you ever stopped to inquire what my sister thinks of these Platonic love letters?"

The feathers of the fan quivered. I could see only Lucrezia's back. Because she did not move, her profile was hidden from me. She had squeezed into a brocade bodice for the occasion. Through the veil which covered her neck and shoulders, I could see the sallow, waxen color of her skin.

"Your thoughts are ugly. So must I give up everything—habits which don't hurt anyone, good friends . . ."

"Yes, we know those habits, those friendships! . . . Will this performance go on forever? . . . Ah, that's well done, that dolphin, the symbol of Venice . . . By the way, didn't our friend Messer Bembo the Venetian have a dolphin in his coat of arms? Speaking of Messer Bembo, I want to invite him to come here again. He's a great man now! Made a handsome career for himself. The purple will be very becoming to him. It can't do us any harm to be on a good footing with the secretary to His Holiness, can it? And more than that, it'll be pleasant, after ten or twelve years—you know how long ago it was better than I do—to renew our acquaintance. Come, what do you say to that? He left in such a hurry that he didn't take leave of me. Did he have some reason to be afraid of me, do you think?"

I did not hear Lucrezia's answer. I only saw a shudder shake her shoulders. Alfonso didn't find it necessary to lower his voice; the music on the stage was quite loud enough.

"Would you be less averse to Monsignore's coming if I gave you the opportunity to continue with those secret lovers' trysts which began in Carpi? That surely was where you met each other? Now after all these years there's no harm in your admitting that. But whether Alberto Pio and his wife are still willing to act as procurers . . . And anyway perhaps Bembo has lost the desire to make love. One and all we are growing older . . ."

I bent over to pick up the fan. The handle was broken. Lucrezia took the pieces from me and smiled with a graceful gesture of self-reproach—a show intended for the many eyes which were looking in our direction—but the trembling of her lips, the wild blind gleam in her eyes, did not escape me.

More than once during the months which I spent in Ferrara I was a witness to a similar conversation between husband and wife. It seemed impossible for Alfonso to leave Lucrezia in peace. Her melancholy patience, her silence, irritated him. I could understand that up to a certain point, although I found his desire to harass her contemptible. All the same, I did not believe that he persecuted her with insults and insinuations out of malice alone. It was he who suffered the most from the thoughts and feelings behind his words.

They managed to maintain the appearance of a good relationship. On official occasions, Alfonso treated his wife with the greatest imaginable formality. He gave her precedence, exhibited satisfaction whenever people cheered her—Lucrezia was, especially after the war years, popular in Ferrara—asked her advice, praised her insights for everyone to hear. Lucrezia had the good sense to play the same game. She knew how to cut a figure in public. Whenever I saw her like that, carefully dressed and coiffed, hung with jewels, I could believe in the existence of that other, legendary, Lucrezia.

In her own chambers, she relaxed. I always found her there lying on a couch in loose clothing without stays, her hair bound up in a kerchief like the women of Rome. Never once, the entire time I was in Ferrara, did I see that famous golden hair uncovered. After her death the rumor circulated that during the last years of her life she had worn a wig.

She had me summoned to her two or three times a day. We always began with an exchange of the usual pleasantries: she asked me what I had been doing in the last few hours, what I thought about this or that in the town and castle. She wanted my opinion of poetry and pieces of music by famous artists from every country who were in her service; about the color and cut of her garments, about the decoration of her apartments. My Latin and my knowledge of literature left much to be desired, I knew little of mythology and nothing about fashion and art. She laughed at my lack of cultural development and said that she would educate me. Then she would take me into her confidence. I could scarcely get a word in. She had an uncontrollable need to talk about herself. Even as she spoke, she seemed to be releasing herself from a burden; she often sighed, squeezed my hands, smiled her childish apologetic smile. Because we were speaking Spanish, she ignored the members of her retinue who walked in and out of the room. She called me her gift from God, said that she could finally be herself again.

"My husband agrees to your staying in Ferrara. You don't know what that means to me. He has always made life impossible for those whom I loved and who loved me. O God, if I could tell you everything."

Her stories allowed me to catch a glimpse of the family affairs of the Este. What I heard roused me to scorn and indignation: and that man dared to speak of Borgia scum! In Italy and also outside it there was and still is—I have since noticed—enough talk about the mysteries of Ferrara. But because the Este belong to a distinguished old family that is still powerful, they are forgiven behavior which in the Borgia would be considered outrageous. Lucrezia spoke; I listened. Her naïve manner of narration revealed her grievances and rancorous feelings to me. Thus sharp pebbles are visible in clear shallow water. I have forgotten most of it. Despite her loquacity it was never possible for me to form an opinion about the life which Lucrezia led in Ferrara.

"Always suspicion, always hostility. They have never forgiven me for being better than my reputation. Whatever I did was wrong. The people here hate the Spaniards. I had brought a Spanish retinue with me from Rome. Many Spanish customs were prevalent at the court of my dear papa the Pope. After all, we come originally from Spain, from Xativa near Valencia, did you know that? I loved to linger in the bath, being salved and massaged by Moorish women. What harm is there in that? My damsels were pretty and refined. Is it my fault that the men here in Ferrara are too clumsy for light amorous banter? My retinue was sent away. So then I was all alone without friends. Four miscarriages, one after the other. O God, the things I had to listen to then! They said that this came from my past, the way I lived. My husband had contempt for me because I couldn't have a child. But he never left me in peace—less than ever when I was pregnant. And I was always pregnant. *He* chose my servants, my company. If I had a confidant, he had to go . . . or worse. The court poet Strozzi, my good, trusted friend, murdered, slaughtered like an animal. O God, my whole life has been like that, whatever is dear to me must always be taken away or killed! I can't talk about it, I can't think about it. Forgive me, I don't know what I'm saying. Forget about it, Juan!"

Later I heard that on the precise spot where the murder was committed, Lucrezia had founded the convent of San Bernardino where she would often retire. Does anyone grieve like that over the loss of a cheerful poet, who provided a measure of consolation and amusement? I made inquiries about this Strozzi, but no one in the Castello was prepared to give any information. As if by agreement, nothing was said about him, just as no one spoke about the two Lords of Este who were shut up in the tower. It evolved that orders had been given from higher up not to speak about my presence in Ferrara either—at least not to outsiders.

Lucrezia gave me, by the way, another explanation for her periods of seclusion in the convent. She fled there from Alfonso. A passage led from his chambers to hers. His many love affairs apparently did not prevent him from regularly honoring his wife with visits. Presumably he distrusted her less when she was pregnant. After that I always had to laugh to myself whenever Alfonso sneered at the Duchess's pious inclinations in front of me. Lucrezia spoke to me about these things with complete frankness. She said that talking like this gave her relief, revived her. She seemed as happy as a child with compliments and friendly words.

"You must love me, love me a great deal," she repeated often, with a smile. "There is nothing in the world which I need so much, nothing I long for so much."

Day in, day out I listened to her with a patience which cost me a distinct effort. I told myself that I wouldn't learn anything until she decided what her attitude toward me really was. My presence excited her, threw her into confusion—that was very obvious; it didn't surprise me. How could it be otherwise? I understood that she wanted to put off answering my questions. But at the same time I strained to catch anything from her stream of words that might serve to solve the riddle which embittered my life. After a while I began to notice that her loquacity was less spontaneous than I had thought at first. The most important things, the things which were really worth knowing, she kept hidden. The grievances she aired were not those which constantly tormented her. She never talked about the years before her arrival in Ferrara. She mentioned her father Pope Alexander only in passing, I never heard her pronounce Cesare's name. Equally striking was her reticence concerning her correspondent and brother-in-law the Marquis of Mantua, or Pietro Bembo the Venetian to whom Alfonso constantly alluded. Sometimes I had the impression that the face which she turned toward me was a mask. Hadn't she herself boasted about her ability to appear to be different from the way she really was?

Time passed; I became no wiser. She evaded my questions and hints. When I noticed that she was not as naïve and defenceless as she wanted to appear, my feelings toward her changed. By withholding from me the truth to which I was entitled, she ranged herself with my enemies. There were moments when I hated her with a ferocity which surprised even me.

Alfonso once mentioned the name of Carpi in connection with Bembo and the role which this man seemed to have played in Lucrezia's life. This had not escaped me: I had drawn my own conclusions from it. Once when I was sitting with Lucrezia, I asked her directly whether anything would come of the proposal by Alfonso that the papal secretary should come for a visit—by chance, earlier that same day I had heard Alfonso declare with scorn that Monsignore Bembo would not dare to accept the invitation. Lucrezia was looking into a mirror which she held in her hand. There was a long pause before she spoke, and her answer seemed directed more toward her own reflection than to me.

"I don't think so. He is kept very busy in Rome."

She ran her finger thoughtfully over the slack soft skin of her neck and cheek. "Listen to me, Juan. If you ever love a woman, leave her before she becomes old and ugly. Speak of love in your letters to her for ten, twenty years but don't attempt to see her again. Never let shame, regret, disappointment or boredom spoil the happiness you have enjoyed."

"That's self-deceit," I said, to wound her.

"Call it what you will. Pretend that things are different from what they really are, that is surely the one weapon against reality, which is ugly, so ugly . . ."

I began to talk about my stay in Carpi. I looked at her significantly as if it were an accomplished fact that we had met each other there. She kept looking into the mirror. I saw that she was seeking an escape. I had to admire her self-control.

"Alberto Pio and Madonna Emilia were my friends. But I never see them any more. . . . Yes, you were brought to Carpi at my request."

"Why?"

"They told me that you resembled Rodrigo. I longed for him. He was still an infant when I went to Ferrara; I could no longer imagine what he looked like. I did not dare have him brought to Carpi. My husband was in communication with the court at Bari. If *you* took a journey, it would be less noticeable. But even that leaked out. On my knees I begged to have Rodrigo with me. After that my husband went to Bari to get him."

"But Rodrigo did not want to go," I said harshly.

I had struck her more deeply than she had struck me. She turned her face away and said nothing. Unmoving, silently, she wept. Those tears which she always shed in such abundance whenever the subject of Rodrigo arose: they were not in mourning for her dead son. The more I witnessed these outbursts of grief, the more firmly I was convinced that she cried from self-reproach. Not because she had allowed him to grow up far away from her. Her weeping and hand-wringing had a deeper cause. The thought of him signified something else for her. She had not known him; she knew nothing about him. She could remember only the time when he was in his cradle, when she bore him in the womb, when he was conceived. Her feelings of guilt had to reach back that far.

Bona had accused Cesare of murdering Rodrigo's father. I understood that if I could find the connections between those things, I would be coming closer to the truth about my own origin. I believed Lucrezia only partially when she gave her longing for Rodrigo as a reason for our meeting in Carpi. Had she really hoped to be able to exorcise certain ghosts in herself if she, when she thought of Rodrigo, could call up his face, his form, in her mind's eye? If it were true that I looked like Rodrigo but I have never looked like Rodrigo—she might then believe that she could call up his image by thinking of me. That explanation did not satisfy me. For what went on inside her when she saw *me?* The tense attention of the woman in Carpi, her kisses and caresses were not intended only for Rodrigo. There must be a reason for the restlessness which overcame her constantly whenever I was with her.

I asked her why she had come wearing a veil at that time. She did not want to be recognized? Not by me or not by Messer Bembo? Without answering, she shrugged, her face still averted. Next to the couch stood a gilded cage in which a parrot sat on a perch. From time to time the bird moved as if he wanted to spread his wings. The gaudy feathers quivered for an instant, and then he sat still again. Lucrezia had been given the parrot when she was still a child. Its wings gleamed like peacock feathers, seeming now green, now blue, but over its breast lay a brown-red glow with a greenish luster, the color of dried spots of blood on metal. The parrot was able to speak; it liked to repeat the first lines of a Spanish canzone: *Si los delfines mueren d'amores, triste di mi . . .* when the dolphins pine away from love, ah, pity me . . .

I often wondered how Lucrezia could put up with that croaking next to her. I realized eventually that this noise did not sound like a parody to her, but like the echo of a beloved voice.

I wasn't going to let myself be put off any longer by vague replies. I determined to force Lucrezia to answer me. I knew her well enough now to expect that she would avoid my troublesome questions by claiming illness or fatigue and then going off to her convent or the pleasure house of Belriguardo. After the conversation in which Bembo and Carpi were mentioned, she had refused to receive me for three days. I knew that I must attempt over and over to bring her to the point where suddenly she would have no way out except to tell the truth. Under the guise of confidences and friendly banter, we played a game of attack and defense.

A soon as I broached those forbidden topics—the past in Rome, Pope Alexander, Cesare, Bembo—she drew into her shell. It was this silent duel which made me realize quite well that she was by no means guileless. I could understand Alfonso's helpless rage at her passive resistance. In her inimitable fashion, she knew how to use weakness as a weapon; subterfuge was her element. In those twilit apartments of hers where she burned perfume in the Moorish custom, her hidden passive power was more clearly noticeable than anywhere else. But she gave nothing away. She had learned to protect herself.

When she noticed where I was heading, she began to give me copious details about the papal palaces, ceremonies and banquets in Rome. She described the Carnival, the celebrations of the Holy Year 1500, the weddings of her two brothers and herself, the triumphal procession of Cesare after his victories in the Romagna. Rome was a colossal backdrop for the Borgia's chief actors. She became excited, deluged me with a stream of details as if she wanted to dazzle me with images of might and splendor. I didn't bother to hide the fact that all this didn't impress me. After all, I could remember something of that lost magnificence. She tried another tack, enlarging upon the background of a great many events which I had witnessed as a child. I listened attentively to this: her words added depth to certain memories. Suddenly, without warning, Lucrezia addressed me directly.

"Why are you looking at me like that? I can't bear being stared at that way. There's mistrust, hostility, in your eyes. Oh God, Juan, you haven't turned against me? Why has everything changed between us? I was so delighted when you came. I have talked with you as I always wanted to be able to talk with a brother."

"And Cesare then?"

She gasped as though I had slapped her across the face. After that she complained of a headache and sent me away.

That same day, at noon, she rode with a small retinue to San Bernardino. Alfonso let it be known that the Duchess, driven by the need for reflection upon spiritual matters, had retired for an indefinite period to the Clarissas. At mealtime he was unusually quiet. He drummed his fingers continually on the table. When I greeted him, he gave me a long, close look. I didn't like that look. I was aware of how uncertain my position was at the court of Ferrara. I had been received into the ducal retinue, I enjoyed hospitality, was treated with courtesy. I had been given a valet and a groom. Lucrezia saw to it that my purse was always full, gave me gifts in the form of clothing and useful objects. She even went so far as to make me a present of one of her dwarves, a brother or cousin of Anna la loca.

Out of politeness, I kept the monster with me for a while. I gave him permission to do whatever he wanted, if he spared me his tricks and grimaces. When I noticed that he—quietly and as unobtrusively as possible—followed after me everywhere and even into the chamber where I slept, I began to suspect that he had been assigned to spy upon me. I made use of Lucrezia's absence to send the dwarf, on a pretext, back to the retinue where he belonged. This was taken amiss by the other dwarves and fools. Presumably they felt that their professional honor had been injured. Whenever they saw me, they mimicked my bearing and gait in a manner that was far from flattering, while emitting unsavory noises. I heard that I was being blamed for Lucrezia's departure. La loca languished, refusing food and drink. Once when I was walking through a dusky passage, she sprang out of the shadows and bit my hand. I needed all my strength to shake off the crazy creature. Although I didn't talk about this incident, it became known. The courtiers who didn't understand my dislike of their famous fools smirked over the attack. Ercole, the eldest son of Alfonso and Lucrezia, took the dwarves under his special protection.

Ercole d'Este had a flat nose, the result of a difficult birth. Without that defect the youth would have had a pleasing appearance. He was at the age at which one takes those things most to heart. His own disappointment and his father's—Alfonso could sometimes not help showing how much he was bothered by the deformity in his heir's face—made him surly, haughty, overly sensitive to any sign of appreciation or its opposite. Ercole was very close to his father. Naturally they discussed me together.

Their conclusions—which Alfonso diplomatically hid behind a benevolent mask—were clearly written on Ercole's face. He seldom or never had anything to do with me. He had his own retinue, he rode out to the hunt with them or to practice his skill in the meadows around the Castel Ducale.

In time Alfonso d'Este traveled to Venice on affairs of state. As his representative in Ferrara he left his half-brother, Cardinal Ippolito, the most conceited and unreliable boor I have ever seen. Lucrezia, who had promised to come back, stayed in the convent. I knew that she hated Ippolito. And she probably preferred not to meet me again yet. There was great unrest in the Castello at that time: intrigues and fights were the order of the day. Compared to Ippolito's profligate and perverse habits, Alfonso's coarse sensuality seemed like child's play.

One day I was asked by one of the courtiers, who was a good friend of the captain of the watch, if I wanted to have a close look at the two imprisoned Lords d'Este. After I had promised him to keep quiet about it, he took me to an abandoned part of the Castello where all the windows had been walled up except one. This window commanded a view of the tower where the prisoners were exercised every day: a barred gallery high above ground level. Between the towers and the walls of other buildings of the palace, a space like a deep narrow well.

I did not have long to wait. Something moved behind the bars; a man pacing nervously back and forth. Eventually I detected another who seemed to be staring, immobile, at us, his face lifted in our direction. I wanted to give him a gesture of greeting.

"No need for that," my companion said from behind me; he pulled me back. "That's the blind one. A long time ago—before he was put in prison, Cardinal Ippolito had his eyes put out because one of the Duchess's Spanish damsels admired them— Cardinal Ippolito had an eye for her himself. Some people think that's why he plotted against Alfonso and Ippolito . . . because Alfonso didn't avenge him. They're all brothers, after all . . ."

Not long after that brief and apparently pointless visit to the tower, I was riding one evening with some other courtiers—

among them the man who had taken me to see the prisoners—across the square in front of the Cathedral. Suddenly, out of the shadows under a portico, armed men fell upon us. A short, confused melee. The assailants vanished as quickly as they had appeared. One of them was left lying for dead in the piazza. It was later discovered that this man belonged to the retinue of Ercole d'Este.

This incident caused a great commotion in the palace. Lucrezia returned from San Bernardino. She called me to her, adjured me to tell her why I had gotten mixed up with a conspiracy. I assured her that I knew nothing about it. Because I realized that I needed her intercession, I told her about the visit to the room opposite the tower. Her obvious terror convinced me that I was in danger; I reproached myself for my carelessness. Lucrezia hinted at the possibility of flight. Alfonso d'Este was on his way back to Ferrara; I could guess what reports he had had. But flight would be an acknowledgement of guilt. At last I saw through the comedy that was being staged here. They wanted to get rid of me. If I fled or let them drive me away, I would be an outlaw. I had to try to use the tension between the D'Este to my own advantage. So I awaited Alfonso's homecoming.

What was discussed between him and Lucrezia before he finally summoned me, I don't know. The grim attitude which he adopted toward me was as false as the joviality he had evinced months earlier.

"You should consider yourself fortunate, Messer. Others before you who have conspired to help my lord brothers to escape haven't come off so easily."

I defended myself as a matter of form and complained of the attack in the Cathedral square.

"My son Ercole is impetuous. He can't wait. Deliberation comes with years. He believed he was rendering a service to me and Ferrara."

I knew that my companion of that evening had not been accused. Alfonso knew that I knew it. His accusation and my defense were both purely formal. When he understood that I was ready to leave if he would give me further help, and when I ascertained that he would really reward my willingness to oblige, the conversation flowed more easily. Since then I have thought a great deal about what lay behind that game. The simplest explanation is that neither Alfonso nor Lucrezia trusted me. Each thought that I was a secret accomplice of the other. They preferred their own mutually tense relationship to whatever might come to light because of me or through my presence there.

Alfonso told me that he was going to hold discussions with the King of France on behalf of Ferrara and Venice. If I travelled with him, he would introduce me to the French court. I was much taken with this plan. It would—I thought then—give me the opportunity to begin again far from Italy, to turn over a new leaf in unbiased surroundings.

There were preparations to make for our journey. I didn't see Lucrezia in those weeks. I heard that she had to keep to her bed. Finally Alfonso sent me to her to receive the gifts which I was to deliver to the Queen of France in her name.

Lucrezia sat at a table covered with jewelry. The skin of her face was pale and yellowish with brown discolorations on her forehead and near her lips. She sat in her chair as if she did not have the strength to move. She pointed to the gifts she had selected and told me what I must say when I presented them.

"Now choose something for yourself, a memento."

For the first time since I had come there, a smile softened the light-blue brightness of her eyes. I expressed my amazement at the treasure on the table.

"That's nothing. Not even the hundredth part of what I had with me when I came here. Much of it was pawned and sold in the war. My papa thought nothing was pretty enough for me. Now I don't care about them so much any more."

I opened a case. There, on dark velvet, lay the green dolphin.

"This," said I. But before I could touch the stone, she held it hidden in her hands which she clasped together.

"That doesn't belong there. I won't give that up. When I die, it will go back to the giver."

The sight of that jewel released a flood of memories in me. At the same time I became aware that my stay in Ferrara would have been in vain if I could get no answers to the questions which were my key to the past as well as the future.

"Who am I? Tell me that at least before I go away."

She stood up and clutched me hard. I felt her nails through the stuff of my jacket.

"I don't know. I had a child, my first child, that was taken from me after it was born. No one would ever tell me what became of him. He was never mentioned again, never more. He might never have existed."

"Because he could call his father grandfather as well?"

"Oh God, who put that idea into your head? I swear to God that it isn't true. My papa loved me as he would love his most precious possession. Why must that tenderness be besmirched by filth? The child came at a time when I had to declare that I was a virgin in order to get my first marriage dissolved. It was in the interest of my father, my brothers, that I should be a virgin. It was in the interest of my father, my brothers, that I should re-marry an Aragon. I had no choice."

"That child who might be me—who fathered him?"

"Don't ask any more questions. Whatever I could tell you would only increase your uncertainty. What's the sense of that? I never said—did I? that *you* were that child. My papa had other sons by various women in Rome. The bull in the Chancellery . . ."

"There are *two* bulls."

She stood silent for a while, pressed against me. Although she didn't move, I had the impression that she was fighting to regain her self-control.

"I know nothing. Believe what you will. What does it matter? You are a Borgia. You are near and dear to me. I shall always look upon you as a brother, the youngest, the only one who is left to me."

By taking a step backward I forced her to look at me. I asked her why she had hated Cesare. Her eyes, with huge fixed pupils, stared into mine. Again I had to think of a trapped animal which, mortally frightened, helpless, fixes its eyes in fascination upon its enemy.

"Hated, hated? How dare you utter that word? Cesare did everything for me, everything. He said that he would protect me. That he would intervene like God Himself whenever I was in trouble or in danger. 'The course of your life is a symbol of our triumph, dearest little sister, but let me judge at which point fate needs a helping hand . . .' "

Again that laughter which was indistinguishable from sobbing. She put both hands against my chest and rose up on her toes. Staring into those light dilated eyes, I suddenly thought that in

Lucrezia a lifelong struggle was going on between herself and the powers which had controlled her youth. Pope Alexander, Cesare, dead and gone to dust, but something of them still existed, had taken possession of that willing spirit, tried to condense itself into a personality which would live in Lucrezia's body after having driven out her own thin self. Her fitfulness was the residue of her struggle with the demon. Against Alfonso, me, all other mortal souls, she had a weapon indeed: she carried with her everywhere the evil that was destroying her.

"I have always accepted my lack of wisdom. I trusted blindly the insight of my papa, my brothers. I was certainly too stupid to understand the how and why of things which happened in my interest and in the interest of my family. I was quite contented with a little happiness and comfort . . . I have never been very ambitious. I have come far, it's true, but God, how many tears have I shed on the way . . ."

She was straying from the subject again. I repeated my first question. "Who am I?"

In a sudden fit of anger she tried to thrust me away.

"When you act that way I think that you are Cesare's son. You won't let go of your prey; you must always have your own way; you torment me . . ."

"I torment myself the most. I live in uncertainty. I am vulnerable on all sides. What am I, a walking riddle, an absurdity . . . Everywhere I come up against silence, against contradiction. To me, the worst truth is preferable to doubt . . ."

Now she wanted to caress me again. With her arms thrown around me, she whispered comforting words.

"I can understand that. I'm not happy either. You and I, we carry our burden onward. You have so much less to drag along than I do, perhaps you can still free yourself. You're young, you're going away from here. If you want to, you can forget. Your will is perhaps still strong, not weakened by corruption . . . Don't look at me like that. If I had it in my power to help you . . . Forgive me. Think of me with affection. This is the last time. I'm pregnant again—this time I won't survive it . . ."

She was right. Seven months later the news of her death reached me in France. Alfonso wrote to me personally, called himself inconsolable. According to rumor, when the corpse was being laid out, a hair shirt was found under her clothes, along with a girdle with sharp points on the inside, such as penitents wear.

In essence little has changed since I left Ferrara. From time to time my suspicions have been encouraged by words picked up here and there. After much uncertainty and self-torment, I chose finally, mostly as a result of Luisa's influence, the most acceptable of all the possibilities: that I was Cesare's son. When Lucrezia was dead, I could easily accept the explanation I had found for her agitation at the mention of Cesare's name. Her real element was enjoyment, a peaceful life, happiness. Only too often Cesare had disturbed that peace. Her first husband driven away in ignominy, her second husband murdered—probably with the dagger which I owned, the dagger which Cesare as a fiendish joke later gave as a gift to Rodrigo, the victim's son. To find an explanation for all this I had to fall back upon what Lucrezia had told me.

Borgia policy was at the bottom of everything. Lucrezia was a pawn who was willing to be shoved about in the name of paternal, brotherly love, blood ties. Under the spell of his ambitious eldest son, Pope Alexander could offer her consolation only in the form of jewelry, kisses, fulsome flattery. Of course she hated Cesare, but she was so deeply frightened of him that ten years after his death she tried still to hide that hatred. She was both attracted to me and repelled by me—a Borgia kinsman, but also a living part of her dreaded brother. Didn't this explain her extraordinary behavior toward me? In Carpi she had looked me over, felt me as if I were a prodigy: flesh of Cesare's flesh, blood of his blood, and yet harmless, defenseless, in her power.

When I weighed up these arguments, the rest—the infamous insinuations overheard in Bari and Naples—appeared to be nothing but slander. The name of Borgia has always roused hatred, distaste and envy. So what is surprising about the fact that a torrent of muck and filth is flung after the dead?

So I thought: I am Cesare's bastard. Alfonso had personally informed me about the existence of a bull which affirmed that fact. That there was a second bull in which I was named as the son of Pope Alexander, made little difference, I believed. Anyone who examined the Borgia's dynastic policies about the time of my birth could easily find a motive for that discrepancy. Cesare had acknowledged me as his son but had decided almost immediately afterward that that acknowledgement was detrimental to his interests. Then Pope Alexander—willingly or under pressure—had taken the paternity upon himself, but with the cunning of an experienced lawyer had allowed both documents to be preserved, for safety's sake.

That was the sort of reasoning which preoccupied me there in King Francis's convivial court. I succeeded, as I have said earlier, in convincing myself more and more. Only in the darkness and quiet of the night when even the most unlikely things seem possible, I lay sometimes, awakened with a start from an evil dream and brooded on these puzzles with no solution.

That mysterious child of Lucrezia's, from whom apparently neither she nor anyone else had ever received word nor sign— that bastard, born in the period between her first and second marriages . . . had she really believed for a time that I was that child? If I wished, I could find evidence for that from her words and her behavior toward me. For my part, I have always rejected that possibility which thrust itself upon me again and again in my dreams. There was so much in the relationship between Lucrezia and me that I did not understand, that will remain forever unexplained. We never faced each other with complete openness. Suspicion, uncertainty, clouded all our meetings. Even now whenever I think back about her, I am overcome by a feeling that is a mixture of resentment and pity. I still have the tendency—although I know it is unreasonable—to blame her for my fate. Why? Because her attitude toward me seemed to stem from a sense of guilt. I have often told myself that if I were her son, nature would have granted me or her or both of us a sting of recognition; on the other hand, I was aware that too much importance should not be placed upon that sort of thing. I have never heard that a man instinctively recognizes and respects his mother as such if he meets her for the first time when he is an adult. In the Greek tale of King Oedipus . . . No, Lucrezia was not that close to me. She was Cesare's sister. The child she had is no concern of mine. For if I should identify with him, then the question arises of his paternity; then I am forced to consider once again the rumors which I heard in Naples. Unless . . . Who said that Giovanni Sforza was really impotent? They wanted to get rid of him, he had to go. If Lucrezia was pregnant . . . Why not? The possibility of a legitimate birth, of a genuine blood relationship with Isabella and Bona and the Lords of Milan . . . My whole life would change if I could prove that.

In France I put such thoughts aside; there the suppositions seemed too bizarre, too far removed from reality. But since I have returned to Rome, the question presses me anew.

For lack of any better information, my name is Borgia-bastard. I have no past and therefore no future. I am not allowed even the privilege of feeling proud or ashamed of my birth. I know nothing. The question which I have so often asked myself and others is an important one: how can a man know which way he wants to go if he does not know himself? Isn't it difficult enough to find our own way in the trackless wastes of time that lie before us even when we know from whence we come?

I've always envied people who don't have any doubts about their pasts or their goals in life. In France I always liked to make friends with ambitious, self-assured young men, and to make love to the most calculating women in the court. But I wasn't able to learn anything from any of them. Although I did my best to imitate their careless nonchalance and confidence, I knew that I didn't possess the one thing that mattered. I only *seemed* to be what they *really* were. I could mislead others, perhaps, but never myself.

One of them gave me some valuable advice, though. It was the Englishwoman with the barbarous family name—Bullen or Boleyn, nobody could pronounce it. (I can still hear her laughing at everyone who tried.) She was in the Queen Mother's retinue; young and dark, she had defiant black eyes. She challenged and tempted all the men in the court, but she didn't allow anyone more than a few kisses. Naturally I tried my luck with her too. She laughed in my face—I'm not a slut like the others, she said . . . One refusal was enough for me; I left her in peace after that. But evidently she liked that attitude: she and I had some friendly talks then. I remember asking her to tell me the secret of her charm and her growing success. As usual, she laughed.

"Nobody knows me. I never say what I think or what I'm planning to do. But I let everyone know that I have high expectations. I don't have to settle for less than the best. That way my value goes up, into the clouds!"

She was right. I've followed her example from time to time and it always produced the desired result for me. I've heard that she's a person of great importance now at the English court. The King himself desires her. One must be silent about one's thoughts and intentions. Or at least you must behave as if what's concealed is worth the trouble of concealment, give the impression that you're completely sure of yourself.

Of course that kind of pomposity is a continuous strain. All right, the Boleyn has been able to hold a king in her hand that way—but what will *my* reward be? They're not going to come and offer me the dukedom of Camerino, no matter how successfully I give the impression that I'm worth more than the other man. The more I see and hear here, the more galling the thought becomes that I haven't got the right or the power to demand Camerino or Nepi. If it's Camerino, I'd have to drive out that fat sanctimonious bore Varano; if it's Nepi, it's held by relatives of that woman, the Colonna, who are ruling Naples again. But the time's past when you can force lands and cities into submission through daring and willpower and acting as *condottiere* to a handful of soldiers. Before I left France, I discussed my chances with Luisa. She promised me that she would write to our blood relatives in Spain who control the Borgia possessions there. But I've heard nothing more about it. Luisa doesn't answer my letters.

Incidentally, since I've been taken into the retinue of the Chancellor of Milan, I'm getting noticeably more respect. I still keep asking myself who got this post for me. I have decent quarters, good food and drink, my expenses are paid and I've been handed a full purse. So at least now I can ride out in Rome with the other gentlemen of the retinue; I don't have to spend the whole day hanging around the Chancellery, or wandering bored and penniless through the endless galleries of the Vatican.

It's dusty and hot in the city; there's a smell that I remember from the past: smoke, fried fish, street refuse, apricots . . . and all that mixed with another sickening stench which blows across from the quarters where the plague is raging. As I said earlier, there's not much to do. In order to liven things up, amusing contests are organized in the streets: running and long jumping among old men, cripples, blind people, Jews in long gowns and half-naked whores. There are many shouting, whistling people on the roads, the winehouses are crowded, there is dancing and singing just as at Carnival.

I have honestly not been able to discover the reason for all this jollity. In order to distract the populace for a while from thoughts of Pavia and the plague, a few pageants and processions were held, following proven custom. If Lucrezia's tales were not grossly exaggerated, things must have been very different here in the previous Jubilee year, 1500. For that matter, on far less important occasions at the court of King Francis, there were more horses to be seen—handsomer and better-groomed—, bigger and more beautifully decorated floats, and in any case there no one would put up with faded brocade, discolored banners and disorderly loiterers. Rome seems to be populated by prelates of every rank wearing garments of the most divergent cut and color, by bedizened wenches and loafers, by lackeys, clerks, scribes and quacks, and a horde of artists, genuine and otherwise, and for the rest, the most impudent rabble in the world. Bankers and noblemen walk through the city with an army of followers and a commotion and display more appropriate to the battlefield than to a journey of three or four streets.

I enjoy myself more in the vineyards outside Rome, or hunting wood pigeons among the ruins in the neighborhood of the Coliseum. Monday noon we captured quite a lot of these, and after that we had the booty plucked and prepared in an inn on the edge of the city. Over those birds and several jars of wine, we argued until the moon rose about the talk going the rounds concerning Messer Morone's visit to the Marquis of Pescara. A secret that's known to all of Rome: that's a subject for the *commedia del'arte*. But men like Pescara and Morone are not clowns.

On the way back, still in the heat of the discussion—and probably drunk besides—I collided, horse and all, with a palanquin. The gentlemen accompanying the coach—also no longer sober—thought they were being attacked by robbers. There ensued a ludicrous exchange of blows and insults which finally ended in general laughter, embraces, apologies and bows left and right. In passing, I looked into the coach.

There were two women in there—one old, fat, still out of breath from raving, and one young, extraordinarily beautiful, who reclined in a corner, yawning and looking bored. By the light of the torches, she seemed covered from head to foot with gold and glittering jewels. I asked my companions who she was.

A courtesan—what else could she be? A certain Tullia, who—

as these women are wont to do—has appropriated the surname of a famous royal family: D'Aragona.

It might be the sound of that name, so familiar to me, or the young woman's indifferent face, looking white in the moonlight, or the fact that I have been without female companionship for so long . . . I plan to ask Messer Aretino for the introduction which he promised me.

I have been told a few things about Messer Aretino in the Datary's office and in Morone's retinue—I could claim that I know the truth about him now. He comes from Arezzo, that much is certain. His father seems to have been a shoemaker or a nobleman gone to seed, his mother a tart or a nun. Before I came to Rome, he had led an eventful life as painters' helper, highwayman, monk, tavern servant, lackey . . . I've forgotten what else. He's made a name here as a rhymer of epigrams about everything and everybody, he's the soul of the annual festival in honor of Pasquino, the patron saint of anonymous satiric verse. He supplies libels and pornography, poetical surveys and lives of saints to order. He's fond of boys without rejecting women. At various courts he has filled the roles, in turn, of spy, buffoon, secretary, procurer . . . that's right, he told me something like that himself. They say that there's no one in all Italy so quick-witted as he, and so dangerous. Although his record seems unsavory enough, the Pope apparently doesn't dare to drive him away.

All this news throws a definite light on my friend in the peacock blue.

X.

Pietro Aretino and Giovanni Borgia

Ah, Messer, I'm delighted that you're finally giving me the opportunity to show you something of Rome! You shouldn't have any regrets about this evening—Tullia d'Aragona is in a class by herself! You've seen her passing in the street—wait 'till you're in her house: her furniture is the measure of her success. I can tell you an amusing story about that. When Strozzi, the banker, one of her loyal visitors—a rich Florentine, he's used to luxurious living—when he first came to Tullia, he was simply flabbergasted at the magnificence. The moment came when he needed a cuspidor, but he couldn't see anything like that anywhere. So he beckoned to his servant, and spat in his face. Naturally Tullia immediately asked him why he had done that. And Strozzi said, 'Because his face is the least beautiful thing in these rooms; I wouldn't dare spit anywhere else!' Later he rewarded Tullia's favors with a set of solid gold spittoons.

"Apart from anything else, Tullia's a nice girl, and I don't say that glibly about women of that sort. Most courtesans are common sluts who disguise themselves by hook or by crook as great ladies: stupid, impudent, superstitious, walking centers of infection—there's no sickness that they don't have. Scrape off the paint, strip away the finery, what's left is nothing special. I know I'm not telling you anything new, it's the same everywhere, in Rome, Paris, Madrid. . . . But this Tullia . . . really, one in a million! Young, healthy, intelligent and from a distinguished family too. It's worth the trouble to go and look. But first—come and take a glass of wine with me. We don't really know each other well enough, Messer. You must tell me all about yourself. You trust me, don't you?"

"You haven't given me any reason to doubt your good faith yet."

"Ah, I see you're cautious! Well, it's a good habit. And it's especially popular among young people who have something to hide or who are trying to get something or who have an interest in appearing to be persons of great importance . . ."

"What place is this? Where are we now?"

"We're in the annexes to the Vatican, my dear sir. Look around . . . you see no marble here, no murals or colonnades or—praise God—no horrible stone dolls from a bygone day! We're in the labyrinth of the Borgo, Messer—a real rat's nest of houses, towers, alleys . . . all the lesser gods of the court dwell here. Haven't you ever been here? You must live on the other side of the palace?"

"Over the guards' rooms."

"And therefore far from the intrigues of the Borgo rats. Whoever you have to thank for your quarters must have some reason for wanting to keep you out of that neighborhood."

"It seems to me that you're always looking for some motive behind everything."

"Messer, I know the world, I know men, and above all I know life at the court as well as I know the back of my own hand. Ah, here we are! So you'll do me the honor of being my guest for a little while? Matteo, Pirro, open the door! Where are they hiding, the idiots? Ah, finally—unbolted! You clods, what do you mean by letting me stand in front of my own door like that? Come inside, Messer."

"Ah, but I'm afraid we're intruding . . ."

"No, wait, Messer, I can fix this right now. Afrosina, didn't I tell you this morning that you had to disappear? Is my home a public house or a bordello? Do you think you can lie around all day in my bed so you can receive their lordships my servants as soon as I show my heels? Get out! I don't want to see you here again! Go back to the procuress, let her barter you away to someone less squeamish than I. Now be off! Excuse this disturbance, Messer, servants and prostitutes in Rome, all vermin . . . Matteo, Pirro! Make the bed, wipe up the crumbs and seeds and those puddles of wine from the floor! Bring clean glasses and a pitcher of Falerno. Do please sit down, Messer. It's my misfortune that I'm too good-natured and too quick to fall in love. I'm always being deceived and robbed by my servants and my sweethearts. Get out, Afronsina, stop it, get out, those are only crocodile tears! If you were a good cook at least, I might perhaps strain a point . . . but I don't care for your polenta and your finery costs me too much. If I wasn't clever enough to look out for myself from time to time, I'd be begging in the streets now . . . I see through them, you know. Some time when we get a chance, I'll let you read a few fragments of a play I'm writing, a comedy, *Cortigiana*, *The Courtesans* . . . I bluntly disclose the lives and struggles of these females in it . . ."

"But surely it isn't worthwhile to devote an entire comedy to these whores? You can enjoy them or let them alone, but to spend time thinking about them like that. . ."

"And why not, Messer? They're human beings like you and me. Inexhaustible study material for anyone who wants to learn about the virtues and vices of his fellow creatures. The whore and her trade—that's the world in little. You have to interpret my *Cortigiana* as primarily symbolic. It's a satire on society: the whole court's made to look foolish. Now don't refuse, this pitcher must be emptied, Borgia. The wine will only go sour in this heat. So . . . you've been to the Datary's secretariat recently? What do you think of Berni?"

"He's your enemy, isn't he, Messer? Unless I'm misinformed . . ."

"Ah, you *are* well-informed! What did they tell you there, at the office of that intriguer, that gossip-rhymer? They laid bare my past, no doubt? It's all lies and slander, all of it! Berni hates me because I have more talent than he does, because powerful men have made me their friend. Before I came here, he had a fair chance as a poet of epigrams and work for all occasions. Now he might as well forget it. He won't forgive me for that. Not too long ago Pope Clement was actually at the point of giving me Berni's post. At that time I had been distinguishing myself for years in the retinue of Agostino Chigi, the great banker. I was the apple of his eye, his right hand, he wouldn't complete any important transaction without discussing it with me. They begged me to come to the court. It's the tallest trees which are hit hardest by the wind, Messer. Now I'm being stabbed in the back. Giberti hates the sight of me because I know everything and I don't try to hide my opinions. He does whatever he can to undermine my influence. It's lucky for me that at the moment the Pope is somewhat less intimate with Giberti in order to avoid alienating Schomberg, the Cardinal of Capua . . . that Schomberg's a great man here now, after the Emperor's victory at Pavia—I'm sure you've noticed that. If Giberti's prestige hadn't suffered I'd have been shoved out long ago: Pope Clement and Giberti have been friends for years, close friends—they used to call Giberti *il cuor del papa*, the Pope's heart. Anything Monsignore wanted, he got without fail. That's why my feathers were ruffled, because of Giberti. They've taken away part of my annuity, they banned me from court for a while, and when I came back I was forced to find shelter here in the Borgo. Look around you, what kind of environment is this for a poet of genius, a knight in the Order of Rhodes, confidential agent of the Marquis of Mantua? A room, what am I saying, a hole, a pigsty, four walls with a roof on top, nothing more; servants, furniture, my food and drink and clothing—I have to provide these for myself. And all because of a couple of sonnets!"

"I've heard something about captions to certain engravings . . ."

"Ah, so you know all about that! I can just see it, I can hear it, the righteous indignation in Giberti's office. I admit that my verses were highly spiced. But you should have seen Marcantonio Raimondi's engravings. Sixteen variations of love play, exceptionally stimulating, and, what's more, a faultlessly executed engraving technique. Masterpieces, piece by piece, Messer. Isn't an artist free to choose his own subject? Is it forbidden to look at the union of man and woman? Are we less than beasts that we must be ashamed of an act which we have to thank for our existence? I don't pretend to be better than I am. I'm willing to acknowledge that I have blood in my veins and not water. I could honestly not remain calm at the sight of those masterly engravings. When the painter Romano—also not just anybody—who came up with the whole idea, asked me if I would be willing to write the captions, I did it, and with pleasure, Messer! That's all. But here at the court a commotion as if the world were coming to an end. *Dio!* I've certainly heard and seen uglier things since I came to Rome. The beauty of the whole thing is still that the engravings and the verses have been most successful with the members of the Curia. No cardinal who didn't have them under his pillows . . . This is all because of Giberti; he needed a pretext for sending me away. I thought, Messer, that you would know Giberti very well because he's the leader of the French party."

"I know Monsignore by sight, that's all."

"But you must surely maintain contact with France and the French party after having lived there so long. To your health, Messer, and the success of your plans!"

"You seem to know my plans better than I know them myself."

"Only a complete idiot accepts a position at the court of Rome without having plans . . . great plans. Now surely it wasn't out of a sentimental longing for *Italia Bella* or our Eternal City that you deserted the French court where life is most agreeable . . . or at least so I've been told."

"I've been a soldier, Messer. If King Francis's campaign had taken a different turn, I wouldn't be sitting here in Rome now."

"Perhaps you were expecting a fine career in the service of France? Commander of a garrison or even governor of some state or other in the Po Valley?"

"Ah, you show a deep understanding of my ambitions . . . I could almost believe that you regret even more than I do that all chances in that direction have gone for good since Pavia."

"For good! Come, come, you're less optimistic than the French party! Even His Holiness doesn't take such a gloomy view of the situation. Naturally you know that he's secretly—as it's called here—working hard to get closer to France again, and special couriers are going to and from England . . . I'm not telling you anything new, Messer. Let me refill your glass, this is an excellent Falerno, I'm sure you've noticed that. You can talk politics safely with me, by the way, I'm just as well-informed as your connections at court."

"And what makes you think I have connections at the Vatican?"

"Anyone who wants to succeed here must have powerful friends, otherwise he wouldn't even try. A post in the Chancellery that can lead to a cardinal's hat. What else would you be looking for there, my dear sir? You have to be completely sure of yourself if you have an interest in getting a place among the wearers of purple. And all the more because you—if I'm not mistaken—can't boast of legitimate birth."

"My birth is a subject that concerns me alone!"

"Ah, you're easily offended, Borgia! I didn't intend to insult you, I'm only trying to give you some advice. Certainly you don't need me to tell you that illegitimacy is no obstacle to making a career. Name me half a dozen great men in Italy who aren't bastards. It's the same story at the court here: offices, annuities, estates, titles to give out, even if you crept up from the gutter. But as far as the purple goes, Clement isn't so generous with it as his predecessors were. Even for money, he won't make a cardinal. Now Leo would have sold God Himself if he could! Christianity—that's a business that brings in cash! I could name you the names of gentlemen who have offered Pope Clement fortunes for a red hat. But even though he can't make decisions about anything else, this is where he digs his heels in. It's fear of course. With this pope, fear is always the driving force. He's saddled with the evil reputations of his predecessors. And Giberti is presently playing the great Church reformer, so he puts in the necessary word. Take some good advice from me, Messer: if you want to make a career here in Rome, first of all you have to flatter your way into Giberti's good graces."

"In that case, I really don't understand why you keep butting heads with the Datary day in and day out."

"Ah, I'm finished with Rome. I don't want to stay here, I loathe this stinking swamp. Listen, Messer, what I'm going to say to you now is confidential . . ."

"I really would prefer that you not tell me anything if you don't feel certain of me . . ."

"Oh, I've known for a long time where I stand with you, Borgia. You're a nobleman precisely to the taste of Messer Baldassare Castiglione, our expert in good manners. You've stepped right out of the *Book of the Courtier* . . ."

"That's too great an honor. I don't know Messer Castiglione and I haven't read his book."

"Of course, what am I thinking of? He was appointed envoy to Madrid before you set foot in Italy—he's a fervent supporter of the Spanish cause, he corresponds with my most important connection, the Marquis of Mantua. That's how I find out things which are kept normally exclusively within the Emperor's closest circle. Castiglione is like many of those so-called superior natures—he's naïve. Because he is nobility itself, he thinks he can overcome meanness and obscenity with a wave of his hand. Courtly interaction—that's his hobbyhorse. He sees this court, any court, as the center which radiates patriotism and virtue."

"And you, Messer Aretino . . . what do you see?"

"A pigsty, a breeding ground of hate, ambition, envy . . . the grave of our hopes and our honest intentions, a market of lies, a school of deceit and crime, a paradise of vice, the dunghill where talent and worth lie rotting. It's madness to think that anyone can develop real stature living amongst this rabble."

"Well, that leads naturally to one question: why have you stayed in Rome feeling like that, Messer Pietro?"

"Messer Giovanni, because I have to live somehow."

"Oh come, someone like you can always earn his keep anywhere."

"So you think! In these times you can't earn a dry crust of bread by writing, my friend. Look around you. It's the same poverty-stricken story at all the courts of Italy: the princes are over their ears in debt and if they do have any money they'd rather spend it on mercenaries and fortresses than on poets."

"Well, looking at the dangerous situation, I can't really blame the lords."

"Yes, the man who sits peering suspiciously at his neighbors opposite and next door to him doesn't want an epic about his forefathers or a paean of praise for his own heroic deeds. The great lords don't have a *soldo* left over for a solid piece of work. What has happened to the times when a poet got big commissions? When he could always find a Maecenas to give him food and clothing and lavish quarters in return for a couple of hundred couplets? Believe me, there's no chance of that now. A writer is a beggar in disguise and that's all he is. You choose a prince or some other prominent person who has a reputation for being especially generous or artistic or vain, you sing his praises in tercets and quatrains, you compare him to all the gods of Olympus, all heroes past and present, you extol his wife as a heavenly wonder, laud his dwarf, his favorite horse and his lapdog . . . and then you send him the whole lot along with a fawning letter, or you offer him the work in person, kneeling, and preferably with an appropriate speech—and what's your reward?—'Our thanks, Messer Pietro, we're content. We'll have your poetry read to us at our earliest opportunity. You'll hear from us' . . . At the best, you get a handful of gold pieces, maybe enough to pay for pen and paper and a new suit of clothes. But even that's not typical. I can't tell you how many times I've asked, begged, pleaded, and threatened, cursed before I've received a pittance. Your health, Messer, drink to the glory of poetic creativity!"

"Well, be that as it may, from what I've heard about you, you can't really complain about lack of interest in your work . . ."

"Ah, Messer, that's my secret: I know what I want and I know how to get it. No one knows human nature the way I do. I'll pluck the fruits of my genius, believe me, Messer Giovanni, because I can squeeze hard cash from their cowardice, their vanity, their guilt, their lust, their most secret wishes—I've discovered how to do that. I supply what they desire even before they're aware of that desire. I know how to take advantage of generally prevalent moods and feelings even before they're put into words. I catch a rumor when it's still only a thin little cloud . . . I shape it, I color it, I breathe life into it and I present it as truth. *Nothing* is so lucrative as scandal. People want to be titillated, Messer. There's more power in mockery and criticism and in double entendre than in all the poetry of Parnassus. That's what the gentlemen pay well for: to keep me quiet or to encourage me to slander. Believe me, I know how to hold the whole world in the hollow of my hand. I bide my time. I keep my eyes and ears open, I gather information, I'm everywhere and nowhere at the same time. I stake my reputation on knowing everything, Messer, everything . . . the truth, but also lies. Whoever I spin my web around is unfortunate. I try things at random now and then . . ."

"On Giberti and his followers, among others?"

"See for yourself; don't the results speak for themselves? Giberti is enraged, but he's powerless at the moment. If his position weren't so shaky, I'd have been sitting long ago in the deepest dungeon of the Castel Sant'Angelo like my friend Marcantonio Raimondi, the engraver. Giberti doesn't dare to do anything to me, because that would look as though my allegations were true."

"What allegations?"

"My allegations that it is Giberti who's responsible for all the Pope's stupid decisions and prevarications. Don't you think it speaks volumes that he and his hanger-on Berni don't come out against me openly? Think about that, Messer, if they tell you anything else about me in the secretariat. I have much more power than you can even begin to imagine. Listen, I know perfectly well that you're watching to see which way the wind is blowing. That's a sensible attitude! I don't like people who let themselves be talked into things easily. But I'll give you just this to consider: remember that I can render an invaluable service to you. There's nothing you can't accomplish with my help, Messer. Of course you have to put your trust in me above all your other connections . . ."

"Messer Pietro, I can't help admiring the persistence with which you keep attempting to pump me. Let me say to you now, as a reward for your diligence, that I have no single influential connection at court and that my ambition doesn't extend to the purple or to anything connected with the purple."

"We must be honest with each other. No more sparring, Messer! I've taken the first step by telling you one thing and another about myself that I don't usually noise abroad. Naturally you want to make a career for yourself. I repeat, no one who's not ambitious can stand it here for one day. You're a Borgia. You have how could it be otherwise?—a gift for intrigue in your blood, for the going-through-thick-and-thin-to-get-what-one-wants. You surely know means, methods . . . Stay calm, there's not the slightest reason to throw a fit . . . Let me fill your glass again. I know more than you think . . ."

"What do you know? What are they saying about me?"

"Messer, I wouldn't spoil this conversation for any price by touching upon a subject that you'd rather not discuss. Everyone has his sensitivities. What I know isn't common property. Nothing was said about you at court that I would take the trouble to repeat, nothing that you yourself would consider important, I'll wager. And to set your mind further at rest: what I know doesn't pass my lips . . ."

"In the Devil's name, what is it then?"

"Don't take offense. We're living in a sinful age, Messer. There

are things which men of the world—like you and me—can accept
for what they are but at which the average man shudders . . . The
kings of ancient Egypt even prided themselves on being born to
brother and sister . . . Ah ah . . . Put up the dagger, my friend, sit
down!"

"I want proof for what you dared to insinuate just now!"

"*Dio*, you have a Spanish sense of honor, Messer Giovanni. You
feel for your dagger the instant the family is spoken of on any
terms except those of the greatest respect . . ."

"When and where have you first heard those . . . rumors?"

"Friend, the people shouted it from the housetops at the time,
in Rome, in every town, village and hamlet in Italy. I heard it
when I was still a boy in Arezzo. But believe me, today it's almost
completely forgotten."

"And the proof?"

"Proof, proof! If you insist on having proof at any cost, I can
certainly track it down for you. It'll be a protracted and troublesome task, but yes, for a friend . . . If I'd known that you take this
matter so much to heart, I wouldn't have opened my mouth. Don't
think about it any more, my friend. Do you play cards?"

"I'm awaiting proof."

"Of course you play cards. You come from France. I've heard
that there's more passionate card-playing in the French court
than anywhere else. More ducats are set rolling by cards than by
trade in Flanders and war in Italy put together! Will you shuffle?
Take a good look at the cards, by the way; each one is a work of
art. Yes, they were done by Marcantonio Raimondi. The same
man who's been thrust into the dungeons of the Castel
Sant'Angelo. Anyone who can produce the symbols on a pack of
cards that way is more than an artist—he's a philosopher!"

"I'm asking myself what you're driving at with *me*, Messer
Pietro. How is this conversation going to help you to make use
of *me*?"

"Use, use—what a disagreeable word. Have some more wine."

"Wine doesn't make me any more talkative than I am by nature,
Messer."

"All right, listen: you claim you don't have any contact with
Giberti and his clique. But I know the world. It's the custom here
to say A, to do B and to think C and possibly to mean D. . . ."

"If it'll make you feel any better, I'll give you my word of honor."

"Your word of honor! Messer, you really must think I am extremely naïve."

"I lived for seven years in France. There his word of honor is part of the equipage of every nobleman."

"You're going to have to break that habit if you want to succeed in Rome. A man of honor fares here like a fish in hot oil. All right, it's accepted that you have a word of honor. Have you pledged your word of honor that you'll keep silent about the visit you paid to the Marquis of Pescara in the retinue of Girolamo Morone?"

"Do you really believe that Messer Morone would possibly take me into his confidence? I still don't even know why I was added to his retinue."

"But damnation, you must have noticed that something was going on! You don't seem to be an idiot or a dupe! Now look, if you handle this situation the right way, you can make your career. Believe me, something's brewing—and it's going to make a nice stink when the lid's lifted, which it will be before long. . . . What a delightful game! I'm a dedicated cardplayer, Messer. Sleeping and cardplaying—for me those are the two great boons of life, a panacea. . . . Listen, Borgia. In the light of those things we've been discussing, we really ought to join together. With my connections and my experience, I can render you a valuable service. See if you can find out what's going on between Morone and Pescara. Get the information and leave the rest to me. If I'm not mistaken, we'll easily find someone who'll offer us a fortune for this information or to keep it quiet—one or the other. What do you say to that?"

"I had intended to make my career in a more honorable way."

"Don't make me laugh! Someone with your name and background . . . Ah ah, there you go again—as if you'd been stung . . . My God, Messer, do you care about it so much? I assure you, no one here is interested in that old gossip. At least, not yet. Only a man like me could transform those winds of rumor into a hurricane which would blow you and all your plans and dreams away . . . I think you ought to bear that in mind, Messer. But why should you be my enemy? We could get on so well together. I suggest that we work together. But we mustn't let the ground be cut away from beneath us. First arrange your cards, quietly take a look at the hand you're holding, Messer Giovanni. It's still early, we have plenty of time. It doesn't become amusing at Tullia's until the candles have been lit. Shall I bid? What's an ambitious man but a player, Borgia—a player on a grand scale and the world his card game?"

XI.

Tullia d'Aragona

Tullia has retired behind the *altona*, the wooden screen on the roof of her house. She is washing and bleaching her long hair, an occupation which requires the whole day and the utmost concentration. She is alone, no serving-maid, no friend, not even her mother keeps her company in the burning sun. Anyone whose hair does not need washing shuns that shadowless place on the roof until sunset. Tullia sits among basins and tubs, her locks spread out to dry on the broad rim of the *solana*, the crownless washing hat which protects her face and neck against the fierce light. In one hand she holds a mirror, in the other a stick with a sponge on the end. From time to time she moistens the strands of hair with a bleaching liquid.

Venetian blonde, the fashionable color—that's the goal. Tullia, who likes things to be easy, would not of her own accord have taken so much trouble for a red-gold coiffure. But her mother knows what a young courtesan is obliged to do to make a career for herself. Where would Tullia be without her help, her advice, her constant vigilant presence? A hundred times a day that question is asked, to which the daughter can give no answer.

Ah, Tullia, lazy-bones, slattern, dreamer, who wakes you, who washes you, coifs you and clothes you? Who prepares your cosmetics, sees to it that you paint yourself properly? Who makes sure that you don't become too fat or too thin? Who has taught you how you must speak and walk to be pleasing, who is always near you with a nod, a gesture, a word of encouragement or warning? Who makes your connections for you, negotiates over the gifts, receives the gentlemen and then shows them out again later? Who gives you the opportunity to show off your good upbringing and who has given you that upbringing?

Tullia can't do much else than shrug her shoulders. Sometimes she yawns, sometimes she looks out of the window and hums, sometimes she walks to another room. After all, there's nothing to argue about. Her mother is right. This is the only way. When she appears to be unwilling, rises in rebellion, her mother is always there to remind her of the things she is not allowed to forget.

"Do you think that you would have had a cardinal for a father if in my time I hadn't kept myself in hand day in and day out? I knew what I wanted. I worked hard on myself. You have to make yourself irreplaceable, the most beautiful, the most well-informed, the most desirable, the only one. And when you have accomplished that, you still can't let yourself go. You have magnificent opportunities, better than I ever had. What was I? An ordinary girl from Ferrara, without friends or relatives and without money, standing one day on a street in Rome. If I hadn't known how to take good care of myself I would have been dead long ago or forced to lie with beggars for a *soldo* under the Ponte Sisto . . . And you? Your father a distinguished gentleman, I his sweetheart. He wouldn't have anybody but me, Giulia Ferrarese, people called me the queen of Rome. You were born and brought up in a palace. You learned Greek and Latin and to play the harp like the girls from the first families. You can read books, you can discuss any subject. It's your misfortune that your father died early and that his creditors left us nothing. Otherwise you could have had a suitable marriage. You would not have had to settle for less than a country nobleman. But there's no sense in living in the past. We must look after ourselves. I've done what I could. Now I'm too old for love. Your turn, Tullia. Use your head. You can go far. Then you'll be grateful to me."

Tullia knows all these arguments by heart. They keep her company night and day, a troupe of ghosts with the beaks and talons of harpies: greed, venality, lust and intrigue, as vigilant as the old hags her mother brings into the house to cook, to crush herbs, to tell fortunes from the cards.

"Use your head, be wise, make the most of your youth, your beauty. You must be ambitious, sweetheart, be ambitious."

If for a moment she succeeds in driving away the phantoms, in silencing that buzzing and hissing and chortling, then her mother drives the holy terrors back to her again. Aristocratic idleness is dangerous; more dangerous still is the innate Spanish pride inherited from her father, a pride which prefers poverty and death to the loss of honor. Her mother knows how to strike at this self-conscious brooding.

"Your father stemmed from the family of Aragon—I see that as a sign, little daughter, as a safe conduct that grants you entry to the great world which would be closed to you otherwise. What use are your education and your elegant manners if you don't know how to take advantage of them? These are weapons to defeat your rivals with—playing music, reciting poetry, speaking Latin: refinements which spice up your beauty. Men who are captivated by that, men of distinguished taste who have the means to satisfy their desires—these are the patrons my Tullia needs. I know the secrets of the trade, leave it to me. All you have to do is obey."

Tullia is silent. At the same time that she longs for her dead father, whom she reveres as the embodiment of royalty, for the spacious peacefulness of the palace where she spent her childhood, she feels a growing hatred for the fat, dark woman, festooned with clinking jewels, whom she must call mother. When Tullia grew older, they moved from Siena to Rome; from staid Siena where, after the Cardinal's bankruptcy, they lived on the periphery of a circle of poets and scholars—to Rome. On the Campo Marzio in the parish of San Trifone, Giulia Ferrarese rented for herself and her daughter an apartment in a beautiful new house belonging to the Augustine monastery. Their neighbors: downstairs a bishop and upstairs two courtesans, Vascha and Speranza, two ordinary daughters of pleasure, no competition. In back, bordering on the courtyard, a school for children. The first admirers, earlier connections of Giulia's—her fame, still not faded, is the best recommendation for her inexperienced daughter—have paid for the furniture, the clothing, the coach, the servants and the mules.

The *altana* is high; it forms a barrier between Tullia and the yellow, grey, dirty-white smoky roofs of the neighborhood, between her and the stink and the noise rising from street and courtyard. Only her mother's voice comes through from the loggia; she is loudly and slowly counting off the ingredients for a beauty preparation intended to make the skin supple: turpentine, lily leaves, fresh eggs, honey, crushed shells and camphor . . . cook that in a glass sphere over a low fire, later add musk and amber, a remedy second to none; my daughter must bathe her face with it seven times a day. . . .

Tullia puts her fingers in her ears. Through a curtain of shimmering hair, she sees the sky where pigeons are flapping their wings.

The weekly washing and dyeing, the only opportunity to escape Giulia's meddling, the old hags' chatter, the intrusiveness of Vascha and Speranza, who want to exchange experiences and toilette secrets over the balconies. Only here, on this scorching flat roof, half-naked, drugged by the smell of her own sweat and the strong spicy odor of balsam, dazzled by the light, sick from the heat, is Tullia free. She hums a song to drive away even the memory of the sound of her mother's voice, and lets her wooden slippers swing back and forth from her toes. She takes her writing case on her lap and looks for a new sharp goose-quill pen.

One evening, in her reception chambers, among the familiar visitors and their guests, an unknown: Messer Pietro's companion. Dark eyes that see everything, few words, not one smile. What struck her above all was that later, during that miserable altercation, he chose the side of the weakest party, the Spaniard.

Giulia wants her daughter to demonstrate courtliness and erudition in order to dispel the taint of the marketplace from the reception.

"Come, Tullia, a poem, a song on the lute or the harp, a dance, a rosina or pavane; talk about Dante or Plato; create an opportunity for a discussion; don't stand there as if it's not your affair."

So Tullia, after an instant of unnoticed resistance, loudly and smiling: "What do you think, Messer Strozzi, did Petrarch borrow in his work from the earlier Provençal and Tuscan poets?"

Applause, bravo; at Tullia's the mind is gratified as well as the senses. They form a circle. Tullia dutifully keeps the debate going. She remains continually aware of her mother's vigilant eye overseeing the room from a strategic corner.

"The adoption of others' ideas is unworthy of a great poet."

"Petrarch has stolen neither more nor less from his predecessors than the Spaniards have from us. They wear our caps, but they stick their buckles and medals on them and call the thing a Spanish invention."

"The Spanish annex a great deal more than our head-gear . . ."

"Che dizis vos, Segnor, de los Espagnoles?"

Oh God, the one Spaniard in the company! From a distance, Giulia hastily waves her fan in warning. A guest, a foreigner, insulted in her house. Petrarch is forgotten; now the subject is politics. A dispute, an exchange of abuse followed by challenges to combat outside. Messer Pietro's guest stands by the Spaniard. The two are the first to leave. Within a quarter of an hour, the courtesan's chambers are emptied. All that remains for the furious Giulia is a chaos of broken glass and overturned chairs, and for Tullia, the lover who paid for the party.

In his arms, she still thinks about the young man. Why hadn't he spoken to her, asked for an hour, a night of her company, as the others did? She wants to know who he is. Her mother later waves all her questions away with a shrug: Don't think about him any more—not for us, I could see that at a glance. A dark, surly face, a stiff attitude. Have you let yourself be dazzled by that? Two against one that's Messer Pietro's newest Ganymede. He's an all-around man!

But thoughts cost nothing. What Tullia wants to know, Messer Pietro can tell her—he's the friend of the household, the advisor, the confidant. A man of the world, a courtier, someone known in and outside of Rome, who is well-informed about everything, has more influence than anyone can imagine, but at the same time can talk with women for hours about things in which only women are interested: clothes, recipes, love affairs. He can bring a very wealthy client into the house as well as a soothsayer, understands how to invest money, knows where to get any conceivable item, is a fund of jokes and novelties and fascinating gossip—a phenomenon; Giulia, for one, can't get enough of him. Not a gentleman in the usual sense of the word, Giulia sees that clearly, but what difference does that make . . . one must have respect for someone who has known how to work his way up to being an important personage at the papal court—a model for you, Tullia!—but what a companion, what a tower of strength, what an inexhaustible source of amusement this Messer Pietro is! He comes when the door is shut to every other man, in the morning or the early afternoon when the women are having their siesta. He isn't disturbed by uncombed hair, an unfastened chemise, hastily tied petticoats. You can eat or sleep or powder yourself in his presence. He indulges in sweets and wine, sniffs at the pomades and perfumes, even lounges with his feet on the table, humming, juggling a pack of cards, playing with Tullia's monkey.

"Yes, my new friend, a remarkable young man, one worth keeping an eye on. A riddle and so all the more fascinating. But no riddle is so complicated that I can't work it out in the end. A man who's not sure of himself, hiding behind a stiff manner, or a spy in powerful hands—which is he, this Giovanni Borgia?"

Who, what, a Borgia? In her time, Giulia had added her graceful presence to the entertainments given by Pope Alexander and his son Cesare. "*Dio*, there's never been anything like that since. Did you know, Messer Pietro, that I was at the chestnut feast at the Vatican? Fifty women of Rome, the most beautiful, of course. On hands and knees, stark naked, we had to creep along the ground between candlesticks with burning candles . . . That was a competition; it was to see who could pick up the most chestnuts. One of Il Duca's ideas. How we laughed—but you both know that story, I've told it often . . ."

"Too often, Mother."

"Shut your mouth, Tullia! Save the great lady act for your receptions where it has some effect. But about this Borgia of yours, Messer Pietro: a blood relative to Pope Alexander and Il Duca? I think not, one of the many nameless little sons . . . No money? The other Borgias were fabulously wealthy."

Messer Pietro raises his hands in an eloquent gesture.

"Our friend possesses the qualities of his illustrious forebears; he knows how to make himself seem mysterious. In the Chancellery of the Vatican, there's more talk about him than about anyone else. He acts as if he doesn't notice, goes his own way, keeps quiet and provides material for fresh rumors. Maybe you can get him to talk, Tullia *mia?* Who knows—in your arms he might become as expansive as Messer Strozzi. Have you sounded your Florentine yet over you-know-what, my little dove?"

Tullia can't toss her head angrily. The *solana* can't be shaken off any more than the thoughts which trouble her. She is imprisoned under her great hat, burdened by the weight of her wet hair, just as she is at the mercy of Giulia's ambition and Messer

Pietro's curiosity about the political and business secrets of the gentlemen who purchase her favors.

At the court of the Cardinal her father, she had met only distinguished men; for that reason she accepts as a matter of course the tribute of members of the nobility, prelates, bankers. And anyway Giulia rejects anyone who can't satisfy the highest requirements of rank and wealth. But Messer Pietro's interest in her lovers stems from other motives. Giulia urges her daughter to grant the requests of this trusted, worthy friend of the family; we must occasionally do him a favor in return for all his helpfulness to us!

It's not for nothing that Rome prizes Tullia's intellectual gifts. The fact that politics and financial affairs can be discussed with her in bed, that she can share personal and social problems, increases her prestige. Strozzi, the Florentine envoy, calls her Aspasia because when he pours his heart out to her, she makes him feel like a Pericles. Because of her—and against the orders of Florence—he has extended his stay in Rome. He is in love, would like to take her back with him when he goes later, but Giulia doesn't see any advantage in a relationship like that while Tullia is still young. So Strozzi keeps arriving with rich presents and a heart full of worry and grievances that he can't air to anyone but Tullia. She is the Midas-pit into which he whispers what most upsets him: the complaints of his jealous wife in Florence, the sluggish progress of the diplomatic negotiations he's entrusted with, his irritation and disquiet with the situation in general, his republican aversion to the Medici who—for how long now?—rule Florence. Messer Pietro eagerly snatches up the echoes of the nocturnal conversations and gives Tullia instructions for further encounters.

"Tullia, my jewel, I really like to be kept up-to-date about everything. I know a great deal but, alas, I can't be everywhere at once. Tell Strozzi that you've heard that his friend Messer Niccolò Machiavelli is in Rome. Knowing that name will do you credit, it'll make you look like a woman with progressive ideas. Bring the conversation around to Messer Girolamo Morone, the Chancellor of Milan. Show your concern for the fate of our beloved Italy, which you might compare with a piece of meat that two dogs are fighting over. Strozzi will tell you more...."

Messer Pietro knows Tullia's weakness. She is more vain about her intellectual powers than about her body. She is not animated by vanity alone. The mind can liberate, ennoble. It is for freedom, eminence, that Tullia longs, the more passionately the more she feels shoved about like a thing without volition by her mother, by Messer Pietro, by her lovers. Something kicks against the touching of her flesh, the pressure on her mind and will. She endures this forced passivity with deep resentment. Knowledge means power, but creative ability is the magic key which unlocks all fetters. A courtesan, however rich, however famous, remains an instrument of lust. Lust to which one must submit is humiliating. But an artist, who allows one to come to her today and one tomorrow—because she loves or because she must live, what difference does that make?—has the right to say that she *bestows* her favors. Tullia does not want to derive her value from the men who possess her. She wants to give her life a purpose outside the almost automatic service to a godhead in which she does not believe. Her mother's grim, dogged, unflagging attention to the courtesan's trade inspires Tullia only with impatience and contempt.

She gladly puts up with the heat in the *altana*, the weight of the washing hat and wet hair for one day of undisturbed solitude. With a writing case on her knees, a pen in her hand, Tullia sees herself as a poetess and scholar. Her rhymes are not without merit; in Siena they enjoyed a certain reputation. Tullia sings of spring, of love, of the transience of all things, in language rich in the mythological images which every poet from the Alps to Calabria has in his arsenal. Strozzi has courteously memorized the best odes and stanzas; Messer Pietro, less honest but more eloquent, calls them little masterpieces and the poetess a second Sappho. Aspasia, Sappho—women of genius, the models to which Tullia aspires. She wants to have her poetry printed. *Divae Tulliae Aragonensis Opera* in gilded letters on a volume of vellum—how glorious! She will live on that paper, admired, honored still when her body is exhausted, her face faded under its paint. Tullia believes in her talent with a passion which must silence her secret doubt. Whoever praises her work while appearing to be a critical connoisseur, has won the day with her.

Messer Pietro doesn't wait to be asked; he devotes much serious study to the strophes which Tullia brings forth during her hours in the *altana* and on those rare nights which she spends alone. Tullia distrusts his enthusiasm, but she's grateful for every crumb that can nourish her self-respect. In exchange, she talks politics with Strozzi as often as Messer Pietro desires. Giulia allows the writing case in her daughter's hands only when there is a letter to be drafted. To recite verses is an attractive talent in a courtesan, but there's no reason to *make* verses—there are certainly enough poets in Rome already.

High up on the roof, gasping under her washing hat, Tullia feels delivered, at least for a time, from the baths, massages, diets and drinking cures and complicated beauty treatments which are her daily lot. She is writing about dark eyes which hold more warmth than the sun. The couplets become confusing; she sighs uneasily, wipes her face, draws figures on the blank paper: a sun, a laurel wreath, a heart dripping blood. Messer Pietro has assured her on his word of honor that the young man does not perform the service of a Ganymede for him.

"It's beautiful women he dreams of—of the Marchioness of Pescara, if I'm not mistaken—maybe even of you after that evening here, who can say? And as far as I'm concerned, I've mended my ways, don't you know that? I've turned completely to the love which you and your friends know how to make so enticing. . . ."

What is it that drives Tullia toward Giovanni Borgia? His eyes filled with secret resentment and rebellion, the impression he gives of being alone within himself . . . alone but self-sufficient, alone but free: in Tullia's eyes that is a privilege next to which everything she could attain as a courtesan sinks into nothingness. She has heard that he's been appointed to the retinue of the Chancellor of Milan. That tells her something because she knows from Strozzi—secret, secret!—what interests Morone has come to Rome to promote. And Messer Pietro, who, in turn, has been brought up-to-date on various particulars by her, doesn't neglect to point out that everyone in Morone's immediate entourage—including Messer Giovanni—will pluck the fruits if Morone's enterprise is successful.

Tullia has become restless. She walks from room to room of her house as though she is in prison. More strongly than ever she realizes that she *is* a prisoner among the cushioned chairs, the tables laden with candlesticks and costly drinking vessels, the tasselled and fringed carpets, the gilded cuspidors. She goes out only for ostentatious rides through the widest, busiest streets and for occasional excursions, escorted by a half-dozen admirers, to a vineyard outside the city.

All that passed between her and Giovanni that evening was a look. He stood leaning against the wall at a distance from the others, inspecting her and her guests as if they were strange amusing animals in a menagerie. Maybe because he admires the Marchioness of Pescara, he thinks he can look down upon a courtesan. Doesn't he know that she, Tullia, writes poetry, and poetry no worse than what the Colonna writes—the Colonna Messer Pietro says he finds so admirable? Connoisseurs of verse have reassured Tullia on that point. But anyway, she could tell him about that Colonna: a woman cold as a stone. Her husband runs away from her, she doesn't know anything about love. This Colonna, whom she envies for her aristocratic confidence, her stainless birth, her fame as a poet . . . this woman, who is everything that *she*, Tullia, wants to be, would probably move heaven and earth to be able to do what Tullia knows how to do—give pleasure.

If Giovanni Borgia ever comes to her—and come he *must*, because she wills it—she'll give him freely what no man has ever been able to buy from her: unfeigned passion.

She doesn't know why. She is overwhelmed by a feeling that she can't understand. Every evening she seeks for him in vain among her visitors. When she finally asks about him, Messer Pietro gives a most significant laugh.

"My little dove, he's not rich enough to pay suitable court to a woman like you. Perhaps Fortune will smile upon him if that daring plan of Messer Morone's—you know what I mean—succeeds. If I knew everything that Strozzi knows, then I might be able to speed up the pace of the affair through my connections at the court . . . Yes, but the amorous Florentine doesn't take *me* into his confidence. Listen, *bella mia*, if that were so, then I would ask him. . ."

Tullia remembers these questions and knows just the right moment to ask them. She discharges her task with more dedication than before, because she hopes that somewhere her path and Giovanni Borgia's will cross. For the first time, Strozzi exhibits some uneasiness. "Swear to me, Tullia, that this will stay between the two of us."

Tullia, smiling, raises her right hand. Strozzi kisses the hand: she must excuse his agitation, he is no longer master of himself, great transformations are at hand, the deliverance of Italy is approaching, "Listen, Tullia. . ."

When Messer Pietro comes again, she goes to meet him straight from under the hands of the old women, barefoot, face and neck still smeared with a balm for whitening the skin. The Marquis of Pescara won over to the Italian cause. Strozzi was told this by someone who heard it from Girolamo Morone's own mouth. But Messer Pietro only snaps his fingers impatiently: "I've known that for days, all of Rome knows it. You didn't need to keep your Florentine from his sleep for that. Damn it, can't your kisses bring anything more than yesterday's news?"

Later he comes to her in the room where she is being adorned for the evening. In the mirror she sees him pop up beind her. Tullia does not smile, she remains stiff even when Messer Pietro says the sight of her shoulders and breast is more beautiful than the seven hills of Rome. She has resolved never again to do what he asks of her. Let him hire spies who will steal secrets and repeat them for money, Tullia isn't stupid. When Messer Pietro, with his eyes raised to heaven, gushes about his miserably enslaved Italy, she knows that he's playing the hypocrite. He is as fascinating but as insincere as a virtuoso actor on the stage. She has rendered him services without ever asking him what he does with the information which she provides. But she has no intention of putting up with rudeness from him. She is not his daughter, nor his sweetheart, nor his servingmaid.

She will no longer allow herself to be coached by her mother or Messer Pietro, those two parasites. They won't get her to do things any more; from now on she will do what she herself wants to do. They have been using her; now she'll use them.

In the mirror she meets Messer Pietro's eyes, which are contrite but at the same time inquisitive. His curled black beard touches her shoulder.

"Angry, dear Tullia? You have a strange light in your eyes. When I'm upset, I say unkind things. Please forget it. There's a lot at stake for me. I have to know everything. I have a reputation to keep up."

In silence Tullia leans forward toward her reflection and hangs two pear-shaped pearls in her ears. When Messer Pietro tries helpfully to brush away a lock of hair, she evades his hand. He raises his brows.

"May I no longer do that? May I no longer help you to make yourself beautiful for your banker?"

Tullia stares fixedly at him until the mockery fades from his eyes.

"Listen, Tullia. Strozzi sees everything from one side only. This affair isn't so simple. He considers himself the friend and confidant of Morone and Machiavelli, but I doubt whether these far-sighted gentlemen will expose their thoughts to our Florentine. There's more behind all this than Strozzi seems to suspect. It's extremely important that I be well-informed. We must find someone from Morone's immediate circle—preferably one of the gentlemen of his retinue. You surely agree with me about that?"

His wink at her reflection does not escape Tullia. She doesn't react by word or look but goes on calmly spreading her cheeks and forehead with a mixture of red pomade and sublimate. He saunters away, busily talking and joking with Giulia and the old woman, but with sidelong searching glances at the silent Tullia.

She opens her writing case again and rereads, squinting in the bright light, her new verses. But the words are pale and bloodless compared with her bottled-up impatience. She is sure now that the encounter she has longed for is at hand. She is aware of a heaviness in her limbs, an unusual tension along her nerves. For the first time, the acts of love and the caresses which she has dutifully learned and applied, seem to her to be meaningful and even enticing. The air above the flat roof shimmers in the heat; the glow seeps into the pores of Tullia's skin; everything inside her turns to flame. She knows that feeling: it's a warning—now she must flee from the sun. She knocks on the trapdoor in the roof. One of the old women opens it and helps her to descend a ladder into the house. Dizzy, half-naked, with the hurriedly removed *solana* in her hand, her hot, dully gleaming hair hanging tangled over her head and shoulders, she goes into the chamber where she expects to find her mother. She is still blinded by the bright light above. It is some time before she notices Messer Pietro and his companion.

"*Ecco la bella!* I've brought Messer Borgia with me."

She seeks the look which has been in her thoughts since her first encounter with him, but sees that he has eyes only for the thick red-blonde strands of hair which coil like snakes, which radiate the warmth of the sun and give off a strong odor of spices and jasmine. Messer Pietro takes a lock between thumb and forefinger, rubbing it with the gesture of an expert. "Beautiful, beautiful! Not too dry, not too red . . . Not one woman in Rome can manage that."

Giulia approaches with wine and sweets. Her tone of voice betrays that, out of curiosity, she has suppressed her annoyance, for the moment, but that she is not reconciled to this visit. Over the tray from time to time she casts an angry, mistrustful glance at this man who, without the prescribed ritual of acquaintance and negotiation with her, has dared to thrust himself into her house in Messer Pietro's wake, outside the fixed hours for reception. She doesn't allow the direction of the conversation to slip from her control.

"I was just telling Messer that you bleach your hair according to the method used by his kinswoman, Madonna Lucrezia. I knew her personally, I was often in the Vatican, you know. *Dio*, what magnificence, that hair! She always wore it loose. My daughter has exactly the same hair, just as heavy, just as wavy, it's amazing that something like that can repeat itself. . ."

As always, Messer Pietro can discourse on any subject.

"No more renowned hair in Italy at the time than Lucrezia Borgia's. They say that Madonna was capable of letting God and the Devil wait when she sat brushing and bleaching it. Dangerous hair, too. Fatal for a certain Strozzi, among others, a blood relative of your Florentine, Tullia, whom they stabbed in Ferrara because he brought a lock from My Lady the Duchess to her lover Bembo. . ."

Tullia shakes her hair back violently, binds it together, winds it into a thick coil. A singular quartet, there in the dusky stifling chamber. Thin strips of sunlight filter through the lowered blinds. Messer Pietro exhausts himself with double entendres and intimations, but the obstinate Giulia will not heed his hints that the two be left alone. Tullia waits in silence; she can hear the blood rushing in her ears. There he sits, across from her; his eyes are filled with desire, but she knows that it is not she whom he desires.

XII.

Vittoria Colonna

S̆he didn't think much about Messer Morone's visit at first. She knew that Pescara and the Chancellor of Milan were acquaintances. His arrival with that great retinue gave the impression of being official: that wasn't surprising. It was no secret that the Emperor had declared himself ready to reward young Sforza with the dukedom of Milan under certain conditions. Morone's skill at bargaining was proverbial in Imperial circles: he had negotiated in Sforza's name with the Spanish envoys, and it was evident after every conference that the Emperor had been compelled to add more water to his wine. And after the fall of Pavia, Morone had approached Pescara from time to time. So it was perfectly natural that in this Sforza affair, he should seek the mediation of the Emperor's most important army commander. Vittoria considered it a favorable omen that a man like Morone, whose office kept him so well-informed, should rate Pescara's influence in Madrid so highly. This must prove, she thought, that the tension between her husband and the Emperor was not as serious as it seemed—or else that it hadn't yet filtered to the outside world. She thought too that she understood why Pescara, despite his spewing of blood, had insisted on receiving Morone immediately: he was a better match for the Chancellor of Milan than the Emperor's other spokesmen. Every diplomatic advantage he could achieve would help him regain the favor which he believed he had lost.

The discussion lasted a long time. Afterward, she waited for Morone so that she could conduct him out—something she wasn't obliged to do, but she felt that a courtly gesture was needed to round off the interview. Pescara could be violently suspicious when he was racked with pain—mocking and hurtful without provocation. So she searched Morone's face for signs of displeasure, but found, in fact, the opposite. He fell to his knees as soon as he saw her, kissed the hand which she held out to him and addressed her formally in a voice trembling with emotion.

He congratulated her on her husband's complete recovery; it was obvious that the wounds which the Marquis had received at Pavia were entirely healed. Vittoria had difficulty concealing her surprise—less at Morone's behavior than at his words. She looked at him to try to discover what reason he could have for such hypocrisy. But the Chancellor of Milan was exhausting himself in compliments. The sight of Madonna was like a bright light dawning, he had known beforehand that he was going to see the most beautiful and gifted woman in Italy, the noble Colonna, to whom peace was an ideal—but only now that he stood face to face with her did he realize how true that was . . . And more: an inner voice told him that she would succeed where powerful, valiant men had failed. . . .

Vittoria heard him out in silence, confused and astonished at this excessive praise, these allusions to an endeavor which she always remembered with shame at her own ineffectuality. She realized that Morone's flattery had some purpose. What did he want from her? Over his shoulder she could see the members of his retinue standing at a distance, waiting for him. One of them bowed to her; after that she was aware that this man was constantly staring at her.

She searched her memory: Have I seen that face before? The fixed gaze was disturbing; it contributed in no small measure to the uneasiness which Morone's behavior aroused in her.

As soon as the company had departed, she went to Pescara's chamber. There were no servants or members of the retinue in the anteroom. Pescara was sitting at a table with his back to the window, where the midday light was filtered by lattice work covered with red cloth. He didn't hear her come in; when she stood before him he looked up like someone startled from his sleep.

Ferrante has changed since this morning. The man who is sitting there is deceptively like the Ferrante whom I know, but under that shell—that fragile outer layer—everything is disrupted, out of joint. If I hadn't come to him at precisely this moment, I wouldn't have known about it, ever: he would have regained his self-control in solitude, and left me and everyone else ignorant about what was going on behind that stiff mask. But now I've surprised him when he's momentarily helpless, and he can't hide his inner disarray from me. For the first time he's shown himself to me undisguised, vulnerable—for the first time, not pretending but the man himself, naked. His forehead is covered with sweat, his eyes are uncertain . . . What do I read there— the torment of temptation? He's just thought, Get thee behind me, Satan! What were they talking about?

There's a wide table between Ferrante and the chair Morone must have sat in, and a still wider stretch of tiled floor. Was it possible that Morone really didn't see what *I* see, what everyone must see at first glance— that Ferrante is a shadow of what he once was? Ah, now he's within my reach; he always evaded me, kept me at a distance, even when he was sick, when he was in pain. But now that's no longer true: he looks at me as though I were the personification of the strength he's lost. I put my hand on his forehead, he lets me do it. We've never been so close to each other as we are in this silence. He leans toward me; this is no illusion. This partial embrace, without a trace of physical desire, this quiet, motionless listening to each other's breathing and the beating of our hearts: tenderness at last. For the first time, he needs me.

❧❧❧

"Don't speak. Don't move. You're exhausted."

"I have no time to lose."

"What's upsetting you? Tell me in a word. Does Milan object to the Emperor's demands?"

Pescara began to laugh softly, but the laugh ended in a fit of coughing. She supported him while he fought for breath.

"The Emperor's demands didn't enter into the conversation."

"But then what was the purpose of Morone's visit?"

Pescara pushed her arm away and sat up straight.

"Go over there to that chair and look at me. That's how Morone saw me. He let himself be misled by a conjuror's trick—that red light. He sincerely congratulated me on my recovery."

"You don't have any doubts that he was sincere?"

"What came after the congratulations was proof of his good faith, at least in that one respect. Only a complete lunatic would come with a proposal like that to someone whose condition he understood. And Morone isn't a lunatic. By God, I'm beginning to respect that man. I wouldn't entrust him with my soul and salvation—but what a sly fellow, what a daredevil!"

"But what does he want?"

"He wants *me*. And he doesn't expect to get me for nothing. The prospects he's holding out to me are far from insignificant: supreme commander of the Italian armies, King of Naples, if everything goes according to plan. Am I talking in riddles? All right, I'll tell you straight out: he wants me to betray the Emperor. He wants me to have De Leyva assassinated, along with a half-dozen other commanders, to lock up my Spanish officers or dismiss them, to bribe the non-Spanish ones with promises of fame and booty, to quiet the foreign mercenaries in my service with money that my new patrons will send me by the cartload . . . And finally, to disband, disperse and if necessary put to the sword those troops who refuse to recognize my authority to do all these things.

"No, Morone's not crazy. Milan is standing behind him—with Venice, Florence and the Holy Father in his own exalted person. If the plan goes through, France will renounce all rights to Italian territory. That's no trifling offer . . . and it's all just to see His

Imperial Majesty overthrown. If it finally gets that far, if the Spanish are driven out and peace and quiet are restored—one is a logical consequence of the other, as these patriotic gentlemen seem to think—then His Holiness will singlehandedly place the crown of Naples on my head. We can't found a dynasty, you and I, for lack of progeny, but nevertheless . . . I see the honor doesn't tempt you?"

"Oh come, Ferrante—you know you don't mean one word of what you're saying!"

"Did you see Morone when he left? He was trying to control himself, but his face was the picture of triumph."

"But I know you haven't accepted his proposal; you would never do anything like that. . ."

"It would give us peace and freedom. Isn't that your ideal?"

"I don't believe you. You're joking."

"You call this joking? More deadly earnest doesn't exist. This conspiracy against the Emperor is the drop which causes the bucket to overflow. No one can stop whatever happens now."

"In God's name, that's enough! You're bitter because they dared to think that you can be corrupted. Tell me what you said to Morone, how you refused him."

"I haven't refused him. Is that a proposal to reject? To say no and run the risk that tomorrow one of the Emperor's other generals should say yes?"

"I don't understand what you mean."

"I must know what guarantees are being offered to me. Whether it's legally possible for an ex-vassal of the Emperor to accept the crown of Naples. Whether the money they're promising for the maintenance of the armies will be paid promptly. Whether I really will be able to act with full, unlimited powers. I must know more, all details, the names of everyone involved. Guarantees in black and white. Morone understands that I'm not a man who will build on loose sand."

Vittoria leaned away from him with both hands gripping the edge of the table behind her back. Pescara sat erect and unmoving. Staring eyes, deeply sunken in their sockets, his teeth bared in derision. A death's head, she thought, and that thought called up another, still more terrifying to her. She fell on her knees near his chair.

"You're ill. You're raving. Let me call your servant or the physician to put you to bed. Better still, may I do it myself? Lean on my shoulder. You're feverish, your skin is burning."

Pescara wrenched loose his hand, which she had seized.

"Leave me alone. Why are you meddling in this? I haven't asked your opinion and I'm not going to. Bring me pen and ink and writing paper or call a servant to do it. Get up, that position doesn't flatter you. Get *up*, I said!"

Vittoria obeyed in silence. Her feeling of security had slipped away. She stood, as she had in the past, against a wall with no way out. She brought his writing materials and placed them before him on the table.

"Read what I'm writing. It's tremendously important that this be expressed correctly. Secretaries are not necessary for this. A letter to His Imperial Majesty in Madrid."

She read the page over his shoulder. Pescara wrote without hesitation: *"Hieronimo Moron a hablarme por grandes arodeos y ultimamente dezirme que sy yo le prometia la fe de le tener secreto que il me dyria y descubrizia grandes coses. . ."*

Vittoria stopped the hand which held the pen.

"The role of informer is beneath your dignity."

"Still feeling secret sympathy for the saviors of Italy? Before I go any further, I would really like to hear how much you already knew about this excellent plan. Messer Morone couldn't find enough words to praise you . . . Emblem of victory, pillar of peace and quiet, and more florid puns like that on your name . . . Has the Pope or your friend Monsignore Giberti told you to influence me in this matter? Don't equivocate—tell the truth!"

"I swear to God that I didn't know anything about any of this! Maybe they did allude to it, but I didn't understand what they were talking about. You forget that I'm distrusted in the Vatican. Giberti knows me too well to believe that I'd ever try to persuade my husband to become a traitor."

"Not even for the sake of that fatherland which you present in your verses as a wretched, shackled innocent? Italy, violated by intruders—the evil Spaniards in particular. That's your opinion; you should admit it. You can't disavow your blood. How can you understand a people that still has the courage to believe, to discover, to conquer. . ."

Vittoria pressed her clenched fists against her breast in an effort to control herself. She was looking down upon a face distorted out of all recognition by impenetrable hostility.

"Whatever my wishes and opinions might be, I would never undermine your position. I stand behind you; I must take the same line you take."

Pescara's lips twisted in derision.

"And yet you're trying to prevent me from informing my Supreme Lord about this plot against him here?"

"You can leave that to the Emperor's spies, can't you?"

"No spy could ever learn as much as they just handed me on a platter."

"Oh, but don't lower yourself to playing a double game. Either take Morone prisoner or stay out of it altogether."

"I'm surrounded by treachery and cunning. Do I have to suffer for that? The Emperor will know who his most trustworthy and capable servant is. There's really no better way to heap coals of fire on his head."

He grew even whiter and struck the table hard with his left fist.

"*Por Dios,* use your head! This plan wasn't hatched today or yesterday. How do I know what rumors have been spread about me—maybe they're trying to sow distrust against me in Madrid . . . What does Lannoy know, what is he whispering in the Emperor's ear—Pescara is a traitor? The Emperor knows damn well that he's neglected me. He'd be glad to believe Lannoy if only so he could quiet his own conscience. . . ."

A long letter. Sentence by sentence, logical, clear, an exposition of the conspiracy—Morone's proposal, the background for it. I can't help feeling that he would never have become involved in this business if he were completely sure of himself. He's in a dilemma. That look in his eyes when I came in—he must have been on the point of accepting Morone's offer. God forgive me, I think that's the truth. All he ever wished for at one blow—his most ambitious dreams fulfilled . . . It's secret guilt that drives him to this display of loyalty. What other explanation could there be for this? Has his pride been so injured by illness and bitterness that he's ready to creep through the mud to regain the Emperor's favor? How could he stoop to consider playing Morone's game . . . it's incomprehensible. . . .

And what about His Holiness and Giberti? Don't they see any way to peace except through conspiracy? The Pope should stand above parties. He's lost his dignity here. . . . Does he represent those who want to liberate Italy? I want that, but not by these means. They say that deceit and betrayal are the stuff of politics. If politics like this define our age, then our age is corrupt, rotten, doomed to destruction.

So they want to reward Ferrante with the crown of Naples for something which is unforgiveable in the eyes of a man like him, the one deed which always carries dishonor with it: disloyalty to the Sovereign. What kind of creatures would try to tempt him like that—How can they expect to build a free Italy on moral corruption— don't they know that spoiled seed doesn't germinate?

I feel that calamity is approaching. . . .

Ferrante is writing, his pen scratches across the paper. I want to fight beside him, I want to fight for him, I want to preserve his integrity. I would be optimistic about the future if I could believe that jealousy and power lust could be defeated . . . That's a struggle more fitting for me than praying and doling out alms. . . . That feeling I had when I first came in, when I stood next to Ferrante—that can't have been self-deception. Why shouldn't this be a new beginning for us? He needs me, even though he doesn't know it, even though he doesn't want to need me. But he has to realize eventually that he tried to intimidate me with mockery because I have more influence on him than he wants to admit.

He has to stay in Rome to discuss things with Morone. All that time, he'll be near me. I hope he'll take me into his confidence completely; he must believe that all I want is to serve his deepest, most essential interests. . . .

Vittoria picked up the sheet of paper which Pescara had pushed to the edge of the table. The Spanish words, in Pescara's upright, hasty script, seemed charged with the pain and passion which he did not reveal in conversation:

". . . For a moment, I was uncertain whether I should have him punished on the spot because he had dared to make such a proposal to me. But I thought that it would be more useful to gain more information. So I answered that I certainly had reason to be discontented. That what he was offering me was not insignificant, but that I could separate myself from Your Imperial Majesty only in a manner worthy of a nobleman. Finally, that I was prepared to do it, if only so that Your Imperial Majesty would come to realize that He could dispense with me less easily than with those whom He now values more highly than me. Girolamo Morone now believes that I will fall in with his plans. These practices go against the grain with me.

"I allow myself to become involved only because circumstances dictate it. If Your Majesty is not aware of the importance of an energetic action in Italy at the moment, then He has received bad advice from those whom He has taken into His confidence . . . Considering Your Majesty's powerful position, this conspiracy has very little chance of success. But I won't conceal the danger from You. Although Italy fears You, the presence of Your armies is felt to be a loathsome burden. Your friends and servants here are exhausted and disheartened. Unpaid soldiers become deserters, embittered commanders lose their vigilance. I adjure You: send

us money and fresh troops. The King of France is in Your hands.
Force him to an alliance . . . Your Imperial Majesty will forgive
my tone. It is only to serve my Sovereign that I speak thus. It's
a matter now of winning everything or losing everything. . ." Vittoria let the paper drop; it brushed rustling against the front of
her gown. Pescara extended his left hand without looking at her.

"Have you read it?"

"Don't send that letter. Write another one and don't mention
Morone. . ."

"Do I have to make a serious mistake—or even worse, be guilty
of a serious oversight—just because I'm not the noble hero—
fearless, blameless—my wife wants me to be?"

He threw the paper on the table in front of him; his hand opened
and closed convulsively. "We can't resolve this without deceit. Is
it a question of which deceit is the least dishonorable? Here, listen,
I don't pretend to be better than I am. . . ."

With strong emphasis he read, " '. . . for I know quite well that
I'm committing treachery in any case, although it's to prevent
transgression against Your Imperial Majesty, whom I am obliged
by oath to serve . . .' What do you say to that?"

Vittoria did not reply; Pescara heard the soft rustling of her
skirts as she walked to the door.

"If you don't want to be Queen of Naples or even the spouse of
the Emperor's supreme commander, the conquerer of Italy, what
in God's name *do* you want?"

"I want to be the wife of Ferrante d'Avalos, whom I love and
respect."

Ferrante looked up with an impatient shrug; the door was closing behind her.

After that he avoided her for days. She herself made no attempt
to see him or speak to him. She sat in the garden where the falling
water stirred the air, creating the illusion of cool breezes. Sometimes Varano and Madonna Caterina kept her company, but more
often she managed through pretexts to be alone. Ever since she
had once confided in them when she was in despair, she couldn't
shake off the feeling that they—and Caterina especially—expected her to tell them more. They never intruded themselves on

her, never volunteered unrequested help or advice, but their watchfulness was unmistakable, and their concern, which before Pescara's return she had found comforting, oppressed her now and filled her with a vague guilt. During the community readings—Paul's Epistles—her thoughts wandered and she was tired and restless throughout the discussions which followed the reading. Finally, the couple's unspoken but obvious antipathy to Pescara (which had never bothered her during the years of his absence) caused a rift now. Varano's genial indifference seemed to her to be a mask from behind which he spied sharply on her; she thought she detected an undertone of impatient reproof in everything Caterina said:

"Whoever has eyes to see, ears to hear, and still doesn't take sides, won't devote himself to the defense of God's truth in this miserable world, is more despicable than the worse sinner. How can one stand aloof when it's a matter of the life or death of the soul—how can one be busy with one's own problems—success or misfortune—or pleasure and amusement, sheer vanity and transience—how is it possible to worry about those things while the world is falling into ruin because no one cares any longer that Christ died for our sins on the cross? . . . That's reckless, that's indefensible, it's a crime against God and mankind! Those of us who know this are being summoned. The best among us has a duty to make the greatest sacrifice. If I had Fra Matteo's gift for speech, I'd shout out the truth in the squares of Rome. . . ."

"The seed is scattered, it'll come up soon enough," Varano said. "Believe me, we're doing our share, there's no sense in trying to hurry the course of events. The attitudes we're fighting against are beginning to dissolve, that's more noticeable in Rome than anywhere else."

I imagine that their words are aimed at *me*. I have eyes to see with, ears to hear with and I remain aloof. I'm summoned but I don't respond. I want to believe that God's grace is the highest attainment but I love

Ferrante more than God. For the first time, I contradicted them. Varano's involvement in these things comes from self-interest. And if circumstances were different, Caterina would feel just as fiercely about other beliefs. They're not prophets, they're not proclaiming angels; what they believe doesn't have to be what I believe. For every man his own heaven, his own hell. For everyone his own solitary rough way to God.

This sudden insight hit me like a shock; I feel as though I have been torn away from solid ground. Whatever Varano and Caterina decide to do in the future, their task with me is completed. They couldn't rouse me to passion with explanations and arguments; but I feel passionately now about the differences between them and me. I haven't tried to tell them how I've changed. It seems to me that estrangement between me and these two who have been my friends and confidants is inevitable now that I realize I must go my own way alone. More strongly than anywhere else, I feel completely isolated here in the garden enclosed within the walls of the Colonna palace.

Over there's the wing where my brother Ascanio lives. I've been estranged from him for a long time. He's a man who keeps trying to play an important role in politics; he's upset because he has less power and money than he thinks he should have. So he torments his wife and dabbles in alchemy, hoping to make gold. He wants Ferrante and me under his roof because it makes him feel important, but he hates us.

Ferrante's apartment is across the way. Close by and yet unreachable. He's sitting behind those closed shutters waiting for further news from Morone, and for an answer from the Emperor. His servant, his physician, tell me how he spends his time. He stays in his room, they can hear him constantly pacing back and forth. He hardly eats, he can't sleep at night. He has brought up blood again. No one is allowed to see him; they've been ordered to say that the Marquis is working.

I must concentrate completely on serving his interests, which are to remain true to his own conscience and to recover from this sickness which is undermining him physically and mentally. In order to be able to help him, I must give up any desire, any hopes of my own. I've touched him, I've dared to speak to him of love, I've wanted the whole loaf when he offered me only a crust of bread. I should have realized that he would thrust me away, that he wouldn't trust me any longer. I know now that I've deceived myself for years, even when I believed that the time of self-deception had ended for good. I believed that I had taken leave of Ferrante forever. That's not true, my desire is as strong as before, even stronger. The pain I suffer tells me how much I have always expected. All that's left for me to do, what I *must* do for his sake, and to be able to achieve ultimate deliverance, is to forget my desire and my pain. He will allow me to approach him only when he feels that I want nothing more from him, nothing more ever. God help me, the time is so short.

When Pescara sent to ask her for an interview, she lost the courage which she had agonizingly gathered during the preceding days and nights. She saw that he had regained his power over himself, irrevocably defined his point of view.

"I regret that you saw me when I was in a state of confusion. That's over. We won't talk about that any more. Yesterday, I had another conversation with Morone."

He smiled at her quick look of surprise.

"He came alone by arrangement, and through a side door. He brought me the result of the judicial inquiry which I had asked for. As I had expected, everything is in order. There's not a single weak spot there. The most clever heads in Rome have given me an assurance in black and white that I can accept the crown of Naples without scruples. Are you interested?"

He unfolded some documents, held them out to her. She didn't reach for them.

"All right. It doesn't matter. I'm keeping you informed for form's sake because I've already taken you into my confidence. The gentlemen—they are Angelo de Cesis and Cardinal Accolti— prove here that Naples is still actually a papal fief despite three centuries of foreign domination. They show me that I can abandon my estates in Spain without damage. So that's that. Further, Morone brought me written guarantees of the sums of money which were promised to me. Today I could have a large amount at my disposal. In connection with one thing and another, it's important that I return to Novara as quickly as possible. I've given orders that everything be prepared for my departure."

Vittoria looked at the enamelled floor tiles at her feet. On a dull red background, a pattern of intertwined arabesques: snakes and leafy tendrils. Seen from a distance, the flower and leaf motifs, the twisting shapes of reptiles, looked like human bodies wrapped in chaotic embrace. She thought: he goes to *her*, to find peace, to be able to do what he wants to do without disturbance.

Pescara laughed softly.

"Of course my line of action rests on what I've written the Emperor . . . . Poor Vittoria. Is my diplomatic game too much for you? Don't involve yourself in it any more. I should never have bothered you with questions on which a woman can have no opinion."

He coughed and turned away to spit into his handkerchief. When he had recovered, he saw her eyes fixed on him.

"I take it that you know how it is with me. You're one of three or four people who realize this. Be quiet about it. It's tremendously important to me that it shouldn't be known outside. I don't know how long this will go on. I give you my word of honor that I will have you summoned when it comes to that. Do come then . . . to Novara or wherever I may be at that moment."

Pescara was grateful that, at their brief farewell, his wife spared him tears and allusions to personal circumstances. He had expected an emotional scene, considered it inevitable, because he was convinced that after this moment they would never again speak to each other in private. Silent, motionless, she received his kiss on her cheek and on her hand. When he had left Rome behind him, the suspicion rose in him that it was only at that last moment that she had really understood that he was dying.

XIII.

Giovanni Borgia

I should never have known what I know now if I had given in to that first rush of anger and walked out of Messer Pietro's house when he arrived at his version of the secret of my birth. But by then I had drunk a great deal. His revelations kept me so occupied that the full extent of what he said about Morone and the Marquis of Pescara did not immediately become clear to me.

Later I went with him to Tullia d'Aragona. I had little desire to be alone with my thoughts. In the house on the Campo Marzio, there were so many guests that I could exchange no more than a greeting with the courtesan. I saw that she had green eyes and dyed hair. She walked with such exaggeratedly graceful movements of her hips and upper body, that it looked as if she wanted to poke fun at the studied seductiveness of her sisters in the guild. The expression on her face remained, moreover, stiff and injured; she didn't bother to be friendly. On closer inspection, I had little desire to join the noisy company that pressed around her like a body guard. They drank wine from her shoes while they disputed about philosophical and literary questions.

Messer Pietro, even more talkative than usual when he's drunk, stood on a footstool to shout over the heads of the others: Literature, my foot! Literature is dead in Italy, stone dead, imitations of classical glory, aping Vergil, aping Plautus and Terence, aping Boccaccio, aping Petrarch, aping everything—and the language itself, stilted forms, artificial mannerisms, as dead as a doornail, gentlemen!

Then he began to tell one of his favorite anecdotes: how a distinguished lady had once invited him to spend the night with her. He had barely entered her bedroom when her husband returned unexpectedly from his trip. Messer Pietro, still fully clothed, prepares himself for a furious fight, but the master of the house greets him courteously and says: do take off your clothes, make yourself comfortable, goodnight to you both, and discreetly withdraws from the room.

For quite a while after this story, Messer Pietro stood on his footstool, hiccuping and gesticulating, talking into thin air while the fat woman, Tullia's mother, filled his glass every now and then. The others seemed no less foolish, standing with flushed faces, yelling about Petrarch and the secrets of poetic art, like a literary academy seen in a distorting mirror. I grew steadily more sober, stayed cracking nuts at the sideboard covered with dishes and jugs. Whenever there was a space between the excited speakers, I saw Tullia looking at me.

Presumably I would have stood there half the night, leaning against the wall counting the figures in the gilt wall covering and the threads in the hangings, if a quarrel hadn't broken out among Tullia's visitors. If it had been a skirmish among the gentlemen themselves, I would have gone on playing the role of spectator. But something in the attitude of the Spaniard, dagger in hand, prepared to defend himself against everyone, accorded with the feeling I had had to suppress all evening. I drew my dagger and leaped to help him. When Tullia's mother implored us to spare her statues, furniture and other ornaments, we moved in a confused cluster to the piazza. The Spaniard fought, hissing and swearing, continually urging himself on and admonishing himself. Finally we had only three or four opponents; the others looked on with their grooms and torchbearers.

Messer Pietro lay on the ground bawling extemporaneous hymns about the battle of the titans on the field of Mars. After some blood had flowed on both sides—there was no one who hadn't been cut or scratched—those who had given us a fight had had enough. The Spaniard wouldn't consider stopping; he continued to demand satisfaction, but the gentlemen had their horses brought and rode away. Finally he realized that there could be no more fighting, spat on the ground after the departing guests to demonstrate his contempt, embraced me, thanked me for my support and, his wounded arm wrapped in his cloak, limped off with his retinue into the darkness.

That skirmish had restored some of my self-confidence. I left Messer Pietro, who was still holding forth to the stars, to his servants. Back in my bedchamber, I asked myself why I should really stay in Rome. And that night, too, I entertained the notion of leaving the city where too much is known about my ancestry that could be harmful to me. I'm no courtier and I don't want to be a clerk. I shall never find my way among the parasites and sycophants at the Vatican, among the fashionable loiterers and frequenters of winehouses and brothels in Rome. As I lay in bed waiting for the dawn, I considered the possibility of success if I offered my services to an army, to the Marquis of Pescara or to Giovanni de' Medici, who commands a famous band of mercenaries. What finally restrained me from getting up and leaving Rome immediately, was the reflection that without a recommendation or letter of introduction from an influential man, I should always and everywhere have to be contented with a place in the lower rank.

A triviality, a coincidence, can change the way in which one views one's circumstances. An event as relatively unimportant as that fight made me realize that here in Rome I have come to a dead end. By birth and by nature, I don't belong in an environment where success comes only to him who can fortify himself behind a bulwark of name, fortune and patronage, or who has the talent and patience to weave clever intrigues. I'm in my element in a world where things have no beginning and no end, where the present must be used right, where there is action instead of documents of nobility and moneybags, where a man has to show by his immediate deeds who and what he is. Mine is the world of the soldier on the battlefield. Yesterday doesn't count any longer, tomorrow is still unknown. I have neither past nor future in the accepted sense of the word, and I have never felt so complete, so free, as when I was fighting in Navarre and the Dauphiné and later in Lombardy and at Pavia. If only I wasn't always dragging that accursed restlessness about with me, that feeling that I must justify my existence by performing great acts, I would be contented even if I were only a mercenary with no possessions but my weapons and my pay, just one among many, always subject to the order of my superiors. But because I feel secretly frightened, I must keep proving to myself that I'm really somebody.

I was in harmony with my surroundings when I was a soldier, I shared a solid reality, But here in Rome I haven't even been given the chance to do anything. At least I have the feeling— sometimes anyway—that I've accomplished something when I write down my thoughts and memories between my dull clerk's chores. At first I thought that being appointed to Morone's retinue was a prelude to action. If Messer Pietro's information has a grain of truth in it, I've gotten entangled in a Gordian knot of intrigue. That's probably a chance in a million for the man who's clever at that sort of thing. But I'm not clever in that way. . . .

Cesare and Lucrezia . . . That's a possibility that seems more and more feasible to me the longer I think about it. But I'm not going to accept it just because it's feasible; I must have *proof*. Then there won't be any more anguish, any more uncertainty. Cesare my father after all, and my conflicting feelings toward Lucrezia explained. This being a Borgia born of a Borgia *and* a Borgia, both with the same Borgia father—I can accept that, I can endure it, without hope but also without torment. At least then I could view my life from a definite perspective.

When I had reached this point, I decided to call on Messer Pietro again. The man I descended upon, unannounced, seemed very different from the peacock-blue fop and braggart who used to wander through the Vatican. The disorder in his house was even greater than the first time I was there. It later evolved that he had caught his servants stealing and had thrown them out. He sat writing, dressed only in shirt and trousers, surrounded by stone pitchers and glasses, articles of clothing, gnawed chicken bones and fruit pits, wads of paper and all sorts of other rubbish, at a table under the window. At first he was obviously not pleased that I was seeing him like that; later he seemed rather to enjoy

adding to the general untidiness. He kicked a couple of empty bottles to pieces and flung piles of books and papers off a chair so that 'clouds of dust rose up to suffocate us. He kept walking back and forth in his cane slippers, his shirt wide open, scratching and rubbing his chest full of black hair, until the collection of amulets and saints' medals which hung around his neck tinkled like a carillon.

Of course he didn't give me a chance to speak. He began by reading me an abusive letter to the Marquis of Mantua in which he threatened him with a campaign of slander unless certain goods were sent immediately.

"I need some new clothes," he said, after he had let loose that firestorm of threats and insinuations. "They're fairly lax in Mantua about paying for services rendered. But fortunately for me, His Serene Highness attaches great importance to maintaining a good reputation in Rome. And from time to time I take the liberty of drawing his attention to that. This time I'll bet anything that it will produce a couple of berettas and some material for a cloak."

Messer Pietro picked up some papers which were spread around under the table and the bed, and thrust them into my hands, instructing me to read his *Cortigiana* out loud, while he changed his clothes. He became impatient when I had difficulty deciphering his pitch-black, blotchy writing, and started to recite it word for word. Gradually he took fire and ended up playing out the whole drama with gestures and various intonations like an accomplished actor. As soon as he finished, he asked my opinion. Panting, sweating, his glittering eyes dilated, he stood leaning expectantly toward me.

"Well, come on, say something! You've never heard anything like that, have you? That's something totally different, totally new! Creatures of flesh and blood, living dialogue—a piece of reality, Messer, and symbolic, satirical at the same time!"

I told him that I found it really amusing, but that I thought the action was rather thin and confused, and the subject of the piece was not particularly important: whores, lackeys, thieves, impudent misfits and provincial fortune-hunters, innkeepers and swindlers—they were all right for minor roles, but what's the point of bringing the riffraff of Rome to the stage in minute detail . . . their conversations, quarrels and trickery? I prefer plays that

present problems to be solved, or that set an example, or where everything is so carefully stylized that it exists outside reality. You can tolerate heroes and jesters on the stage because they're far enough removed from everyday reality, but anyone who's really interested in Messer Pietro's characters would have a better time on the streets or in a brothel.

Before I could finish, Messer Pietro exploded. The room seemed too small to hold so much noise and agitation.

"Oh, we've got to get rid of those antiquated masquerades! What's wrong with people—why do they accept the truth only when it's recited in verse by kings or saints or gods and demigods or shepherds or satyrs? Yes, heroes and jesters certainly exist, Messer, but there are infinitely more ordinary people who lie and steal and suffer and laugh and make fools of themselves and each other and weep and prostitute themselves . . . that's what these creatures of mine do, the ones you call the riffraff of Rome!"

With tears in his eyes, he begged me to believe that the tragedies and farces in vogue now have had their day.

"All of literature is a corpse, Messer—cleverly embalmed, painted and adorned, but simply lifeless forms and rules. Do we have to go on worshipping a mummy? We can't learn anything from history and mythology . . . Did you say there's no action in my *Cortigiana?* Oh, Messer, it's bubbling with *life*—that's better than action. This isn't folly that makes the audience howl with laughter—it's folly which makes the sensitive man cringe with shame and guilt. Here, maybe you missed this passage. . . ."

I saw that I had really offended him; his excitement had an undertone of rage. He stood in front of me and repeated, with obscene gestures, and forming every word carefully with his wide, moist, mobile lips, a part of the play that—if I remember correctly—roughly presented this point: war, plague, famine and predictions of disaster have driven mankind to the wild pursuit of pleasure, have turned the whole world into one great whorehouse, where parents and children, brothers and sisters, without remorse or regret or shame, with one another. . . .

All right, I didn't allow him to go on. He obviously wanted to pay me back for being so critical. This time he actually played into my hands because I had wanted to introduce that subject. I asked him to produce the proof he had promised me for what he

dared to insinuate now and earlier. He slapped his hands together and rolled his eyes so that I could see the whites.

Ah ah, there I had just asked him for something that was impossible. That wouldn't be easy to sort out. Since we talked last he had remembered other things—Lucrezia had three brothers . . . why should she have a preference for only one of them? Maybe I didn't know how people had tried at the time to explain the mysterious death of Pope Alexander's eldest son, the Duke of Gandia: it seems that Cesare had put his brother out of the way because he too had enjoyed Lucrezia's favors. And as far as number three was concerned, Gioffredo. . . .

Then with a sweeping gesture and a sly peering look full of secret enjoyment, he offered to collect whatever he could that might relate to the Borgia family: epigrams, libels, letters and reports from courtiers at the time. I forced myself to reject his proposal as calmly as if we had been talking about the most trivial matter.

❁

Since that meeting, a secret duel has been going on between us: between *my* will to conceal my deep uncertainty and *his* will to see through me and use that insight to get me to dance to his tune. He came very near his goal. He knows where I'm vulnerable but he's mistaken when he takes me for a coward. When a man has been obsessed year in, year out, with certain thoughts, he won't be easily frightened into losing control of himself. I could spy on Pescara and Morone—the thing he obviously wants—out of ambition, but never out of fear of Messer Pietro. He's generally a good judge of people, but this has slipped past him. He was noticeably taken aback when I didn't become upset at the reference to four-fold incest.

Far from being upset, I'm prepared to consider even that idea in the light of what I've heard and seen over the years. Certain remarks Sancia made, for instance, might make sense now: her abuse and mockery of the constantly bewildered Gioffredo. . . . Once in Naples, when Rodrigo and I were there, he complained about her dissolute behavior. She spread her fingers out above her forehead like horns and said, Go to your sister now, run along to your beloved Lucrezia, let her comfort you, she'll caress you the way she used to! She shrieked at him that he should thank God that she didn't reproach him, that she didn't let people know what sort of man he was. As she swept past Rodrigo and me in a swirl of black skirts, she spat at us. . . . I think also about Vannozza's strange lamentations. . . . I remember moments with Lucrezia in Ferrara when I sensed the existence of a stinking dark world hidden away behind the thin wall of her self-control.

Ten, twenty times, over a glass of wine or a game of cards, Messer Pietro has calculated how much we could achieve if we worked together. And then, as regular as clockwork, he would bring up some Borgia atrocity or profligacy. Each time he apparently thought he could intimidate me into carrying out his wishes. There's a close connection in his mind between possessing power and inspiring fear. He really can't imagine the kind of thing that frightens me. A man like him can understand only tangible reasons for terror or anxiety.

So we continue our sham battle, interrupted by Messer Pietro's reading one of his comedy pieces, or by walks through Rome where he seems to know every moneylender, jeweler, fishmonger, fruit seller, common crier, winehouse landlord and procuress.

I told him that I didn't care to be the last in a long line waiting for Tullia's favors. When he answered that other meetings with her were difficult to arrange when one didn't have much money, I considered the matter closed.

Probably he noticed that it still bothered me not to be able to approach that woman. One afternoon he came to me winking and, with many prefatory jokes, said that I was expected. I enjoyed a privileged position; she herself wished to see me.

So I went with him again to the house on the Campo Marzio. I found her more attractive than the previous time; she wasn't adorned and painted, but wore a shirt and skirt like an ordinary girl and her hair was hanging loose. Neither she nor her mother treated me as a welcome guest, which made me doubt the trustworthiness of Messer Pietro's message. The mother in particular was hostile. Tullia stared at me in silence. If she moved, it was to arrange or brush away a lock of her hair, newly washed and unruly—a golden shimmering weight. I would never have suspected that a woman's hair could be so thick, so long. Even if no one had told me, I would have realized that I must imagine Lucrezia's legendary hair as looking like this.

When Tullia noticed that I kept looking at her hair, she braided it and pinned it up; later she tied a kerchief over it. It irritated me that she forced me to think of Lucrezia and Lucrezia's bent for secrecy. At that moment, it no longer made any difference to me whether I was welcome or not. I had only one wish: to induce her to undo the braids again. When I finally got her to do that (it was hours later; all Messer Pietro's skill was needed to reconcile the mother to my visit), I discovered two things: the first, that her lovemaking was completely earnest, and the second, that I was so bewitched by the touch of that warm, soft, fragrant flood of hair that I couldn't respond as I should have. She didn't say a word about my failure. She leaned on her elbow quietly, next to me. Her eyes didn't leave my face. Because I didn't know what to make of her silence and her stare, I finally assured her that she had no reason to reproach herself. She shook her head with a proud, impatient movement. So we rested there in that dusky chamber, lying like two figures on a tomb. With any other woman, out of shame and anger, I would have found such proximity intolerable. Tullia, courteous and sensible, gave me time to recover.

She had fruit, wine and other refreshment brought, sent away the old hag who dawdled inquisitively on the threshold and served me herself. She asked me no questions but told me about herself. She is the bastard daughter of a cousin of Isabella of Aragon. That breed runs true to its nature: it's reflected in Tullia's bearing and the shape of her hands, her dislike of laughter and boisterousness. She sang and recited her own verses with more animation than when I had first heard her at her reception evening. She let her monkey show his tricks. Later she allowed me to remain while she was dressed and had her hair done. In the course of an hour, I saw her changing from a human being to an idol. Crackling brocade bulged on her hips and arms. Her breasts were pressed up by a tight bodice. Her hair, divided into strands and intertwined with all sorts of finery, lost its disorderly charm. She painted a stiff calculating courtesan's mask over her own serious face. When we parted, I gave her the jeweled clasp from my cap, one of the few valuables which I kept from the past. She asked me to come back, to come back often.

It is certainly not her fault that I retain an unpleasant memory of my hours with her. If her hair were not red-gold, had not smelled of jasmine . . . Every time she turned her back to me and I saw that broad glistening stream flowing over her shoulders to far below her waist, I was assailed by a feeling of indescribable confusion. I curse all Borgia.

❦

A written message from Tullia: is it suspicion that stops me from visiting her? She swears that she will never, never disclose to a third person (this is underlined) what I confided in her during our time together. She begs me to come for her sake, to say nothing to Messer Aretino about that visit. I shall go.

❦

Messer Morone has returned suddenly to Milan. And the Marquis of Pescara seems to have left too, in great secrecy. When I was summoned by Berni to receive both his thanks for my services and the second and last purseful of ducats, I could have kicked myself. In that game—which, going by Messer Pietro's information and from what Tullia whispered in my ear during our siesta hours, I think I now understand—I have been only a spectator. I lost the chance to be more than that because I didn't know in time what it was all about. Compared with my clerk's job at the Chancellery, I considered it a promotion to ride with great pomp on horseback behind a man of importance. Was I perhaps chosen precisely because I suspected nothing? Or was I singled out from the beginning for the role of traitor—and if so, by whom? Tullia has admitted to me that Messer Pietro asked her to draw me out. It would appear from this that he has taken me for an insider all along.

❦

Messer Pietro lies in his house in the Borgo, badly wounded. It seems he is unconscious. The doctors who are tending him and the armed guard at his door will allow no one inside. He was set upon by unknown attackers one night in the street. The rumor is

—262—

going around the city that the murderous attempt was instigated by the Datary Giberti. Here in the Vatican, they dare only to shrug with knowing looks on their faces. Meanwhile everyone knows that the Spanish-sympathizing cardinals have paid visits to Messer Pietro's sickbed and that on orders from Monsignore Schomberg, a number of suspected persons have been thrown into prison . . . even though the Pope has protested against it. It is not difficult to guess what is behind this affair.

I've finally managed to gain admittance to Messer Pietro's house. His life is no longer in danger. Seven dagger wounds have put him out of action for the present, but they haven't silenced him by any means. He lay in the shadow of the bedcurtains, propped up by a pile of pillows, with bandages on his head, chest and arms. His face was grey. His beard, out of curl, hung in uneven black strings over his bloodstained shirt.

He seemed pleased to see me and asked me to sit down at the foot of the bed. His eyes glittering with fever and excitement, he gave me a look that was at once impudent and apologetic.

"Hold on, here's Messer Giovanni too! As you can see. I'm still alive. This time they've done their best to finish me off. What a disappointment for Giberti and Berni that they miscarried. More—much more than a disappointment, I hope. May they suffer for it! Monsignore Schomberg, the Archbishop of Capua, has assured me that he won't rest until these criminals are punished. If only he'd been here half an hour ago. The murderer sat on my bed, there where you're sitting now, asking about my condition: Della Volta, Berni's factotum. As soon as I came to after the attack, I said they must seize *him*, I damned well recognized him even though it was pitchblack in that alley where they assaulted me. But what happens? The prison is full of fellows who don't know anything at all and Della Volta comes unhindered to pay a call on his victim. And a bodyguard is stationed outside to protect me! Tell me, how can that happen?"

I asked him what he thought the reason for the assault could have been. He tried to shrug his shoulders, realized too late that he couldn't and winced in pain.

"Calm down, Messer," I said, "perhaps you conveyed certain facts to the Spanish sympathizers in connection with Girolamo Morone and the Marquis of Pescara?"

"How could you think a thing like that about me, Messer Giovanni? This is the result of something else entirely; it has nothing to do with politics, God preserve me—I'm in love with Giberti's cook and he can't allow that."

He winked and burst out laughing. "Do you really believe that Giberti will ever admit that he's involved in a conspiracy against the Emperor? Especially now that the conspiracy has partially failed? Listen, use what I'm telling you to your own advantage ... why have Morone and Pescara both left Rome? I know from a trustworthy source that Morone still doesn't have Pescara's promise in black and white—even though a lot of papal ducats have been paid through him to the Marquis. Those gentlemen are not crazy. The freedom of Italy, or the power of the Emperor— magnificent words, glorious ideas, but in practice nothing is as important as one's *own* freedom and one's *own* power. Just watch, those two are playing a pretty game. Morone has money at his disposal and Pescara has seasoned troops, and together they know everything that's worth knowing about relations here and abroad. Presently the Pope as well as the Emperor will be checkmated and then we'll have two rulers, King Morone in Milan and King Pescara in Naples."

He beckoned to me to come closer. When I stood over him in the oppressive vapor of sweat and medicine, he pulled at my sleeve and whispered hastily, "If you hadn't been so stubborn, Messer, I might not be lying here like this. Now it's too late. Pity, pity. There's no secret to sell any more since little by little everyone is finding out all about this thing, everyone is talking about it, everyone is doing his best to give more or less obvious hints to the other party so that whatever the outcome, *ad votum* as it is called, they may take advantage of it. We could have been the first, Messer. It's not for nothing that they say strike while the iron is hot. All in all, that hesitancy of yours nearly cost me my life."

I reminded him that he knew quite well how to get information even without my cooperation. Hadn't he hoped to get from Tullia's lips what I had refused to tell him? He raised his eyebrows, acting surprised, but his eyes remained sharp and sly.

"Ah ah. So you know that too? But then she's more in love with you than I thought, Messer. Your gifts as a lover must be extraordinary. If I had suspected that . . . I admit that I wanted to show you up. Now about you—do *you* know anything about that attack? Or this time am I mistaken about everything?"

I reassured him, saying that he should not lump me with Messer Della Volta.

"I came for the proof you promised me."

Apparently in his enforced horizontal position, he couldn't play the braggart as usual. After some reflection, he finally mentioned the names of past informants—a Venetian envoy, a spy from Ferrara, a servant of Pope Alexander's master of ceremonies. Most of them are dead or can't be traced.

"Heaven help me, what a fuss, Messer, about something as unimportant as a pair of parents! You didn't come out of a cabbage, you don't owe your existence to a heavenly miracle. You're alive, what more do you want? In any case, you bear a great name. As far as that goes, you're better off than I am—for lack of a paternal name I have had to call myself after my birthplace, Arezzo. Do I worry about it? Am I any the less for it? I have come far, Messer, and I shall go farther. I shall show them that a man without all that hodge-podge can be the equal—or I should say the superior—of kings and emperors. With my pen I will rule the world. You'll see, they'll call me the scourge of princes. They'll lay treasures at my feet just to keep my friendship. How will I accomplish that? Because I'm a free man, Messer. I go my own way. I'll speak as I please as long as I live. I acknowledge no man as my master. And in any case you will never see *me* become slave to a chimera. Follow my example; to hell with your past—worry about the future and you'll have your hands full."

He peered at me with half-closed eyes. I asked myself what he read in my face. He warmed to his theme. Supported by the pillows, gesticulating with his good hand, he proved his eloquence once more. Now he tried another tack and, with as much facility as on previous occasions he had played up their scandals and crimes, he painted a rose-colored picture of the Borgia family.

Gifted, fascinating personalities, all the Borgia, slandered out of
envy and lack of understanding by a world which no longer knows
how to value affection for close blood-kin and family pride. . . .
Pope Alexander, a diplomat of the first rank. Naturally, he was
too fond of beautiful women, but what do you want? He was an
imposing figure himself, they say, except for his last years when
he got too fat. Tall, dark and strong, most amiable in company,
a brilliant speaker, a man with wit and tact too, he could get his
own way with everyone and everything. He should never have
become pope, that's the thing. Ecclesiastical problems didn't interest him in the least; he hardly knew the liturgy and was always
forgetting the ritual. At official ceremonies, his prelates had their
hands full covering up his mistakes. In the first place he considered himself a worldly prince and he was too proud or too lax to
preserve even an appearance of priestly dignity. You must admit it does him credit that he had no desire to play the hypocrite. . . .

Lucrezia, said he, also had more sense than is usually believed.
Did I know that she had made an appearance as her father's
deputy twice when he was away on a trip? In Spoleto she had
taken over the regency for months and had done well. Since then
her dignity and clever judgment have been proverbial.

"And in Ferrara since her death, she has been revered as a saint.
She established a fund there to pay dowries to poor girls so that
none of them will have to tread an evil path out of need . . . There's
nothing better than marriage, she used to say . . . Besides, she
could dance like an angel and she had more taste in clothes than
all the other women in Italy put together . . . that's not easily
forgiven, Messer . . . Ladies who set the tone and who are afraid
of competition have contributed their share to Madonna Lucrezia's bad reputation. The old Marchioness of Mantua—as you
know, she's the mother of my lord and master— I've heard her
with my own ears making nasty remarks about the dead who
can't defend herself. That it came out of *her* mouth says enough.
She's the sister of Duke Alfonso of Ferrara, you must know that
. . . I know that power-hungry shrew—she always wants to be the
first, the highest, the best, the most famous, the richest. *Prima
donna d'Italia*, don't make me laugh! Patroness of the arts and
sciences. Artists who don't satisfy her nonsensical demands are

put in a tower on bread and water. She'll tell them what they'd better do. Oh yes! If you really know about art, her notions will make your hair stand up. Once I get started on *that* . . . But what was I saying again? Ah, the Borgia, the Spanish twig grafted onto an Italian tree . . . Remarkable family, the world will never stop wondering about them, believe me, Messer . . ."

He described Cesare to me as a man who despised the pompous manners and weaknesses of the court. Taciturn because he detested superfluous talk and meaningless discussions, preferring to be alone because he could not stand flattery and toadies. Strong and deft in the bullring and a hunter and rider without equal. In the Romagna, people still talk about how Cesare would come into any village in the evenings, on foot, without an escort, to wrestle with the strongest yokels, just for pleasure.

"Cruel, cold, unpredictable—well yes, of course, that too, Messer. A real Spaniard. After all, that's what they're like, you know that perfectly well. The poorest beggar wants to be an hidalgo, has his pride, his honor. Sword and dagger are always loose in their sheaths. They're easily insulted and then they fight like devils. Let alone those who belong to great families. I think that the Borgia lords achieved so much here because they were foreigners and had no obligations to Italian families—either through blood ties or feuds. That whole family's a closed unit. They probably always felt threatened, hated. They fought with might and main to hold their own. And as far as incest is concerned . . ."

Messer Pietro threw his left hand up to heaven, fingers spread in a gesture of resignation. "Was somebody else there then, Messer?"

There was nobody else there then, no. As if that were the main point for me. The world's opinion is only important to me as a means of seeing myself. What's said and thought about me would leave me cold if I were a man complete in myself, if I understood who I really am. This poisons my life: the knowledge that I am *not* myself. Those who created me are stronger in me than I am. For that reason, and that reason alone, I want to know them. I want to know what they were guilty of, because their guilt lives on in me. Still, Messer Pietro's advice to look to the future is sound. If it weren't for this brooding over what lies behind me, I might perhaps—although not together with him—have been able to gain the interest of influential people. That must certainly be the first step. If I have support, then I can attract followers. Whoever can count on followers can dare to make demands. That's the level where the game begins. I'm still a long way from there.

What Morone asked of Pescara will be known to the Emperor's people. But Pescara promised his cooperation; the Emperor's people will also know that Pescara made that promise. But Pescara goes free. Morone and those who stand behind him must know that the Emperor's people are aware of everything.

Nevertheless they support Pescara with money. Who's the dupe here? That this singular state of confusion continues can mean only one thing: each of the two parties hopes its representative will ultimately score over its opponent. Meanwhile—according to Messer Pietro—Morone and Pescara are secretly forming a new faction together. Why not? Messer Pietro has often astounded Rome when his bold predictions have come true.

Here at court and in the city, a silly farce—no one ostensibly knows anything but everyone thinks he knows everything. In reality there is not a living soul who knows what is actually happening.

XIV.

Niccolò Machiavelli and Francesco Guicciardini

N iccolò Machiavelli to Francesco Guicciardini

From San Casciano, in alarm. *Vir illustrissime,* greetings. I'm hardly surprised to learn that Morone was lured into an ambush by Pescara and taken prisoner—in the light of all the underhanded manipulations that have been going on in this business and after all your warnings and predictions. Now I hear that Pescara has annexed Milan into the Empire in the Emperor's name and that Sforza has been accused of felony . . . I realize that this must have been the intention from the beginning.

The only reason that Pescara played this game with Morone, with the Pope and with Italy was to get rid of Sforza and make himself master of Milan. You saw this danger from the first; I was blind with my eyes wide open. The Spaniards are behaving like the Devil himself in Lombardy. And new companies of German lansquenets are swarming over the Alps to join together into an army in the north. The stories that refugees from Milan and Cremona and other towns are telling about the Spanish and the Germans are so hair-raising that there isn't a mortal soul who wouldn't rather give houseroom to Satan himself than to those fellows. Why don't they do something about this in Rome? Now, *now!* While there's still time to act!

Word is out that Pescara is lying ill in Novara and Lannoy and Bourbon are in Spain—this would be the ideal moment to attack their troops—while they're scattered and disorganized. We should do it in the name of anything you like, but just *do* it! We need an army and a leader, all the men we can get hold of, under one leader. How about Giovanni de'Medici? A commander of mercenaries is better than no leader at all. Everyone says that Giovanni is a brave, capable warrior. He isn't a Pescara and he's no Cesare Borgia—not by a long shot. But his little army is fast, brave and disciplined. We don't have a better man. He's the one who must have the command of our united troops. With good intentions and the strong central authority behind him in Rome, he will defeat the Emperor.

The Pope will certainly have to accept this plan. After all, it involves a Medici. You could explain to His Holiness what a victory for Signor Giovanni would mean to the whole family. I *can't* keep quiet about it now, Francesco. You told the Pope not to support that plan for a people's militia after I had aroused his enthusiasm for it. Of course I know perfectly well that you did that because you thought it was your duty to do it and not because you were trying to injure me—that's the only reason I was able to forgive you. You serve the Pope, you won't do anything that you think would hurt him. You are proposing a League and the power of the Holy See would play a role in it—but my plan is concerned *only* with the freedom and unity of Italy—and I don't think—as you undoubtedly know—that the Church is included in that.

So even if it does not mean freedom for Italy, you are supporting your masters, the men who wear tiaras, and who are responsible for causing this dissension among us. You wrote me that you place honor and trust above everything; of course it's admirable that you stay utterly loyal to this cause that you have made your own—the protection of papal authority. But that's a bad cause for anyone who wants to serve Italy. I'll even go so far as to say that it's a cause that's contrary to your deepest convictions and so basically you're not really either loyal or a man of honor—you're dishonest and disloyal to yourself and in my eyes that's unforgiveable. I'm fond of you, Signor Francesco, I don't have a better friend than you, but I love my fatherland above everything.

I have a troubling dream which recurs night after night. I'm alone in a vast field full of sheaves of corn. So far as the eye can see—sheaves, sheaves, ripe grain, bread for a whole year. On the horizon appear rolling lead-grey towers of clouds: gusts of wind drive the squall nearer, I see the storm approaching that will annihilate our harvest, but I'm powerless; one man can't reap all that grain.

San Casciano in late autumn is a dead place. Mist and rain obstruct the view of the hills. I spend my days in the house, in the dusk, amid fumes of onion soup. The youngest child is ill, it screams all day, my wife walks around rocking it in her arms. In the kitchen, the servants squabble while the wind tugs at the shutters. Sometimes I flee down muddy and impassable lanes to one of the girls in the neighborhood, if only for a few hours, to do something besides eat my heart out with rage.

I notice now that I'm growing old. Also something is wrong with my insides. I keep going with the help of medicines. Now it occurs to me that you asked me for a prescription. *Et tu, amice?* My God, Francesco, we're two figures from a farce!

I have begun to write again to keep from going crazy and to be able to air my disquiet and bitterness in an indictment of the princes and prelates who have brought us to this pass. So here I sit—a grey-haired fool who has no other weapons but pen and paper, no other sounding-board than this godforsaken hamlet. Why am I in San Casciano again? Because I've resigned the overwhelming honorary post of spokesman for the woolworkers' guild (which was offered to me on my return from Rome) after having rendered my services. A journey to Venice to draw up a three-page report about a couple of merchants who disappeared—that's a commission which is really beyond the power of an historian and diplomat. Besides, I have difficulties with my two elder sons in Florence—one ill, the other in financial trouble...

Francesco Guicciardini to Niccolò Machiavelli

Dear friend, when you receive this letter you will, I hope, be far from San Casciano, back again in Florence and this time given the opportunity to be useful in a more creditable capacity than the woolworkers' trade. I would gladly have sent you a report earlier but at present certain things can no longer be arranged on the spur of the moment.

I'm still in Rome. Pescara's death on the second of December was an event that raised the hopes of many people here. The Queen Regent of France is making important proposals. Now it's crucial to get the Pope to form a League before King Francis is released in Madrid on terms that are very unfavorable to us.

It would be insanely reckless to march against the Imperial forces with a hastily assembled army of citizens and farmers. The Pope doesn't like the idea of naming his nephew commander. He would do it only in case of the most dire necessity. I don't know the reason for his reluctance—family disputes or fear of being accused of nepotism. However, I'm convinced that the matter must be dealt with differently. The net which the Emperor is drawing closed around Italy won't be ripped apart by one heroic effort. It's only with thorough preparation, endless patience and endurance that we might perhaps escape our destiny. Only a League, with the strong support of France and Venice, can give us the necessary self-confidence.

Don't let yourself be fooled by appearances. Perhaps the Spanish and German companies in Lombardy are not very numerous, but they consist of hardy, experienced soldiers, tough fellows who aren't afraid of hardship and adversity and who will stop at nothing. And as far as the Emperor's diplomatic methods are concerned, can you still say after the Pescara-Morone affair that they're transparent? Why is Morone being handled with velvet gloves after his arrest, why is he being catered to in every conceivable way? True, he's being kept under lock and key, but I hear his quarters are princely. De Leyva and other captains of the Imperial guard visit him regularly. His money and his property haven't been confiscated; not a hair of his relatives' heads has been touched. Why didn't Pescara put Morone to death? Think about this: before Morone made this last—and what looked like fatal—visit to Novara, he was warned against it by everyone. But still he went. Later, his confession—written in his own hand and not brought about by coercion—was precisely the license that Pescara needed to occupy Milan.

We hear that Pescara put in a good word for Morone with the Emperor, in his will. The explanation for all this has gone with Pescara to the grave. But I'm afraid that Morone, thanks to his ingenious twisting and turning, will soon become one of His Imperial Majesty's most trusted advisors.

Your bitterness makes you unfair, my dear Niccolò. You're accusing me of being disloyal to myself. But do you think I have chosen this course out of self-interest? I am deliberately sacrificing the satisfaction of openly acting out of my deepest convictions so that I can reach—secretly and indirectly—the same goal that you want. I don't care for fame, but I do want real influence and some control. I don't want the appearance of power—what I want is power itself.

You said once that I pull the strings of the papal puppet show. It isn't necessary for the spectators to know and see the man who pulls the strings. By the way, marks of honor don't matter to me. I love what you call the fatherland no less than you do. If that weren't true, where would I get the patience and courage to lead this nerve-wracking round dance—hop, skip, jump—one forward, two back—toward a League?

I've given some thought to that dream of yours. The worst isn't that the sheaves are lost, but that the people on the road stand around and watch that cloudburst as if nothing special were happening. What is wrong with Italy are the Italians themselves. And there's no cure for that. I hope you won't be bothered by nightmares now that you're back in Florence.

I have a personal request to make of you. Would you please do me the honor of acting as intermediary in a family affair. . . . It concerns a possibility of marriage for one of my daughters. . . .

The Scarlet City

Niccolò Machiavelli to Francesco Guicciardini

. . . no, this time I won't complain. I thank you from the bottom
of my heart for helping me get this appointment. They've commissioned me to make a study of Florence's defenses . . . that
comes down to the question of whether the city walls are still
serviceable. Last year when I was in Rome I happened to mention
this to the Pope. His Holiness said that the walls should be extended around San Miniato—of course that's a silly plan; that
hill is an obstacle—the wall would be too long and thus too weak
or else a whole part of the town would be left undefended. Now
I'm instituting a careful survey: I'm hoping that my report will
show that the best thing to do is to reinforce the existing walls
with new towers, forts and ramparts. My head is so full of bastions
that I can't think about anything else. But at last I have a job
to do that will bring instant benefits. Without these walls of Florence to think about, I'd burst with rage.

I knew perfectly well that nothing much would come of the
League. In my opinion, the fact that the King of France has made
a compromise with Madrid in order to be released, means that
the League will never be formed. That treaty between France and
Spain means that war is inevitable. Why aren't we assembling
troops? Why isn't anything being done even now? Do you people
expect a miracle there in Rome? You've seen your dream of a
League go up in smoke; now you certainly have to admit that I
was right.

I don't understand what you are waiting for. You formulate
things so nobly, so peacefully, at your writing table. When I read
your levelheaded letters, I feel like an excited lunatic. But now
I'm asking myself: what's the basis for that calm? Is it some
insight which escapes me, or is it perhaps the result of a quality
which I seem to have noticed often—a sort of haughty dispar-
agement of everything that goes on around you—that damn *sprez-
zatura*, we call it here—an aristocratic disdain for kill-or-cure
remedies. . . . That's all well and good, Excellency, that philosophical resignation to one's destiny—that's splendid for your
private life. But now there are greater things at stake.

I'll send you an account of the negotiations which I conducted in your name with the relatives of the suitor for your daughter's hand. They're planning to squeeze the last drop out of you, you know, like the honest Florentine bankers that they are. They don't respond to my counterproposals, they just keep up a courteous skirmishing with words. Let me give you some good advice: ask the Pope to lend you some money for a dowry, if you've really made up your mind that you want this alliance. He'll never refuse you. . . .

Francesco Guicciardini to Niccolò Machiavelli

. . . refuse no, but I could never even think of making a request like that of the Pope. I've always been frugal with my money and with other people's money. So now I'll offer what I can afford and that's going to have to be enough. If it doesn't suit the gentlemen in Florence, then I'll call the thing off.

You're jumping to conclusions: I haven't seen the plan for a League go up in smoke. On the contrary, I consider the Treaty of Madrid between the Emperor and the French King to be a serious political blunder on the Emperor's part. He makes demands which the French will never comply with—they can't, out of regard for their own self-preservation. The Pope has already promised King Francis absolution in advance if he violates the Treaty and joins the League. Vettori has left for Fontainbleau for further negotiations. So you had better wait before you start talking about a failure.

And you're wasting too many words guessing about my character, my dear friend. I'm a dry, sober, conscientious person, and I do appreciate a certain decorum, I grant you that. But am I haughty, do I disparage the world around me—that bewildering panorama of disasters and human inadequacy? Oh, no! I just happen to have been created differently from you, dear Niccolò. I was born without the gift of spontaneity.

That prescription you sent me for constipation is no good. I can understand why remedies don't relieve you if you trust that sort of quackery. Consult a good doctor, take care of yourself.

Francesco Guicciardini to Niccolò Machiavelli

By express courier so that you may be the first in Florence to know this—favorable news from France. The League is an accomplished fact. *Sis felix.*

XV.

Tullia d'Aragona

Mother and daughter are kneeling next to each other in one of the chapels of San Trifone, in front of the altar where the mass is being read. Giulia's kneeling-cushion is once again pushed up close to Tullia's, the folds of Giulia's dress touching Tullia's full drooping cloak. Tullia's eyes are fixed steadily on the altar lights. She gives no indication through look or gesture that she is aware of the presence of her mother who, with a fan in one hand and a rosary in the other, between her loud agreements with the responses, whispers, whispers incessantly.

"Lorenzo, that blockhead, didn't listen again to what I told him, past San Cosmo's shrine is what I said, on the mosaic of the Destruction of the Innocents, and here we are kneeling on the Adoration of the Wise Men, right in the draft, Amen, I'll develop rheumatism and you'll get a stiff neck, wind your veil around your neck, pray Heaven that it won't still be raining when we come out, all that mud makes me sick, look, Pantasilea is wearing an ermine stole, I can count at least five, six dozen tails, tomorrow they'll all be sitting here with furs on, mark my words, Amen, remind Strozzi again about his promise to send those marten skins, if we don't get them made up *now*, they won't be any use to us this winter, you must have a red lining and I'll take black, you might as well ask for clasps and chain fastenings to go with the rest, he didn't mention them, but an ordinary cord or braid fastening is no good, we must look regal if we want to stop them from yelling after us that you're past your prime, there you are, that's what I mean, we never had to worry about things like that before, that's what comes of your crazy choice, you just talk about that fur with Strozzi, he can't refuse you anything, Amen, look, there is Messer Petrucci again, still somewhat green around the gills but apparently the cure has helped him, say Tullia, I've heard that the French call the *mal francese* the disease of Naples, did you ever, now Italy gets the blame for it, Amen, you didn't eat any of the marzipan again this morning, it's delicious, with Indian nuts, melon seeds, essence of roses, be careful about getting too thin, that ugly bastard of a lackey isn't worth it, letting yourself pine away just because you're lovesick for him, take a look at Imperia there right in front of you, what shoulders and arms, plump, white, she's worked hard to accomplish that, I can tell you, she keeps bragging that all your lovers are running to her, Amen, you're all skin and bones, Messer Strozzi doesn't like that . . . Oh God, oh God, if we had never seen that Borgia, what a lot of suffering we would have been spared. . .''

After Giovanni's first visit, Giulia tried every argument she could think of to convince her daughter that she was risking her career by entering into a love affair with someone who had nothing to offer. When neither stamping her foot nor screaming angrily had any effect, she changed her approach: words came rolling out of her mouth in an endless stream of reproaches and admonitions and complaints; she made an appeal to Tullia's common sense, to the filial love which she ought to feel for her mother; in the end she resorted to pointing out to her all the things that had been won: fame and success, and even more tangible, the house, its valuable contents, the gold and silver, the art work, the jewels and perfumes and clothes of brocade and silk. She painted in the darkest colors the fate of the aging whore who lives in stinking poverty and dies like a dog. All that eloquence, all that passion, wasted on a silent, shrugging Tullia.

After a few days, that Borgia turned up again and from that moment he became a regular visitor until . . . Ah, when Giulia thought about it—that in her own house she had to flee from that undesirable intruder; as soon as she heard his footsteps she hid, to avoid seeing him, to avoid greeting him. She never, as she had always done with Tullia's other guests, personally brought wine and pastries to the bedroom, laughing, joking, behaving with a mixture of officiousness and servility, here arranging a fold in

Tullia's shift, there a lock of hair on her bare shoulder, as if her daughter were an object that was being brought out for inspection.

When the door of Tullia's chamber closed behind her and Giovanni, Giulia remained, sulking, brooding, alone in the ornate apartments among the piled-up treasures which in her eyes made life worth living. With a proprietary air she patted and fluffed up the cushions, arranged goblets and dishes on the sideboard, shifted footstools and spittoons—one of Strozzi's new distinctive cuspidors adorned with gilded cherubs. Meanwhile she strained her ears in the hope of catching any sound from the locked room.

Each time he comes, she has spat at the door he goes through, that Borgia. She has racked her brains over the question of why she hates and loathes that young man so much. Borgia, Borgia. He certainly bears that name, but what about it? Bastards of prominent families can usually name their fathers and mothers or at least one of the two; it's an open secret that Messer Giovanni *cannot* do that. Giulia has the unpleasant feeling that there is something she should remember . . . she cannot think of it.

Thus she wandered about the house during all the afternoon siestas of October and November, restless and peevish, kicking the cat which ran in front of her feet, cursing the parrots asleep in their cages, the autumnal chill of the chamber. When she could finally stand it no longer, she descended to the floor below, ostensibly to scold the two old women there for some omission, but in reality to warm herself at the good fire in the kitchen. There she sat, surly and brooding, among pots and pans, under bunches of garlic and onions and dried herbs which hung from the low vaulted roof, rubbing her forearms inside the sheltering folds of her shawl. . . .

"You can see perfectly well that she's using false hair in her coiffure, that Imperia, it's a totally different shade, she'd give ten years of her life to have hair as thick as yours, that's why it's an everlasting sin and shame the way you neglect it, oh the rubbish you wash it with, Heaven help me, I could scream with misery when I look at that brown mop of yours, stiff as a horsetail. Amen, and then *you*, who had the most gilded hair in all of Rome, why did you do it, and especially after Monsignore Bembo wrote that beautiful poem about it, how did that go now, like the locks that once bound my soul and senses in a net of burnished gold, isn't that splendidly phrased, imagine hearing that out of the mouth of a great man, and then to think that he compares you to the late Madonna Lucrezia who was once his mistress, Amen, that's what *you* could have been if you hadn't so grossly insulted him by sending his gift back to him, an uncommon jewel at that, a beautiful pendant, that emerald dolphin ... how could you act so stupidly, the Cardinal was madly in love with you, that was our chance, Tullia, our best chance, but no, you had to listen to that jealous good-for-nothing of yours and his raving, he came to you nine times out of ten with empty hands, and as if that isn't bad enough, you cut your hair and wash it with something without asking my advice about it first, trash, filthy nut juice, and now you walk around with a head, God help you, like every peasant and tramp, Amen, amen. If only I knew someone in Rome who had some influence over you, I'm only your mother, you dare to throw my advice to the winds now that you think you know better yourself, ah ah, that's the way things go, and I have only your welfare at heart, glory and power and riches for my Tullia, and that you should be queen of Rome as *I* was in my heyday, I would give anything for that, I smooth the way for you, I let you profit from my wealth of experience. Now listen, child, stop acting like a stone statue, you're breaking my heart and Messer Strozzi's too, oh, he doesn't complain to me, but I can certainly see it, I can certainly notice it, he's at the end of his rope too, watch out that we don't lose our last trusted friend, that he doesn't desert you for Pantasilea or Antonella or Maddalena, as the others have done ... Right *now* he still gives you gifts and courtesies to coax you into a better mood, but keep this up and he'll seek his pleasure where it's offered more smoothly, you can thank Heaven on your bare knees for that patron, there aren't many girls who are able to take the sort of liberties that you've been allowed to take lately, and don't forget your obligations, either, you owe something to Messer Strozzi, he doesn't know you have repeated the secrets of his heart and his official business to Messer Pietro, the devil take him, that sly dog, he intentionally shoved that Borgia under our roof, ah, I let myself be dazzled by his pretty speeches and his helpfulness and his pranks and jokes, *dio*, that's what he was after, to have us in the palm of his hand, in his pocket, he ate and drank

with us, we washed and mended his clothes, we lent him money
and let him walk around as if he owned the house, we told him
everything, yes, we pumped our most distinguished guests and
pried into their affairs and bribed their servants just to please
him, the sneak, and how does he thank us, he ruins your career
by making you fall in love with that damned friend of his. . ."

In her rage and bitterness, Giulia had thought a great deal about
Messer Pietro since he had fled to Mantua or Venice, no living
soul knew where. His life was not safe any more well, yes, that's
the price that a man must pay for shady practices. She never
poked her nose into his business, although she believed in a certain silent confederacy—no questions, no explanations, but we
understand each other. I serve your interests, you serve mine. She
felt comfortable with that arrangement. Always somebody near
at hand with whom a few words were enough for mutual understanding. She had shrugged off anything in his behavior or remarks which did not fit that image of the omniscient, adroit
advisor, the amusing friend of the family. Looking back, she has
the uncomfortable feeling that it had not actually been "between
you and me" but rather that she had been made to look like a
fool. Giulia, who knows better than anyone else her own little
world, the realm of alcoves and lovemaking and love potions and
secrets of the toilette, of the byways and roundabouts of physical
passion, who believed that she had summed up Messer Pietro
when she classified him as "an all-around man", realizes suddenly
that the hidden recesses of his character had escaped her notice.

She remembers all sorts of things: the rapture with which he
handled satins and velvets, lace and ribbons, letting them drift
in folds from his arm; how he—apparently in jest but it went on
too long to be a joke—stood before the mirror studying the effect
on his own body of jewelry and various colors; his curiosity about
what even a courtesan would seldom discuss with a man; the
secret smoldering attention with which he watched Tullia as she
moved about and stood and bathed and dressed, with which he
stayed near her, close to her, touching her and sniffing at her,
completely without erotic interest but rather as if what he wanted
was to creep into her skin, to *be* Tullia herself . . . and often in his
eyes that quick fierce light, flashes of an inquisitiveness that
seemed self-tormenting, filled with unmistakable envy. Giulia,

thinking her own thoughts about that now, sniffs with scorn and contempt. A man who envies women for the one thing he cannot have—their sex—she identifies irrevocably with the hybrid vermin to whom, if only by virtue of her profession, she feels vastly superior.

A woman like Giulia doesn't see that as a reason to hate anyone. But she considers the arrival on the scene of Giovanni Borgia to be an expression of Messer Pietro's long-suppressed need for revenge and provocation. She can react only with hatred to that underhanded attempt to destroy her success and happiness. He is the evil spirit who has used Giovanni Borgia to draw Tullia away from her influence. She blames him for her daughter's intractability, the incidents which drive the guests one after another away from her house. Gradually in her mind Messer Pietro and that Borgia have become apparitions which constitute one hostile creature. Messer Pietro is beyond her reach, but in striking at the other man she hopes to hit him too.

It was a long time before the inspiration came to her, that blessed lucid moment when she was able to put her bottled-up rage into the words that drove that Borgia away. He is gone (please God forever, amen, amen, Giulia prays quick as lightning at the thought, with a forceful glance at the altar filled with candles and wax flowers) but does that balance the account?

Looking back on the time which has passed, Giulia can point out with certainty the very evening that the life she had built for Tullia and herself began gradually to collapse. Before that, Tullia's rebelliousness had shown itself in a stubborn silence and a cold look of dislike. Her afternoons were reserved for that Borgia, but in the evenings she received, as she always had, the gentlemen who had arranged a visit with Giulia. Nevertheless Giulia thought she smelled trouble. She has never been mistaken in priding herself that nothing can remain hidden from her for long. A question here, a question there and she had found out that a rumor was going the rounds of the clients; embracing Tullia was like taking the living dead into your arms. Giulia then tried a strategem to ward off imminent displeasure: my daughter is a poetess, gentlemen, sensitive and high-strung; could it be that one of you has given her reason to believe that her character is viewed as un-

chaste, that her talent as a courtesan is considered to reflect a
lack of virtue?

Immediately the faithful visitors to the house in the Campo
Marzio, while enjoying the delights of a good deal of wine, drew
up a manifesto: Tullia the most virtuous woman in the world,
and anyone who dares to doubt that fact to be challenged forth-
with to single combat by Orsini or Rinuccini or Urbino or Mattei,
impressive-sounding Roman names. Then the document was read
loudly to Tullia, who despite her resistance had been enthroned
on the shoulders of two or three future champions of her honor.
The joke ended in discord, when Strozzi (who had entered during
the ceremony), white with rage, had torn the paper from the hand
of the reader and ripped it to pieces. This incident and the scuffle
which ensued from it caused a noticeable decline in visits to the
house in the Campo Marzio. A second, more serious, event was
responsible for the dreaded silence in the reception rooms.

When one evening, masked and in civilian dress, Cardinal
Bembo, with a small retinue of trusted friends, came in unannounced—he wanted, he said, to kiss the hand of the most discussed woman in Rome—it seemed to Giulia that the heavens
had opened. This friend of princes and popes, a man of the world,
a great scholar and poet, rich and powerful, destined perhaps to
receive the highest honor some day ... who knows what un-
dreamed-of glory might be awaiting Tullia? The grey-haired Cardinal with his slim, elegant figure, a head taller than the rest of
them, is known to be a fastidious and refined connoisseur of
women. A person like him does not visit the house of a young
courtesan of his own volition, without a reason. Even before the
first goblet of wine had been drained, Giulia had worked everything out in her mind: even Strozzi will have to resign himself,
Monsignore comes first ... surely Tullia can't help but feel flattered now—didn't she learn to read from Bembo's famous dialogue about love, the *Asolani*, wasn't it under his influence as a
writer that she became a poetess, didn't she, time after time,
fervently defend the Cardinal's work against Messer Pietro, who
had the nerve to call Bembo a pedantic fool, a half-baked hypocrite, a rapist of the language?

Giulia urged her daughter to recite her poetry; she herself, in
the background, was a witness to Monsignore's benevolent nods.

She called on all the saints, praying that Tullia's desire for literary fame might be stronger than her passion for that Borgia. Praise and encouragement from Bembo himself, what more could she want, her name will be made. Later, when the Cardinal, reciting in his turn, improvised in carefully chosen words praise for Tullia's red-gold hair, the feeling of triumph rose to Giulia's head like wine.

Why did that Borgia have to be with Tullia the next day when Bembo's Moor came to bring her a gift, Monsignore's thanks for that first pleasant meeting? A pendant, an emerald dolphin leaping from a wave of pearls. He, that Borgia, tore the jewel from her neck, called it whore's finery and Tullia's gilded hair whore's hair. Tullia, pale and wild with fear, ran after him to the courtyard: I'll throw the dolphin at Monsignore's feet even if he has me driven naked into the street by the *sbirri*, if that's what you want, but don't go away, stay with me, Giovanni!

She kept her word and in spite of Giulia's threats and lamentations (a villa, a princely allowance, lost through your stupidity and wilfulness) gave the jewel back that same evening to Monsignore who, with apparent joking nonchalance, but with a set face, departed immediately afterward. Tullia bribed one of the old women downstairs to bring her something that would restore dyed hair to its original color. The following day *sbirri* came with orders from high authority that Giulia Farrarese and her daughter were forbidden to receive guests for the time being.

Holding her breath, Giulia listened every day at Tullia's door, trying to guess the lay of the land from fragments of their muffled conversation. What do these two want in there, what are they doing? It's as if they know she's listening, for she can rarely hear anything and what she hears she can't understand. Once she hears Tullia say clearly: "I'll do anything you want, haven't I proven that? I'll go away from here, I will go with you, it doesn't make any difference to me where. Today, tomorrow, you only need to say the word."

Wild terror seized Giulia. Tullia will run away, one day she will leave, taking money and valuables with her to have something to live on with her Borgia. She, Giulia, can drop dead. She is as sure of that as if her daughter had shrieked it at her. Tullia will not put up with her any more, never any more. And then? Oh God, the things that she had heard and seen when she was a young woman—before her days of glory—wandering about Rome alone and unprotected. Creatures who come creeping at twilight from secret hiding places, like animals frightened of the light. Under rags and tatters, revolting corruption. Squatting in the shadow of doorways and church porches, begging for alms. Scrabbling in refuse heaps in search of food. Begging at public houses and brothels, hoping to entice a drunkard. Scarecrows, all skin and bone, covered with rashes and festering ulcers, with sagging breasts and toothless mouths, roaming the brothel quarter desperate with hunger, clutching at young prostitutes there: "Take me in service, dear heart, I will be your *ruffiana*, I know secret cures for the *mal franccso*, baths which will make you a virgin again, I can read palms, I know this, I know that, I will tell you everything for a plate of food and a mattress to sleep on. . . ."

How often had she herself, with a shudder and a curse, yanked her gown out of the hands of a creature like that, who screeched vindictively after her, "I've got the evil eye, you'll rot, slut, hang, burn!"

Tullia will have no mercy on her, she will let her go that way, to the slums at the Ponte Sisto, to the hovels and holes among the ancient ruins, to the whores' prison at the Torre Savella, and finally to the lazaretto and the charnel house.

Giulia can't sleep, her food sticks in her throat. It has become quiet in the house, a thin layer of dust covers the furniture and the carpets in the reception rooms. In the kitchen, the old women sit whispering near the fire, they hush and poke the ashes as soon as Giulia enters. Gusts of rain lash the pavement in the courtyard. Only at night there is still laughter and song in the part of the house where Vascha and Speranza live; during the day a flurry of children's shouts rises from the school. Without these signs of life, Giulia would go mad. As long as she can only keep moving, as long as she can talk, talk. . . She has intentionally never had anything to do with the other inhabitants of the quarter. She knew the value of a haughty attitude. Now she would give anything for heart-to-heart talks with the neighbor women and market vendors.

There are no more reception evenings, there is nothing to arrange, nothing to prepare for. All the long day, nothing to do but huddle by the fire, brooding on approaching disaster, watching Tullia: how she goes calmly and proudly on her way, issuing instructions to the old women, to the page Lorenzo and the groom, having meals prepared for herself and that Borgia, in dry weather ordering a palanquin and mules for a ride through Rome. None of the former lovers shows any signs of life. Only Strozzi sometimes sends a messenger for news: still no hope? Tullia doesn't answer and Giulia sobs and curses in helpless rage.

In the silence of the night, a new idea takes possession of her. Tullia is bewitched. Didn't the Borgia have their will of every woman, weren't they able to put all their enemies out of the way? In the Vatican at one time, Il Duca had a cabinet which held collections of dead men's bones, exotic beasts, abortions preserved in alcohol, carnivorous plants and bizarre finds. Giulia tosses sleepless in bed. Whoever heard too much, said too much, was no longer invited to the papal feasts. Giulia Ferrarese, the rising courtesan, had taken careful note of that. Nothing passed her lips but praise for the Borgia and their court. But if she had wanted to . . . They insulted her too. Il Duca was good at holding courtesans up in one way or another to public ridicule. Once during a game in company, she had reason to believe that it was he who in the darkness . . . When candles were carried in, he was standing in a far corner, laughing at the top of his voice, and next to her she discovered Perotto Caldès, the Spanish servant, the Pope's pet. For the first time in years, she tries to call up that face; she remembers him as combining Messer Pietro's impudence and the dark, irritatingly elusive quality of Giovanni Borgia.

What Giulia will never know: that although Tullia received him every day, each time Giovanni Borgia was a stranger to her anew, that the brief moment of intimacy following lovemaking when they lay together in peaceful silence, never brought a feeling of empathy which lasted to the next meeting. She asks him no questions. It doesn't trouble her that he's not talkative. She has had to talk and laugh too much with lovers. She peels fruit for him, plucks her lute, feeds the birds in the aviary, throws wood on the fire in the hearth. She realizes that it is just this ability of hers to maintain a distance that draws him to her. She would like to know whom he has loved, whom he has hated and why. But she doesn't dare to begin. She once made a hesitant first attempt by admitting that she despised her mother. While she was speaking, she saw in his eyes that he fully understood her. So he knows what that is, hatred of your own flesh and blood. And he's not eager to hear anything about his relatives. He and she had this trait in common, along with a distrust of enthusiasm, of smooth, easy talk.

The only rules for the game of love which Tullia knows are those her mother has taught her. These don't apply this time. She gives herself without reservation. She has forgotten the life she used to live. Let her mother sob and rave about the chances which are gone forever, that has no effect upon Tullia. What can it matter to her that men stay away from her evening receptions because they are afraid of losing Cardinal Bembo's favor by visiting a house where he has been insulted? What does she care about Strozzi's letters and messages? He has always been good to her, but she has repaid him for that with her body. She has no reason to feel sorry for him. Only Giovanni Borgia exists for her now— he who comes without protestations of love, who leaves without thanking her, who does not primarily seek pleasure in her arms, whose essence and intentions are a mystery to her. She has patience, she can wait. For the time being their enigmatic meetings are enough; his presence, which has set her free.

She notices that her mother's pent-up tension is verging on hysteria. But what can she do about it? Tullia's happiness and Giulia's happiness cannot be reconciled with each other.

Late one afternoon when she and Giovanni are coming out of her room, Giulia springs toward them from a hiding place where she has been awaiting this moment. She threatens him with fingers curved into claws, she shrieks abuse at him.

"Come," Tullia says. "Leave her alone. It sticks in her throat that there isn't as much money as there used to be. Day after day she sold me—never less than a small fortune for each embrace. Now what a loss there is since I've loved you."

Sobbing, Giulia clutches at her daughter's skirts, embraces her knees, tries to prevent her from walking past. "You, you, you don't know what you're doing, you call that love, he works through sorcery, you're in his power, he does what he wants with you, the devil, he belongs in the Tiber with a stone around his neck, just like his father!"

Giovanni has been listening silently, indifferently, to this invective. But at Giulia's last words, Tullia sees how his face changes, goes slack, becomes vulnerable. Giulia senses insecurity and, quick as lightning, takes advantage of his weakness. She no longer weeps, she no longer kneels, now with her arms akimbo she can respond to her enemy.

"Deny it if you dare, you servant's bastard, even if your mother was a hundred times a great lady with the pretensions of a princess, the apple of Pope Alexander's eye, his porcelain Lucrezia, they thought no man in the world was good enough for her. . . ."

Roughly he shakes off the hand which Tullia places on his sleeve.

"Give me proof of what you're saying."

"Oh yes, get around Tullia d'Aragona, who receives only the nobility and the great bankers and the purple, acting as if you're better than all those lords put together and thinking that there is no one left in Rome who remembers how Madonna Lucrezia had to hide away for nine months to conceal the trick that Pedro Caldès had played on the Borgia. I can prove that too if I have to, before I met Cardinal d'Aragona, didn't I live with a woman who took big bribes to help with a delivery in Monna Vannozza's house and I could give the names and family names of people who were there when Perotto was hauled out of the Tiber tied hand and foot along with a lady's maid of the pure Lucrezia, those two didn't fall in the water by accident, believe me . . . I don't have to keep my mouth shut now, there aren't any of Il Duca's assassins walking around to finish off anyone who dares to say an ugly word about his sister."

Tullia doesn't understand why he stands staring at the malicious distorted face in front of him, why he doesn't check the stream of Giulia's abuse—by force if necessary. What she sees happening fills her with boundless amazement. He pays Giulia the sort of close attention that she, Tullia, no matter what she did, no matter what she said, had never been able to rouse in him. He doesn't seem to be concerned about Giulia's jeering attitude permeated with gloating enjoyment of the misfortunes of others. He leads her to a chair, sits himself down opposite her. Leaning toward her, his clenched fists pinned between his knees, he puts questions to her which Giulia, sobered by his composure, answers. When he suddenly stands up, Tullia takes a step toward him, but he doesn't see her, he brushes past her on the way to the door as if there were someone waiting for him outside.

After a week Giulia notifies Strozzi. "He's gone, she doesn't eat, she doesn't sleep, she doesn't say a word, do come, Excellency, *per misericordia.*"

But what can Strozzi do? She won't look at the presents he brings her, she won't touch the delicacies, she refuses his caresses. She stands before the window where she can overlook the square. A hundred times she leans over the bannisters listening to sounds in the courtyard. She walks back and forth, back and forth. When Giulia comes near her she bares her teeth like an animal which feels the approach of an enemy. Bewildered by this unsettling situation, Strozzi makes a proposal that fills him with shame and self-mockery. He, a Florentine nobleman, will play the procurer. He sends a trusted servant to the Vatican with a message for Messer Giovanni Borgia. The man comes back without having been able to accomplish his mission.

Messer no longer lives above the guard rooms, he is not to be found in the Chancellery nor anywhere else in the papal palace, he has been seen riding through the city, but where he is and what he is doing, no one knows.

Strozzi gives this news to Tullia himself in carefully chosen words. He sees her unnatural tension suddenly relax; it's as if a spring has snapped, a mechanism stopped. Her eyes become dull. Strozzi talks and talks, in the hope of rousing this doll to life, of striking a spark that can suggest the warmth of their past intimacy.

"Do you know, Tullia, that because of you, I have received a rebuke from the Signoria, what do you think of that, *bella mia*, I have visited you too often and they think in Florence that my fighting for you that time was not in keeping with the dignity of a man in the service of the state. When I can't choose my own sweethearts any more, they can find someone else to take my place henceforth. That's not pleasant by the way, that squabbling, that qualifying and hair-splitting that's called diplomacy . . . and all the while God knows what's at stake. It's not good, it's not good, Tullia, things are not going as we expected, I am over my ears in worry, child, and you have refused to comfort me for so long now. . ."

Later Strozzi makes his wishes known to a submissive Giulia: the house must remain closed to the other visitors, even if the captain of the Torre Savella raises the ban on receptions. Mother and daughter must hold themselves in readiness to travel with him when he returns to Florence. Meanwhile he provides some diversion: an artist is coming to paint a portrait of Tullia. Strozzi chooses the pose, Giulia the attire. In silence Tullia endures the arranging and draping of her body. She sits for hours in the desired attitude, her head slightly tilted, a smile on her lips, her empty green gaze directed at the same spot. The painter, who has heard that his model writes poetry, gives her portrait a background of laurel branches so that she will be immortalized in that legendary forest where fame is for the plucking.

"How cold it is here, how cold it is, we'll catch our death, Tullia, in God's name pull your mantle over your chest, here now, let *me* do it, are you so lost in your devotions or are you asleep or are you thinking about something that's over, be sensible, see things as they are, your whole life is in front of you, you'll forget what's happened, you have Signor Strozzi, you have me, what more do you want, when I was your age I was standing all alone. Perhaps we'll go to Florence one of these days, that will be a change, you must have a change of air. Strozzi will see to it that everything is done to your taste there, you know how he is. Your future is assured, your whole life long you will be his sweetheart, but I haven't given up hope for something more for my Tullia, listen, powerful gentlemen will see your portrait when it hangs in Strozzi's palace and they'll ask: who is that beauty, where does she live? Believe me, you're still a star in the ascendant. Amen, amen. Thank God, we can get up now, here, Lorenzo, the cushions, and remember, you ass, next time on the Destruction of the Innocents."

XVI.

Giovanni Borgia

W hat is it that led me to visit Pescara's wife in order to get a letter of recommendation to him? I thought then that the moment had come for me to leave Rome. Actually I was obeying a blind urge to confirm the best in myself, or at any rate what I took then to be the best, in surroundings that were completely free of court intrigue and whore's favors. I managed to gain access to the Marchioness of Pescara a few days after it was learned in Rome that Girolamo Morone had been arrested.

She received me standing in a draughty little chamber, a connecting space between two rooms. When I told her who I was, she looked directly into my eyes with cool inquiry. I had to use all my self-control to keep from throwing myself at her feet. I wanted to cry out to her that she must not despise me, need not fear or distrust me because of my name, since in reality I was no one, with no possessions, since I had just begun to live, as it were, at *that* moment. She did not have much time for me. She asked me what I wanted. So I said without circumlocution that I wanted to serve her husband and that I hoped she would give me a recommendation that I could take to him in Novara.

"I can't recommend you, Messer; I know nothing about you." She shrugged, smiling slightly. "Why do you want to serve the Marquis?"

"I'm looking for a cause to live or die for. I respect the Marquis. The goal which he sets for himself is certainly good enough for me."

"A cause to live or die for. That's a great deal to ask, Messer. You're placing a heavy responsibility on my husband."

I expected her to send me away because I suddenly realized how ridiculous my request was. But she stood absorbed in thought. Through the open door behind her, I saw a series of empty dark rooms.

"I've seen you in the retinue of the Chancellor of Milan. Isn't it odd that you're seeking out the Marquis now? After what has happened, everyone who supported Signor Morone will turn away from my husband. Explain that to me. What qualities do you admire in the Marquis?"

While I was speaking, she looked at me steadily. Her face was tired. She wore a dark dress without ornaments and a transparent cloth wound about her hair. A chaste costume for a nunnery. I remembered that I had found this woman desirable the last time I had seen her. Since then she had changed in some subtle way. The outward charm remained: her quiet regal bearing, her bright eyes, the repressed passion of her mouth. But that beauty no longer spoke to the senses. She seemed to me much more than a beautiful woman.

"Serve me first," she said, when I stopped talking. "I must go on a journey. I give you the command of my armed escort."

❦

These days I am a different man from what I was when I wrote down my memories so prolifically in the library of the Vatican. The conviction that I was the product of incest between father and daughter, between sister and brother, and, moreover, a Borgia, has, I see now, paralyzed me for a long time. Add to that the exhausting idleness, the sauntering about the papal palace in the expectation of a commission, the visits to Tullia d'Aragona. She was willing and tranquil; I have no regrets about that relationship. I believe that her expressions of affection were sincere. She gave me more than I expected, more too than I wanted. In the end one feels oppressed by a love to which one can't respond with love in return or with princely open-handedness. Besides, it's not possible to embrace the same woman when one doesn't love her, day in and day out without becoming subject to boredom. Apathy tormented me like a disease. Lying on Tullia's bed, I contemplated a hundred and one different possibilities, but I decided nothing. I lacked the courage and the willpower to shake off the past. A shock was necessary to get me to move.

When I first heard certain things from that shrew, Tullia's mother, I was beside myself. It all fitted so damned well with what I knew from my own experience. That I too didn't vanish into the Tiber, that Pope Alexander made me the gift of a dukedom, that Cesare took me under his protection—every fact had an explanation. They hoped in this way to safeguard their precious pawn Lucrezia from suspicion. The bulls in question were of course drafted later, when Lucrezia was to marry Alfonso d'Este. The Borgia needed male descendants to be able to consolidate their power in the long run.

If Pedro Caldès is my father, it becomes understandable why after the deaths of Alexander, Cesare and Lucrezia, no one wanted to support me. The members of the family who live in Spain now, descendants of the Duke of Gandia and Gioffredo, wouldn't want to recognize me. I'm writing all this down in complete peace of mind. I've stopped being absorbed in the question of my origin. I know enough now. Messer Pietro was right when he said I would do better to look to the future. But in order to come to that realization, I had first to be convinced that I could find no hints in my past about my future.

In the beginning, I wandered aimlessly about Rome. I was rebellious and bitter at the trick which fate had played upon me. It seemed to me that my birth had been sufficiently proven by the life I had been leading for the past few months. That I had spent a part of every day lazing about in the apartments of a prostitute, which in a way I found pleasant; I felt at home in the midst of her finery, her parrots, her monkey and in a bed where half of Rome and Florence and Siena had lain before me, and not as a guest, a patron, but only as a favorite, a sort of house pet; this miserable behavior undoubtedly resurrected the lackey Pedro Caldès in me. Thus my flight from Tullia's house was an attempt to rid myself of an undesirable element. In my blind rage I forgot that I carry that element with me wherever I go.

But when I came to my senses, I realized that what I had taken for a fresh setback was in reality a gift bestowed on me by fate.

Pedro Caldès released me from that other elusive, ominous possibility. I'm not afraid of the Borgia in me since I now have reason to believe that half of my being is anti-Borgia by nature. A lackey who seduces the daughter of a lord—in itself that deed expresses rebellion and resentment.

Although I cannot and will not be heir to the mentality of a servant, nothing prevents me from acknowledging a debt of thanks to Pedro Caldès for the antidote which I carry in my blood.

The obligation to unravel that Borgia-knot, whatever the cost, has fallen from me. I am nameless in the fullest sense of the word. I am not a link in a chain, nor am I the end of one. I could, on the other hand, be a beginning. I'm not defined by the history of a family. I don't even belong to a family. I carry the name Borgia for lack of a better one. Traditions, privileges, duties don't exist for me. The awareness of my freedom came over me like a revelation.

Farewell, Camerino! Never again the spasmodic feeling of regret and impotence because, once started, I failed to hold the line. I have no role to play at that level where the Varano and the representatives of royal families make their moves.

I want to seek my self-affirmation in an environment where those qualities triumph which I hope were given me at birth: inner discipline and assurance, the ability to act purposefully, and, above all: the gift of finding the meaning of life in the continual necessity to choose. Just as the Marquis of Pescara chooses from a number of political possibilities, just as Madonna Vittoria obviously makes one choice after another in the hidden world of her soul.

Certainly it was well-done to draw a line through everything that lay behind me. I have no friends—Messer Pietro is gone, at the Chancellery I was only one of many hangers-on. Tullia will surely forget me.

❦

Still another period of my life has closed. Once again I see myself facing the necessity of seeking my destiny. Pescara is dead. She must have known how it was with him when she took me in service. She never intended to send me to Novara. I take it she realized what a state I was in when I came to ask her for a favor. She felt it necessary to protect me from myself.

She visited a number of estates one after the other to the south of Rome, which she and the Marquis owned together. She never stayed anywhere longer than a couple of days. After she had held discussions with governors and stewards (I think now that because of Pescara's approaching death, she wanted to put their affairs in order) she gave immediate instructions to travel on.

There were balmy days in the late autumn. She sat in an open palanquin. I rode alongside her. She was friendly and courteous to me, but she spoke little. I have never been so consciously absorbed in the shapes and colors of the landscape as I was during those journeys. The sun shone on the flame-red leaves of the vineyards. The brooks, swollen by the rains, foamed white between patches of meadowland and cypress groves in the valleys. At elevated spots she would often call a halt. Then she stood for a while, wrapped in her mantle, silently looking out over the land. The armed men in the escort, mostly from Ascanio, Colonna's household, grumbled and sighed to express their displeasure over these delays. They asked me to persuade Madonna to stop in villages or towns where there were inns, instead of on deserted hilltops.

I didn't want to disturb her in those moments of quiet which she allowed herself. I shared some of that peace or whatever it was that she found there. In those days I wanted nothing more. I breathed deeply; I could feel the blood flowing through my veins. It was enough for me to lead the little procession from stopping place to stopping place. I thought I had finished with fear and uncertainty. I inhaled the odors of earth and water and trees as greedily as if I were a freed prisoner or a convalescent.

When we stayed at one of the country estates, she sometimes invited me to spend the evening playing chess with her in the room where she sat with her women. She was an expert player. But what I admired even more was the roundabout way in which she gave me the opportunity to talk about myself, without asking me questions. I always told her more than I really wanted to. But after all I noticed that, time after time through that talk, I purged away the remains of disquiet which I had still felt. I don't know how much she understood. She listened to me as if we were having the-most normal conversation in the world. I felt no discomfort or shame about telling her so much. It is also possible that what I said didn't really penetrate to her. What I took to be attentiveness could also have been something wholly different, the reflection of an inner tension. Even when no one spoke to her, she looked as though she were waiting, listening.

One day she sent for me. I found her standing motionless before the window with a letter in her hand. She said that the Marquis had requested her to come to Novara. I considered that favorable news. I was convinced that she would speak for me in Novara.

In order to travel faster, we left the wagons and palanquins behind. In addition, at her request we rode day and night. The weather had broken. We sat our horses in the streaming rain. She spoke no word. In Viterbo, the first stopping place which we allowed ourselves, a courier was waiting. She was about to dismount when the man spoke to her. I saw her moving her head as if she were gasping for breath. Before I or anyone else could reach her, she fell sideways from the saddle.

A man who has the opportunity to act loses the taste for speculating on paper. Of course there was some sense in my putting into words certain events in my life and my thoughts about them. When things are seen in black and white they become less menacing.

But I don't see any sense in giving a day-to-day account of the things which define my life since I entered the service of Ascanio Colonna. I'm no diary keeper. What difference can it make to me later to know whether it was on a Tuesday, Thursday or Saturday that I conducted an exercise in sharp-shooting in the courtyard, supervised the men strengthening the outer walls and bricking up the windows and entrances of the ground floor. These and similar duties have been (and are) assigned to me.

When Madonna Vittoria, after Pescara's burial, had withdrawn to the convent of San Silvestro in Capite (it was said here at first that she wanted to become a nun but the Pope apparently forbade it), I was taken into the retinue of Signor Ascanio. He has gathered a staff around him of male blood relatives, uncles and nephews, bastards, an army of nothing but Colonna; Marcello and Giulio and Sciarra and Marziano and whatever the rest are called. In addition, there are many supporters of the Ghibelline party here from other families. Despite this show of importance, Ascanio is not the head of the Colonna family: that's Cardinal Pompeo (a bitter enemy of Pope Clement, and himself a candidate for the triple crown) who, after a dispute with His Holiness, has entrenched himself in the Castel Marino. He doesn't come to Rome any more, but incessantly sends messengers with instructions.

Among the Colonna—who are convinced that the Emperor will shortly rule Italy—no one believes that Pope Clement will really dare to form a League. Apparently they expect that there will soon be an armed conflict: Cardinal Pompeo and Ascanio Colonna have secretly had weapons brought into the palace from outside the city. Here the dominant mood is like that which precedes a siege. We go into the town only in groups. Since the League was proclaimed, the houses of the Emperor's sympathizers and of Spaniards are being kept under guard. It's forbidden to carry weapons.

So now I find myself in the camp of those who boast of being the Emperor's most important domestic auxiliary troops. No one here cares about who I am or where I come from. For them my past spans only the time since I led Madonna Vittoria's armed escort. They have accepted me as one of their own. I carry the colors of the Colonna.

Every day members of the family come with their supporters to seek shelter in the Palazzo. It seems that soldiers in the service of the Pope are stationed all over the province in the neighborhood of the Colonna estates: apparently His Holiness intends to cut off the Colonna's communication with Naples so that they cannot link up with the Imperial army in case of war.

I hear it said that the Emperor expects the Spanish sympathizers in Rome to intervene in good time to prevent the League party from taking advantage of changed circumstances. In the Vatican, conferences go on all day long, but here there's no sign of the new decisions and measures which we are awaiting, weapons in hand.

(✦)

The Spanish envoy, Don Ugo de Moncada, has come to Rome. People in the palace held the opinion that the grandee, one of the Emperor's most capable advisors, could undoubtedly talk His Holiness out of the idea of a League. It was said afterwards that it was Giberti who was responsible for the failure of this visit. The Pope was noticeably uncertain during the interview and impressed by the letters from Madrid which De Moncada had delivered to him; but Giberti did not budge from his side, kept whispering in his ear. Finally the envoy had to depart without having accomplished anything. His retreat was a disgrace unequalled here for a long time. Moncada's face, as he left the Vatican, was inscrutable.

His fool, whom he had taken up behind him on his horse, spat and let wind and urinated on the pavement of the papal courtyard and in the square in front of San Pietro. Don Ugo de Moncada has taken up residence at the Castle of Marino with Cardinal Pompeo Colonna.

It looks as though something is about to happen now. The papal and Venetian troops appear to have received orders to advance upon Lombardy. The day before yesterday, Francesco Guicciardini, whom the Pope recently named Lieutenant-General, left the city; all the League's hopes are now pinned on him. Uneasiness is growing in the city from day to day. There is always rioting. Agitated prophets and forecasters of doom wander about: Varano's proteges—monks who call themselves Capuchins because they wear a sort of hood—are preaching penance on all the street corners. The death bells knell continuously for victims of the plague. The Pope has now strengthened Rome. All commands are given by the Orsini: His Holiness could not have thought of a better way to irritate the Colonna.

It seems that the Pope has become frightened at the Colonna's menacing attitude and preparations for war. He wants to restore Cardinal Pompeo's honor, give back the lands which had been seized. He has proposed to partially disband the army occupying Rome and to send the Orsini home if we and our supporters will vacate the city. On Ascanio's orders, we're holding our horses and weapons at the ready. To depart at the first signal? I don't think so. I have the impression that this obedience to the Pope's orders has quite a different reason behind it.

❦

I wrote this on the nineteenth of September. On that same night, Cardinal Pompeo and Don Ugo de Moncada with three thousand foot soldiers and eight hundred riders (mainly recruited from the provinces), forced their way through the gate of San Giovanni in Laterano, to enter the city. They bivouacked around the Colonna Palace among the ruins of the Forum, a stone's throw away from our walls.

We, Ascanio's men, joined them. After dawn we moved through the city. We encountered no opposition. People stood along the way to see what was happening. We advanced unhindered to San Apostolo as if it were a parade. I was a part of the troop which was sent over the Ponte Sisto to Trastevere to reconnoitre the situation there. The two hundred papal defenders hastily gathered together and then after a brief skirmish rushed about in every direction. Then Cardinal Pompeo and the rest of the Colonna army also moved across the bridge with loud cries: *Imperium!* Colonna! Freedom!

It seemed a repetition of something that I had experienced as a child long ago: the closely-packed snorting, stamping horses, the soldiers crowded together shoulder to shoulder, the dawn sky yellow above the houses of the Borgo and the battlements of the Vatican. As before, the gates of the forecourt were smashed in, armed men swarmed over the staircases and galleries. At the last moment, the Pope had fled through the escape passage to safety in the Castel Sant'Angelo. Most of the cardinals went into hiding in the city.

The Vatican lay open. A couple of the Swiss guard fought until they fell—more, I suspect, to save their reputation than from any rational motive. Out of deserted rooms and loggias, lackeys and functionaries scattered like rats from a fire. Cardinal Pompeo, who probably imagined he was lord and master here, was so busy looking through the papers of the Chancellery and the Datary's secretariat that he forgot to forbid plunder. For that matter, it is a question whether the men would even have obeyed such an order then. From the instant that we entered the Vatican, not a single Colonna had authority any longer over the mercenaries and the farmers wooed from the Romagna with promises of booty.

The papal reception rooms, the apartments of courtiers and prelates, the basilica and the sacristy of San Pietro, everything was looted. Hangings were torn from the walls, statues smashed to pieces, doors and windows kicked in, and the horses from the stud farm driven in a stampede directly through the palace to the outside. Giberti's costly porcelain services burst into a thousand splinters on the pavement; shreds of Berni's correspondence and the librarian Giovio's manuscript collection fluttered about on the wind as far as Trastevere.

In a futile attempt to collect some men together, I came right into that part of the palace where Alexander and Cesare had lived. The looters had broken the seals on the doors. Complete silence reigned there. There was nothing to take away from there because these rooms had been empty for so long a time. The floors were covered with dust and grit, cascades of splinters lay under the window openings.

For the first time in twenty years, I stood again in the Borgia apartments where Rodrigo and I once came to pay our respects. I remembered the blue and green floor tiles, the mass of gilded ornaments, tiaras, keys, bulls and other Borgia emblems on the vaulted arched ceiling. I remembered too the murals—especially the one of the Santa Catarina dispute. Standing before it, I received a shock. Those whom I wanted to forget were staring out at me, dressed as sacred and Biblical figures. Cesare, Lucrezia. It was she especially whom I saw, at full length. I knew that it was she although I had never known her looking like that. A slender body, a proud and melancholy girl's face.

It was in these rooms that she met him for the first time, Pedro Caldès, Perotto. Behind Alexander's chair, serving at bed and table. Bringing in food, buttoning up the shoulder cape, putting slippers on the papal feet. A good-looking dark youth who could play the lute and cut a good figure in the fives court. Moreover, a Spaniard. A favorite of the Pope. Bearer of private messages and letters between father and daughter. He knew the family secrets, could speak with her confidentially in her palace of Santa

Maria in Portico. She had warm blood and Sforza was impotent. It is entirely possible—more, probable.

Standing before the fresco, I told myself that I now had no reason at all to go on doubting. Nothing remained for me of my past at that moment except dust and splinters and the colorful ghosts on the wall. The seals were broken. I could settle accounts with what lay behind me as with these empty chambers. I remembered where I was and what I was doing there. In the distance, I heard the shouts of the plundering troops echoing in the corridors.

As I was turning away to leave, I saw, on a medallion above a door, the portrait of a madonna. At least, she had a child on her knee and a halo was painted behind her head. She looked down at me with a sidelong gaze filled with secret contempt. And there was laughter in her eyes which seemed to me to ridicule my desperate desire to believe something that I couldn't prove, just to have some certainty at last. Representations of the Mother of God are supposed to bring peace and comfort.

I was standing there wondering how Pope Alexander had borne this cold critical stare night and day, when there was a sound of voices and footsteps in the adjoining apartment. Through the door came Don Ugo de Moncada, followed by a young man in armor who was holding the Pope's silver tiara in his two hands. Don Ugo de Moncada joked and played with his gloves as though he were at a feast instead of in the shattered Vatican. He looked at me and then at the madonna above the door.

"Ah, the charms of Giulia *Bella* make the *capitano* into a dreamer," he said in Spanish to his companion. "That was a most enchanting woman, your relative, Farnese, I still remember her perfectly."

"If I had my hands free, I would scrape her face from the wall," the other answered. "We're not proud of having a Borgia whore in the family."

As he passed me, he looked at me over the top of the tiara with the same eyes as the woman above the door.

I have heard talk about Giulia Farnese. I have never seen her. At the time that Rodrigo and I were here in the Vatican, she had been out of favor for quite a while. I knew that Lucrezia hated her: she asked me once if I could imagine what it meant, for love of her father, to have to live in a sisterly relationship with the "bride of Christ". That was how Giulia Farnese—I remember that quite well—was generally known.

Toward sunset we succeeded in assembling the booty-laden men and inducing them to turn back to the encampment which lay all around the Colonna palace. It was high time too. If we had not departed then, the people, who were indifferent in the morning and filled with mortal fear at noon, would probably, out of indignation over the plundering of the Vatican, have listened at last to the desperate calls from Giberti and the other cardinals, and taken up arms.

So nothing came of the Colonna's intention that there should be a general uprising in Rome in favor of the Imperial party—a plan cunningly and quickly worked out from an idea of Don Ugo de Moncada (who, according to his own words, had learned this art when he was still a member of Cesare's staff) but which failed because it was impossible to control the soldiers, who were unfit in every respect.

The only thing that was finally attained: the Pope, literally and figuratively driven into a corner in the Castel Sant'Angelo, wanted to conclude an armistice with the Emperor. Convinced that the promises of His Holiness cannot be relied upon, the Imperial forces have taken hostages, who left the city yesterday for Naples under heavy guard. Among them is Filippo Strozzi, Tullia's Florentine patron.

❦

Pierluigi Farnese is the bastard son of Cardinal Alessandro Farnese, who was called "the Petticoat Cardinal" because he owed his elevated position to the fact that his sister Giulia mentioned his name to Pope Alexander. This Pierluigi is, in spite of his youth—I would say he's about twenty-five years old—a person of importance in the Colonna party. His father has warned him that he must disappear from Rome as quickly as possible. It seems that something is brewing in the Vatican. Excommunication of the Colonna and all their supporters, confiscation of all their property? That would only be possible if the Pope were veering once more toward the League. However that may be, Pierluigi Farnese is about to move with the young members of the Colonna family to Naples, where the Viceroy has promised them posts in the Imperial army.

At first I tried to get permission to join that group. But I changed my mind. I don't want to be in a subordinate position to Pierluigi. I don't want to watch him operating effortlessly on a plane which I can never reach. I have never spoken to him. Beyond that brief moment in the Vatican, when he passed me carrying Pope Clement's tiara, we have never even been near each other. He belongs to the close circle around Cardinal Pompeo; I am after all only one of the men in the Colonna retinue. What I feel about him isn't easy to express. He could be my best friend or my bitterest enemy. I follow all his actions with intense interest and at the same time I'm eaten up with envy.

He's everything that I want to be, everything that I *could* have been. The bastard of a distinguished family, but not hampered in the least by his illegitimate birth. A free, self-assured, strong-willed man. They say that he has a great future before him. Without striking a blow he could well become a general in the Emperor's army. He has money, friends, a powerful father. If I were near him, in my inferior position, I would have no peace. But in God's name how can I live when I can't be content with what lies within my reach? Pierluigi Farnese—that name alone, which he bears with such self-assurance, makes me rebel against my destiny. His presence here is a reason for me to consider leaving the service of Ascanio Colonna.

XVII.

Francesco Guicciardini and Niccolò Machiavelli

F rancesco Guicciardini to Niccolò Machiavelli

From Piacenza. *Carissime.* The League has failed, failed.
A great plan has been shipwrecked through impotence, unrelia-
bility, mutual distrust. All the effort of the past year for nothing.
The advantages won in Lombardy lost because the Pope in his
cursed treaty with the Emperor has promised to pull his troops
back over the Po. The help from France—nothing more than beautiful words on a rag of paper. I no longer receive money from
Rome for payment and maintenance of our men. They're deserting by the hundreds. The Emperor's fleet, with seven or eight
thousand men on board, has reached Gaeta. Bourbon has left
Milan with a great army of half-starved and mutinous Spaniards.
And who accompanies him as his right hand and advisor with
the impressive title of Commissioner-General of the Imperial
troops? None other than Messer Girolamo Morone, scarcely a year
ago the champion of Italian unity and independence. After this
nothing can surprise us.

We have received news from Brescia that the roads which lead
down from the Alps are black with lansquenets, without money,
artillery, provisions or horses. What they need they steal on the
way. Giovanni de'Medici has been killed. Urbino, who has now
taken command, is a nonentity. Rome seems to be fermenting
with riots. Since the Colonna's infamous assault on the Vatican,
everything there is chaotic—prices are high, the plague is raging

and the Pope has invented some new taxes in order to pay the Emperor what he demands. His Holiness writes heartbreaking, desperate letters. He doesn't know which way to turn; for the first time he realizes the danger. But it's too late now, I can't give him any more advice. He wants to negotiate an armistice. Whatever he does, he should do it quickly.

Lannoy is advancing from Naples, and the Duke of Ferrara is helping the Germans to cross the Po. It's clear what kind of man he is when he deserts us at this moment. I can't do anything with the troops I have here if I don't get cooperation from Urbino. Every day I send express couriers to Mantua, every day I beg him, I order him to come here, but he won't lift a finger. I have his latest reply on the table in front of me: His Highness thinks it's better to stay there with his army and guard the Venetian territory in case the lansquenets should change their course and turn back. Turn back! Those people will never let anyone or anything deflect them as long as they are heading for the rich cities of Tuscany. If they're not opposed in time, they'll go on plundering and burning all the way to Táranto if that's necessary. It's not a question of right or wrong for them—it's only a question of booty.

Really, now there's only one solution left: we have to defend ourselves to the end any way that we can. But everywhere I look, all I see is confusion, halfheartedness, cowardice and hesitation. I'm tired. I wish I could throw it all away. But I've practiced self-control; any form of letting-go is impossible for me. So even now I'm able to keep up an attitude that prevents my entourage from becoming panic-stricken.

In spite of the imminent danger, Carnival is being celebrated here in Piacenza with more excitement than I've seen in years. I'd have been happy to have seen your *Mandragola* performed again so that I could laugh and forget everything for a while. I've never needed to do that as much as I do now. But it's the duty of the Lieutenant Governor to remain vigilant and hardheaded. Every night, after the usual mealtime hour, I've been sitting up with my maps and dispatches . . . the last vestige of hope I had has been killed by the shouting and drunken bawling which rises from the street. I wish I wasn't doomed by nature and circumstance to stay at my post until the bitter end. Then for the rest of my days I could settle down and operate a little shop selling festival goods.

Niccolò Machiavelli to Francesco Guicciardini

Excellency, when this message reaches you in Piacenza, I'll just
have left Florence on my way to your headquarters as envoy of
the Signoria. They have someone else in mind to take my place
as *proveditore* of the fortifications—Messer Michelangelo Buonarroti, the sculptor, an admirable person as you know.

I hope with all my heart that he'll succeed in bringing this
matter of fortifications to a quick, satisfactory conclusion. I've
had to struggle with constant difficulties: my building plans are
criticized, the citizens don't want to help with the work—the
fortifications still exist only on paper. Nobody has any money to
give and the Pope hasn't sent the support he promised. Don't ask
me how this could have happened; I wouldn't know how to answer
you. I'm coming to you now as the representative of a desperate
city where the people discuss the latest rumors, wringing their
hands and calling upon the saints, without realising that they
themselves must *do* something. You know better than anyone else
what will happen to Florence if that locust swarm of mercenaries
and adventurers descends on us. Without instant action, Florence—all of Tuscany—is lost.

What will become of us if even you waver, Francesco? I'm
ashamed that I ever dared to scold you, to criticize your ideas. I
was the helmsman on the shore, *you* had the hard job of piloting
the ship through the breakers. Now how can I make a stand if
you lose your courage? Let me hear from your own lips that it
isn't true, that you haven't given up all hope. I know perfectly
well that I'm a hothead, a fantasist. But if my presence, my ideas,
can still encourage you somehow, help to overcome your dis-
couragement, rouse your fighting spirit—then let me stay with
you through thick and thin, as secretary, messenger, fool, whatever you want. All my life I've steeped myself in politics. I've
examined all kinds of questions on paper, laid down lines of action
for war and peace: words, words, all most exalting for the man
who sits in his study, but worthless now when it's a question of
life or death.

I'm ready to repudiate all my work, my *Principles*, my *Discourse*,
my *History*, all of it, to destroy it in exchange for one thing: to

be able to act now that the situation is desperate. I can't express my feeling in theory or in literature any longer. Whatever I have, whatever I am, I want to offer up completely. I'll never put another word down on paper, never again.

I'm not a leader in any way. But I can talk. Send *me* to the Duke of Urbino. I'm writing you this so you can have a decision ready when I arrive at Piacenza. I swear I won't give Urbino any rest until he and his troops begin to move. I swear to you that I know how to accomplish this. If not, then I'll be your partner and we'll sell masks and false noses together.

Francesco Guicciardini to Niccolò Machiavelli

What's Urbino doing, what's he saying? The day before yesterday the Spaniards under Bourbon joined up with Frunsberg's lansquenets at Mortara. I've left Piacenza; I'm on the way to Bologna. I'll risk a siege there. Make Urbino understand that without him and his troops, it will be impossible for me to stop the Imperial armies.

He *must* break camp *at once*, immediately. I'm depending on you.

Niccolò Machiavelli to Francesco Guicciardini

Excellency, best friend. I received an urgent call to return to Florence. Meanwhile you'll have received my report that Urbino has promised to depart as quickly as possible. When I was leaving Casalmaggiore the day before yesterday it looked as though he was about to keep his promise.

Here at home everything is in a state of uproar. The Pope seems to have bought an armistice for eighty thousand ducats—Florence apparently must supply the lion's share of it. The Signoria has had the church plate melted down to provide cash in hand when the Imperials arrive before our walls. The people are prepared to make sacrifices out of their insane fear of the lansquenets which they wouldn't make to defend themselves. Now they're sending me to Rome to explore the question of money with the Pope. When it's a question of money, the organization leaves no stone unturned.

An armistice will give us time to prepare for a decisive trial of strength. This is the last chance. If it isn't taken, then all is lost. If I hadn't broken myself completely of the habit of praying, I'd fall on my knees and beg Heaven to make it come true that Urbino is on his way to Bologna. But experience has taught me that prayer is less efficacious than putting one's own shoulder to the wheel. As soon as I complete this mission, I'll try to convince the Signoria that they must send me again to your headquarters. Then you empower me to travel around Tuscany and the Romagna and hammer at the city governments, at the lords high and low: to arms, to arms—one Italy or *no* Italy!

Francesco Guicciardini to Niccolò Machiavelli

I'm entrenched here in Bologna, still waiting for Urbino. For three weeks, in the streaming rain, the Spanish and German armies have been camped in the fields near San Giovanni, close to the town, exhausted and demoralized. They've completely plundered the countryside far and wide along their route—there's no food to be found anywhere. Bourbon sent a herald to us at Bologna to demand provisions and free passage. But since I hadn't received any confirmation of the armistice, I refused both demands. That was the moment when Urbino should have attacked the Imperials from the rear. If we don't get any help here, all we can do is defend ourselves. What's Urbino doing? He promised to come and he doesn't do it! Is he crazy or more stupid than a mule or is there some plan behind his damn hesitation? I don't trust him any more.

The Spaniards and the German lansquenets have been mutinying and rioting every day since they heard that the Emperor and the Pope are negotiating an armistice. They're camped so close to the city walls that we can hear them shouting for bread and pay and the booty they were promised: they're threatening their commanders, they've plundered Bourbon's quarters and they've driven out the envoy from Rome like a dog. Frundsberg was trying to put down the rebellion—he's apparently had a stroke.

Now the camp is broken up, they're leaving. They're not going back to Lombardy—they're taking a circuitous route past Bologna, violating the conditions of the armistice and the Emperor's commands. Bourbon isn't doing this of his own free will, and that can mean only one thing: he can't control these hordes any longer. He has the choice either of being killed or of leading them wherever they want to go. From the Castello, I am watching them disappear into the mist . . . disorderly mobs of soldiers and riders and servants and their following of tramps and adventurers. They are starving; they feed on unripe olives from the trees. And they're in a hurry.

The last act has begun, Niccolò. Cato's Italy, and Scipio's, Dante's and Petrarch's Italy, is finished—the Italy of our youth. ... God knows it was careless and reckless in its wealth, but I mourn it now as a lost paradise.

Guicciardini and Machiavelli

Niccolò Machiavelli to Francesco Guicciardini

On the road. Rain, rain, a piercing wind, a new attack of my cursed stomach trouble which makes sitting on a horse into a martyrdom, worse than what I suffered on the rack in the dungeons of the Stinche. I thought then that I couldn't have hated the Medici more bitterly. But what's hatred, what's bitterness, compared with the feeling that chokes me with rage now that I have to watch this Pope, this Medici, limp back and forth between his advisors, not able to wage war or even to conclude a peace— and then sit counting his ducats in fright when he must know that there are twelve thousand heretical lansquenets on the march who've sworn to reduce the new Babylon of Rome to ashes, armistice or no armistice.

In Florence they're crying for protection. My wife and my children write me desperate letters from San Casciano. Every time they see the trees swaying in the wind, they think that the Spaniards are coming. But I can't go to them, not yet. I'll just keep on riding around with senseless letters and messages until I drop. A few weeks ago I endured everything—the mud, the cold, the rain which seemed to trickle into my bones—with joy, yes, with joy, Francesco, because I was convinced that my efforts could accomplish something. Now the doubt which is engulfing me is causing me a thousand times more suffering than this eternal bellyache. I don't believe any more in what I'm doing.

It is folly to go on fighting when the battle is already lost. I suppose you can admire the resolute man who perseveres even though he is prepared to accept the consequences of his actions, you can admire his courage because he's taken a course that isn't for wavering malcontents, or weaklings or blockheads. But what use really is courage when there is no way to attack or defend? Isn't it only irresponsible fools who talk about war but can't conduct it in a way that limits the possible sacrifices? I was a fool like that, I was an instigator.

Francesco, you're the only one who can understand what I've been going through to be forced to come to the decision that I'm writing here: we must conclude a peace at any price . . . humiliate ourselves, surrender ourselves, pay the barbarians whatever they want, to save the country from a bloodbath, from unequalled devastation.

There's no other way out now but negotiation—and don't leave it to the Pope and his clique of weathervanes who let Bourbon deceive them with their eyes wide open—but you must do it, Signor Guicciardini, because everyone knows that your word is your bond. Negotiation—before it's too late.

What could be more shameful for you than your recent helpless cringing before the Imperials? There's no shame in pleading for peace when you can't go on fighting. But to neglect doing whatever one can, one's utmost, to prevent a cruel slaughter of defenseless and mostly innocent people—to neglect that would be *more* than shameful, it would be criminal!

Command me as you think fit. I only have one desire now: that Italy may be spared a second Vandal atrocity. Let the Emperor be lord and master, let us just pay, pay. But don't let us have a repetition in town after town of what happened in Lombardy— a hell of murder, rape, torture, senseless destruction. . . . I'm sitting writing here in an inn on the road, in a bar room full of chickens busily scratching around and little children solemnly staring at me, and it seems to me that that idea—that degrading human terror *must* be avoided no matter what the cost—that idea is more worthwhile, more worthwhile, Francesco, than all the work I've done in my life, all my missions and diplomatic speeches, all the hundreds of pages of ideas and treatises and theories. Francesco, what have I been living for?

Francesco Guicciardini to Niccolò Machiavelli

Your demand for peace is as passionate and as detached from reality as your call for war two years ago.

Do you want negotiations? With whom? Bourbon doesn't negotiate. He can't. Even the desperate cat-and-mouse game he seems to be playing with the Pope is nothing but a desperate camouflage of his own impotence. There's only one will: the will of that army, that hydra with twenty-five thousand heads, which has already smelled its prey. . . .

I've received a secret letter from Messer Girolamo Morone, who is offering to mediate with the Emperor in exchange for cash. Well, Niccolò Machiavelli, my friend! In our great need, do we have to entrust ourselves to *this* negotiator? Nothing shows more clearly than that precise offer how hopeless our condition is. When the vultures circle, the end is near.

There are still two alternatives: flight or resistance to the death. The ultimate result will be the same. It's only a question of state of mind. The choice won't give much trouble to you or me.

Now that the Imperials seem to want to leave Florence until later, I'm moving with our men on the shortest possible route to Rome.

Farewell.

XVIII.

Michelangelo Buonarroti

He scarcely knew how many months had passed since his return to Florence. He had buried himself in his work like a mole in its burrow. He was blind and deaf to the outside world. When he had finally put his signature to the new contract with the Lords della Rovere in Rome, urged on by Pope Clement's fatherly nods and encouraging gestures, he had realized that he had irrevocably condemned himself to hard labor. He was prepared to be a slave, nothing but a slave, to toil doggedly at his task. He knew quite well that he would never feel free of guilt until that task was completed. But why wasn't he granted a period of grace to perform in peace what he considered to be his duty, to atone in peace for an ancient oversight? In a final word before the audience had ended, the Pope had pronounced judgment on him aloud:

"The tomb will be completed, my lords, that's now a fact. Our worthy artist here has just affirmed it in black and white. Now we hope that this disagreeable matter is settled . . ."—and, whispering so that only *he* could hear him: ". . . but in the meantime, don't forget the work on the Medici chapel; I'm counting on you holding to the contract that you signed with *me* too. . ."

Since then he was inwardly torn; next to that any other sorrow sank into nothingness. In his dreams, Julius's mausoleum rose up before him, swollen to enormous dimensions, a group of figures reaching into the clouds—Moses, Paul, Rachel and Leah, marble giants thrusting up through the earth itself, just as mountains are created. In the folds of their garments, colossal stone promontories, he attempted to climb to the top: an ant, a poor weak creature on trembling legs, higher, higher to where the personifications of Heaven and Earth supported the sarcophagus in which his tormentor slept—Julius, whose pride had done this to him! To glorify the power of the Conqueror-Pope more than ten years after his death, at the moment when papal authority was a mockery and the conquered territories shuddered at the prospect of a still more frightening enemy—that seemed to him worse than stupidity: it was a libel, a lie!

Back in Florence, he had destroyed the old design approved by Pope Julius himself. Away with the symbols of the vanquished provinces, of the seven arts, the seven virtues! He made a new sketch of the figures which had to support the tomb: shackled slaves, bowed under the burden of the stone colossus which threatened to crush them, the eightfold embodiment of his own state of mind. While he was freeing the figures from the marble, he felt their pain, their mute despair. He worked in blind rage, now on this statue, then on that one, as if it were his peace of mind which he must free from that oppressive stone. Moisture dripped continually from his red-rimmed eyes, bloodshot from lack of sleep and the irritation of fine grit; dust and dirt clogged all the pores of his skin; his hair clung in damp strands. He couldn't remember the last time he had taken his clothes off. He didn't allow himself time to eat or sleep. Leaning against a chest, his eyes fixed unmoving on the block he was working on, he took some bread, onions and wine, and when everything went black from exhaustion, he just dropped down somewhere, on a pile of sacks or on the bare floor among splinters and fragments.

Sometimes an uncontrollable longing for fresh air drove him outside. He walked about through the streets of Florence without knowing where he was or what was going on around him. He heard bells sounding, noticed the glow of the evening or morning sky, he felt cold or warm, he recognized the familiar outlines of certain buildings. Once he went deliberately to a spot outside the city walls in the direction of Fiesole, past San Miniato, assimilating the broad flowing lines of the landscape. His body, his hands, rested for a moment. But never and not here any rest for his thoughts. His body, his hands, slaves in the service of the slaves who must support Julius's tomb. . . .

His spirit took flight in visions of the work for which he now longed as for eternal bliss itself: the Medici monument in San Lorenzo. What he had not been able to find before he went to Rome, the meaning and thus the ultimate form of the composition, he saw now before him with supernatural clarity. An answer to the call which had reverberated within him for years: Adam, rise. Rise from life on the other side of the secret of death, to the eternal truth. Rise from that prison which is the body, rise from the power of inexorable fate, rise from the constraint of space and time, to the real life of the soul. Life on earth is a dream. After that, awake amazed in the day, in the lucidity of the world of ideas. Waking and dreaming, falling asleep and waking up,— mysterious state of the soul, corresponding to day and night and sunset and daybreak.

While he continued to chisel free the torsos of the bound slaves, the urge burned in him like a fever to give form to the new ideas. He felt that his burden had doubled. He no longer gave himself up to toil on the tomb. At his work, he had to contend with his most dangerous opponent, his own aversion to his task and the force in him which drove him to the creation of those other figures which would *not* symbolize his servitude, his carrying of a hated burden, but the only possible deliverance. He had put the words of Pope Clement—don't forget the Medici chapel—out of his thoughts so that he wouldn't be tempted, but now they couldn't be pushed aside any longer, he couldn't stop his ears against them. They were like the wind which fans the flames.

One day he threw down his tools, covered the unfinished torsos protruding from their marble blocks and went to the table which held the draft of the design for the chapel. He surrendered to ecstasy. He saw, coming to life under his hands, the figures he had dreamed about. For two or three whole days, he forgot all about his slaves. But then the inward struggle began again, the pain that couldn't be suppressed for long.

His desire to work was poisoned, his concentration was disturbed, by those stone bodies behind him and the invisible burden which they bore. He was tortured by thoughts of his unfinished work. Not to finish—that didn't mean just an incomplete piece of work—oh no, it meant he had failed those who had given him the commission, and that failure was symbolic of his inner world:

chaotic, not fully formed. And, too, he was more and more afraid that he wouldn't be able to make his inspiration visible, he wouldn't be able to make it tangible, before he kept that promise he had made years ago to complete Pope Julius's tomb to the last detail.

In the deserted workroom behind Santa Maria Novella, he kept talking to himself aloud. He hadn't tolerated any companions or assistants there since his return to Florence. The old woman who brought his food came and went without his noticing her. Finally, he couldn't go on. He collapsed and for twenty-four hours, he slept the sleep of exhaustion in mind and body. When he woke, he felt as though the ability to concentrate on his work was lost to him forever.

Some time during those days he received a summons to appear before the Signoria. With difficulty he pulled himself out of his mood of immobilized brooding. He washed and dressed himself carefully and reported to the Palace at the appointed hour. Members of the Council were meeting there with the Committee of Five which had the responsibility for the upkeep and fortification of the city. Notable for his absence was Niccolò Macchiavelli, who had recently been named *proveditore* of the bastions. To his stunned amazement, after some introductory talk, they offered *him* the post. Messer Niccolò had received another commission.

Walls, fortifications. He shrugged in silence and stared over the heads of the Council members at the blood-red lilies of Florence on a banner hanging on the wall. A new task for him which would take up his time day and night when he didn't have an hour to spare! Immerse himself in architectonics and military questions *now*, when all he could think about was the riddle which dominated the life and death of people on the earth! Those arguments should settle the matter, but he could advance other objections: time was pressing . . . in face of the danger, old walls were better than new walls still under construction . . . besides, he knew that the post of *proveditore* would be a long martyrdom because of a dearth of workers and money . . .

While the members of the Council and the Committee assailed

him with proposals and urgent requests, he sat still, his eyes closed, the fingers of his left hand spread against his cheek. From time to time he nodded, to indicate that he understood what they meant. Finally he sighed, stood up and asked for time to think it over.

When he walked outside, across the square, he looked up involuntarily as usual at his David, which had been standing here now for twenty years. His first sensation was one of pleasure at the harmonious lines of that great stone body. This time he couldn't walk on. For the first time in a long while, he realized that for him, for the city, this David had once meant more than the perfectly sculptured statue of a young man: strength, courage, noble indignation at injustice and violence . . . the symbol of the brave people of the Republic of Florence . . . He remembered how, during the revolution, many had regarded the statue as their visible protest against the tyranny of the Medici. David, defender of freedom.

He twisted his lips as if he had a bitter taste in his mouth. Suddenly, the belligerence of the young colossus with his sling seemed to him to be incredibly naïve. David belonged to a world without shadows, where everything stood sharply outlined and brightly lighted in classical equilibrium. Had the ancients in their golden age really known a world like that? This Florence, this Italy, needed a more complicated kind of heroism.

He turned back. On the other side of the entrance to the Signoria Palace stood an empty pedestal. Since he had come back to Rome, he had avoided the square so that he wouldn't be plagued by feelings of resentment and humiliation which were indissolubly connected for him with that place opposite David. When he had completed that statue, the city administration had asked him to do a Hercules as a counter piece. He had not brought it farther than a rough draft. How could he find time in those years of papal commissions to begin work on the Hercules? It seemed to him to go without saying that Florence would set that task aside for him, if only out of aesthetic considerations. The design stayed alive in him, it was his spiritual possession, a part of himself. Just as David personified the struggle against external violence, so Hercules represented for him the fight against the enemy which is a part of everyone. These two giants on either side of the gate through which the rulers of Florence entered their council building, would form a unit: internal and external vigilance.

As recently as '25, before he left for Rome, the Signoria (to dispel rumors that someone else would be given the commission) assured him that only *he* would ever be entrusted with its execution. What he had often heard but hadn't believed during his first days in the Vatican, turned out to be true. Pope Clement had assigned Bandinelli, one of the court sculptors, to provide a Hercules.

He remembered the humiliating audience as if it had happened yesterday. When his vehement protest was stopped dead—"You have enough work with the tomb in the Medici chapel, my friend, and we've been waiting for the Hercules for twenty years"—he had offered to create the statue for nothing if he could only be given the time and the opportunity. The Pope had smiled and shrugged. Bandinelli received the commission.

The thought of Bandinelli recalled once more those weeks in Rome. He had felt like a prisoner in the Vatican. There too he was always confronted by unfinished work. In the Sistine Chapel, he was tormented by the conviction that a counterweight of some sort was needed for the painting which seemed to roll across the ceiling, to drift like clouds or undulate like waves on the sea. He had not yet found the key to what he wanted to portray there. He would not go into the chapel any more. Each time anew the sensation of impotence, the restlessness from which he could find no release in shaping his art. . . .

He roamed around the galleries, in search of himself. He didn't notice the mockers, the slanderers, the inquisitive. He spoke aloud to himself as he customarily did when he was alone, reviled himself as worthless because he could never seem to exist anywhere without self-torment. Why couldn't he stop this struggle to tie himself to a vision that was beyond his strength? Wasn't it a delusion, that belief of his that he had been singled out to paint what had never yet been depicted, man's agonizing journey between beast and God? Standing in the square in the cold wind which swept down on Florence from the hills, he thought he saw, on the bare pedestal across from David, his own Hercules, wrestling—as in the design—with the giant Antaeus: two bodies entwined in a struggle that will never come to an end, symbol of the duality of the human spirit.

In the days following his visit to the Signoria, he could not get back to work. Impotent and irresolute, he went again and again into the city, which seemed real to him for the first time since his return: a place seething with unrest, full of feverish, agitated life. He saw the long procession of refugees from the territories in Lombardy ravaged by the Spaniards, moving through the streets: farmers and citizens from small towns, with their families and as much of their goods and chattels as they could take with them on foot, on horseback, in oxcarts.

From a leaden sky, rain and snow gusted over Florence. In the Cathedral, in San Lorenzo, San Giorgio, Santa Trinita and in all the churches and chapels which he walked into, the people were thickly packed together, kneeling in prayer. He heard sobbing and wailing and supplications for mercy; he was brought back in time thirty years when in these same places Fra Girolamo Savonarola cried from the pulpit: "Repent, the hour of judgment is approaching, do penance, great catastrophes will overwhelm you. . . ."

Now as then an ominous ferment as if the destruction of the world were approaching. While he stood in the twilit nave of the Cathedral, staring at the candleglow on the distant altar, the sensation came over him that all those who were with him here praying really would witness the destruction of the world. A world of careless enjoyment of beauty, of human pride and self-satisfaction, of doubt and mockery, a world of ironic indulgence of cowardice—one's own and others'—lies and opportunism. That world was at the point of bursting like an overripe fruit. Was that the disaster which Savonarola had foreseen? Was a new world evolving, with new standards, new convictions, a new awareness of life? A world where the meaning of human existence, the inner struggle for grace, would no longer be denied, concealed, disguised, but would be passionately affirmed and transformed into art. . . .

He hurried through the center of Florence as though he were preparing to leave it. It was on this pavement, under these very arches, that the footsteps had resounded of those whom he had revered in his youth—those statesmen, philosophers and artists who had made the city great. Their shadows had moved across these walls; he touched the cold stone. The colors had been richer then, the light had been brighter. The glow of youth and joy and the freshness of spring had illuminated everything. Under the cypresses and pomegranate trees in a park, or at festively covered tables in some palace hall, listening to speeches and discussions about the divine Eros and his all-pervasive power, he had believed that there was nothing in existence that was more exalted than this wisdom, and that this world in which he and his companions lived would last forever.

Now he sought in vain for a last reflection of that lost world, that Florence of his youth. He remembered the words and melody of a song written by Lorenzo the Magnificent: ". . . enjoy youth and beauty, for no one knows what tomorrow will bring. . . ."

While the wind blew the mist into his face, he looked up at the towers and roofs against the great sky. The outlines remained the same—so how could the picture have changed so irrevocably?

A similar feeling had caught him by surprise in Rome, but there it had not touched his heart.

Among packed crowds of shouting, gesticulating people—word was out that the German lansquenets had crossed the Po—he made his way quickly back to his workroom.

The sight of the figures of the slaves, of the two statues, only very partially completed, of the two Medici dukes, of the papers with sketches of the figures of the night, the day, the morning and the evening dusk, took away the last vestiges of his self-confidence. He ran his hand over the marble in which his dreams were sleeping, that lay stretched like a hard white shroud over barely defined forms. While he leaned his forehead against the cold stone, it seemed to him that the task which he had set himself was directed by its nature toward the world which was about to come into being. He would never be able to complete the work if he wasn't ready, wasn't able to abandon a part of himself to annihilation. He too awaited the crucible. He too must be born again.

XIX.

Giovanni Borgia

1527

I 'm still alive. When I trouble to stand up and look out a window, I see piles of rubble overgrown with weeds, the ruins of devastated burned-out houses . . . like islands between churches and palaces with defaced, fire-blackened walls. There's a persistent stink of putrefaction. The ground must be saturated with blood. Rome is silent.

I limp. I've lost an eye. My health is ruined. I can scarcely call myself a man; I'm not fit to be a soldier any more. Pierluigi Farnese and the Colonna . . . those of them who were spared . . . are still with the Emperor's armies. They're proceeding to Naples, to Lombardy, through the Romagna—without me. But I'm still alive.

I have—presumably on Cardinal Pompeo's recommendation—been given a post in the secretariat of Cardinal Alessandro Farnese. I'm living in his palace which has suffered only slight damage. I'm left in peace here.

I almost never venture outside the gates. For me Rome is a panorama of decay and devastation which I can look down on from my window on an upper floor. It's enough for me to travel several times a day, leaning on my crutch, between my bedchamber and the apartment where I now sit writing. Always writing, writing. I can still hold a pen.

I want to record what I've been through. Quick, quick, before it slips away. There are days when I can't remember it all Then again, suddenly, everything that happened flashes before me as quick as lightning, in a series of pictures. I must hold on to that, even if it's only to be able to say later: that was the turning-point, after that everything changed.

❦

As soon as the first Spaniards pushed their way into the city through a breach in the gate of San Spirito, the defenders deserted the walls and raced away as fast as they could go, shouting, "The enemy is here! Save yourselves if you can!" We of the Colonna party were just at the point of rushing out when the stampede passed by us—the Pope's captain Renzo da Ceri with his gang of cowards in front, and behind them a crazy excited crowd of men, women and children, burdened and loaded down with whatever they grabbed up in their haste. People were pouring out of every building to swell the stream. None of us had time to go back into the courtyard. I was sucked, horse and all, into the mob sweeping toward the Castel Sant'Angelo. The crush in front of the citadel defied description. Soldiers, nobles, courtiers, prelates, peddlers and shopkeepers, hundreds of women too, fought side by side with the lowest people from Trastevere and Ripa for their life's salvation: a chance to enter the Castel gates.

My horse was maddened with terror; when it tried to rear, it was seized by three or four fellows at once and slaughtered, after they had dragged me backwards out of the saddle. All this accompanied by the screaming of the people who were pushed up against us on all sides by the pressure of the mob and who were afraid of being hit by the convulsive movements of the horse. They restrained me forcibly, but by then I wasn't thinking about my mount, I was fighting desperately just to keep on my feet, because anyone who fell was immediately trampled to death. I wasn't even a yard away from the gate when the iron portcullis fell down with a rumbling crash. From behind the bars someone cried out to us over the shrieks of the wounded that there were more than three thousand people in the castle; if any more came in, the walls would burst.

The mass of people didn't fall back a hair's breadth—that was impossible in any case—but stayed under the walls screaming and wailing. That supplication for admission broke into curses and raving when a couple of cardinals and other high lords who happened accidentally to be in the forefront of the crowd, were hoisted up in baskets and on rope ladders. I saw the Datary Giberti and Monsignore Schomberg high up against the wall dangling and swaying next to each other like two fat purple fish on a line. I couldn't move or turn. I hung, gasping for breath, among those desperate people who were begging to be hoisted up too or who were spewing out curses at the nobles and prelates who had bought themselves asylum in the nick of time in the Castel Sant'Angelo. Close to me a man went mad. He rolled his eyes and foamed at the mouth but was instantly pushed down. He vanished as if he had fallen into a whirlpool. I shouted, "Disperse! Why don't we defend Trastevere? Close off the bridges!" but I fell silent when I saw the wild suspicious looks of those around me—I didn't want to share the lunatic's fate.

All at once the crowd began to move; screams rose out of the tumult and confusion. A strong suction commenced pulling toward the opposite direction. Everyone who had fled headlong toward the Castel now had to go over the bridges, back into the city. Hundreds plunged into the water and swam to the other side. There was no sense in resisting. This time too I had to let myself be dragged along, past the convents and the palaces of the Spanish-sympathizing nobility. Anyone who saw the chance pushed or climbed his way inside the buildings, hoping for safety there with the nuns or under the colors of the Emperor. I tried to get into the Palazzo Colonna but the gate was forced shut before I was able to free myself from that wild wriggling ant heap.

I no longer knew where I was when I heard the first cries: "*Viva Spagna! Amazza, amazza*, kill them!" There they came in closed ranks over the whole breadth of the street, marching in a cloud of dust, left and right, mowing down whatever they found in their path. Those who went to meet them with their hands above their heads or crawling on their knees in supplication—no mercy. Among the desperate shrieking people there was no one who thought of selling his life dearly. To offer resistance by oneself was completely senseless. I succeeded in pushing my way into a narrow alley, where I climbed up a wall and ran stooped over as fast as I could across the roofs.

I remember those hours as a nightmare without end. The sun burned in a cloudless sky. It was the sixth of May in the forenoon.

In the glaring light I shoved myself on my stomach across roofs
and terraces, while from the streets below me rose bloodcurdling,
marrow-piercing screams. I have no words to describe what I
heard and saw while I hung over the cornices of roofs, hid behind
balustrades and chimney stacks. All my life I had believed in the
discipline and control of the Spanish. The last remains of my self-
respect rested in that belief. Now I know only one thing: in Hell
I hope to find devils, not Spaniards.

During the advance of the Imperial troops on Rome, the Colonna had planned to join the Spaniards as soon as they entered
the city. It was taken for granted that there would be looting. But
no one had any notion that that entry would degenerate into a
bestial bloodbath. I know that soldiers are cruel. In Navarre and
Lombardy and at the Battle of Pavia I have certainly experienced
that. But never anything that can even remotely be compared to
that lust for murder, torture, rape. Among the Spaniards, I saw
officers and men from the papal army of occupation and the
Colonna party. I realized that they had joined the Imperials to
avoid being struck down themselves, but I did not understand
how they could join in the killing with equal frenzy.

I crept over the roofs, leaped across the narrow deep gaps over
alleys, to the heart of the city, still hoping to find a group offering
resistance. With the death cries of women and children ringing
in my ears, I had only one desire: to go for the murderers. In the
piazza di Gesu, armed citizens had gathered together from various quarters of the city—not, as I first assumed, to fight to the
bitter end, but to throw their weapons in a heap and hold up
white flags. From one side Spaniards advanced upon them; from
the other, German lansquenets. Before the mass slaughter began,
I fled once more over the rooftops. If I had known then what
awaited me, I would have tried to accomplish the impossible and
get out of the city.

I stayed hidden until sunset. When I heard that the signal for
assembly was being sounded in the Campo di Fiore and the piazza
Navona, and that soldiers were moving with drum-rolls toward
these points, I assumed that order had been restored and that the
senseless slaughter was over. I went to the piazza Navona and
found a group of Colonna men there lined up behind the Spanish
ranks. They stank of blood, they were spattered with blood from

head to foot, like butchers. I heard then that there were forty thousand Imperials in the city—Spaniards, Germans, troops of the Colonna and the Gonzaga, and a veritable army of scum which had built up along the way.

We stood there in the square all evening in order, it was said, to be prepared for a possible counterattack. The sky was red from the fires in the Leonina quarter. The Spaniards were impatient. Their commanders rode back and forth before the ranks, but couldn't keep order. What I saw standing there in the torchlight were certainly not the pick of Spanish foot soldiers, but a hastily recruited batch: thick-set, sinewy fellows, brown as Moors or gypsies, filthy, savage and arrogant. Toward midnight, they flung down their standards and heavy weapons, bawling at the tops of their voices that they had had enough and streaming off in all directions to go back to the city in search of plunder. I had thought that we of the Colonna, now that no general orders could be expected for the time being, would return to the palace, where they must be in serious need of armed men. But with a few exceptions, they all joined the plunderers. At that moment this could still throw me into a rage. From the Campo di Fiore came the lansquenets, who had also broken loose.

I tried to find my way through streets filled with the deafening roar of splintering wood, falling stones, screaming and yelling, where flames shot out of windows and ruddy smoking torches swayed and danced above the tangled grubbing horde. Drunken soldiers—casks of wine were being rolled out of houses everywhere—bodies and smashed furniture blocked passage. In order to avoid attracting attention, which would have meant certain death, I could think of nothing better to do than to go along from house to house in a zigzag movement with a bunch of looters crying *Spagna! Spagna!* while I held my sword in one hand, and in the other a gold object—I don't remember any longer what it was—which I had hastily picked up from the ground.

Here my memory begins to fail me. The sequence of events after that is no longer clear in my mind. I don't know if I pushed my way into ten, twenty or a thousand houses, churches and chapels. Looking back, it seems to me, as in a nightmare, as if it were always the same occupant who was knocked down and beaten to death on the same threshold, as if I had to listen to the same

pleas, shrieks and death-rattles again and again and again and
yet again. Over the same bodies, we burst incessantly into the
same house, always kicked open the same door, tore down the
same curtain, smashed the same mirror to splinters, everywhere
poured the same gold out of treasure chests and jars. After that,
an infinite repetition: the same panting and cursing struggle for
a handful of ducats. In most of the churches, the lansquenets had
been there before us. I don't know any longer how often—that
wading through blood and fragments of statues and windows,
that stepping over the bodies of priests and people who had come
there seeking refuge in vain, to the smashed, defiled, pillaged
altar.

It must have lasted for a day and a night. I remember that I
saw the sun rise and set again. The image of the town had been
altered so greatly through fires and devastation that I didn't know
where I was. Troops of lansquenets moved about with all the
whores in Rome, dead drunk, singing and shouting, black from
gunpowder smoke, draped with plundered finery, jewels twisted
into their hair and beards, glittering chasubles around their
shoulders. In both hands they carried their caps, filled to the brim
with gold. The Spaniards had their booty tied into bundles made
from cloaks and flags, and hanging on their backs: they always
kept their hands free, their eyes and teeth flashed like their knives,
they were covered to their groins with clotted blood.

Bugle calls and drumrolls sounded here and there in the city.
Perhaps the commanders thought that the soldiers had had their
fill of plunder. The worst hadn't yet begun.

I saw everything, heard everything. It seems absurd to me now
that I have been a witness to these things, and still live.

I wandered that night like a madman through the hell that was
Rome. The burning. The stink of the corpses of people and animals. The sounds coming from the houses that had been broken
into. The long rows of soldiers, like beaters driving game by torchlight, scouring the wastes of Palatinus and Campo Vaccino for
women who had hidden among the ruins. Echoes rose up from
underground holes and passages. At daybreak grotesque processions: guarded by shouting lansquenets decked out in purple
and vestments: prominent cardinals and bishops, manhandled,
bound, on asses, in open coffins, dragged forward by the feet, or

hanging head down between sticks like shot game. On street corners and in squares, over still-smoldering fires, on stakes and in chains: naked, mutilated bodies. I recognized among them supporters of the Colonna. That whole day without pause, gorging and orgies and dice-throwing in the open air with torture of the richest and most distinguished prisoners as amusement at the banquet. Always, everywhere, the same dialogue between tormentors and victims:

"Your money, your money, tell where you've hidden your treasure!"

"Mercy, have pity, I've given up everything, it's all been taken from me. . ."

"Where is it hidden, buried, who's keeping it?"

"God in Heaven is my witness, I don't have a *soldo* left, believe me, spare me, mercy!"

Anyone who was finally released tried, groaning, to creep away; he was stopped at another table and the game began anew.

As long as the sun was shining, I stayed in the vicinity of large gatherings. They must have taken my unsteadiness and distracted mumbling for drunkenness. I didn't stand out in the midst of that nameless mob from every region. Being with them was my salvation. I was with the crude pack who went around all the marketplaces and squares to see the nuns and priests dressed as women being sold at auction to the brothels. I was with the troop of Spaniards who, obsessed by the idea that valuables must still lie hidden in graves, moved from church to church, lifting up the tombstones to grub about in the darkness beneath. I was with the Germans who belched forth blasphemies, marching with relics and hosts stuck on their lances, to the Vatican—now transformed into a gigantic barracks—to have their brother Martin Luther declared pope. I was with the baggage servants who had to fit up the Sistine Chapel as a stable for their leaders' horses; since they had no hay or straw they covered the floor with torn pages from the papal manuscript collection. Later I was with the bands who wanted to smoke out the strongly defended palaces, or blow them up. I saw the Spaniards and Germans forcing their countrymen to deliver citizen refugees to them by the hundreds. Spanish prelates were murdered by the Germans; the Spaniards tortured and robbed German bankers and merchants. Toward evening, the bacchanals broke out anew, while they fought savagely among themselves for possession of the booty.

I wanted to go to the Tiber in the dark to try to get out of the city by swimming across. Once again a haunted journey through a maze of streets and alleys full of corpses. Was there really still the sound of moaning everywhere, or did I imagine it in my feverish state? A few times I entered a ruined house because of the plaintive cries I thought I heard, but I found nothing except debris and bodies and scurrying rats. Those districts were a city of the dead, deserted because there was nothing left to steal. Perhaps there were others like me, hiding there. Perhaps they were waiting in deadly fear in an air hole or behind a wall, until my footsteps had died away.

On the main roads which led to the Ponte Sisto and on the wharves along the Tiber, Lannoy's Spanish and Neapolitan companies were holding their saturnalia within sight of the Castel Sant'Angelo, but out of range of the cannonballs which the papal garrison fired off from time to time. Above the booming of the guns could be heard the screams and laughter of the army whores, and the wailing of the prisoners who were being tortured there, as they were everywhere in the city, to get ransom. I walked through the burned-out slums running parallel with the Tiber, in the hope of finding a point somewhere beyond Trastevere where I would be able to reach the river without being noticed. When I saw a light approaching and heard the clatter of hooves, I hid.

Slowly a mule came past, with two riders: a snoring lansquenet holding a woman in his arms. The woman was more than half naked. She had a bishop's mitre on her head and a burning taper in her hand. She was staring at the flame with fixed, empty eyes. I saw that she was Tullia d'Aragona. She remained sitting hunched over when I pushed the drunken fellow off the mule. I spoke to her, and touched her, but she didn't recognize me. I don't believe that she even understood what I was saying. Was she drunk or numb or had she lost her senses? I didn't know. For safety's sake, I had to put out the candle. For the first time she made a sound and moved weakly. I soothed her, begged her to be quiet, assured her that we would escape, although I knew that it was hopeless, that my words were not reaching her and that I couldn't hope to think about escaping with her. I led the mule forward by the bridle. I wanted to try to reach the wastes of the Palatinus without being seen, so that I could hide there with Tullia in the ruins called Caligula's Palace.

I remembered that she had once offered almost daily to forsake everything to go with me wherever I went, even if it were to encounter only sickness, poverty, death. What I had then rejected because her devotion oppressed me, seemed to me—there in that dark alley, under the night sky glowing red from the fires—an undeserved blessing. I realized that I had never possessed anything in the world so completely as I did that helpless creature on the mule. I, who had never been able to discover any meaning or purpose in my life, recognized both while I walked silently beside her.

Then at a crossroads, that band of Spaniards. They became enraged because I wouldn't hand Tullia over. I fought like one possessed, I wanted to fight to the death. But they overwhelmed me and dragged me away. I screamed her name. The words which I had never said to her, which I can never say any more, choked me. She still sat motionless on the mule and let herself be carried away in a different direction. She didn't even look back.

۞

Oh God, the rest. A deep vault, a torture chamber like the vision of a mad executioner, full of hanging, racked, spectral figures. Those who had brought me there took me—bitter irony of fate—for a rich and distinguished man. I said in Spanish that they had better kill me at once because any torture would be a waste of time. They didn't believe me. They took my Borgia dagger. They tried every possible means to wring information from me about where I had hidden my treasure and who my powerful kinsmen and connections were.

I have always had a strong body, a robust constitution. I must have suffered for a long time before they destroyed that. I don't know how many centuries it lasted before they untied me and poured water over me. I could no longer see, couldn't move. Later I found myself, dizzy from weakness and pain, outside somewhere in the heat of the sun. I was given some food. After that I toppled forward and slept. When I came to myself, I could see again with the one eye that was left to me. I saw that I was in a courtyard with a number of other filthy men, all covered with wounds.

Spanish soldiers gave us more food and then drove us through an unrecognizable Rome, through streets full of loathesome putrefaction, black scorched houses—no other living creatures besides soldiers and ragged, begging ghosts—over the Tiber to the walls of the Castel Sant'Angelo. There, like convicts sentenced to hard labor, we had to throw up ramparts for the approaching Imperial assault on the fortress, where the Pope was still entrenched. We were continually fired upon. In self-defense we threw the earth up as rapidly as possible. The Spaniards stayed out of range in the Borgo.

When the plan for the siege was abandoned because the Pope was ready to negotiate, we were forced to carry the bodies, now in an extreme state of decomposition, out of the city and fling them into the Tiber or bury them outside the gates. We had to crawl through the *cloacae* to see if gold were hidden there anywhere. In my half-stupefied condition, I did what I was told to do. The pain in my empty eye socket kept me from thinking. But one day someone pointed out to me the Imperial spokesman who was on his way to the Castel Sant'Angelo to begin discussions with the Pope on the conditions of his release. Surrounded by armed men, he rode past, the most powerful man in Rome, perhaps in all of Italy then: Messer Girolamo Morone.

When I saw him, I realized where I was and what I was doing. That same night I fled with a couple of my companions in misery. We found shelter in the mountains with farmers on one of the Colonna estates.

❧

For everything that happened, I feel guilty, guilty. The Borgia in me, the Spaniard in me, the servant in me—guilty. Whatever I, consciously or unconsciously, had in me of greed, cruelty and envy: guilty.

I have resigned myself to the fact that I must atone.

❧

Giovanni Maria Varano is dead. Not fallen in battle, but succumbed in his bed, a few weeks after he had fitted up the Castle of Camerino as a sort of pesthouse for the populace. His child is underage. It seems that there are many rivals in the field who want to possess the dukedom.

Cardinal Farnese himself told me these things. He knows that I once had an interest in the destiny of Camerino. In fact, he knows still more about me. He seldom speaks openly about me or my past. But I can tell in a number of little ways that he is thoroughly well-informed. He has me summoned to him often. He is sixty years old, a thin old man with a sly face, sharp dark eyes, the eyes of that sister of his, Pierluigi's eyes. The Petticoat Cardinal. No name for him could be less fitting. Even without the support of the beautiful Giulia, he would have become what he is: legate of Rome, and since Giberti has fallen from favor, the Pope's confidant. It's said that he is a clever diplomat and that he will certainly receive the tiara after Pope Clement's death. No one has nearly as much influence on the court of Rome as he.

Why is he being so affable to me? There's no trace of condescension or hypocrisy in his attitude. What reasons can he have to give such consideration and support to someone like me, inferior to him in every conceivable way? He seems to be fond of me. God knows why. I'm not pleasant company. When I entered his service, he had his own physician tend to me as carefully as if I were a guest or a blood relative. I enjoy every freedom in his palace. I'm treated with respect.

There was a certain alert tension in his look when he told me about Varano's death. I told him that for a long time it had been a matter of complete indifference to me who held Camerino and who did not.

❦

The Emperor is coming to Italy to receive the crown of the realm in Bologna. Cardinal Farnese told me this. He added with emphasis that the Emperor was going to hold audiences here and provide opportunities for the presentation of petitions.

Suddenly Farnese said that I should sit down, a sign of unusual familiarity. Without looking at me, he advised me to plead for my rights to Camerino before the Emperor. He gave me no opportunity to object. I must consult the documents from the time of Pope Alexander in which I was named Duke of Camerino. He would engage the most capable lawyers in Rome to sort the matter out and put it in writing.

When I refused, his head jerked up. For the first time I saw a flash of anger in those eyes.

"Come, there are certainly bulls, aren't there?" he said impatiently. "Write to Ferrara; Duke Alfonso will certainly send them."

He knows so much, why shouldn't he know about the existence of those damned bulls?

He leaned toward me. "Write now, today. I'll send a special courier."

I said that I didn't expect any good to come from such an attempt. The Emperor wouldn't deprive Varano's daughter of her dukedom in favor of a wreck like me. I could no longer beget heirs, I was no longer capable of governing a property like Camerino properly or of defending it if the need arose. My claims were questionable. I had no relatives, no supporters. I didn't possess one *soldo*.

Again the fierce black look.

"That will be arranged. Everything will be fixed. That Caterina Cibo can't hold her own in Camerino in the long run. Everyone knows that, even she knows it. Varano and she stripped themselves out of pure charity. She would undoubtedly be glad to receive a princely dowry for her daughter. If not willingly, then by other means. Oh, no force—that's not necessary. Litigation, litigation. Bring a lawsuit before the Rota; this is a matter for the papal law court. What do you have to fear with me behind you?"

Why does he want to dazzle me? This plan is senseless. With all his money and influence, he can't make me into what I've never been. I can't get to sleep tonight. I don't know whether I have to thank him or to curse him because now when I have no prospects he has brought an element of unrest into my life again. What good does this hope do me? What use can I make of the chance he's offering me? His support comes too late for me. It's not only my body that's sick and impotent. That vague darkness which has tormented me all my life, that canker in my mind—I recognize it now for what it is: an inheritance of guilt and shame and feelings of unworthiness. With that feeling inside me, I shall always doubt my rights to anything no matter what. It's indissolubly bound up with my birth. Cardinal Farnese can no more free me from that feeling than he can change my birth. Even with a dukedom, I can't be Pierluigi's equal.

Why does he want to do so much for me? I don't believe that his own interests are prompting this offer. If he wants power over Camerino, he would do better to betroth one of his sons to Varano's daughter. I don't understand his motives. I take it that for this matter too I must revisit the past. There's no escape. I'm always forced to that damned investigation that can only add to my burden. I must dig, dig, in order to go on living.

XX.

Vittoria Colonna

1 5 3 4

S he lived with a small retinue of women in a few rooms in the convent of San Silvestro in Capite. She received no one and seldom came to Rome. When the visit of Caterina Cibo was announced, her first thought was: I don't want to see her, her least of all. Later she was ashamed of that cowardice. She sent a messenger with a word of welcome to the Duchess of Camerino, who was staying with relatives in the city.

Caterina came on a mule, surrounded by a handful of shabby servants. She wore a threadbare, shrunken robe of state; her large feet protruded from beneath it. Her face was as brown and weatherbeaten as a farmer's or a soldier's. She took long strides, her footsteps thundered in the loggia of the convent. She looked slovenly and pugnacious.

"You haven't changed," she said when Vittoria had greeted her. "I have, as you see. That's from a life of struggle and constant vigilance. A man carries that well, a woman becomes a scarecrow. Not that I care about externals. What does physical privation matter? I'm not afraid of poverty or filth or discomfort. I know there are probably worse things awaiting me than a few sieges, a famine and a plague. I'm prepared one day to walk the streets and beg, for the sake of my convictions. I ask nothing better than to be tested in this way. These last years have been a school for me: I know now what I can bear. I know too that one can maintain one's peace of mind despite reverses and injustice, if only one believes."

Vittoria took her to a little inner court where an awning was opened out against the sun. Damaged columns, patches of smashed pavement—reminders still of the destruction and plundering of seven years ago.

"Only wish me luck. That Borgia—you know him too well, didn't you have him in your service for a while?—has lost his ridiculous lawsuit. I didn't doubt that outcome for a moment, even though he had the Emperor's favor and the Farnese's gold behind him. He didn't have a single piece of evidence, even apart from the fact that his claims are nothing next to the Varano's. The bulls they wanted to shock me with, where he's named with titles and everything, are forgeries executed at the time in Pope Leo's Chancellery on instructions from Farnese for that Lucrezia, the Duchess of Ferrara. My lawyers sorted that out. That has silenced him for good, I think. But my troubles are only beginning. Farnese will never forgive me for exposing his bungling before the Rota. I'm the first one he'll strike at when he becomes pope. Before that happens, I must make Camerino safe. I'm going to marry my Giulia off to Urbino's son; that's one of the reasons I've come to Rome now. I want to talk with His Holiness before his condition deteriorates to the point that he no longer knows what he's saying or doing."

She leaned forward and grasped Vittoria's right hand in her own hard dry ones. Her eyes began to glitter with zeal, a look that Vittoria remembered well.

"Listen, I need your help. I can manage Giulia's marriage myself; besides, His Holiness is well-disposed toward Urbino, he won't put any stumbling-blocks in my path—on the contrary. But there's still something else. You don't live so immersed in meditation here that you don't know that the Capuchins were driven out of Rome. Naturally you know that. Driven out like dogs on the most slanderous accusations. Farnese's behind that too, believe me. He's worked against the Order from the beginning. He has even dared to mention the word heresy. It speaks volumes that that word should come from him. You know how he used to live and, God knows, probably still lives. I've always considered him the personification of everything which is rotten and corrupt in the Curia. All the mockery and slander of our *Compagnia* come from his closest circle. Listen to me: when Farnese is pope, he will reform the Church in his own way, if it's only to dissolve the

Compagnia and accuse the Capuchins of heresy. That has nothing to do with faith, it's pure politics. I can tell you still more. . . He himself favors an Order, a handful of French and Spanish priests who preach in the streets near Venice. They seem to have an especially zealous leader, a certain Loyola, a Spaniard. It's possible that they do good work. But why do they let themselves be used by Farnese? They're telling people that we in the *Campagnia* and the Capuchins are infected with the German heresy. . . My God, there isn't a nobler, more pious man than Fra Bernardo, the head of the Order. It's a comfort to the soul to hear him speak, about how we must seek God out of our own will. . . If I didn't have Giulia and the responsibility for Camerino, I would follow him from city to city, just to hear him, to gain courage and strength from him. . ."

"Where is Fra Matteo, your old friend?" Vittoria asked, with a smile. Caterina shook her head impatiently, like one speaking with a dull child.

"Fra Matteo has been dead for more than six years now, I wrote you that. Did you forget? Oh yes, you were in Ischia then, you were busy with other things. I haven't read your poetry about your husband; I don't read anything any more except the Word of God and the Letters of the Apostles. You must forgive me for being out of touch. . . But I've heard you praised to the skies by people who understand such things better than I do. Listen now . . . Fra Bernardo is a prophet, a preacher, a man of God like no other. He possesses the truth and he knows how to open the eyes of the sinners and the indifferent. . ."

"You said that you needed my help?"

"No, I'm not straying from the subject. It's all connected with Fra Bernardo and the Order. At this moment they're living like exiles outside the city walls in San Lorenzo. If something isn't done, greater humiliation may well be in store for them. They have many followers among the very poorest, the lame, the paralyzed and the sick. But what can the poor things do but lament or keep their mouths shut? Help must come from the Vatican. And now that the Pope's condition is growing noticeably worse, no soul dares displease Farnese.

"There's still no place in Rome for truth, righteousness, charity. Rome has learned nothing, nothing. . . The same immoral ambitious clique in the Curia as before '27. . . Oh, so long as there were heaps of rubble to be cleared away, dead to be buried, the sick to care for, the afflicted to be comforted, plague, suffering, hunger—the Capuchins were welcome. Now that no one needs them any more—except beggars and the banished—now that their presence reminds people of things they want to forget, they would like them to go up in smoke. But they're not going to go up in smoke, they follow in the footsteps of Christ, and that's why they've been driven out. Don't you see that we must do something? Come with me when I visit His Holiness. They say at the court that no woman has a greater gift for words than you—not since the days of Catherine of Siena. They call you the greatest poetess in Italy because you have rendered the spirit of our age. So now they'll listen to you. You can convince His Holiness."

"That I *cannot* do," said Vittoria stiffly. "Further contact with the Pope is impossible for me. After my husband's death, he wanted me to marry a Medici. That's how much worth he attached, apparently even then, to my influence. He forbade me to take the veil. He pursued me with proposals even after I had asked him to leave me in peace. Then I went to Ischia."

"Yes, of course, yes, but you have also come back from Ischia. That can only mean that you felt that your place was here, where you have a task to perform. I have never given up hope that you will someday become one of us. Come, you've mourned long enough: we don't ask you to be faithless to the dead but to give yourself up, with everything you think and feel, and thus also with your sorrow, to God. You are behaving selfishly burying yourself like this. Whatever existed between you and the Marquis is over forever. No more growth, no more development, is possible there. Step over the border to your love of God, that love encompasses all others, even your love for Pescara. You're clinging to a withered branch, Vittoria. You're condemning yourself to a living death. But the world outside moves onward and, believe me, it's a different world from the one to which you've closed your eyes since '27. People whose opinion I respect highly have told me that your poetry, although it is love lyrics, is important because you have found words to express that longing that lives in all of us, that longing to escape from the morass of self-indulgence and spiritual and moral indifference, from doubt, hatred and envy. . .

In the work you dedicated to your husband, you say that it's possible to conquer sensuality, to come through love of a mortal being to an awareness of the immortality of the soul.

"That's all very beautiful. But you must go further than Plato. We need more than Plato's teachings. It's not enough to believe in the power of deliverance of the human spirit alone. If you paid attention to what's going on outside your refuge, you would know that the world is crying out for stronger support than the 'noble' and the 'beautiful'. That cult of the noble and beautiful which we all took up so passionately hasn't prevented us from drowning miserably. Redemption is God's grace. Whoever knows that is reborn. With your great gifts, you could achieve infinitely more if you would devote yourself to serving the truth."

Vittoria was silent for a long time. She freed her hand from Caterina's forceful grip.

"I should be deceiving myself and others if I did that," she said finally. "I would pile deceit on deceit. I know how great the influence of the written word is, I know that better than you might imagine. I don't sit here sunken in myself, in grief; I live here separated from the world precisely in order to reflect on all the rash uses of words. You don't understand me, that's to be expected. I must know myself and the motives behind my thoughts and actions before I venture to preach to the world. Believe me, there's no more horrible punishment than to become gradually aware of what one has done unwisely, driven by hidden feelings. You once said to me years ago that one can purify oneself only through the most rigorous honesty. If your belief in God is built on honesty, Caterina, then I take it that you possess the grace you spoke of. But when I examine my own soul, I find this at the bottom of it: that God has no reality for me. I use His Name, I call upon Him in prayer. I don't know what that Name means. I don't know whom I am calling upon. I don't have the power to give up my demand that God must be comprehensible to me. I can't stop believing that there's a connection between God and my intellect. It's impossible for me to surrender myself completely."

Caterina had sat nodding vigorously. She drew closer.

"You're ripe for the metamorphosis and you don't even realize it. You're still trapped in that blind worship of the intellect—as if the intellect could provide salvation! Listen to what Fra Bernardo says. . . ."

She talks, all she does is talk. I've heard all of it before. Ten years ago, she sat next to me just like this: Fra Matteo says, Fra Matteo is right. . . . That's her life, following these men who proclaim the faith, believing everything they preach, to the letter. She finds satisfaction in that. I can't arrive at a faith on somebody else's testimony. Caterina can't convince me, neither can the pious nuns here. Caterina says that she possesses grace, but the sisters—who lose themselves in a ritual which Caterina dismisses as unimportant—seem to be as sure of grace as she is.

I might have taken the plunge, before Ferrante's death. I remember before his last trip to Novara, there was a moment when I felt ready to embark on a spiritual journey. But his death changed everything. Caterina doesn't know what I've been through since then. I'm certainly less inclined now to let myself be carried away. Something about her zeal repels me, even though I do respect her. There's a germ of fanaticism in that fierce enthusiasm to save the world and redeem mankind—a touch of coercion and relentlessness that's frightening to me. She wants to fight evil or what she sees as evil—but couldn't that combativeness degenerate into an evil itself? My intellect asks that question and I can't silence it. My intellect argues too against that irrational impulse of aversion which I felt when I first saw her just now . . . Do I have the right to criticize her? At least she *does* something. I think I see the dangers and limitations of her enthusiasm, but I stand idly looking on while *she* is devoted completely to her beliefs.

While I think and think about myself, *she* acts. Maybe it's necessary to be so single-minded, so zealous and energetic in order to accomplish worthwhile things in a crisis. But that doubt which holds me back, that tend-

ency to consider everything, is my most precious possession. It compels honesty. At the last, I have to reject
Caterina's militancy for reform, along with the sim-
plistic piety of the nuns here—and as I reject the hypocrisy of that Messer Pietro Aretino who dared—
purely for commercial reasons—to send me the *Life of
Mary Magdalene* which he wrote and dedicated to
me. . . .

I can't explain all this to Caterina—she doesn't pay
any attention anyway to anything outside her obsession. How could I make her understand that what she
calls my great gifts would be useless here because I'd
be using them to deceive others, and myself? It's un-
fortunately true that I've been praised throughout Italy
because my love has glorified Ferrante. Those verses
are passed from hand to hand and they do their
wretched work. No one knows the truth except me. I've
never loved Ferrante, never.

If he had lived, I should have had to learn to endure
my loneliness. But death gave him back to me—at least
I thought so then. He was mine alone; the world had
no share in him any longer. I wanted him to go on living
in me, *with* me. I wanted to serve him with all my
strength; I wanted to clear his name of suspicion, to
erase his guilt, his failings. But that Ferrante whom I
wanted to honor had never existed. I was dedicating
myself to a ghost; I set up an idol because I wanted to
give meaning to my life. I built the figure of Ferrante
out of my unfulfilled longings, my dreams, the suppressed desires of my youth and that figure dominated
me so that I forgot the real world around me. Friends
and relatives have pitied me and called my widowhood
heroic and exemplary. But what they didn't know was
that I have never been so happy as I was at that time.
I was at Ischia, where every stone, every tree, every
view, reminded me of the past. The years fell away from
me, I felt young and resilient. I could see in my mirror
that I was reviving. I was stealing from the dead. I was
alone in an enchanted silence, peopled with images I

had created myself. The dream was my reality; the world outside that island was a distant haze.

But gradually I awoke, I had to outgrow that serenity, I had to recognize the world which I had so long forgotten. Guns were booming on the Spanish galleons in the Bay of Naples. Refugees from the wasteland were huddled in makeshift hovels outside the gates of my park. I saw that I had things to do, and in that instant I realized that all that remained of the years which I had spent at Ischia after Ferrante's death was a bundle of papers covered with lies. It took all my courage to read carefully through the sonnets and canzoni again one by one. I was horrified by the transparent self-deceit I found there. I read love songs to the mysterious divinity Eros . . . I said that Eros had withheld the pleasure of complete physical union from me and Ferrante so that we could attain a happiness that would endure beyond the borders of death . . . I said that Ferrante's pure love for me had annulled all the sensual desires in my heart and prepared me for deliverance from earthly passion . . . I said I lived in him and he in me, I said that that unity existed for eternity, it was a rock which could not be dislodged. We were childless, our love did not become flesh, but spirit—another, higher form of immortality. Our marriage did not dissolve on Ferrante's death since death can destroy matter only and matter filled no role in our relationship, none whatever. . . .

When I read all that, I realized that there was no salvation for me, unless I unravelled that cocoon of lies with my own hand.

I haven't been easy on myself: night and day I forced myself to live with the bare truth until I accepted it, until I no longer wanted to use my imagination to escape the pain. I realized that I had never loved Ferrante—certainly not in the way that I had celebrated during his lifetime and not in the way that I had celebrated after his death. How could I have loved him when I didn't know him? What had always separated us was the phantom Ferrante, whom I had created and whom I *willed* to love.

Now I realize more: that the key to all our misunderstandings and estrangement lies in my own inability to give and accept love which is not supernatural, not spiritualized. This is a mysterious inability because—even in those long years when any reconciliation seemed out of the question—have I ever really desired anything but that very passion which tempted me, but of which I was ashamed? I had to repudiate my feelings, deny my body; I couldn't do otherwise. The shame and reserve, the secret fear and loathing of the urge of nature, was inborn in me. And although it made what happened between Ferrante and me inevitable, if I had to begin again, I couldn't choose otherwise than I have chosen. I was created to behave in a way that would repel Ferrante more and more deeply, and he himself could not help exciting me so that I reacted with a desperate rejection.

When I first grasped that what I called my love had been a puffed-up sham which I had imagined in order to justify my life, I felt empty, shaken-out. And then the other, worse torment began. I became aware that the Ferrante who had taken shape in my verses was not just my property alone—after all, I had consciously given this idol to the world as the true Pescara. I was deliberately trying to drive out that other Pescara whom people remembered—the calculating, ambitious man, the traitor, the Emperor's cunning agent. So I allowed and even encouraged the distribution of my poetry, and the praise that reached me made it clear that I would accomplish what I set out to do. I had started an avalanche which couldn't be stopped: because of me, Ferrante is considered the perfect knight. The Imperials revere him as the glowing example for every man who serves the concept of Empire. Anyone who dared to rake up old rumors would be sued for slander.

This fervid gratuitous hero-worship is my fault. Fer-

rante has become immortal in a form which is utterly
alien to him. There's no trace of the man he really was—
I didn't know that man—perhaps no one did except
Delia Equicola, with whom he chose to die. No trace
remains of that man. I don't begrudge him his fame,
but the falsity, the strident spurious colors of that his-
torical portrait which I called to life, make me shiver
before the power of the written word, which goes its
own way and spreads among the people like a plague.

Before I left for Rome, I went once more to visit the
grave in San Domenico Maggiore in Naples where Ferrante rests under a trophy of weapons and banners. I
left behind in the tomb in a leaden case the documents
which had just been sent to me from Madrid: the Imperial recognition, in black and white, of the service of
"Ferrante Francesco d'Avalos, Marquis of Pescara, commander and diplomat, through whose courage and insight We have at long last been crowned in Bologna
with the Crown of the Empire which is Our legal inheritance."

Kneeling on the tombstones, I put these questions to
the emptiness around me:

"Are you satisfied now? Is it these few pieces of parchment with the Emperor's signature and with red seals,
the phrases about esteem and fame and eternal glory
for which you lived, for which you died?"

I would have cried out to him if I had known how
my voice could reach him: "I have done more for you
than the Emperor and his ministers. I have returned
your honor to you. I have given it back to you to an
extent that must satisfy even the Castilian nobleman
in you. You are the greatest hero since the legendary
Roland. For that I shall atone every day and night of
my life to the hour of my death."

After that, I returned to Rome. I believed it was my
place to be in the ruined city. The devastation, the emp-

tiness, the laborious attempts at restoration, seemed to me to reflect my own state of mind. What do I seek here? Community with others who, like me, must live on amidst a heap of ruins, who must start to rebuild with empty hands; a feeling of unity; the awareness of equality in suffering that might flower into acceptance, even into hope. Because it's a privilege to realize that one has survived a catastrophe and been given insight into one's own guilt and error.

It's amazing how quickly one can become accustomed to the sight of ruins. In spite of ruins, in spite of poverty and pestilence, the people's festivals are celebrated the year round. Many of my former friends, prelates and nobles, have opened their palaces again; they're living in great style. I visited some of them at first. But I can't feel comfortable in the courts of old acquaintances and in those transformed streets. After every visit, after every conversation all I wished for was to be completely alone again.

How can I explain to Caterina that at this point in my life my salvation seems to lie in closeness to my fellow men rather than in closeness to God? I've never really loved anyone, there's never been a bond of deep familiarity between me and any other being. But I know that I exist as a person only by the grace of my neighbor whom I may love as I love myself. My being will only be fulfilled, my life will achieve meaning, only through that love. And only then will I be able to seek God. When I have earned it, I hope the grace of such a perfect love will fall to me.

After she had shown Caterina out, she walked back through the series of cells where she lived with her women. She entered her own room and sank onto a small bench facing a wall hung with a crucifix. She looked at that body, bloodless, exhausted, tortured to death. Michelangelo Buonarroti had made it for her at her request. They had never met, although he was living in Rome—he was working in the Sistine Chapel on a fresco, The Last Judgment, intended to be the last of the Chapel frescoes. She had written to him to explain what she wanted: a suffering, humble Christ in his most bitter hour on Golgotha, deserted by God and man. He had kept her informed on the progress of the work in short, business-like reports. Finally, with the completed crucifix came a note: "I am in my bitterest hour, but I am not humble. I have been forsaken by God and man and I suffer; I am tortured by the thought that everything I make is transitory—paint, wood and stone, and that in the long run there will be nothing left, nothing, nothing. This realization takes away all my strength and courage."

She was deeply moved by this unexpected outburst. She had immediately written to him to thank him copiously and praise his work; she felt painfully inadequate. That ended their correspondence.

She sat upright on the little backless bench, her hands clenched in her lap.

Every day, every hour of her life, she had to struggle anew for self-affirmation. As she sat there in that moment of deep contemplation, she knew she was ready to wage that eternal struggle. But outside of that certainty, she possessed nothing.

She rose, fetched pen and paper and then wrote:

"Will you, respected friend, draw for me once more the figure of Christ on the cross, as only you can do it? Don't depict him as a dead man as he is usually portrayed and as you have already done at my request—but living, his face raised at the moment that he calls upon God: *Eli! Eli! Lamma sabbachtani!* That is the meaning of the Crucifixion for me—not the impotent surrender, the collapse into death, the end of torture, but conscious suffering, the torment of body and soul which never ceases, never. Deliverance lies only in the acceptance of that suffering. I have a request to make of you. Will you come and bring me the design yourself? Forgive me this indiscretion. I would like to talk to you. I have wished that for a long time, but have not dared to ask."

She sealed the letter and sent it to Messer Michelangelo Buonarroti in the via Esquilina in Rome.

XXI.

Giovanni Borgia

During that accursed lawsuit, the opposing party made certain insinuations.

And there are facts which have come to light. *Farnese* had had the two bulls made, in '18, for a great deal of money. It was *Farnese* who protected me in the court at Rome, after my return from France. And it was *he* whom I had to thank for my appointment to Morone's retinue.

At my request Messer Pietro sent me from Venice the results of the investigation of which he seems to possess the secret: for a while in '97—the year of my birth—a bastard infant of Farnese's was looked after in the joint household of Lucrezia and Giulia *Bella* in the palace of Santa Maria in Portico.

Son of Farnese, brother of Pierluigi. . . I *will* believe that.

Then why should I be upset over my defeat before the papal court? Even my mutilation, my impotence, would be bearable if I could know for certain that I have no involvement with the Borgia or with Perotto Caldès.

But why won't he—Farnese—look me directly in the eye when I turn the conversation in a certain direction? Why does he evade my questions?

I must know. The answer will determine whether I exist or do not exist.

Farnese am I, Farnese. . .